MW01060260

Empathy

By Gloria Goostray

Copyright ©2014

Empathy by Gloria Goostray

Cover design/photography by Kelly Mann

ISBN 9781495963315

All rights reserved.

This book is a work of fiction.

To my grandchildren

Jessica, Brendan, and Eric

Many thanks to my daughter, Linda Harmon, and W.N. for their assistance and patience. Thanks to my mentor, Helen Monahan, who encouraged me to write this book.
Final thanks to M. H. for his words, which describe me to a 'T': "The secret inner Gloria is unveiled." Who would have guessed?

Chapter 1

Lucinda could hear the gurgle of blood coming from his throat as she slid the knife across Andrew's soft tissues. His shirt was immediately stained bright red. He slid down, off his plushy leather chair onto the floor, his crystal cocktail glass momentarily raised in a morbid toast. His hand then dropped, shattering the glass. The shards sparkled like diamonds from the reflection of the flames in the fireplace.

She stood there looking down at him for a few moments, then slowly walked into the bathroom. She wiped the knife clean with a facecloth, removed the top of the toilet tank, and dropped the knife into the water. Replacing the cover, Lucinda then folded the bloody side of the cloth inward and set it on the edge of the tub. She washed her hands thoroughly, drying them with the matching towel from the rack. She then proceeded into the kitchen and tore off several sheets from the paper towel roll and went back to the bathroom. Within minutes, she had replaced all of the towels with new ones from the vanity and given a thorough paper towel scrub to everything. Using the bath towel as a sack, she gathered everything up and went off in search of a trash bag. She found a kitchen sized one under the sink, put everything in it, rolled it up tight, and stuffed it in the bottom of her large pocketbook.

Lucinda returned to where Andrew's body lay, careful not to step in the pool of blood slowly working its way toward the bearskin rug. She couldn't help but stare at him, amazed that a person could have that much blood. Pouring herself a glass of scotch, she sat on the chair opposite his. She held up her drink for a moment, as though returning his earlier dying gesture, and then quickly emptied the glass.

Chapter 2

Andrew was a partner in a thriving legal firm in downtown Santa Barbara, California. His salary was in the high six-figure category.

Lucinda was a paralegal in the same office. She was single, well educated, had traveled the world some, and enjoyed playing classical music on the piano. When she was first introduced to him, there was a magnetic chemistry between them. Many times he would ask if she could stay after hours to help him, and naturally she jumped at the chance to be alone with him. In the beginning, it was strictly professional. He had her researching long into the night, often thanking her as he headed out the door. As time went on, however, he began checking in with her more often, seeing how she was doing and offering to help. Working dinners became dinners which became breakfast. This went on for almost two years. Lucinda never pushed for more, as she had never known a man who was as kind and generous as Andrew, even though she knew that he was giving as much as he ever would.

One evening, while dining on a sumptuous meal of filet and shrimp, he slid a small velvet box across the table. She opened it and saw a stunning opal and diamond bracelet. She reached across the table and took his hand. She knew he was a married man, but he had never mentioned his wife's name or anything about her. She never asked. He often said that he was married in name only.

"Andrew. Thank you so much. I love it." And she did. She understood that this was an enormous step for him – a tangible token of what she meant to him. As they held hands across the table, he said that he had another surprise for her. He slid another item across the table. It was small and silver – a key. Stuck to it was a small label with the number 617 on it. He told her that he had bought a condo overlooking the waterfront at Stearns Wharf, here in Santa Barbara and not far from where she lived. The number, he explained, was the code to open the front door. He asked that she memorize it and dispose of the sticker.

Lucinda didn't know what to say. A thousand thoughts ran through her head at once, with the loudest one wondering what the gesture meant. Was this a reach for a commitment she never expected from him, an entrance to a life of comfort that she always hoped to attain? She was beyond excited, but didn't want to put Andrew off with the dance that she wanted to perform right there in the dining room. Instead, she pursed her lips in a "Mona Lisa" smile and tucked the key into her purse. The conversation then switched to small talk. They stayed in the dining room for another half hour before adjourning to the lounge for an after-dinner drink. Lucinda's mind was whirling, thinking of how the next few hours would unfold. Would tonight be the first night for them to spend in "his" place? She was barely conscious of the time passing, and soon they were in his car. Although his condo was thirty minutes from the restaurant, it passed in an instant for Lucinda. She watched the lights zip by on the freeway until they turned down an off-ramp and into a neighborhood. Each condo had a personal garage, which was already opening as they turned into the driveway. Andrew brought the car to a stop and, seemingly in one fluid motion, had the car off and was at her door with his hand out. She glided with him to the elevator, where he pressed the button for the sixth floor.

When Andrew opened the door to the condo, Lucinda was greeted by an elegant entryway, with marble floors and a collection of artwork lining the walls that would have looked completely at home in the Louvre. Ten feet from the entrance stood a small wooden table. She saw a tray with a bottle of champagne and two flutes. Andrew opened the bottle and filled the two glasses. After handing one to Lucinda, he silently raised his glass in toast and the two drained them in one motion. Without putting his glass down, he moved in and put his hand on the small of Lucinda's back. Simultaneously, she felt the tender kiss and the unzipping of her dress.

Chapter 3

It was all business Monday morning when Andrew called Lucinda into his office. "There is an important meeting on Wednesday in Chicago and I need you to be there with me." Andrew was shuffling papers on his desk with a rather stressed look on his face. Lucinda resisted the urge to comfort him. "What do you need me to prepare?" she inquired. He was definitely in the work zone. "I will need the files on Bowler and Jennings, as well as the Terrance Corporation reports. We will be leaving tomorrow afternoon at three, so bring your luggage with you. We'll be flying back on Thursday." She nodded. "Anything else, Mr. Lowe?" Without looking up, he shook his head.

Lucinda became aware that they had company. Theodore, another partner in the firm, was standing behind her, listening to the conversation. Not surprisingly, he turned and left without saying a word. She knew that he was miffed at not being included in this trip, and she wondered how much he knew about her relationship with Andrew. Still, Theodore was not about to rock the boat, as business was going very well. Lucinda had heard that he was hoping to hire two more lawyers to handle the workload.

The rest of the day was busy and Lucinda had little cause to see Andrew. She headed home that night and packed for a couple of days in Chicago. Lots of wool and sensible shoes to go with the cold weather she knew she would encounter during the trip. What made her smile was the possibility of a warm fire and a romantic interlude in a hotel room far away from any office politics.

Tuesday proved to be impossibly long. The flight from LAX to Chicago was delayed for an hour by inclement weather, and then further complicated by seat changes. Lucinda ended up sitting between two rather large gentlemen intent on arguing over whether or not the Bears' defense was good enough to get them to the Super Bowl. She couldn't get off the plane fast enough, almost running to the baggage carousel, where she saw Andrew standing with both of their bags already on a cart. Wordlessly, they hailed a cab and headed for the hotel. While Andrew checked in, Lucinda made a quick pit stop in the ladies' room. As exhausted as she was, she was still going to be ready for anything. Their rooms were across the hall from each other, but she was only in hers long enough to change into something more comfortable and freshen up a little more. She was glad she did, as they spent the night in Andrew's room.

Wednesday morning brought the all-business mentality again, as Andrew was in the shower when she woke. She headed back to her room and quickly got herself ready for the day. They shared a brief breakfast downstairs and caught a cab for the Terrance building. The meeting ran through lunch, well over the allotted three hours. Lucinda arranged for lunch to be brought in and, before she knew it, the meeting was over. There was a part of her that was mulling over the possibilities for that evening, but they were both so tired that it took away the anticipated pleasure. Ten minutes in the room and they were both fast asleep.

The ringing of the phone at six the next morning brought violent thoughts to Lucinda's mind. She wondered why wake up calls can't be just a little less jarring. Andrew didn't seem to mind, as he took the call and was quickly in the shower. She headed back to her own room and hastily prepared to leave. She had heard Andrew order breakfast for two in his room and she didn't want to be late. Fifteen minutes later, she was showered, dressed, packed and ready to go. When she got back to his room, a steaming breakfast was waiting. While everything was delicious, it was over too quickly for her taste and they were soon looking out on a cold and dreary day while waiting for the taxi to the airport. The winds were whipping lustily that day, which caused a rather turbulent flight back home. Even the most seasoned travelers seemed uncomfortable, but for Lucinda the flight was especially excruciating. She was never fond of flying, even in the best of weather. The bump of tires on the runway was a most pleasing feeling.

When they walked out of the airport, there was a company car waiting for them. Lucinda thought a huge thank-you in Andrew's direction. Taking a cab after that flight would have just been the icing on a very bad cake. The driver took their bags and placed them in the trunk as they slid into the back seat. Though traffic was heavy as usual, Lucinda noted that the driver was deftly maneuvering at a high rate of speed. She would be home very soon.

When the door opened, she slid over and took the drivers' hand. Over her shoulder she said, "Don't forget the concert tonight." Andrew did not respond, but she assumed that he had heard her and was just eager to get home. As she gathered her bag, she heard him through the open window instruct the driver to head to Stearns Wharf.

As she entered her apartment, she kicked off her shoes and hung her coat up in the closet. She then poured herself a scotch, making sure to add exactly five ice cubes. She dropped down into her favorite chair and clicked the remote for the electric fireplace. The scotch went down smoothly and warmed her up comfortably. She put her feet up, closed her eyes, and allowed herself to dream for a bit – dream about what a life with Andrew might be like. It wouldn't have to be a secret, though the sneaking around did always excite Lucinda a little bit. Her life up to this point had entailed a lot of dreaming, of wanting, keeping secret many things. She wondered if this was why she was so good at keeping her affair with

Andrew quiet for such a long time. Then one secret drifted into her mind, one from long ago. One involving the best friend she had ever known. An image of Marlene, clear as day, dominated the inside of her head.

Chapter 4

Marlene and I were inseparable. We had lived next door to each other as long as I could remember. On the outside, I imagine we made a curious pair. Marlene was always tall and lean, while I had a short, solid, tomboyish build. She had long blonde hair that looked fabulous even in the simple ponytail that she threw it in every day. I, on the other hand, hated my short, brown, unruly hair enough that I constantly changed its color. I used food dye until my mother finally relented and let me use real coloring products. Magenta was always my favorite, but the neon green ran a close second. For all of our physical differences, most people we met thought we were sisters, since we were never apart and often finished each other's sentences. In the beginning, our home lives were nearly identical. Both of us grew up as only children, living in comfortable though conservative homes, with two conservative parents. That all changed when we were twelve years old.

I had never seen my grandmother look so serious. She sat me down next to her on the couch in my own living room. She had started a fire in the fireplace, which was unusual. When she would babysit, I would always beg her to start one, but she would just change the subject. She looked at me for a long time without saying anything, so I listened to the Johnson's dog barking madly at something, probably the Johnson's cat. It was then that she hit me with it. Mom and Dad had died that morning in an accident. She was going to take care of me. I haven't forgotten how the tears rolled down my cheeks, burning small grooves in my skin, marking me with my anguish. Those tears changed me, changed my life, changed my relationship with everyone around me. Especially with Marlene.

She tried consistently to be there for me, but I was having none of it. For some reason, I just couldn't picture how this beautiful girl with the perfect life could ever understand what I was going through. For the first time, I truly felt like the ugly stepsister next to Cinderella. I pushed her away, frequently using less than lady-like words, until one day she just stopped trying. This just made me hate her more, as she was now playing the "too-good-to-be-friends-with-someone-like-me" role that I had created for her. At the time, I wanted nothing more than to be somewhere else, away from her. However, as fate would have it, moving in with my grandmother meant moving from next door to the other side of the street and one down from Marlene. We would still be on the same bus, go to the same school, although we would be in different home rooms. The next six years saw us circle around each other, careful never to cross the other's path if it could be helped.

By the time we graduated, we were on completely different paths. Marlene had gone on to be captain of the chess club and a regular in the drama club. I, on the other hand, was a card carrying member of the detention club, an exclusive group of five that met every day after school for one reason or another. While my four companions were far more advanced than me, I was nonetheless accepted as one of them. It amazed me that I ever even qualified to graduate, although I wondered if they just shuttled me through so that I would be someone else's problem. I took a job working in a local ice cream shop and didn't see Marlene again until the day I was arrested.

I remember getting up that morning, thinking how beautiful it was and how much I was dreading going to work. I was sitting in the backyard when I thought I heard the doorbell ring. The sound of quiet conversation reached me, followed by my grandmother almost yelling, "You leave her alone!" Two policemen appeared at the back door. I was soon in handcuffs and being walked across the front yard to a waiting cruiser. Out of the corner of my eye, I saw Marlene sitting on her front doorstep, watching the entire scene.

I found out, in bits and pieces, that the detention club had been using my job at the ice cream shop to sell some merchandise. Apparently, I was the drop. My "friends" would often come by, grab a single scoop cone and leave something with me for someone else to pick up. One time it was a book bag left at someone's house. Another time it was a birthday gift that needed to be hidden from a brother or sister. Once it was even a bag full of dirty clothes. Being that it was summer and we were busy, I never thought too much about it. Besides, I liked my place with them and wasn't about to jeopardize my status by asking questions. That mistake cost me two years in a women's prison.

As disappointed as my grandmother was, she was still the one waiting for me on the sidewalk when I got out. I was soon back in my old room, looking just as it did the day I left it. The big difference was that it wasn't just the two of us. My grandmother had taken on a boarder to help make ends meet. When she introduced us, I couldn't tell if the feeling in my stomach was fear or butterflies. His name was Bill, and he was an imposing figure. I was shocked that my grandmother would have welcomed someone like him into her home. He was about six feet tall, with broad shoulders and built lean, like a swimmer. He had jet black hair and eyes that were almost as dark. It wasn't long before he started being just "around" when I came home. We began dating soon after and those were the happiest days of my life. Then one day I woke up to his voice, low and terse. I couldn't imagine who he was talking to. I went to the window, as it sounded as though he was in the back yard. Bill was pacing back and forth on the grass, with one hand on his cell phone and the other firmly woven in that thick, dark hair. I remember thinking how appealing that intensity was, until his voice reached me again. "God no, Marlene! How could you ever think I would get involved with an ex-con?" I don't remember much after that. I fell back on the bed and it seemed as though I lay there for hours. Sadly, my first thought ended up being my final one as well, with much wasted time in between. It was dark by the time I stood up, decision firmly made. Marlene needed to go. Then Bill could see the kind, sympathetic side of me instead of the troubled side.

I got up and quietly headed downstairs into the kitchen. I knew my grandmother had a key to Marlene's house for bringing in the mail and feeding the fish when they went on vacation. The rattle in the sugar bowl told me that I was on the right track. I removed the key and silently slipped out the door. It was cold and damp as I crossed the street between the houses. I felt the fog engulf me like a chilling shroud. With a shiver, I unlocked the back door. As I stood in the darkness, I could hear soft music playing. It was coming from upstairs, accompanied by the sound of splashing. Perfect. She was in the tub. I silently crept up the stairs. I could see the glow of candles in the doorway and peeked around the corner. Only the top of her head was visible in the tub. She was surrounded by small votives on plates all around the tub. On the vanity stood two brass candlesticks. I stepped quietly in, blew out one of the candles and removed it from the brass. One hard swing to the back of her head sent water flying and candles sputtering. I grabbed the bloody hair and held her head under water to make sure she was gone, but there was no struggle. When I let go, she floated upwards. It was then that I discovered that the woman was not Marlene, but one of her friends with whom she had done a school play.

With a surge of panic, I used my sleeve to quickly wipe the candlestick holder and anything I could remember touching. I thought I smelled smoke as I backtracked to the door, but was too afraid of getting caught there to worry about it. I sprinted across the yard, into the street, heading towards home, fighting nausea all the way. I hadn't been in my room more than a few minutes when I was startled by sirens outside. I ran downstairs and found my grandmother in the picture window crying. Past her, I could see Marlene's house being completely consumed by flames. I could not take my eyes off the inferno, even when my grandmother wrapped me up in a huge hug. The two of us just stood there for what seemed like forever, until there was a knock at the door. She went to answer it, then came back into the living room, followed by two police officers. They were asking the usual 'did you see anything' questions, and I waited only long enough to not appear guilty before excusing myself and heading to my room. When I woke late the next morning, feeling more like I blacked out rather than slept, I found my grandmother on the couch. She had passed after I had gone to bed. The paramedics said she suffered a massive coronary.

It was at that moment that I made a decision. It was time to start over. I found the box where my grandmother kept all of her important papers. She had told me when I got out of prison where it was. There were specific instructions for everything, including her burial wishes. She had left a letter stating that she was to be buried in her favorite green dress, but she wanted me to press it first so she would look her best. Through tears, I pulled the dress out of the back of the closet and laid it on the bed. The funeral director will take care of that. I needed to prepare for my new life. Jeanette "JJ" Jenkins was gone. I had never liked that name, could never understand what would make my parents hang such an awful moniker on their new bundle of joy. It was a name that, at this time in my mind, brought images of sadness, frustration, isolation, and loss. This would be my opportunity to start anew. It was time for Lucinda Preston to get her chance.

Chapter 5

Looking at Andrew's body, Lucinda noticed the coagulation starting in the pool of blood. She poured another scotch, sat back in the chair, and just stared at him for a bit. *I'm glad you're dead*, she thought to herself.

Earlier that evening, there was a concert at the Art Museum. Her friend Gregory had performed his latest original piano compositions. The museum hosted a fundraiser each year for a local charitable organization and this was the sixth year that he had offered his services. Lucinda had been just about finished getting dressed when the phone rang. Something had come up and Andrew was not going to be able to join her. Though she was dejected at not having his company, she decided to go anyway and support her friend.

When she arrived at the concert, there was a group of both friends and co-workers, all having cocktails and soon she was handed a glass of wine and she joined the conversation. Lucinda could see Theodore, Andrew's partner in the firm, moving through the crowd toward her. She could tell he was already well lubricated by the way he kept bumping into and apologizing to almost everyone he passed. He sidled up to her, feeling no pain, and leaned in close. She could smell the pungent alcohol as he whispered into her ear. "I know why Andrew is not here. Did you know he has a new girlfriend?" Lucinda was caught completely off guard and spun around. "What are you talking about?" It dawned on her that Theodore knew about them. Why else would he seek her out with this information? Before he could say anything else, the lights flickered to signal that the show was about to begin. The crowd started moving toward their seats. Ted snatched a glass off a passing waiter's tray, toasted Lucinda, gulped the wine down and proceeded to enter the hall.

Lucinda's stomach turned upside down and she quickly headed for the ladies lounge. She wet a paper towel and patted her face, took a deep breath, and tried to regain her composure. *If he's been playing me for a fool, I'm going to....* The sound of a toilet flush behind her broke her concentration and she turned toward the door.

After she left the lounge, she got her coat and practically ran out the door and down the sixteen marble steps to the street. She quickly walked to her car, unlocked the door, got in and just sat staring ahead wondering what she should do. Finally, she dialed Andrew's cell phone number. He picked up after two rings.

"Hello, Lucinda. Sorry I missed the concert. I'm working at the condo."

Lucinda barely let him finish before responding, "Andrew, I have to see you now. I'm on my way." She thought she heard a woman's voice in the background, "I'll see you next week." Lucinda could feel the heat spreading across her cheeks. "Is someone there with you?"

"It's the TV." Andrew sounded exasperated. "Lucinda, I'm really busy. Will you take a rain check?"

She could barely contain the rising anger. "NO! I'm on my way."

"I told you I have a lot of work to do." Cutting him off again, she blurted out, "I don't care. I'm coming!"

In one motion, Lucinda started the car, threw it into gear, and stepped on the gas. Leaving a small patch of rubber in the parking lot, she headed for the freeway. It was after nine-thirty when she pulled into the driveway. There wasn't a soul around, as most of the condos were unoccupied. Only a handful had been sold so far. The prices were not cheap.

Lucinda couldn't help but think of that night in the restaurant as she punched in the code to the door. She heard the click and grabbed the handle. Taking the elevator to the sixth floor, she slowed her pace as she got closer to the door. She quietly knocked, tried the knob and found the door unlocked.

Andrew was standing by the fireplace with his back to the door. She wondered if a guilty man would leave himself so vulnerable. Without turning around, he said, "Lucinda, I'm tired. I don't feel like getting into this with you now. I told you I have work to do. I wish you hadn't come." At that point, he turned around and sat in a leather chair. She gently settled into the chair directly opposite him. He did indeed look tired. Her anger was abating. Then she noticed the glasses on the coffee table. One of them had lipstick marks on it.

"Where is your friend?" She was keeping her tone as even as she could. He just sat there, sipping his scotch, not uttering a word.

"Is it true that you are seeing someone else?" Andrew's eyes lifted up from his glass to meet hers.

"Who told you that?" He seemed genuinely inquisitive and not just buying time. She felt a small touch of victory at his lack of a denial.

"Your partner, Teddy boy, that's who." Andrew shook his head from side to side. "He never could keep his mouth shut. He was probably three sheets to the wind when he told you that."

Ignoring the last comment, Lucinda continued. "I want to know why you are dumping me." Andrew's voice rose up at this. "Lucinda, for crying out loud, look at the time! I wish you would go."

"I'm not going anywhere until I know why." She folded her arms for emphasis. Andrew slammed his left hand down on the arm of the chair. "Why, why, why! You are more of a pain than my wife!!!"

"Oh, that's a nice thing to say to me after all I've done for you." She was playing the guilt card, but Andrew wasn't buying it. "You're just like all the others. Take. Take. Take."

When she was younger, such a comment would have stung Lucinda but she didn't even pause before she responded, "Hey, you take what you want, when you want."

Andrew put his head in his free hand. As he was rubbing his eyes, he said almost under his breath, "Please go."

Lucinda stood up. "Fine." Instead of turning toward the door, she headed for the kitchen. Andrew never looked up when she quietly opened up the silverware drawer and slid out a knife. Closing the drawer, she circled around his chair where he still sat, pinching the bridge of his nose. By the time he realized she was behind him, it was too late. Just as he lifted his head, she slid the knife across his throat.

Chapter 6

Lucinda was exhausted as she drove back to her apartment. It was close to midnight when she pulled into her garage. She changed clothes quickly, throwing her evening wear into the washer in case she had gotten something on her that she might not want found. She padded into the bedroom and was asleep as soon as her head hit the pillow.

The shrill ring of the alarm rattled her awake at six-thirty. She lay there for a few moments, going over the events of the previous night. There would be no run this morning. She would have her hands full just getting ready for work and putting her recent deeds out of her mind. By seven-thirty, Lucinda was on the road, having been rejuvenated by a long hot shower and two cups of coffee. Wearing her favorite grey suit, she felt a little better about the upcoming day.

When the elevator doors opened, revealing a bustling office, Lucinda stepped out and almost immediately ran into Theodore. He was looking rather ragged this morning, lacking a shave and hugging a rather large coffee mug. "Good morning, Theodore." She became aware of how perky she sounded and tried to modify her tone. "Did you enjoy the concert last night?" Theodore looked at her through his eyelids. "Morning. Lucinda, please call me Ted. Sister Mary Anne called me Theodore in the third grade. I hated it even then. Yes, the concert was nice. Where were you, anyway? I looked for you as we funneled in, but you were no longer behind me."

Lucinda's stomach lurched a little. "I had to use the facilities and there was a line. By the time I got out, the doors were closed. I had to wait until the first song was done before they would let me in. I sat in the back so I wouldn't disturb anyone else." She decided to change the subject, but was sorry as soon as she heard what fell out of her mouth. "Has Andrew come in yet?" She couldn't believe that she brought that topic up, but Ted didn't even blink. "Not yet. Something I can help with?" She breathed a small sigh of relief. "No. I just have some briefs that need his attention before we go to court." Ted didn't pursue it, and Lucinda wondered to herself how such an unmotivated person could have ever made partner.

Morning gave way to afternoon and the office bustled on, even in Andrew's absence. Lucinda kept herself busy with paperwork and phone calls, but the nagging feeling in the pit of her stomach maintained a presence. When Ted passed her desk on his way to a late lunch, she caught his attention.

"Did Andrew ever check in?" She hoped she sounded nonchalant. Ted checked his watch. "No. You know him. Some days he is here, and others…who knows. I'm not worried, are you?" She wondered if she should pursue it. "Do you think we should call and at least make sure he doesn't need anything?" Ted just shrugged his shoulders and said, "If he wanted us to know where he was, I'm sure he would call. Don't worry your pretty blonde hair over it."

The rest of the afternoon dragged on. At six, Lucinda felt as though she had given enough to the company for one day. She tucked some papers into her briefcase and bid all a good night. On her way home, she stopped at The Deli and bought a few pieces of fruit, some cheese, and a bottle of wine.

The first thing Lucinda did when she walked in was to check the answering machine, although she wasn't sure what she was expecting to hear. Still in her favorite suit, she cut up some of her bounty of food and brought it and the wine into the living room. She dropped into her favorite chair and flipped on the television. The local 24 hour news station was in the middle of a story about a baby monkey at a zoo in Los Angeles. She poured a glass of wine, closed her eyes, and listened rather than watched. An hour went by with no mention of a murder anywhere in the Santa Barbara area.

The nagging feeling in her stomach relented just a bit. She poured another glass of wine and held the glass up. *Here's to you, Andrew. May you rest in peace.*

Chapter 7

Early Monday morning, Ernie the maintenance man was vacuuming the carpets in the hallways. He had reached the end of the cord length and went back to unplug the machine. When he bent down to plug in at the next receptacle, he noticed a foul odor coming from suite 617. He headed back to the maintenance office to call the manager. When the manager, a quiet and elegant man named Joseph Costa, met Ernie outside the suite, he winced at the smell. After knocking on the door twice gently, then once rather forcefully, he took out his passkey and opened the door. What greeted them was nothing short of horrific: a body lay on the floor near the fireplace, surrounded by a large pool of blood and shattered glass. Quickly, Mr. Costa shut the door behind them and pulled out his phone. Dialing 911, he found himself speaking far too loudly. "I am Joseph Costa, the manager of the condominium complex at Stearns Wharf. It's located on the corner of State Street and Cabrillo Boulevard. I need to report a death here. There is a body on the floor of suite 617."

"Are you sure he's dead?" The voice on the other end of the phone was impossibly even. Mr. Costa tried hard to keep his emotions in check. "Yeah, I'm pretty confident that he is." The next question set him off. "Did you check for any signs…" Mr. Costa couldn't take it anymore. He was now yelling. "No! I can tell that he is dead! D. E. A. D., dead!!"

The voice on the other end was quiet for several moments. "Please stay where you are, sir, and don't let anyone in that suite. A unit is on its way. Clear?" Mr. Costa took a deep breath. "Understood." Then he hung up and carefully tucked the phone into his pocket.

Chapter 8

Elsewhere in the city on that same Monday morning, Lucinda was going about her normal routine. Years ago, she had trained her mind to block out everything that bothered her. Not to mention, a weekend without any mention of a death on the news had steeled her nerves considerably. She flew through her morning routine and decided to head to the office early. Similar to Friday, she met Ted as she stepped off the elevator. However, he was looking much more well-rested.

"Good morning, Lucinda." He came to a stop a few feet from the elevator. "Good morning, Ted." She glanced at Andrew's closed door and thought out loud, "I wonder if he is in. I didn't see his car downstairs, but the door was open on Friday." Ted shrugged and said, "I will check as soon as I grab a coffee." Lucinda sat down at her desk and began to unpack her briefcase. Soon, Ted was back with two cups of coffee. He placed one on the corner of her desk. "Cream only, if I remember correctly." Before she could say anything, he was already ten feet away and heading for Andrew's office. With mug in hand, he knocked and opened the door. She could see that the light was still off in the room and Ted quickly reappeared in the doorway, minus the other cup of coffee. He saw Lucinda looking at him and shook his head.

She raised her eyebrows and said, "Maybe you should call him at home." She was trying not to be too pushy, but this was her alibi after all. However, if Ted knew about them, he would surely give up that information when Andrew was eventually found. Still, she felt compelled to keep up the ruse. Ted shook his head. "He told me never to call his house unless it was an emergency." He clearly didn't want to cross some line in the sand that Andrew had drawn. She persisted. "Just call his cell." He dug in his heels and crossed his arms. "Look Lucinda, if he was sick, his wife or one of the kids would have called me." Lucinda felt like she had been slapped. "He has kids?" Ted continued. "Four. Two are in high school, one is in middle, and the youngest is in grammar school. Great looking kids. Definitely take after his wife. Didn't he ever mention them?" Lucinda looked out the window for several moments before realizing that she hadn't answered. "No. I mean...maybe. I can't remember. I'm just surprised that it never came up in conversation." *That son of a...*

"Don't worry about Andrew. I'm not." Just then, Ted's phone rang. He pulled it out of his pocket and looked at the screen. "Speak of the devil," he said before answering. Before he could say a word, a loud voice came through the speaker. She could hear that it was a woman, but it was too distorted to make out anything she was saying. Ted was listening, then nodding, then listening some more. His face turned ashen. This went on for a minute or two, before he ended by saying, "Keep me in the loop." He looked her square in the eye and said, "He's dead."

Though Lucinda knew that he would have to be found eventually, she still found herself surprised when someone else said those words out loud. Her stomach jumped, but not out of guilt. She wasn't second guessing her actions one bit. She was just waiting for Ted to start questioning her about her relationship with Andrew. "Did she say what happened?"

"No. She only said that the cops called her early this morning and said that they needed her to come to the medical examiner's office to identify the body. She couldn't understand why Andrew was here in town at a condo she didn't know about, when he told her that he was going to be away on business in Philadelphia through the weekend. She's going to call me later when she has more information about what happened." Ted slumped into the chair next to her desk.

As they sat there letting this information sink in, Lucinda was already thinking about the future. Would she even have one? Was Ted playing with her? Why wasn't he bringing up their relationship and what happened last week at the charity event? What would happen in the firm now? She was afraid to pose any of these questions, but the last one sounded the most logical and innocuous to ask. As she steeled herself, Lucinda became aware that the work day was in full swing now, with the entire staff bustling away around them. It seemed like forever ago that they were the only two in the office. She took a deep breath. "What is going to happen here?"

Ted rose from his chair, suddenly looking even more tired than his hangover morning. "Well, I am going to have to have a meeting with all of the employees and let them know what happened. I am sure that the police will be here soon to start interviewing people and looking through his office. Then I will need to arrange for an emergency meeting of the Board of Directors." With that, Ted left her office and headed down to his own. Lucinda was left to her own thoughts, first and foremost being when the bomb was going to be dropped.

For the rest of the morning, Lucinda aimlessly shuffled through papers and read through her emails several times, acting on none of them. Every time the phone rang, she jumped right out of her chair. When Ted had the meeting with the staff, she barely heard anything he said but she was acutely aware of every gasp and groan in the room. The afternoon came slowly that day and Lucinda's confidence from that morning had completely dissolved. A knock at her door practically stopped her heart.

She turned to find Ted leaning through the doorway. "You have company."

Chapter 9

Lucinda was afraid to even open her mouth, for fear that her stomach would leap out. An image of her being walked out in handcuffs swam before her eyes. There seemed to be no way around it, so she just sat back in her chair.

Ted disappeared from the doorway and was replaced by a tall, thin, handsome man wearing a dark suit. He had very close-cropped brown hair and wore a serious expression. He turned back to the door and thanked Ted for showing him in. "May I?" he asked as he pointed to the chair next to the desk. "Please," she replied, feeling a little more confident when none of her internal organs exited when she spoke. Maybe she could do this after all. Why hadn't any of this occurred to her before she executed her lover?

"You are Lucinda Preston, correct?" She nodded in assent. "I don't know if you remember me. My name is Detective Carl Nelson and I work for the Boston Police Department. We actually met a number of years ago." Lucinda's feeling of panic quickly turned to confusion. What the heck did this have to do with Andrew? Or did it at all? Then the feeling of her stomach coming out her mouth came rushing back. *Oh my God. Please don't let this be about Marlene's friend!* Detective Nelson had been Patrolman Nelson at the time and had interviewed her grandmother about Marlene's family after the fire. "Yes, I do believe I remember you. How did you find me after all these years?"

Detective Nelson chuckled. "That would take quite a long time to tell you. Suffice it to say, it has been a long search. However, what I am here for is quite worth the effort. I see you have changed your name." He looked at her quizzically. Lucinda was almost ready to burst wide open.

"Yes. After the fire and my grandmother's death, I felt it was time to start over somewhere else and put my past behind me." He nodded and looked down at the floor. "I get that. With everything that happened to you and the trouble you had gotten into, a fresh start was almost necessary." She was crawling out of her skin at this point. "Well, you found me, so now what?"

"I don't know if you remember my partner, Anthony Harmon. He and I came onto the force together and became detectives together." Lucinda stretched her mind back and did recall an attractive man in uniform standing in the living room during the interview. He never asked a question directly, but frequently leaned into his partner's ear to whisper things. "I have a vague recollection of him. What about him?" She was starting to get more curious than nervous. If he was here for the Marlene situation, wouldn't he have just gotten right to the point and slapped the cuffs on her? "Well, Anthony dated your friend Marlene for a while after you left. During that time, he was killed by a car bomb." Lucinda remembered hearing about the bomb, but didn't know who died in the explosion. "How horrible! I am very sorry for your loss."

Detective Nelson smiled slightly. "Thank you. It was a difficult time. Anyway, I inherited a box of his with all of the stuff from his desk and locker. I couldn't go through it right away, as his death was still too fresh. Eventually I decided that it had to be dealt with. As I was going through the paperwork, I found this envelope with your name on it." He placed a manila envelope on the desk, about half the size of a piece of notebook paper. "He had told me that he was looking for you, but never said why. I felt that he would have wanted me to finish this for him. I must say, you REALLY disappeared. It took a lot of time and work for me to track you down." She could see her old name chicken-scratched on the front as he slid it toward her.

Looking at the envelope, Lucinda said, "I have to give you a lot of credit. I thought I had done pretty well to, as you say, 'disappear'." She reached out and picked it up. Whatever was in there had some weight to it. She opened it up and tipped it. A small cloth pouch slid silently out. She looked at him. He just smiled and said nothing. She untied the top of the pouch and poured the contents onto the desk. A small card fell out amongst a collection of sparkling jewels: diamonds, rubies, sapphires, and others. Detective Nelson chuckled as she looked at him and gasped. She picked up the card and turned it over. All it said was, "Your legacy. Love, Mom." She could not catch her breath. "Did you know what was in here?" Her voice was almost a whisper. "Where did they come from? Are you sure they are mine?"

The detective stood up. "Yes. I don't know. My partner said they were." He began to move toward the door. "Sorry I don't have more information than that." She just sat and looked at him incredulously. As he grabbed the door handle, he turned back toward her. "There is something else in that envelope that might make more sense to you than it does to me." Lucinda was trembling now. What other surprises could be in there. "Please stay." He stopped, but didn't move back into the room. She squeezed the envelope by the two sides, creating an opening shaped like a football. Stuck to the inside was a business card. She shook it out onto the desk and read it. Her feeling of shock was replaced by confusion. It had the name of a Boston lawyer on it, a Ricardo Azulai. She looked up at the detective and shrugged her shoulders. "Does this mean anything to you? I've never even heard of him."

Detective Nelson shook his head. "All I know is that, at one point, that man contacted my partner looking for you. While I never knew why, I got the impression that it was somewhat important." He looked at her solemnly for a few moments before continuing. "So what are you going to do now?"

Lucinda couldn't even wrap her mind around the question. "Right now? I...I don't know. I need time to think." Detective Nelson grabbed the doorknob again. "Well, I hope you get good news from that lawyer. I would hate to be the messenger for bad news. Obviously, the gift will be beneficial. I wish you well." With that, he stepped through the doorway and was gone. She quickly placed all of the stones and the note back into the pouch, then put the pouch and business card into the envelope. Finally, the envelope went into the bottom of her briefcase.

Just as she snapped the clasp shut, Ted appeared in the doorway and asked what all that was about. Lucinda answered abruptly, "Personal business." She softened her tone. "I'm sorry, Ted. This has just been a day of surprises, first with Andrew and now a family issue. If it's okay with you, I would like to just head home. My head is splitting and I'm just really tired now." Ted had a very sympathetic look on his face. "Go on. Not much work has gotten done today anyway. The police won't be in the office until tomorrow." Lucinda had almost forgotten about all that would go with the investigation of Andrew's death. "Will you call me later if you hear anything from Mrs. Lowe?" Ted nodded. "I'm probably going to be here for quite a while. There's a lot of paperwork to get ready for the Board of Directors. They are all flying in tomorrow morning." Lucinda nodded. She stood, picked up her briefcase, and mouthed a silent thank you as she passed by him and out the door.

Chapter 10

As she pulled the car out of the parking lot, Lucinda was having a hard time concentrating. She was still reeling over Detective Nelson's visit, not to mention shocked that she had completely forgotten about Andrew. She forced all of it out of her mind and tried to concentrate on the traffic.

Once in her apartment, she dropped five ice cubes into a glass and bathed them in a large helping of scotch. She carried the envelope and her drink into the living room and sat in her chair. Spilling out the contents of the envelope and the pouch, questions and thoughts ran through her mind. *How did my mother get all of these jewels? Did my father know about them? How did Anthony Harmon get them? Could Marlene have had something to do with them?* This last question was perplexing. Detective Nelson did say that his partner was dating Marlene. Maybe she had given them to him, hoping he could find her old childhood friend. Still, how would they have gotten from her mother to Marlene? She thought briefly about the business card, but had little energy to give to something that was probably just some formality regarding her grandmothers' estate.

Her mind drifted to Andrew. She took a long sip of scotch and closed her eyes. She went over all that happened in his condo last Thursday night. She got rid of the facecloth and towel. She purposely left the glass with the lipstick marks on it. She wiped the bottle from which she poured the scotch. She washed the glass she used and put it away. She never did look in the bedroom, but imagined it must have been in disarray. She retraced every step she made there and felt confident that she had covered her tracks. She felt certain that there wouldn't be a fingerprint of hers anywhere, or any DNA of her own in the bedroom, since she had only spent the one night there. Andrew would likely have had the sheets changed since he was having another guest over. She winced at that last thought. She was thankful that the complex was new, as there was no one around to see her coming or going. She even wiped all the buttons and door handles in the foyer. There should have been no trace of evidence to prove she was ever there. *I hope the police pin this on his 'new girlfriend'. Serves them both...* The thought of a built-in scapegoat made her smile. If only she knew what Ted knew.

Opening her eyes, Lucinda's thoughts turned back to the jewels. She didn't believe that they had any sentimental value, but likely came from the old "family business". She knew that her grandfather worked in organized crime, although her parents worked hard to shield her from that. When she had gotten older, after her parents died, she found out that he was actually known as "The Godfather", the head of the South Shore Mob based in Quincy, Massachusetts. She glanced over the pile of stones on the coffee table and wondered how much they were worth. She also wondered what she could possibly do with them. Lucinda wondered if it was possible that these stones still belonged to the mob. Maybe they were even looking for them. How could she ever use them? Selling them quietly seemed to be the only way. How would she know what fair value was? She remembered a woman, back when she was in jail, who talked all the time about her days as a jewel thief. *What was her name? Carmela something.* Then Lucinda remembered hearing about her dying while racing the police up the Mass Pike. It occurred to her then that one of her friends in jail had also been friends with Carmela. That name was much easier to come up with. Stella Birch. Stella had been essential for getting her through those two awful years. She had protected Lucinda, introduced her to people, taught her how to survive inside. Stella had to be out now.

Lucinda flipped open her laptop and did a quick Google search. There she was, back living in her old neighborhood. Name, address, phone number. Lucinda took a quick look at the clock. Three hour time difference would make it six in Boston. She dialed the number. After three rings, a raspy voice answered: "Hello."

"Stella, this is J.J." Stella practically exploded into the phone. "Oh my gosh! How are you doing kid? I never thought I'd hear from you again once you got out!" Lucinda breathed a sigh of relief. Stella went on. "My caller ID said Lucinda Preston and I thought, 'Who the heck is that?'. What did you do, change your name?" Lucinda laughed and replied, "Long story. I'd love to see you and I could tell you all about it. Will you be around and up for a visit this weekend?" She was thrilled at Stella's enthusiasm. The years can do funny things to friendship, but clearly Stella was happy to hear from her. "My social calendar is wide open, but why wait until the weekend?" Lucinda informed her that she would have to fly there, since she was on the other coast. "California?? Land of sunshine and movie stars! I'm single if you are friends with anyone hot and famous!" Lucinda laughed out loud. "I'll leave Friday night. I'll call you when I get to Boston on Saturday morning so we can set up a time to meet. I already have your address so I'll come to you." After quick goodbyes, Lucinda hung up the phone.

She closed her laptop, poured herself another drink, and turned on the TV. The breaking news story was on several channels. "Again, our top story tonight: the body of Andrew Lowe, an executive at the Lowe and Maher law firm in Santa Barbara was found murdered early this morning. The police are not releasing any more information at this time. We will let you know if and when any new developments arise."

Lucinda clicked off the television. She sat, staring at the blank screen, trying to piece together all of the events from the past week, preferably in a way that didn't involve her going back to jail.

Chapter 11

On Tuesday morning, Lucinda stepped out of the elevator and into bedlam. There was simply no other word that came to her mind. She had seen the office at its' busiest moments, but they paled in comparison to what greeted her eyes on this particular morning. The usual business was trying to go on, with phones ringing, potential clients waiting, and office staff scurrying in all different directions with armloads of paperwork. However, there were also newspaper reporters conducting interviews with several of her co-workers, while television crews from at least three different stations were setting up lights, microphones, and wires in a number of rooms.

"Morning, Lucinda." She turned quickly, only to have Ted pass her going in the other direction. He was moving faster than she had ever seen, barking orders and asking questions, trying to keep this dog-and-pony show moving along. "Rosaleen, did you call the caterers?" From somewhere in the room, Lucinda heard her shouted answer. "Yes, they said they would be here at ten, on the dot." Going in the other direction now, Ted addressed Lucinda again. "Could you get the latest files from Andrew's desk and bring them to me? His wife never called me, so I have no idea what's going on. The board should be here by nine-thirty. I'll touch base with you later. Leave the files on my desk." As he turned to go, he was greeted by a reporter with a humongous microphone stuck right in his face. Even though he was not facing her, Lucinda could imagine the blood rushing into his face. She knew what was coming next. "Will you get that blasted thing out of my face? I have no time for interviews right now!"

The reality of the situation came rushing back to Lucinda. *Wow. To think that I caused all this.* Her stomach seconded the motion with a small lurch. She had seen the newspapers that morning and Andrew was the headline on all of them. When she was at the coffee shop, the TV had the sound off, but she didn't need to hear the voices of the reporters, as they were standing in front of Stearns Wharf in one of the scenes and her office building in another. A phone number was on the bottom of the screen, presumably asking for a call from any potential witnesses.

Lucinda turned to head to her office to drop off her coat and briefcase, but was cut off by two men that seemed to come out of nowhere. They were dressed in black suits and carrying matching briefcases. They introduced themselves to Rosaleen, who had found her way back to her desk outside of Ted's office. Lucinda strained to hear what they said, but the noise in the room made it all but impossible. Her stomach gurgled in response as she moved toward her desk, with one eye still on the men in black. She quickly threw her stuff on the chair that her visitor used yesterday and headed off to get the files for Ted. She was also hoping to catch any information about the mystery guests, although she had a pretty good idea who they were.

The men were still standing at Rosaleen's desk when Lucinda passed them on the way to Andrew's office. She reached the door and didn't even hesitate going in. However, once she stepped inside, she immediately felt uncomfortable. It was as though she had never been in the room before. She scanned the room and several things jumped out at her. The most prominent of these were the several photos meticulously placed along the credenza behind Andrew's desk. The largest, right in the middle and flanked on both sides by smaller frames, showed six smiling faces all huddled in close to the center. Andrew was in the center of the circle, being embraced by a stunning blonde with a megawatt smile. Two boys stood in the back, leaning down over their parents while two girls were seated in the front. All four had almost identical hair as their mother. Ted was right. For a moment, Lucinda almost laughed. Andrew looked like the black sheep of that particular family. The kids did indeed take after their mother. Still, they looked ridiculously happy and she couldn't understand what would make a man risk losing that. Thinking of her own teenage years minus a father and mother, she felt a brief pang of guilt, knowing what it would be like for the four of them. Quickly, though, this passed and was replaced by the resilient and defiant attitude that she developed so long ago. *A tough lesson to learn, that nothing is permanent and life is unfair.* She had overcome it, and they would as well. Suddenly, the feeling that she had trespassed swept over her, and she felt as though she would be caught any minute. This was exacerbated by the presence of the two men waiting for something less than thirty feet from where she stood. Lucinda quickly stepped over to the desk, grabbed the files from the basket marked "current", and left the office, quietly closing the door behind her.

Lucinda strode past the men in suits, much more confidently than she felt, knocked lightly on Ted's door and stepped in without waiting for a response. Ted was on the phone, but gestured toward the empty chair in front of his desk. No sooner had she settled in than there was another knock on the door. She spun around to see Rosaleen and the two men standing so close to each other that it appeared as though they were doing a three person sack race. Ted looked up, wearing a rather uncomfortable look on his face. She wondered if he ever got this rattled in court. He quickly ended the call and said, "Gentlemen, please come in." Without saying a word, they moved into the room but ignored the two additional chairs along the far wall of the office. Taking out small notepads, they introduced themselves and presented credentials indicating that they were part of the CSI team investigating Andrew's murder. They began firing questions at the two of them regarding their relationship with the deceased, when they had last seen him, whether Andrew had any enemies of whom they were aware. They asked Lucinda specifically about the previous Thursday. She told them about how Andrew was supposed to be escorting her to the concert, but called just prior to the show and said that he had a late appointment, so she went alone. After about fifteen minutes, they seemed to be satisfied and tucked their notebooks back into their jackets. They presented two cards, handed them to Lucinda and Ted and were gone as quickly as they came.

They looked at each other, but before a word could be spoken, the phone broke the silence. Ted answered and immediately took on a soft tone. Lucinda surmised that it was Andrew's wife, calling with an update. She was impressed with Ted's bedside manner, comforting and reassuring, all while being decisive in regard to what the company would be doing to assist her during this difficult time. It was a side of him that she had never really seen before. She had always seen him as the frat boy who never grew up, chasing girls and drinking beer. She waited patiently for the conversation to end. When Ted finally hung up, his brow was deeply furrowed and he gave a deep sigh. "Poor thing. She has no idea where to go from here. Andrew was apparently very secretive about a lot of things, money being one of the biggest. She has a lot of paperwork to go through in order to find out what their financial status is. Her brother flew in from Tennessee this morning to help. Funeral arrangements are pending. Given what happened, I am guessing the services will be private."

Lucinda leaned forward in her chair. "Have any decisions been made regarding the office?" Ted was still looking down at his desk, but she couldn't tell if he was actually focusing on something. "Well, I spoke to a guy I know in the corporate office, and he tells me that they are sending someone out with the board. He is going to take over Andrew's position for the time being. I am guessing that they will still need to vote on whether or not to make it a permanent change. His name is Roger Powers and he currently works out of our Chicago office." She pressed on. "Do you know this man?" At this point, she guessed that Ted was going to need some time alone before he had to greet the board members and get that meeting going. When she asked the question, he turned to stare out the window, as though he was sorting out some important details that had just come to mind. Before she could suggest that they continue the discussion later, Ted answered. "I met him several years ago at a meeting in their offices. He seemed like a real down-to-earth kind of guy, but what can you tell from an hour?" Lucinda felt this was a reasonable place to excuse herself and get back to her work. "I will leave you alone so you can get ready for the meeting." She silently stood up and moved to the door. "Oh, by the way, Ted. Would you mind if I was a little late coming in tomorrow? I have a personal matter to attend to." Without looking up, Ted waved at nothing and said, "No problem. Take whatever time you need."

Lucinda spent the rest of the day staying out of the spotlight as best she could. Other than having to slam her door on one poor rookie reporter, she was able to get a sizable amount of work done without interruption. The next morning, Lucinda was waiting at her bank fifteen minutes before it opened. In half an hour, she was standing in a private room with a safe deposit box on the table in front of her. She dug deep into her inside jacket pocket and retrieved the manila envelope. Briefly marveling at the weight of something so small, she dropped it in the box and locked the lid. She buried the key where the envelope had been and rang for the attendant. She soon found herself back on the sidewalk, feeling slightly lighter and breathing much easier.

Chapter 12

As she was driving to work, it occurred to Lucinda that just one week ago, she was in Chicago with Andrew, having breakfast and getting ready to come home for the concert. Amazing what can happen in a week. When she arrived at the office, Ted was not at his desk. Rosaleen gave her a weird look that she couldn't figure out when Lucinda asked where he was. Apparently, Roger Powers had not made the flight with the board yesterday and Ted was picking him up from the airport. An awkward silence told Lucinda that the conversation was over. She thanked Rosaleen and headed for her office.

The morning flew by quickly, as Lucinda had let work back up quite a bit because of the events of the previous week. A knock at the door stirred her from her diligence and she looked up at the clock. Eleven-thirty. Her stomach growled as though it had just woken up. She looked toward the door to find Ted standing with easily one of the most handsome older men she had ever seen. Powerfully built, tailored suit, a full head of salt-and-pepper hair, and no wedding ring. She felt the same tingle that had occurred the day she met Andrew.

"Lucinda, I would like you to meet Roger Powers. Roger, this is Lucinda Preston." She stood up to greet him and became instantly aware of her appearance. She was thankful that she had taken a little extra time that morning in getting ready. She had chosen her favorite periwinkle suit, perfectly professional and yet very inviting. As he extended his hand in greeting, she noticed him giving her a once over. She felt herself flush slightly. Ted broke up the moment by informing her that they were going to head for a working lunch, so Roger could be brought up to speed on what needed to be done to get the office back on track after the recent diversions.

Lucinda ate at her desk, trying to get back into the flow that she had that morning. The presence of Roger Powers, however, made that far more difficult. As soon as he and Ted had returned from lunch, the tension in the office seemed to explode. She hated closing the door to her office because it made her feel somewhat claustrophobic, but Ted was making her seriously consider it. He was running around frantically, gathering files and information, with Roger in tow looking increasingly anxious. Whenever they would pass her office, Roger would look in at her and roll his eyes. She just gave a slight smile and shrugged her shoulders.

When five o'clock rolled around, Lucinda packed up and headed for the elevators. She had had enough for one day and was looking forward to putting her feet up and wrapping her hands around a glass of scotch. As she stood waiting, she could feel eyes burning into the back of her head. Turning quickly around, she caught Rosaleen staring at her with a rather venomous look. What had Lucinda done to tick her off so badly? Lucinda had never really cared for her, with her high-and-mighty attitude, but she was starting to outright dislike her. Images of what she wouldn't mind doing to her filled Lucinda's mind. She smiled and, with the ding of the elevator, she turned and stepped out of Rosaleen's view.

Chapter 13

Friday proved to be amazingly quiet and without incident, and Lucinda soon found herself on a late flight to Boston. Even though she was a most reluctant flier, the trip flashed by and Logan Airport appeared outside her window without incident. It was a little after nine in the morning by the time she reached a coffee kiosk, and she felt that it was certainly late enough to make a phone call.

Stella picked up on two rings, sounding remarkably wide awake. "Hey, kid. I'm making a fresh pot of coffee. How about picking up some muffins or doughnuts?" Lucinda looked at the cup in her hands and laughed. "Sounds good. I could use a cup. See you soon." She went back to the kiosk and picked up two muffins and two jelly doughnuts. She nursed the coffee until she was ready to head out and catch a cab, then dropped it into the trash. She knew a second cup of coffee wouldn't sit well in her stomach and she wanted to enjoy one with an old friend. She left the terminal and soon was on her way to Quincy.

When the cabbie pulled over to let her out, she looked at the building in front of her. It was an old brick building, though it was surprisingly devoid of the intricate brickwork that was usually found in the early Boston construction. Not surprisingly, there was no elevator and Lucinda knew that Stella lived on the sixth floor. She headed into the stairwell and was soon standing in front of her destination. She knocked on the door. In one motion, Stella opened her door, threw her arms around her, and gave her a big bear hug. Lucinda noticed how thin and frail Stella was. This unnerved her a little bit. She handed Stella the muffins and doughnuts. Lucinda closed the door behind her and watched her friend head into the kitchen, where the table was all set for a casual breakfast. From this position, she could really see how bony Stella had become.

"Give me your jacket, stay awhile." Stella took her coat and wrapped it over a hanger and hung it on a doorknob. "I'd hang it in the closet, but I can't even put a postage stamp in there. It really is jammed tight. I keep telling my daughter, Denise, to stop buying me stuff. But does she listen?" Stella gave a low chuckle. "Kids will be kids."

Lucinda sat down while Stella brought the coffee pot over and poured out two steaming cups. It smelled good. Hazelnut, maybe, but she wasn't sure. She ripped open the paper bag so they could see what the choices were without having to rummage around. Lucinda waited until her friend chose a muffin before doing the same. As casually as she could, Lucinda asked, "So how are you doing?" Stella laughed a raspy laugh, ending with a rather juicy cough. "Hey, it would take a month of Mondays to tell you my troubles." She cut her muffin into four equal pieces. Lighting up a cigarette, she offered one to Lucinda. She shook her head no and Stella shrugged. Settling back into her chair, Stella blew out a long blue plume of smoke. "Your call the other day really got me thinking about the past. I hadn't thought about your grandmother in a while. I do miss her. She was a good friend. We had some good times together." Lucinda remembered when she found out that the total stranger who kept her safe through two years in jail ended up being an old friend of her grandmother. She never really knew what the connection was, but she wasn't a big believer in coincidence. It had been karma. "I miss her too, Stell. It's hard to believe it's been ten years."

Stella blew out another plume and stared out the window. "Ten years. I can't figure where the time goes." Turning her head toward Lucinda, she cut right to the point. "So, kid, how come you flew all the way cross country to see me? Must be important. You could have enjoyed my sparkling personality and conversational skills over the phone."

"I don't really know where to begin." Lucinda took a deep breath and a quick sip of the still steaming coffee. She told Stella about the visit from Carl Nelson, inheriting the jewels, and the law firm that had been looking for her. She could tell that the jewels intrigued Stella, as she sat up and let out a low whistle at the mention of them. "So why me? Why come here? It sounds to me like you should be planning some trip or buying an island or something."

Lucinda hesitated for a moment. "I need to sell the jewels. I remembered that butch girl, Carmela, was always talking about her 'work' in the jewel field, but she died some years ago. I knew that you were close with her and I thought that maybe she had mentioned someone who could take them off my hands, quietly, for a fair price." Stella mashed out the last of her cigarette and immediately lit another one. She was quiet for a moment, seemingly in thought. A couple of hard coughs later, she spoke up again. "Well, kid, you weren't wrong. I do know a few people, although it's been a long time since we've spoken. I may need some time. How long are you in town?" Lucinda informed her that she had a flight scheduled for tomorrow morning. Stella went back into deep thought. Lucinda heard a noise behind her and turned around. An orange tabby was coming toward them. Its' right rear leg was missing.

"Wow. What happened to her?" Lucinda was amazed at how well the cat was moving. "Her is actually a him. Got hit by a car. Nearly lost him, but the vet was one of the best." Stella used her second cigarette to start up a third. Her eyes lit up and she said, "Wait right here. I've got something to show you." She headed down the narrow hall behind her and Lucinda could hear rummaging, maybe in that closet that wouldn't even fit the postage stamp. Stella came back holding a small, oblong box. "Open it."

Lucinda ran her fingers along the sides until she found two small grooves. She pried open the box and placed the cover on the table. In the box was a wooden plaque, engraved with the following words: I've Finally Stopped Smoking. She looked at Stella, who was trying hard to stifle a laugh. "That is going to be placed in my casket next to me when I croak." The two of them burst out laughing.

After the business end of the meeting, the two old friends shared an hour or so of small talk. Lucinda stood up, stretched, and looked at her watch. It was pushing noon and she was hoping to walk some of the old neighborhoods before heading to a hotel. She thought briefly about the business card in the envelope and was sorry that she hadn't brought it. Lucinda couldn't come up with the name of the firm, so there was no way she could even see if it was still an active practice. She made a mental note to skim names in the phone book and see if one jumped out at her. She thanked Stella and told her to do the best she could with the request. She took out a business card, turned it over, and wrote all her relevant numbers on the back. Stella walked her to the door and gave her another big bear hug. "It really was great seeing you again. I'll be in touch when I have something."

Lucinda headed back down the six flights and quickly hailed a cab. A sudden wave of exhaustion told her that the neighborhood walking would have to wait. She checked in at a hotel not far from Stella's and made reservations for dinner that evening in the hotel dining room. She headed upstairs, dropped onto the bed still in her shoes and jacket, and fell fast asleep. An early dinner, then a long and deep sleep brought Sunday morning and a trip to the airport. Aside from a two hour layover in Chicago, the trip went smoothly and she arrived at her apartment by early evening. As she unpacked her bag, Lucinda felt buoyed by her trip. She was already looking forward to a call from Stella.

Chapter 14

In the aftermath of Andrew's death and the subsequent investigation, life in the office had gotten far more difficult. Ted was beginning to look rather sickly, as the annual audit of the books was coming up and the transition from one partner to another was more work than anyone had anticipated. Lucinda was pulling more hours than she ever had before, but this was turning out to be a blessing in disguise. It had been two weeks since her visit to Boston and staying busy was keeping her from agonizing over the silence.

Lucinda had taken a stack of old files down to the shredder and when she stepped out of the elevator back on her floor, she could hear her phone ringing. She picked up the pace and grabbed on the fifth ring. "Lucinda Preston," she breathed into the phone. "Hey, kid. It's Stella. What did I drag you away from that has you breathing so heavy?" She could hear the sarcastic tone in her friends' voice. "Nothing like that, sorry to say. I was just down the hall when I heard the phone, so I had to run a bit. Funny you would call, as I was just thinking about you." She could hear Stella exhale loudly. Obviously she hadn't quit smoking just yet. "Yeh. I bet you thought I had forgotten all about you. I was working on it, but these things take time, you know." Lucinda was just about to assure her that she wasn't thinking that at all, but Stella continued. "After you left, I started making some phone calls. I wasn't feeling too good, but I figured that it was just the pot and a half of coffee I had that morning. Every morning, actually. Anyway, I ended up in the hospital with a bit of a stomach problem and I only got out a couple of days ago." Lucinda thought back to her first impression of Stella and how skinny she was. It made her wonder if there was something more going on that she wasn't being told.

"I understand. I don't mind waiting a little longer." Lucinda only half meant this, as she was really hoping to both get the jewels out of her possession and get that money in her pocket. "You don't understand, kid. I didn't say that I didn't have what you needed. I was just telling you why I haven't been in touch. Hang up and find a pay phone. I'm calling from the one in my lobby. Here's the number. Talk to you in a bit." Lucinda jotted down the number. On the way to the stairs, she told Ted that she was heading to the pharmacy to pick up pills for her migraines. "If you need to go home…" She interrupted and assured him that wasn't necessary. "I'll be better once I take the pills. I have a lot to do here. Thanks anyway." She headed down the stairs taking two steps at a time. She wasn't sure why she was running, as Stella never said that she needed to hurry. When she got to the sidewalk, she started thinking about where she would even find a pay phone. With everyone having a cell phone, she never even noticed those little booths anymore. Scanning the street, she saw one in the far corner of the parking lot of the gas station on the opposite corner. She fished for the number in her pocket as she weaved through the stop-and-go traffic outside her building. Breathing heavy once again, she dialed the number.

"Hey, it's J.J. How come I had to call you from a pay phone?" Stella coughed loudly. "Listen, I got you a contact. It wasn't easy. I can't take the chance of this conversation being traced back to me. I'm going to give you a number. Whoever answers, say "This is agent 1820" and then give them the number of the phone you're calling from. Wait five minutes. Let the phone ring three times before answering. You'll get a name and address, then go from there. Good luck. Love ya."

"Stella, I promise. I owe you big and I'll make it worth your while. Hope you're feeling better. When this is all done, I'll be in touch."

Lucinda hung up the phone and immediately punched in the number that Stella gave her. A sultry female voice answered, and Lucinda followed her friends' instructions. After hanging up, she waited and fidgeted. On more than one occasion, she needed to tell someone that they couldn't use the phone because she was waiting for a call. She was amazed that this thing got so much use. Suddenly, the phone rang out behind her and she waited impatiently for three rings before grabbing the receiver. A deep male voice gave her a location in San Francisco, near the Cannery Row Company. She was to be there on Saturday. She hung up the phone and headed back to the office. She couldn't tell if the nerves were from excitement or fear over the cloak-and-dagger meeting she just set up with a total stranger. Even though Stella would never knowingly put her in harm's way, some of the people she had done business with in the past might not be as benevolent.

Within minutes of sitting back at her desk, Ted poked his head in. "Better?" He genuinely looked concerned. "Better. Thank you." She smiled. No sooner did he leave than there was a knock at the door. Roger Powers was standing there. "I hear you have migraines too. How are you feeling?" *Ted really can't keep his mouth shut about anything.* "I'm fine. Not to worry." Roger continued to stand there, making Lucinda a little nervous. She looked back up at him inquisitively. He coughed a small cough, as though he were about to make a big announcement. "Any chance you would be interested in dinner with me tonight?" That was not what she was expecting. She quickly skimmed her calendar on the desk and said, "Looks like I'm free for the evening."

Roger smiled. "Good. Well, I did the asking, but since I'm not from here…." Lucinda found herself laughing. "You like seafood or Italian?" Roger's eyes lit up at the choice. "I love seafood." Lucinda was thrilled with his pick. "Me too. There is a great seafood place not far from here, called the Lavender Turtle." She never really got the name, but Roger didn't bat an eye. "Sounds great. Do you need to go home first or should we just go from here?" Lucinda always kept a little bag in her office for instances like this, so she didn't even have to think about it. "Let's leave from here. It will be easier to get a reservation if it's earlier. I'll call it in." Roger winked and said, "Wonderful. See you at the end of the day."

Lucinda thought to herself that it would be good for her to go out with someone else for a change. After a couple of years with Andrew, she was actually excited about the dinner date. For a moment, she thought about Ted and what he might say. *The heck with him. Let him think what he wants.*

At six, Lucinda was standing in Andrew's doorway. Roger was just packing up some paperwork. The trip to the lobby and outside was silent, as though each was feeling out the situation. Roger was just about to hail a cab when Lucinda said, "Don't bother. I have my car." They settled in and she pulled out into traffic. She turned on the radio to fill in the quiet a bit. They listened for a minute before Roger cleared his throat and said, "I hear you and Andrew were an item." Lucinda winced. She had almost forgotten that Ted might have known and said something to the police. "I suppose Ted told you that." Roger was staring straight ahead. "Yes," he said carefully. "Well, I thought we were too. I have since learned that I was apparently just one of many. Still, I am sorry that he is dead, especially for his family." They let these words sink in a bit and rode in silence. Then Roger blurted out, "I wonder why he was killed." Lucinda began to worry. Maybe this was why he asked her to dinner. Maybe Ted suggested it. Maybe Roger was just fishing for information.

"Could we not discuss Andrew? I'm really just looking forward to a simple and quiet evening." Roger did not answer, but just nodded his head in assent.

The rest of the ride was silent and Lucinda couldn't stop thinking about the motivation for the dinner. As she pulled up to the restaurant, she decided that she needed to be careful with what she said, but she felt she had covered her tracks well enough. She handed the keys to the valet and stepped up to the curb. Roger stood waiting with his elbow out to her. *Ah, an old fashioned gentleman.* She took his arm and they walked up to the front door, where he opened the door for her with a smile. *A gentleman, indeed.*

They entered the restaurant and found themselves standing in front of a wall to wall mirror. She couldn't help but think what a good looking couple they made. She looked at him now and realized that he was more salt than pepper, with striking green eyes, and a very aristocratic look about him. The maitre'd walked over and greeted them. "How delightful to see you again, Ms. Preston." She noticed Roger glance at her with a smile on his face. "Petar, I would like you to meet my friend, Roger Powers. He recently joined our firm." Petar immediately bowed slightly and then extended his hand. "Mr. Powers, so nice to make your acquaintance. Please, follow me. I have a lovely table for the two of you." He led them to a small table in a quiet corner with a view of the entire restaurant. The dinner crowd had yet to come, so they had the place mostly to themselves.

Before they could even peruse the menu, the waiter was at their table. He handed Roger the wine list. He turned it to her, thinking she might like to choose. "I would actually love a scotch on the rocks." He smiled, handed the wine list to the waiter, and said, "Make that two, please." After the waiter left, Roger turned back to her. "Well, Lucinda, I'm dying to know more about you. Theodore has told me how invaluable you have been to the company, but I am sure that there is so much more to know." Lucinda smiled, but inside she was squirming a bit. She reminded herself to be careful and not reveal too much, but Roger was such a calming presence. She would have to be continually mindful. "Why don't we start with you?" He followed her redirect willingly. "Ah. Well, I've been married five times." Lucinda coughed. "Five times? Are you serious?" Roger laughed heartily. "Of course not. Just thought I would break the ice." She took a quick sip of her drink, which had magically appeared at her right hand when she wasn't looking. "Heck of a way to break the ice." She laughed also.

"I must confess, however, that I do have my vices. I drink my share. I like to gamble. I work hard and I enjoy the benefits when they come. I like the challenges that come with my job, as they force me to be my best every day. I have even been working on writing a book." Lucinda was surprised at that last comment. "Really. What kind of a book?" Roger looked sheepishly at her. "I guess it's a bit of a cliché, but I have been working on a whodunit." She was genuinely impressed. She added, "I have always wanted to write a book, but nonfiction. Maybe a little spiritual, about life." At that moment, the waiter appeared at the table. They ordered another round, along with their dinners.

Lucinda looked around and noticed that the restaurant had filled up considerably. She also picked up the sound of a piano being played. She knew there was a small dance floor and asked Roger if he would do her the honor. He smiled, extended his hand, and led her to the floor. He gently took her hand and rested the other on her hip. He gracefully moved her to the rhythm of the foxtrot, and Lucinda melted into a state of oblivion.

When the music suddenly stopped, Lucinda found herself considering giving the piano player a piece of her mind. However, Roger led her to the table and her frustration dissipated when she noticed that their dinners were just being set out on the table.

Lucinda was never disappointed when she dined here, but tonight easily surpassed all others. The very first bite of her stuffed calamari sent her eyes rolling back and, from the look on his face, Roger was experiencing the very same thing with his scallops wrapped in bacon. She couldn't help but think that this much silence on a first date is normally a bad thing, but she was reluctant to break the reverie with conversation. They were both about halfway through their entrees when Roger finally spoke up. "I have to say, Lucinda, that I have eaten in countless restaurants around the world, and this ranks right at the top." She couldn't help but laugh at how he punctuated this statement with a forkful of Delmonico potatoes. "This was a fabulous place to recommend." Before she could reply, Roger continued. "Did Andrew take you here?" She winced at the name. It also reminded her that she needed to be careful, as she still wasn't sure what Ted knew about the two of them and didn't feel like handing him a rope to hang her with. "Please, Roger, could we not discuss that? The evening has been so lovely." Once again, Roger nodded his assent and quickly changed the subject. While he gave her a brief summation of his history with the company, Lucinda couldn't help but think again about why he had asked her to dinner. She didn't get the sense that he had ulterior motives, or that either he or Ted suspected her and was trying to corner her, but it didn't feel entirely like a social dinner either.

The next hour flew by, accompanied by lively conversation, dessert, and another quick spin around the dance floor. As the last plates were being cleared from the table, Roger took a quick glance at his watch.

"Time truly flies when you're having fun. I should get you home."
Thinking about the driving arrangements, he chuckled and added, "Maybe
it is you who should be getting me home." He stood up and came around
behind her, putting his hands on the back of her chair. He gently slid it
back as she stood up. She wondered for a brief moment about the check.
Then she remembered hearing Roger call over the waiter when she excused
herself before their last dance. *A gentleman and smooth as silk.* When
they arrived on the sidewalk, the valet was already there with her car
waiting. He held open her door, took her hand as she got in, and closed it
gently after her. She noticed Roger shake the young man's hand and she
knew that a generous tip was inside that handshake. Then he was beside
her.

She pretended to pull on a pair of driving gloves. "Where to, sir?"
Roger laughed aloud and asked if he should be sitting in the back seat.
"Truthfully, I have no idea where to take you. What hotel are you staying
at?" She was curious just how generous the firm would be with one of its
executives. "Actually, I am staying at Ted's." Lucinda was shocked at
this. She never expected that someone like Roger would have to bunk with
someone while he was in town. However, she hid her surprise and put the
car in drive. "Very well, sir. Now if you can just tell me how to get
there…" She truthfully didn't know where Ted lived and was curious to
see his home. She had always figured it was some old apartment,
surrounded by bars and barbeque joints. Frat boys would kill for a place
like that. "It's down by the water. Are you familiar with the area near
Stearns Wharf?" She stifled a cough and replied that she was not. "Take
the highway south to Cabrillo Boulevard and I'll direct you from there."
As she got on the highway, she couldn't help but be surprised. Stearns
Wharf and the area around it was certainly not where she expected to find
Ted. It was mostly newer construction, though even the older houses in

the area were sizable and well maintained. Roger broke her train of thought. "Slow down. The Cabrillo Boulevard exit is coming up." *Oh, Roger, don't you worry. This isn't exactly uncharted territory.* She pulled off the highway and down into a very elegant neighborhood. Roger directed her through two quick turns before bringing her to a stop at a patch of woods. She looked at him with a quizzical look. "Are you two sharing a tent or did you splurge for two?" He laughed again and said, "No, it's the white house on the hill up ahead. I just need to walk off some of that incredible meal." She looked up ahead to a beautiful old Victorian with a long, sloping front lawn. The landscaping was subtle and meticulous. *Wow. Ted certainly is full of surprises. He has done well for himself.* She could see the Pacific Ocean in the distance and wondered how much better the view was from up on his hill. She also knew that she was no more than a mile away from Andrew's condo.

She turned to look at Roger. He smiled and took her hand. "I had a really good time tonight. You have been exceptional company and I thank you for saying yes to the invite." He kissed the back of her hand and started to open the door. She held his hand firm and he turned back to her. "Roger, forgive me. I am confused. We just had an incredible meal, wonderful conversation, and some heavenly dancing. Now, I am leaving you not at a beautiful hotel room, but at the home of one of the partners, not to mention at the very bottom of the hill." She was confused about so much more, but that would do for now. Roger looked at her for a moment, then kissed her hand again. "I will let you in on a secret, and I do hope you can keep it a secret." He shifted in his seat to face her. "We have had an exquisite time tonight and I truly enjoyed your company. However, I am thinking that I might have given you the wrong impression." She looked at him curiously. He then added, "I am afraid that I am spoken for." She waited for him to continue, but he was clearly waiting for her to process what he just said. Roger looked first at her, then up the hill, when suddenly it dawned on her. "Oh my God! Really? I mean, that's great! I'm happy for you. How long have you been together?" Roger laughed gently. "We met at a business meeting in Chicago several years ago. Everything just seemed to click between us. We both knew it right from the start, but felt it best to keep it quiet. You can never tell how such information might influence co-workers or clients, especially in this field. We see each other at least once a month, alternating flights, and so far it has worked out reasonably well. This business with Andrew, as sad as it is, has allowed us to spend a lot more time together without questions being asked." He stared intently at her, trying to gauge a reaction. Lucinda's mind was going a mile a minute with all sorts of thoughts, but there was one question that she had to ask. "Why are you telling me all this?"

Roger answered without so much as a pause. "You are a lovely lady. Given the circumstances, I guessed that you might be getting the wrong signals from me." She fired off a second question without thinking. "What is Ted going to think about our 'date'?" Roger chuckled. "Not to worry, my dear. It was his idea." Lucinda's mouth dropped open. Her perception of Ted continued to be decimated. "Why on earth would he suggest that?" For a moment, she thought that maybe she was right, that Ted suspected her in Andrew's death and was using Roger to peel for information that he wouldn't be able to get on his own. However, Roger squashed that thought with his answer. "Ted thinks very highly of you. He knows that everything in the office has been wearing on you, between the workload and this recent tragedy. He could tell that you were interested romantically in Andrew. Ted also knows that Andrew had an insatiable appetite for women. He had a tendency to keep several on the hook at a time. He couldn't bear to see that happen to you. That is why he told you about Andrew's new girlfriend the night of the concert, although he is sorry about the delivery." Lucinda continued to stare at Roger open-mouthed, so he went on. "He felt that a night out might give your mind a break. He is counting on you to help move the firm through all this." The silence stretched on after his last statement, as Lucinda tried to come to terms with what all of this meant. However, Roger decided it was time to go. With a final kiss of her hand, he bid her good night and got out of the car. Before the door closed, she asked one last question. "What will I say to him tomorrow at work?" He turned briefly and said, "I'm sure you'll do just fine. Like Ted, I have faith in you." She watched him go up the hill. As he neared the front door, it swung open and Ted stood there. He had a wine glass in one hand and made a small wave with the other. She instinctively knew that the wave was for her, not for Roger. As she put the car in drive, she saw them embrace and then disappear inside the house.

Lucinda drove home in silence. So many things to consider. Roger and Ted. Who would have seen that coming? Ted thought so highly of her and her work. Clearly there was more to him than she had picked up on. One thing stuck out above all the others, though. Ted knew that Andrew was a player. He knew that she was interested in that player. He knew that Andrew would leave her hanging. He didn't want to see that happen. So he told her about the girlfriend, hoping to intervene before that could happen. Ted was trying to protect **her** from **Andrew**.

As she pulled into her garage, she smiled. She felt better than she had since the Chicago trip. Lucinda had a good feeling that all would be well soon.

Chapter 15

The next morning, Lucinda cruised through her routine and found herself at the office a half hour early. She had already put a sizable dent in her workload for the day when she heard the elevator open. Moments later, Ted poked his head in the door. "Good morning, Lucinda." She kept her eyes on the work in front of her, but acknowledged the greeting. "Morning." She knew Ted was still standing there. Waiting. "Well?" The tone in his voice told her that she should know exactly what he wanted. However, Lucinda was feeling quite playful this morning. "I should have that paperwork on your desk within the hour." She could feel his eyes boring into the side of her head. "Whatever. Well?" She was struggling to stifle the laugh. "Oh, and everything you will need for your ten o'clock meeting is already in the conference room." Ted let out with a loud, "Lucinda!" and she burst out laughing. "Thank you for suggesting that Roger take me out to dinner last night. I really enjoyed his company." At this, Ted smiled. "I figured you could use a night out after all that's been going on around here." Without looking up, she added, "I can't wait to see him again. He's a marvelous dancer."

"You keep this up and I'll make sure you never have time for another night out." Ted's tone was stern, but she knew he was enjoying the banter. "I'm guessing that you and Roger had a lot to talk about? He is a very worldly individual." Finally Lucinda turned to him. "Yes, Ted. He shared a great deal with me, both personally and professionally." Ted interjected with a question. "I trust that you can keep a secret?" She nodded and moved her fingers across her lips like a zipper. "Honestly, Ted, I couldn't be happier for you. It was a bit of a shock, but then there's been a lot of that around here lately." Ted gave her a quick smile and ducked back out of sight. She could have sworn that she heard him click his heels when he left.

Around ten, Roger stepped off the elevator. He too made her office the first stop. "Good morning. How did things go?" Right to the point, she thought. So different from Ted's coy, foot-shuffling approach. "Like you said, I would do just fine. I believe that I handled it quite well." He smiled and said, "I had no doubts whatsoever." With that, he turned and headed off to Andrew's old office.

Lucinda worked through lunch in order to finish the rest of the days' tasks, knowing that she had a couple of errands to take care of before her trip on Saturday. Her first order of business was to make a stop at the bank. It only took five minutes for her to retrieve the pouch and get back on the road. She then stopped at a fast food drive-thru and ordered a hamburger. Pulling into a spot in the back of the parking lot, she took out both the burger and the key to Andrew's condo. Wiping the key clean with a napkin, she stuffed it into the meat before rewrapping it. She put the burger back in the bag and wrapped the entire thing into a tight ball. She stopped at a trash bin near the exit so she wouldn't have to get out of the car. She threw the bag, burger, and key into the trash before slipping into the mid-afternoon traffic and heading for home. *Almost there*, she thought to herself, with just a hint of a smile.

Chapter 16

Friday proved to be uneventful, although Lucinda found herself getting excited about her trip the next day. She did her best to stay in her office and busy, hoping that fewer diversions would keep the time moving. Still, the day crept along, but finally she found herself in the elevator and heading for her car. Her itinerary for the night was simple: a quick run, a light dinner, prep what she would need for the trip, and into bed.

When the alarm rang the next morning at four thirty, she was thankful that she had turned in earlier than normal. It was still pitch black outside when Lucinda headed off for a shower. She was out in record time and threw on a pair of jeans and a sweatshirt, finishing off with a pair of sneakers. She grabbed her jacket and threw on a pink baseball cap. It was going to be a long drive and she wanted to be as comfortable as possible. Lucinda noticed the business card on the kitchen table, where she had thrown it last night before packing the pouch. She wasn't sure what to do with it, but knew she didn't want to lose it. Sliding it off the table, she held it to the refrigerator door with one finger and put her favorite magnet on it, the one she had made using the only picture she had of herself and her parents. She smiled wistfully, as she had little memory of where the picture was taken, but that didn't matter. All that mattered was that the three of them were together. She picked up her backpack, with the jewels tucked in the bottom, and headed out the door.

Getting into the car, Lucinda threw her backpack on the floor, but then retrieved it and put it on the seat next to her. Even though it was only a few feet, she still felt better having the bag, and the little cloth pouch, right up against her. She had chosen the backpack instead of her handbag because she thought it more appropriate with her casual attire, as well as for the fact that it would be harder to get off of her shoulders than a single strap bag. She backed out, hit the door lock button, and headed for Route 101. She figured she would drive to Los Angeles, a ninety mile trip from Santa Barbara, before stopping. After a quick breakfast and bathroom break, she could then finish the two-hundred-forty-eight miles to San Francisco.

Lucinda felt a little uneasy about having the jewels in her bag and continually put her hand down to make sure that it was still there. She tried to keep her speed below the limit, fearful of either being pulled over and having to get out of the car or getting into an accident. However, traffic was light and she reached her final destination a half hour earlier than expected. She parked her car in the lot of an old chocolate factory. Appropriately enough, there was a pay phone in the corner of the lot. She put her arms through both of the straps on the bag, feeling a bit like a college student as she strode quickly to the phone. She called the number that Stella gave her and heard the sultry voice from her first phone call. The woman gave her an address just around the corner from where she was. As she hung up, Lucinda thought for a brief moment about driving the car there, given what she was carrying, but surveyed the area around her and decided that she would be okay with the short walk.

She found the building less than fifty yards from where she parked her car. It was an old brick building, with a fish market taking up most of the first floor. There was a door with a buzzer at the far corner. She pressed the button and was surprised to be buzzed in without so much as a question of who was there. It gave her the feeling that she was being watched from the moment she stopped at that door. She walked down a dim hallway and was even more surprised when she reached the end and stepped into a modern and clean foyer. She crossed over to the elevators and pressed the button for the fourth floor. A smooth ten second ride later and the doors opened to perhaps the biggest surprise. She was standing inside a breathtaking apartment. Beautiful handmade furniture, exquisite paintings on every wall, and an impressive pastel flowered design Oriental rug covered a large section of beautiful hardwood floors. She was greeted by a male voice, less imposing than the one with whom she made this appointment, but equally confident. "You must be Ms. Preston." She turned to the voice and found a handsome man, she guessed in his forties, standing with his hands clasped behind his back. He wore gray wool trousers and a neatly pressed blue dress shirt. When he reached out in greeting she noticed well-manicured hands graced only with a silver watch held by a black leather band and a matching silver wedding band. "My name is Oliver. Please, step into my office."

He passed by her and through a door that she had not noticed when she came in. She followed him into a smaller room, but no less elegant than the first. A large oak desk stood on the far side of the room looking formidable, with a small coffee table and two wingback chairs off to the right in front of a fireplace. Oliver gestured to one of these. "Please have a seat. Our mutual friend Stella told me about your recent good fortune." Oliver sat down in the seat almost opposite her. Lucinda took a deep breath. "She is a very good friend. I appreciate you taking the time to see me, especially on a weekend." He smiled and leaned forward. "It is my pleasure. Shall we get down to business, then?" Lucinda reached into the bag, down to the bottom, into the ball of lacy underthings she hoped would dissuade anyone who went rummaging. She found the pouch, removed it, and silently handed it to Oliver.

He spread out a black velvet pad that looked like a place mat and poured the gems onto it. He spread them out and, with very delicate fingers, rolled them this way and that without actually picking them up.

"Beautiful. Beautiful. And what are your plans?" She came right to the point. "How much will you pay me?" She immediately felt awkward at the less than graceful delivery, but Oliver seemed to pay no attention. He had picked up a jeweler's loop and was looking at a large blue sapphire. She sat back in the chair and watched as Oliver went through each of the many stones.

Suddenly, he stood up. "Lucinda, pardon my manners. Can I get you something to drink?" She wasn't sure what time it was, although she was pretty sure it wasn't noon yet. Still, her nerves hadn't abated entirely. "I could certainly use one. By any chance, do you have any scotch?" Oliver smiled and crossed the room. "Only the best. I will join you." He stopped at a paneled wall by the door and pressed a button hidden by the intricate woodwork. The panel opened up to a well-stocked bar. He filled two beautiful crystal glasses that were quite similar to the one Andrew was drinking from the night she killed him. Oliver handed her a glass and they made a silent toast.

He moved around to the other side of the desk and sat down. Leaning back, he took a sip of scotch and began to swivel from side to side. "I remember the Southern Artery Gang in Quincy. My father owned several restaurants on the South Shore. That gang extorted a lot of money from him." Lucinda took another sip of her drink, but the knots that had untied in the last few minutes began pulling together again. She did not know what to think. Was Oliver a friend or foe? "I am very sorry to hear that." Oliver stopped swiveling. He looked at her a moment before saying, "You seem nervous. Don't worry. I'm glad your father ripped them off. A little bit of justice, not to mention irony, has brought you here today." He then pulled a drawer open and pulled out a small yellow pad. He wrote something on it and tore off the top sheet. He slid it across the desk. "Here is my offer." She stood up and moved to one of the chairs in front of the desk. She flipped the paper over, looked at it and smiled. *This is just like in the movies!!* "Agreed."

Oliver stood up again. "I assume that cash is acceptable? I do not deal in checks." She nodded. He opened up the bottom drawer of his desk and proceeded to count out four hundred fifty thousand dollars, all in large bills. He then produced an empty candy box. "Please excuse me while I get your candy purchase gift-wrapped." He was gone for a very short time before re-appearing with an exquisitely wrapped box adorned with the name of the chocolate factory in whose parking lot her car now sat. "Drive carefully and please don't hesitate to contact me if you need to satisfy future sweet tooth needs." He smiled and handed her the box. Understanding that the meeting was over, she stood and shook his hand. He escorted her to the elevator, where there was a tall, muscular man inside. Although he was as well-dressed as Oliver, something about him made her nervous. Before she could say anything, however, he addressed her. "Ma'am, please allow me to escort you to your car. It would distress Oliver greatly if you were to have any problems getting home." She nodded, although she still wasn't so sure about this arrangement. He proved to be a perfect gentleman, though, walking alongside of her, holding each door and waiting until she started her car before turning back down the sidewalk. Oliver truly was a professional, regardless of what businesses he may involve himself in. She wondered for a brief moment what brought together two people who were complete opposites like Stella and Oliver. Not finding much of an answer, Lucinda took a deep breath, pulled out of the parking lot, and headed for the highway.

Traffic had gotten heavier since that morning, but she was thankful that it was at least moving. Traveling on I-5, she could see the exit sign for route 101. As she headed up the ramp, her stomach reminded her that she was running mostly on scotch and that food would be a welcome addition. She wasn't thrilled with stopping, as having all that money in her bag was as unnerving as having the jewels. Still, she knew she wouldn't be able to make it home otherwise, so she made a plan to travel as far as San Luis Obispo before stopping. Lucinda had heard of a famous Chinese restaurant there and figured that, since she wasn't out this way often, it was an opportunity she shouldn't pass up. When she got off the highway, she quickly found the street the restaurant was supposed to be on. Given the reviews, she was looking for a large building. However, she caught a glimpse of the sign at the far edge of what looked like a vacant parking lot, complete with large tufts of grass growing through the pavement. She turned in apprehensively and saw a building no larger than a two car garage at the very back. It made her wonder who wrote that review. Still, she was here and hungry, so she pulled into a spot and parked.

Twenty minutes later, she was sitting in her car with a large bag, filling the car with steam and a wonderful smell. She couldn't bring herself to sit inside, given what she was carrying, but her stomach had no intention of leaving without satisfaction. Lucinda tore into several of the containers, eating a forkful of this and a forkful of that, savoring each bite. She made a mental apology to that reviewer for her negative thoughts from earlier. The food was even better than it smelled. After what seemed like hours, Lucinda put her fork down and moved the seat back a couple of notches. She noticed the two fortune cookies that were sitting on the seat. Her curiosity got the best of her, wondering what the Chinese thought tomorrow held for her. She carefully opened the first one and read, "*The lemon will be sweet.*" She then opened the second, pulled out the small white paper and read, "*A new adventure will unfold soon.*" She couldn't help but smile. All that delicious food and prophetic words, for the bargain price of $8.95. She packed up all the containers and put them back into the bag, along with the two fortunes. Wiping her hands and mouth with one of the included wet naps, she was soon back on the highway heading home.

The rest of the drive flew by, as the midday traffic had abated, and she soon saw the sign for the Santa Barbara city limits. As she pulled into her garage, Lucinda noticed she was holding her breath. For how long, she wasn't sure, but she breathed a sigh of relief at finally being home. She was surprised at how far away her pre-dawn departure for this trip felt. Opening the door to the apartment, Lucinda headed straight for the bathroom. She kicked off her sneakers, got out of her clothes, and jumped into the shower. She stood motionless for almost ten minutes and let the hot water wash away several hundred miles of driving before finally washing up and getting out. Slipping into her favorite cotton robe, she went into the kitchen and poured herself a scotch. On her way back to the living room, she checked the answering machine. Nothing, but she wondered what she really could have expected.

Once in her easy chair, Lucinda found herself both exhausted and excited at the same time. She reached over and picked up the backpack, unzipped it quickly and found the candy box at the bottom. She stared at it for a long time, almost afraid to open it and find only candy, and instead read all the ingredients on the bottom of the box. Finally, she unwrapped it and flipped the cover off. Thousand dollar bills stared back at her, unblinking. She suddenly felt conspicuous, sitting there with all that money out in the open. She put the top back on and headed back into the kitchen. She stood there thinking for a moment. Putting the box on the counter, she found some scissors in the junk drawer. She dug a box of frozen pizza from the back of the freezer, cut the end open, and replaced the pizza with the candy box. She put the pizza into aluminum foil, while taping the box closed. She reburied the box in the back, while putting the pizza right in the front. She closed the door to the freezer and had a silly thought – *cold cash*. With a smile, she shut the lights off and went to bed.

Chapter 17

Lucinda woke to the sound of bells. She rolled over onto her back and stared at the ceiling, listening to the clanging as a service was starting at the church up the hill from her apartment. The irony of being woken up by God after what had transpired over the past weeks was not lost on her. She lay there for several minutes, both enjoying the peace of the morning and thinking about all that money. For the first time in her life, Lucinda was not going to have to worry about what tomorrow would bring. For once, she would have control over what would happen. She could hear rain beginning to fall outside, a sound she always loved. *Washes away all sins, brings a clean slate.* Tomorrow, Lucinda would start planning for the future. She decided that, for the time being, the money should go into her safety deposit box. She would take care of that during lunch, along with getting a check out to Stella. The thought of Stella receiving a check as large as the one she was going to send was thrilling to her. She would now be able to pay off all the help and kindness her friend had shown her, both in jail and in the last twenty four hours. Lucinda made up her mind right then – ten percent. That should cure most of her ills, maybe even cure whatever seemed to be eating away at her. This last thought made Lucinda sad. There were things that money couldn't buy, but she hoped that wasn't one of them.

Chapter 18

Monday morning found Lucinda up and heading into work a half hour early once again. She hoped to get ahead of the workload, so that she wouldn't have to feel rushed while she ran her errands at lunch. When the elevator doors opened, she was surprised to find both Ted and Roger standing there, talking to a gentleman whom she did not recognize.

Ted looked over and saw Lucinda standing there. He smiled and waved. "Good morning, Lucinda. May I steal a moment?" Looking the stranger over quickly, she walked over to where they were standing. "Good morning, Theodore. Good morning, Mr. Powers. Of course. What can I do for you?" Ted turned so she could join the circle and said, "Lucinda, I would like you to meet Carlton Pedersen. He will be joining the firm starting next week." She turned to him and extended her hand. "Mr. Pedersen, it is very nice to meet you. Welcome." He received the handshake and, with a touch of a Swedish accent, said, "It is a pleasure to meet you at last. I've heard so much about you, I feel that I already know you." Lucinda's thoughts about what Ted knew sprung up in the back of her mind, but she pushed them back down. "I hope it was all good. I know you will enjoy working here. If you will excuse me, I have to take care of a few things before the day gets going."

With that, she went into her office. As she logged on to the computer, she thought about all the changes that were happening because of her. Most of them were good, such as her better relationship with Ted, the addition of someone like Roger, and her new knowledge of the importance of her role in the company. However, she found herself feeling more like a stranger in a strange land with every new face. Carlton Pedersen seemed nice enough, but she couldn't help feeling more conspicuous by the day. She shook her head, trying to clear those thoughts and get down to work. She wanted to make sure she would have time to run her errands at lunch and there was a growing pile of paperwork on her desk.

The morning flew by and Lucinda was shocked to see that it was after noon when she took her eyes off the computer for the first time. She quickly finished her current task and signed off. She found herself walking at an unnaturally brisk pace for the lobby and made a conscious effort to slow down. Knowing what she was carrying, it was hard not to break into a run. Hitting the sidewalk, she was thrilled to find a cab sitting empty and jumped right in. Even though the bank wasn't all that far, she had no intention of making herself a target in the busy rush of lunchtime. In less than twenty minutes, she found herself outside the bank, having secured her money in the safe deposit box. She had also gotten a bank check for Stella, which the bank assured her they would send by certified mail. Lucinda found it amazing how helpful people can be when you have money. She felt relieved by having these two tasks done, and she decided to walk back to work. The air seemed so clean after all the rain yesterday and the sun was shining brightly.

As she entered the lobby of Lowe and Maher, the rumble of her stomach reminded her that she hadn't actually eaten lunch during her lunch hour. A glance at her watch revealed that there was time for a quick bite. She stopped at the small café located on the first floor of the building. She ordered a cup of tomato bisque and a half of a tuna salad sandwich. She spotted a small round table by the window and settled in. As she was eating, she heard a voice next to her. "Soup looks good. What is it?" Startled, she looked up and saw the smiling face of Carlton Pedersen. She responded, "Tomato Bisque. It's really good. I always get it when it's on the menu." He nodded and walked off to join the line. He was back quickly, carrying an identical cup and a sandwich that looked like salami, with what she recognized as their hot mustard dripping out in all directions.

Sitting down with her, Carlton wasted no time in starting a conversation. "So, Ms. Preston. How long have you worked here?"

"Several years. I have learned a lot and really enjoy the pace. I'm sure you will as well." Since Carlton had a mouthful of sandwich, she continued. "Have you found a place to live?" Wiping hot mustard off his mouth, Carlton replied, "Ted told me about a condo near the waterfront, not far from where he lives. It's a place called Stearns Wharf. Ever hear of it?" Lucinda kept a straight face and said, "I have a general idea. I have heard that the condos are quite elegant and the views from the balconies are breathtaking."

"Ted gave a similar description. I am meeting him and the realtor there after lunch. It will be nice to settle in quickly, if possible. There is nothing I hate more than living out of a suitcase for months." Lucinda nodded her head in agreement. She had spent her fair share of time living in transition when she was younger. "Mr. Pedersen, I am sure you will be quite happy there, as well as at Lowe and Maher."

"Please, Ms. Preston. We will be working together and have now eaten lunch together. Would you call me Carlton?" He gave her a pleading look which made her laugh. "Only if you agree to call me Lucinda." Over the soup, he offered his hand, which she took in hers. "Agreed." She noticed then that they were both indeed finished with lunch, so she pushed back her chair. Carlton stood up as well and grabbed the two trays. "Allow me." She smiled and nodded, then he headed off to dispose of the trash. When he returned, they headed back out to the lobby together. They said their goodbyes and Lucinda walked toward the elevator while Carlton went out the front door to look at his potential new home.

When Lucinda stepped off the elevator, she practically ran into Ted stepping on. With a smirk, she said, "Not busy enough, Ted, that you need to dabble in real estate too?" He looked at her quizzically for a moment, then laughed. "News travels fast. How did you find out?"

"We ran into each other in the café downstairs and had lunch."

As Ted pressed the lobby button, he said, "Hopefully he is still here so we can share a cab." When the doors slid shut, Lucinda headed to her office, where the phone was ringing. "Lucinda Preston," she answered. A familiar voice boomed back. "Lucinda, would you get me a cup of coffee, black?" Before she could tell him where he could put his coffee, Roger laughed. "Just joking. I need the update of the Anderson files, when you get a moment."

"Give me about fifteen minutes." Lucinda chuckled and hung up the phone.

Chapter 19

The following day was gorgeous. Lucinda had been sleeping well lately, and last night was no exception. She had time for a run and a quick breakfast before work and hit the ground running as soon as she got to the office. She knew she had an appointment at the courthouse at eleven and wanted to get her paperwork in order first thing. She kept her nose buried until ten-thirty, then called Ted to let him know she would be out of the office for a while and that it might be a long session. However, when she got there, the meeting took far less time than she anticipated and she found herself with extra time on her hands. With such beautiful weather, she decided to try a new indoor-outdoor café called 'Eviddas'.

Lucinda seated herself at a table right on the sidewalk and began to peruse the menu. When the waiter came over, she ordered an iced tea. Though she was sitting under an umbrella large enough to keep her entire table in the shade, the glare forced her to put on her sunglasses simply to choose a meal. As she did so, Lucinda noticed a tall woman walking down the sidewalk toward her. She thought she knew that stride from somewhere and, by the time the woman reached her, she was sure of it. As the woman was about to pass her table, Lucinda spoke up. "Johanna?"

The blonde stopped and looked down at her. "J.J., is that you?" Lucinda got up and gave her old friend a hug. "I can't believe my eyes. What are you doing here in Santa Barbara?" Johanna held her at arm's length and gave her a once over. "I could say the same thing to you." Lucinda gestured to an empty chair and the two friends sat down.

"I was just about to have lunch. Interested in a bite?" Lucinda was hopeful that Johanna would have time for a quick catch-up.

"I'm not hungry, but I could use a drink. What do they have here?" Johanna grabbed a second menu off the table and began scanning the fare. Lucinda shrugged and said, "I don't know. This café only recently opened and I just sat down." She signaled for the waiter. When he arrived, Lucinda requested a second iced tea and Johanna ordered a lemon drop martini. Lucinda thought back to the fortune cookie. *The lemon will be sweet.*

As they toasted each other, Johanna said, "You just seemed to vanish into thin air! No one knew what happened to you. Obviously the years have been good to you. What's with the blonde?" Johanna twirled her own hair around her fingers for emphasis.

Lucinda just laughed, but never answered the question. "So you never said. What brought you to Santa Barbara? Are you living here?" Johanna stirred her drink and smiled. "No, I'm here on business. I'll be here for another two days."

"Where are you staying? There are some really great places, but some of them only look good on the outside."

Johanna laughed. "Yeah, I've gotten stuck in a lot of those over the years with all the traveling I do. This time I got lucky. I'm staying at the Villa Resort, down by the lake."

Lucinda was slightly jealous. She had heard many good things about the Villa. "Ooh, very classy. I hear it's also pretty expensive. If you want, you could stay with me. That would give us more time to catch up."

"As great as that would be, my company is picking up the tab, so I plan on enjoying every bit of the experience. Besides, my schedule is crazy and I wouldn't want to disrupt your life. How about dinner tonight?"

Lucinda pulled out a business card and Johanna did the same. They each wrote their cell numbers on the back and Johanna included the number for her room at the Villa. When Lucinda slid her card across the table, her friend picked it up and flipped it over. "What's this? Lucinda Preston? Since when?"

"Long story. Let's save it for tonight, give us something to talk about if the conversation lags." Johanna threw her head back and laughed. "Like that was ever a problem with us." At that moment, the waiter came over to see if they were ready to order. Johanna finished the last of her drink and stood up. "I'll let you eat. Until tonight…" She started to open her purse, but Lucinda offered to take care of her drink. "First round tonight is on me, then." Johanna turned and quickly disappeared into the crowd. Lucinda gave her order to the waiter and sat with her drink, thinking about the first time she met Johanna.

Eleven years ago, Lucinda was in Boston's famous North End, waiting to get into a well-known Italian restaurant. As always, the line extended out the door and down the front steps. It was a long wait, made longer by the fact that she had chosen to dine alone that night and had no one to pass the time with in conversation. Still she enjoyed people watching and Bostonians never failed to provide entertainment. Once she worked her way up to the hostess' podium, she was informed that it would still be almost a twenty minute wait for a table. As she was standing there, she noticed two women sitting at a table not more than twenty feet from her. Their eyes met and, for some reason, one of the women motioned for her to come over. At first she ignored it, as she didn't recognize either one of them. However, the woman kept beckoning her and finally her curiosity got the better of her. As she walked over, she kept trying to figure out if she should know either one. Not wanting to feel dumb for not recognizing them, she simply sat in one of the empty chairs and said, "My feet are killing me!"

As it turned out, she did not know them, but they simply saw someone in need of a seat. They were two friends, Johanna Newlin and Joan Spencer. They both had top jobs at the same computer firm in New York and were attending a one day seminar in Boston. They shared an apartment in Centerport, Long Island when they weren't travelling for business. Lucinda was amazed and appreciative that they would invite a total stranger to join them, but they hit it off immediately and were soon chatting like old friends, which they eventually would become. On occasion over the years, Lucinda had lamented leaving such a good friend without so much as an explanation. She often wondered what happened to the people she left behind, and was thrilled that this chance meeting would give her the opportunity to find out.

It struck Lucinda as ironic that Johanna would show up again in her life, on the edge of another potential direction change. It also dawned on her that lunch was long over, and she finished the last of her iced tea, left her money on the table, and headed back to the office.

Chapter 20

When Lucinda stepped off the elevator, Ted happened to be walking by. With a quick glance up from some paperwork, he asked, "Everything go okay this morning?" She nodded and said, "Business as usual." Ted headed into his office, while Lucinda headed toward hers. When she sat down, she found herself suddenly feeling out-of-place. Her chair didn't feel quite right. The office walls seemed a little bit closer than normal. She started thinking about recent events. Her inheritance, her "legacy"; seeing Johanna; the second fortune cookie: 'A new adventure will unfold soon.' She could hear the ticking of the clock, insistent and unchanging.

Lucinda counted sixty ticks before she made her decision. As soon as she stood up, she knew it was the right one. She headed over to Ted's office, shutting the door behind her. Ted looked up with a puzzled look on his face. "Something I can do for you?"

"Ted, I am leaving the firm." The look of shock on his face bothered Lucinda. She didn't really think about this part of her decision, the people she would now be leaving behind. She had only been looking forward to what lay in her future. Still, she knew she had to be firm in her decision.

"You're kidding, right?"

"No, Ted. I'll have my letter of resignation ready before the end of the day." She felt badly about how abrupt that sounded.

"Is it salary? I'll give you a raise." Lucinda smiled inside. *Mom already beat you to it.*

"No, it's just time for me to move on." Before Ted could say anything else to dissuade her, Lucinda stood up and headed back to her office. As she walked, she couldn't help but smile. She had just quit her job over a cookie. Well, that and several hundred thousand dollars' worth of jewels.

The first thing she did was type her letter. Then she went through the current files on her desk, grouping them into two piles, one for Ted and the other for Roger. She packed her personal items into a box, which she left on the chair by the door. Picking up the first stack of files, she headed over to Roger's office. He was not there, so she left them on the corner of the desk, so he would be sure to see them. She thought for a moment about leaving some sort of note, but thought better of it and left the office. Besides, she knew that she would be the topic of conversation at Ted's house that night. When Lucinda went back to Ted's office with the stack of files and her resignation letter, he was waiting. "Are you sure about this?"

She answered immediately. "Absolutely." And she was. "I want to thank you, though, for everything. For the opportunities that this job has given me, the knowledge I have gained, the friends that I have made." She reached out her hand and smiled. Ted looked at her for several moments before silently nodding. He took her hand and, rather than shaking it, held it gently for a few seconds before letting her go. Lucinda turned toward the door and, as she left the office, looked over her shoulder and said, "Take care of yourself. And Roger."

It only took a few minutes for Lucinda to gather her things and she was soon standing at the elevator. While waiting, she turned and scanned the office. For being only mid-afternoon, she was surprised at how few people she saw. It was almost as if everyone was giving her privacy for her exit. She was glad for this, as she wasn't much for tearful goodbyes and promises to keep in touch. Not that she had ever really connected with anyone here other than Andrew and, more recently, Ted. The ding behind her announced the arrival of her ride and she stepped into the elevator with no hesitation. The excitement of what waited for her outside was beginning to grow.

When Lucinda stepped through the lobby doors onto the sidewalk, a sudden breeze engulfed her. It was exhilarating. She strode briskly to her car and, as she was putting her work belongings in the trunk, thought it might be about time to buy a new one. She decided to take the scenic route home and contemplate what that might be.

By the time she arrived home, it was just after five. She chuckled at the thought that all of her co-workers, make that 'former' co-workers, would be just leaving the office. She opened the door to her apartment and flopped down onto the couch. It just dawned on her that she hadn't made any arrangements for dinner with Johanna. She thought that tonight should be something special, something that reminded them of the old days. The idea came fast and she immediately grabbed the phone book. She looked up the number for the Wildwood Steak House. She had known Gerry, the owner, for years. He had the original Wildwood restaurant back in Massachusetts. He was a real down-to-earth guy with a smile you would die for. His place wasn't all that far outside of Boston and was considered the best steak house in the area. The restaurant was originally just a small place run by Gerry's father. In the early days, Lucinda would enjoy the 'Soup and Salad" luncheons for just $1.75. There were always loaves of freshly made bread near the salad bar. A cloth napkin would be placed over the loaf, keeping it warm as well as keeping hands off it when you would cut slices off. So many of the meals were a bargain and a half.

Gerry used to work there and, when his father retired, he took over. He remodeled the place and turned the small, family style restaurant into a very classy, upscale one. Reservations became necessary and rather hard to get. Years later, Gerry decided to move to California and left the original in the hands of a friend and business partner. Lucinda remembered that, soon after moving, he started the Wildwood II, only a twenty minute drive from where she now lived.

Finding the number, she called and made reservations for six-thirty. Lucinda then called Johanna and left a message that she would pick her up at six. She jumped into the shower and washed off her old life with Lowe and Maher with a good hard scrub. She chose a rather short black dress with spaghetti straps, something she rarely pulled out of the closet as a paralegal. With a quick, satisfying look in the mirror, Lucinda headed off to pick up her old friend.

When she pulled up at the Villa, Johanna was waiting outside. She was in the car before Lucinda could even find a parking spot. She was wearing a remarkably similar dress and looked spectacular. "Buckle up." Lucinda put the car in gear and headed for the highway. "I'm hoping to add a little touch of home to our reunion tonight." Johanna looked at her quizzically. "As long as the food is good and the drinks are strong, I'll be happy." It was a short drive to the restaurant and Lucinda was soon pulling into the parking lot. Johanna looked up at the sign on the restaurant and exhaled. "It can't be the same place, can it?" Lucinda smiled and nodded. "The owner started up another one soon after moving out here. It's just like it was back home, with some accommodations for California cuisine, of course."

While they waited at the hostess' station, Lucinda scanned the dining room to see if Gerry was around. A lovely woman dressed in a long black skirt and a highly starched shirt approached them. A small metal name tag told them that her name was Pauline. Lucinda gave her name for the reservation and asked if the owner was around. As she directed them to a table by the windows, Pauline informed them that Gerry was off for the night, but would be back tomorrow. She laid two menus on the table, as well as a wine list and told them that their waitress would be over momentarily. It was a good thing that they knew what they wanted for drinks, as the waitress arrived before they could even crack open a menu.

"Could we have a lemon drop martini and a Scotch on the rocks, please?" Johanna smiled at Lucinda when the waitress left. "You remembered my drink!" Lucinda couldn't help but laugh out loud. "Well, you did just order one this afternoon." Johanna became serious then. "So. Long story. Let's hear it."

"Well, as you know, my grandmother passed away just before I left. At that point, I was just drifting in life, not really knowing what I was going to do. I had some legal troubles before I met you and was trying to move on from that. I hid a lot of my life from the new friends I had made and it was getting harder to do. My grandmother was my one anchor, my sanity. I thought it would be better to just start over somewhere else. As much as I hated to cut ties without even a word, a clean cut seemed the best way at the time. My grandmother left her estate to me, which wasn't a huge amount, but the sale of the house allowed me to move away and have some money to live on while I figured out my plan."

During her story, the waitress had come and quietly left the drinks. Lucinda was thankful for that and took a healthy gulp of her Scotch. "I moved to Yuma, Arizona and changed my name. While I was just aiming to go somewhere warmer than Boston, it ended up being a really good choice. In the beginning, I just worked odd jobs, often making less than my monthly bills. I was spending my inheritance and living the same life that I had in Boston. My grandmother had always harped on me about getting an education, saying that doors don't open for people without one. There was a local college with a great selection of courses and, given my legal scrapes, I thought it would be funny to take some law courses. I ended up loving them, taking one right after another, and I soon earned enough credits for my Associate's degree. I was looking through job listings in the career center and found a position for a paralegal with a small but growing law firm here in Santa Barbara. I flew out for an interview and, within a week, I had a new job and a pretty nice apartment."

As though waiting for a break in the story, the waitress showed up to take their order. They each ordered a steak and another round of drinks. Johanna picked up the story again. "So are you still in the same law firm, having worked your way to the top in a cut-throat manner?" Lucinda hoped that her wince at that expression wasn't as obvious as it felt. "No. That first job was a good stepping stone, as I was learning right along with all the others there. However, I was limited by my inexperience and could see that I wasn't going to be able to grow within that firm. I was lucky to make some good contacts, though, and eventually moved into a larger firm, one that would provide more opportunities to broaden my knowledge base." She paused for a quick drink before continuing. "I had a great boss," she thought of Andrew first, then Ted, "actually, two great bosses who let me tackle many tasks not normally worked on by a simple paralegal." A pang of sadness hit her at the thought that one of those bosses was dead, and the other she had left in the lurch less than eight hours ago. "It was a really great experience. At least, up until this afternoon. I quit."

"You quit? Seriously?"

She nodded. "It's something I had been thinking about for some time now, and today just seemed like THE day."

Johanna's jaw dropped. "I am so jealous. What I wouldn't give to be able to just up and quit my job." Then she looked serious at Lucinda. "I hope you at least have some sort of nest egg to keep you going."

"In fact, I do. I was pretty responsible with my money. Plus, my mother had an investment that I only recently found out about, one that left me enough money to keep me off the streets for a while." Lucinda downplayed exactly how long *a while* could last.

The look on Johanna's face gave Lucinda a small amount of satisfaction, as she had always looked at her friend as being in the place she wanted to be. While Lucinda had struggled for as long as she could remember, often just making ends meet, Johanna seemed to be a magnet for good things: beauty, good job, opportunity for travel. Lucinda seemed to remember a really handsome boyfriend just before she skipped town. For all she knew, Johanna could be working as a model and living the good life with the dashing husband carrying her luggage. "So you said you were here on business. Still in the tech field?" Lucinda couldn't resist. "Or did you become a glamorous model here for a shoot?"

Johanna laughed at that. "Neither, although that second one sounds really good. I am working as a pharmaceutical sales rep. It keeps me on the road eight months of the year, but I love getting the chance to see the world, especially on someone else's dime. I was just in Japan a couple of months ago and absolutely loved it. Maybe someday I will be able to go back for a vacation. The people are wonderful and there is so much culture and history."

Just then, the meals arrived and Lucinda became suddenly aware of how much her stomach had been grumbling. The two friends dug in and ate ravenously. The meal was interspersed with a little more catching up and general observations on the state of the world, but most of their focus was on the delicious meal in front of them. After polishing off their dinners, along with a cup of coffee, they found themselves in the car and heading home. Lucinda asked Johanna if she would like to see her place and maybe have a nightcap before taking her home. "As much as I would love to, I will have to take a rain check. I was tired before dinner and all that good food has really made me miss my bed. Besides, I need to get up early for a meeting."

"No problem. How much longer will you be in town? Lucinda glanced over at her friend, who was battling to keep her eyes open and losing. Badly.

"Two more days. I'll call you tomorrow after I look over my schedule." No sooner had Johanna finished her sentence, then Lucinda heard the sound of faint snoring coming from the passenger side. She chuckled quietly to herself and enjoyed the rest of the ride in silence.

Chapter 21

The next morning, Lucinda woke to the sound of birds chirping and dogs barking. She had not set the alarm the night before and it was wonderful to get up when you wanted to instead of when you had to. Sleeping late, she decided, suited her perfectly. Rolling out of bed, she threw on her enormous terry cloth robe and headed for the kitchen. She was thrilled to smell the coffee, which she always programmed the night before, waiting for her. Lucinda poured out a cup, grabbed a cranberry scone and moved into the living room.

The feeling of absolute contentment was disturbed almost immediately after turning the TV on. A local newscaster was in the middle of saying that the ongoing investigation into the murder of Andrew Lowe was now being turned over to the FBI. The positive events of recent weeks had allowed her "indiscretion" to slip to the very back of her mind, but this news brought it screeching back to the forefront. The newsman added that Mr. Lowe's partner at the firm had been hospitalized after an apparent heart attack. *Oh, my God. This is unbelievable. I have to call Roger.* She dialed the office. The phone rang almost six times before Rosaleen answered. She sounded exhausted. Lucinda asked to speak to Mr. Powers. Without a word, she was put on hold.

"Roger Powers here."

"Roger, it's Lucinda. I just heard on the news about Ted. Is it true?"

"Yes. It was a mild heart attack, and they are keeping him for twenty-four hours for observation. He had been feeling pretty good until recently. The doctor had him watching his diet and working out more, which had gotten his weight and cholesterol levels down. However, I guess the stress of you leaving in addition to all the business with Andrew was just too much for him." Lucinda immediately felt guilty at the reference to her sudden departure. "Is there anything you need?" The line was quiet for a moment, and Lucinda had the panicked feeling that he was going to ask her to admit to her crimes so they could get back to their normal lives. However, all he said was, "Any chance you could meet me for lunch?"

She breathed a sigh of relief. Even though she was feeling some apprehension over the fact that she had not actually said goodbye to Roger when she left, Lucinda knew that he just needed a friend right now. "Any place in particular?"

Roger was quick with his answer. "How about George's Clam Shack?"

"I'll pick you up at noon in front of the fruit stand around the corner from the office." She didn't want to run into anyone from the office right now, and sitting in front of the building just felt too weird. Roger agreed and hung up the phone.

Lucinda looked at the clock. It was only ten-thirty. She was feeling somewhat flustered at this recent news, but she knew that she had to stay focused. There were still things to do, even though she now no longer had a job. She took a quick shower and picked out something that still looked professional. She wasn't going to turn into someone who lived in sweatpants and hung around all day. She put on a pair of black slacks and a black-and-white print blouse before slipping her feet into a comfortable pair of flats. A look in the mirror said that she was ready to go.

Lucinda quickly dialed Stella's number. She answered on two rings. "Hey, kid. Thanks for the mail."

"Good. I was calling to see if you received it. I'm thinking about flying out to Boston again. Any chance you'd be up for another visit?" The card stuck to her refrigerator crossed her mind.

"I don't know if I can. I'm due for surgery in a week and a half. I might not be suitable for visitors at that point." Lucinda frowned at the thought of frail Stella going under the knife. "Is there anything I can do for you?"

"You just did. Besides, with nine kids, I'm sure I'll be taken good care of. I appreciate you asking, though."

"Well, you have my numbers. I am here if you need me." With that, she hung up the phone.

Chapter 22

Lucinda drove up to the fruit stand at exactly noon. Roger was standing there waiting, looking fairly out of place surrounded by a menagerie of shopping moms, college kids, bike messengers, and blue collar workers making their daily wages. He was perusing the sidewalk displays when he noticed her and headed over to the car.

Sliding in beside her, he buckled up his seatbelt and gave her a smile.

"How is Ted doing? I feel really bad that this happened to him." She didn't mention the guilt she was still feeling. Roger replied, "He's doing just fine. He looks a whole lot better than he did yesterday. He came into my office after you left and I thought he was going to faint. He ended up doing a whole lot more than that."

Lucinda pulled into traffic and headed for George's Clam Shack. "I'm sorry that I didn't get to see you. I just didn't feel like it made sense to hang around the office. I was planning to leave at the end of the month, but yesterday just seemed like it was time."

"So what are your plans? Did you get an offer for a better job? You certainly deserve it." Lucinda smiled at the kind words. Keeping her eyes on the road, she just said, "Let's say that I won the lottery and leave it at that."

Roger gave her a puzzled look for a moment, but then smiled and said, "Good for you. I wish I could just pick up and go." The restaurant wasn't all that far and Lucinda soon was pulling into the parking lot, effectively ending the conversation for the time being. She parked the car and Roger quickly got out, running around the back to open her door for her. As before, he extended a hand to help her out and then offered an arm for the walk. Even though a clam shack didn't warrant such chivalry, she accepted it willingly. As they walked to the door, they could smell the aroma of seafood wafting toward them.

The owner, George, originally came from a small town in New Hampshire. He had been the head chef at a well-known restaurant near the waterfront in Portsmouth. He always wanted his own place, and a friend who had moved out here told him about an opportunity to buy that he couldn't pass up. Hence, "George's Clam Shack" came to be.

There was a short line waiting to be seated when they walked in. However, they found themselves at a table in less than five minutes, with two glasses of water and two menus sitting in front of them. Lucinda had always laughed at the name of the place, as it was hardly a shack and the quality of food was as good as any classy restaurant that had a seafood menu. Looking over the menu, Roger said, "I love their fried calamari. It comes with crispy sweet potato fries and coleslaw that you would die for."

Lucinda was amazed that Roger had found the time to eat here and be able to offer suggestions. She did not let on that this was one of her favorite places and replied, "That sounds good. Maybe I'll try that. A friend told me that they had the fried clams once and that they were so good, he tried to get them to give him the recipe."

"Did he get it?" Roger asked.

"They just laughed and said that it was their secret."

The waitress came over and asked if they wanted something to drink. Roger gave her a smile and said, "A light beer would be great." She looked at Lucinda and she replied that she would have the same. They also gave her their orders and were soon sitting alone again. Roger looked at her and said, "So no scotch?" With a wry smile, Lucinda answered, "Somehow it seemed very out of place with a plate of fried calamari. Besides, beer really does go with anything." Roger laughed and said, "A million college kids can't be wrong."

Lucinda looked across at him thoughtfully, finally asking the question that had been on her mind. "So, why lunch? I would have expected that you wouldn't have much of an appetite, not to mention that you would likely want to spend this time with Ted." Roger gave her a sheepish smile and told her that he was just lonesome and didn't want to eat alone today. "Besides, Ted can be such a demanding little sissy when he isn't feeling well." Lucinda couldn't help but laugh out loud at that comment, with Roger joining in. Before that moment, she couldn't have imagined liking Roger more than she did. Ted really had done well for himself. She found herself being somewhat envious of them, having found someone who complements them so perfectly. While she had had boyfriends over the years, she never really felt like any of them was "the one". Maybe now that she had the time, not to mention the means, Lucinda might be able to take more time out for that endeavor.

Suddenly, Roger broke into her inner monologue with a topic change. "There is another reason why I suggested lunch. The FBI has kicked up the intensity searching for Andrew's killer. They have re-interviewed everyone in the office and dug into all of his files, looking for some connection that might give them a new lead. You are going to be hearing from them, as they were surprised that you left so abruptly. Rosaleen gave them your contact information. See what you have missed in such a short time!"

This information unnerved Lucinda. She knew about the FBI, was worried that they might take it further than local law enforcement would, but had hoped that she had slipped out quietly enough that they wouldn't take notice. To hear that they specifically asked about her and the sudden departure was disconcerting. As she was considering what her next move might be, Roger continued.

"No one suspected Andrew of commingling funds and padding his clients' bills. Just think about it: his kids are in private schools; his wife is very involved with the 'girls' at the Country Club, as well as charity work; he owned a sixty-five-foot yacht; lived in a mansion with a pool, not far from Ted; he recently bought a condo on the waterfront. Ted always suspected that Andrew might be involved in something, but since everything seemed on the up-and-up in the firm, he didn't want to stick his nose into Andrew's private life. He was aware, as well, that Andrew had several mistresses," he paused and said, "including you."

Lucinda could feel the blood rushing to her face. "I did some work for Andrew after hours and accompanied him on several business trips. While we did get to know each other pretty well, which can be expected with all the time we spent working together, it was strictly professional. Yes, he was handsome and charming, and any woman would have found him attractive, but he was also still my boss." She had no desire to keep this conversation going and quickly changed topic. "That was so nice of Rosaleen to offer me and my contact information up. I can just picture her running around, trying to make a good impression for the FBI agents, like she is superlative to the other four secretaries there." Roger gave a slight smirk and said, "Well, you did nail that one right on the head."

When the waitress showed up with their drinks and dinners, Lucinda was thankful for the distraction. The light tone of earlier conversation was gone and the two of them dug quietly into their meals. She couldn't help but think about what she was going to do about the ongoing investigation. Clearly, Roger had other things on his mind as well, and dinner passed with minimal conversation. When he excused himself for a moment, Lucinda noticed that he passed his credit card to the waitress on his way by. Smooth, indeed. When he returned, he gently suggested that work still beckoned him. The trip back to the fruit stand was quiet and uneventful. As he got out of the car, Lucinda said, "Give my best to Ted." Roger gave her a small smile and replied, "Don't be a stranger." At that moment, Lucinda felt that she may have to soon become just that.

By the time she got home, Lucinda's head was spinning. Thoughts of the FBI coming to question her, dig into her life, analyze everything about her was pushing her to panic. She knew she needed something to get her mind off it for the moment. Trying to think of someone to call, it dawned on her that she really had no one. Her job and Andrew had consumed most of her last few years. Stella was on the other coast. She couldn't even call her newfound friends, Ted and Roger. Out of the blue, a name came to her. Then several others. She had forgotten about her old group of girlfriends, the ones she met soon after moving here. Lucinda tried to remember the last time she talked to any of them, but couldn't come up with an answer. It made her nervous, thinking about calling, but she really needed some company. She opened her junk drawer and fished out an old address book. Scanning pages, she found what she was looking for.

With a trembling finger, she dialed the number. As the rings piled up, she remembered that Krystina was a flight attendant, with ever changing schedules. She was just about to hang up when a sunny voice appeared on the other end.

"Hello?"

"Krystina, you're home! I wasn't sure that I'd get you."

Lucinda was pretty sure she heard dogs barking when her friend answered. "Oh, my God! Lucinda! Where the heck have you been?" Lucinda couldn't help but laugh. She wasn't sure if Krystina was this full of energy before she became a flight attendant or if they had brainwashed her for the job.

"Always been here, just always working."

"It's so great to hear from you. Is everything okay?"

Lucinda loved that about Krystina. Even after not hearing from someone in forever, she was happy to get the call and was concerned about how that person was. "Everything's fine. Actually, I just quit my job and was wondering how I was going to fill all this free time." Before she even finished the sentence, Krystina started up again.

"You have to come over. I'm having some friends over tonight for a drink. You'll know a couple of them, but they are all really great people. You can't say no. We need to do some catching up."

Lucinda's spirits lifted. She was somewhat surprised how down she felt before the phone call, considering she was newly wealthy, rid of the cheating boyfriend, and had nothing but time to do what she wanted. "That would be great. I assume you're still living in the same place. Can I bring anything?"

"Yes, same place. Can you still get a hold of those hot pickled string beans? I loved those."

"Consider it done. What time?"

"Any time after seven. Whoops, got another call. See you tonight!"

Just like that, Krystina was gone. Lucinda hung up the phone laughing. She was looking forward to tonight. As she cleaned up a little, she found herself thinking out loud. "Well, that takes care of one night of my retirement. I'm going to need a plan, though, because I will go bonkers if I am not busy doing something other than having lunches, dinners, and drinks. Not too good for the waistline. Although, I will have plenty of time to hit the gym and burn some of those calories." She laughed at this last thought. She really was going to need to think this out. Her decision to quit the job was far more spontaneous than she was making out to everyone. Still, that thinking could take place tomorrow. Tonight was all about old friends.

Lucinda puttered about for a couple of hours before realizing that she needed to freshen up. A quick look in the mirror told her that the outfit was holding up nicely, so no need to change. She washed her face quickly and finished with just a little blush. A brush of the teeth and she felt like new. It was now six-forty, so she headed out to pick up the beans and then off to Krystina's apartment. She actually didn't live all that far from Lucinda, which made her feel that much more guilty for dropping the group so abruptly. As she turned onto Tremont Street, she immediately recognized her friend's building and was ecstatic to see that there was a parking spot right in front. *Wow, my lucky night!!*

When Lucinda got to the apartment, she found that she was nervous about the reception she would get. Beside the fact that there would be people here that she didn't know, the ones she did might not be as happy to see her as Krystina was. However, those feelings were dispelled almost immediately. Krystina must have been timing her from when she got buzzed in, because the door soon flew open and Lucinda found herself the recipient of a rather suffocating bear hug. She was dragged into a room with about six women standing and chatting while picking at a selection of cheese trays on the kitchen table. It was an eclectic group, with what appeared to be a wide range of ages and ethnicities. The one constant was that they were all in phenomenal shape, as each was wearing an outfit that proudly displayed a body that had spent many an hour in the gym. This was immediately confirmed by Krystina, who came up behind her and whispered in her ear. "I met all of these girls in the gym. I can't wait to put your beans out. Let's see how healthy they eat then!" She cackled as she headed off to put the jar on the table.

Lucinda followed her into the kitchen and was quickly introduced to everyone. She was sorry that there were no familiar faces, but maybe it would be better for her new start if she practiced creating new social circles. Krystina called out, "Still drinking scotch?" Lucinda nodded. "Still five ice cubes?" Lucinda laughed. Who would have ever remembered that detail? A blonde to Lucinda's left asked, "What is with the exact count of cubes? I had a boyfriend who did the same thing. Got all upset once when a bartender put in six." A short haired brunette answered, "Less than five makes the drink too strong. More than five waters it down." Lucinda could see herself really liking this crowd.

The doorbell rang and Krystina disappeared for a moment, only to return with two more tall, beautiful, and toned women in tow. She didn't get to meet these two, as no introductions were needed for anyone else here. Lucinda stood quietly, watching the room and getting a feel for where she might be able to slide in. As she sipped her drink, she overheard a conversation that peaked her interest. Before she knew which group it was, she knew that a Casandra was telling an Elizabeth how satisfied she was with the private investigator she had hired to track down her ex-husband. Apparently, he followed the ex for two years before catching up to him, but it was worth it in the end. By law, she was entitled to half of all they owned, which included a house, boat, plane, and a sizable bank account. She mentioned some other things, which Lucinda couldn't pick out over the rest of the conversations, but that was certainly enough. He had everything transferred to his private account weeks before the papers were served and took off for an unknown destination. She was left with a house she couldn't sell because he wasn't there to sign the paperwork, and no one had been able to locate the boat or plane. She borrowed money from her family, but the P.I. found the ex living on some exotic island, with servants and all, enjoying the good life. She, in the interim, had been forced to get a job to make ends meet. In the end, she got her half and he got to spend substantial time in jail, as the P.I. also discovered some illegal side businesses that her ex had been running.

Lucinda found herself grinning at this story. She felt good knowing that she wasn't the only one who had to deal with a relationship that turned badly. However, Casandra had been able to deal with hers through far less violent means and didn't have to worry about the FBI coming to talk to her. In fact, she had done law enforcement a favor. Lucinda laughed to herself at the thought that she could sue Andrew over being a bad boyfriend and a two-timing husband. She wondered if Ted would have represented her.

The rest of the night went very well, as Lucinda got a chance to talk to almost everyone at the gathering. Numbers were exchanged and promises were made to get together soon. She knew, however, that she was unlikely to ever follow through with any of it, as a location change seemed inevitable. Another name change was also a distinct possibility, but for tonight at least Lucinda could enjoy the company of a pleasant group of women with no agendas beyond food, drink, and good conversation.

Chapter 23

The next morning, Lucinda made a mental note to monitor her drinking. It had been a long time since she woke up with a marching band playing in her head. She got up and headed into the kitchen for a cup of coffee. The pot was empty, and then she remembered that she had gotten in late and gone straight to bed. After setting it up and starting the machine, she made a quick call to the office to get an update on Ted's status. Rosaleen picked up quickly.

In a deep voice, Lucinda said, "Roger Powers, please."

"I'm sorry. He is not in the office at the moment. Would you like to leave a message?"

"No, thank you. I will call him later." Lucinda abruptly hung up the phone.

She then called the hospital. She still felt bad about what had happened to Ted and wanted to see how he was feeling. When she asked to be connected to his room, they informed her that he had been discharged that morning. As she hung up, she felt more at ease. *At least I know he is better. That's probably why Roger wasn't in the office.*

Lucinda looked in the refrigerator and realized that she needed to do a little shopping. She had been eating out so much lately that she hadn't bothered to pick up any groceries, and a diet of ketchup and salad dressing just wasn't going to cut it.

One quick shower later and Lucinda found herself shopping not at the local supermarket, but in all of the specialty shops that lined the streets near the common. Santa Barbara was well known for these, but Lucinda could never bring herself to spend such money on food. Today, however, was different. She splurged on imported cheeses, a wine whose name she couldn't even pronounce, and a cut of filet mignon that she swore smelled like it had already been cooked to perfection. *I could get used to living this sort of easy-going way of life.*

As she opened the door to her apartment, the phone began ringing. She dropped her bags on the counter and ran to answer it.

"Hello."

"It's Roger. Why do you sound like you've been running?"

"I was just coming in. How did you know I called?"

"Rosaleen told me. Didn't you leave a message?"

"No, I just said that I would call back." Lucinda was confused for a moment, but then realized that she had called from the land line. *Damn that caller ID.* "I was just calling to see how Ted was doing."

"He's fine. Still milking it though. I picked him up at the hospital and he told me that the doc told him not to lift anything or do anything strenuous." Lucinda could picture Ted clearly, complete with melodramatic hand gestures. "He's lying on the couch right now, but I could have him call you later."

"If he feels up to it, but it's not important. I just wanted to check in. Good luck with the recovering patient." As she hung up, she swore she heard him say, "God help me."

Chuckling to herself, Lucinda started unpacking her food and putting things away. She was tempted to dive into almost everything she bought, but resisted the urge. After checking to make sure it was after noontime, she did allow herself one glass of the wine. She held the glass under her nose, taking a deep breath, enjoying the heavy scent. She took one small sip and held it in her mouth for a few seconds before swallowing. While delicious, she still found herself thinking about a glass of good scotch. She put down the glass and moved to the refrigerator to put away the cheeses. As she bent down to open a drawer, she found herself eye to eye with a card. It was the business card that she found with the jewels. Lucinda slid the magnet over and held the card between her thumb and index finger. With all of the events of the past weeks, she had completely forgotten about this loose end. She felt pretty confident that it was some little detail, maybe a signature that would allow them to file that last piece of paperwork. Turning the card over and over in her hand, she almost put it back on the refrigerator door. The name on the card said Ricardo Azulai. It seemed a rather exotic name for a lawyer.

Impulsively, Lucinda strode over to the phone. She held it for several seconds, thinking, before finally dialing the eleven digits. After several rings, a pleasant sounding woman answered the phone. Lucinda identified herself and asked to speak to Mr. Azulai. The woman asked if she could put Lucinda on hold. After about a minute of classical music, the line clicked to life once again.

"Ms. Preston? My name is Joshua Kendell."

"Mr. Kendell? I needed to speak specifically to Ricardo Azulai."

"I understand. However, Mr. Azulai passed away several years ago. I was working for him at the time and took over the firm."

"I'm sorry to hear that. However, I don't know if you can help me. I recently received possessions of my grandmother and found his business card among them. I was told that he was looking for me."

Lucinda could hear the tapping of a keyboard and realized that Mr. Kendell was searching through files for her name. "I see no evidence of records regarding anyone by the name of Preston."

"Try searching the name 'Jeanette Jenkins'. I legally changed my name some years ago." More clicking. "Ah, here we go. Yes, there is indeed an active file for you." She could hear more clicking, along with a few 'hmms' from Mr. Kendell. "We actually have something here for you. However, this is a matter that needs to be done in person. By any chance, are you still in the Boston area?" She told him that she was not, but could be if it was absolutely necessary. "Unfortunately, it is. We have something for you that needs verification of identity and signatures." Lucinda's curiosity got the better of her, though in the back of the mind she could picture getting to Boston only to find out that they had her grandmothers' old bingo set, with cards and ink markers. She made an appointment for the 24th of September and thanked Mr. Kendell for his time. As she hung up the phone, Lucinda wondered what could be waiting for her in Boston and why they couldn't just mail it to her. She almost couldn't wait for the two weeks to pass so she could find out.

Chapter 24

Lucinda found herself constantly thinking about her trip. To help pass the time, she decided that the new start needed to apply to everything. She had been saving stacks of magazines, promising that she would one day read all of them. Instead, she bundled them together and dropped them in the recycling bin around the corner from her apartment. She cleaned out her closets and filled three trash bags full of good clothes, pocketbooks, and shoes. She called one of the local charities and made arrangements to have them picked up.

The night before her flight, Lucinda packed a small suitcase for the trip. After double-checking to make sure she had everything, she decided that she had done enough and would go to bed early. She wasn't a huge fan of flying and never felt enough at ease to sleep on the plane. A good night's sleep would be essential.

She was at the airport well before her departure and breezed through security. She was thankful that the flight was on time and wasn't too tightly booked. She had only one neighbor and a seat between them. The weather at take-off was beautiful, but unfortunately that didn't last. The seatbelt light stayed on for most of the flight due to pockets of turbulence, which created a fair amount of turbulence in Lucinda's stomach. When the plane finally landed at Logan Airport, she thought she might actually kiss the ground when they disembarked.

Lucinda made a quick trip through the airport and was soon hailing a cab to go to her hotel. The cab driver made a few efforts at conversation, but she was in no mood to talk. Exhaustion was quickly taking over. When she opened the door to her suite, Lucinda dropped her bag on the floor, dropped herself on the bed, and proceeded to fall into a deep sleep for the next two hours.

When she woke up, Lucinda felt surprisingly refreshed and had no interest in spending the night in her hotel. She thought about what she could do to entertain herself for the evening. There was so much to do in Boston, but she was more interested in the company than she was the activity. Right now, a nice dinner with old friends would trump a Broadway show attended alone. She knew Stella was recuperating from her surgery and likely wouldn't be able to go out. She made a mental note to check in with her and see how things went. Wracking her brain for someone from her past, she was surprised at the names that popped into her head. She was, at one time, friendly with Beverly and Virginia, who were friends of her grandmother back in Quincy. The idea of reconnecting with someone from her earliest days here made her more than a little nostalgic. She found a phone book in one of the desk drawers, along with the usual copy of the Bible. Searching through the listings, she was more surprised that Beverly was still alive than she was at the fact that her grandmother's friend was still living in the same place. She punched in the phone number and then tossed the phone book back into the drawer.

A familiar voice answered the phone. "Hello?" It made her smile immediately. "Hi, Beverly? It's J.J."

"My God! How are you? It's been forever since I've heard your voice!"

"It's been too long, that's for sure. The reason I'm calling is that I am in Boston for a couple of days on business. I thought it would be nice to catch up over dinner, if you were able to make it."

"I would love to." Lucinda could actually hear her smiling from ear to ear. Of course, that was Beverly. She was probably the happiest person that Lucinda had ever known.

"By any chance, is Virginia still living in the area? Do you think she might like to join us?"

"She's still alive and kicking. Would you like me to give her a call?"

"Can you give me her number? I would rather surprise her, if that's okay with you."

Beverly gave her the number and said she was going to get ready. She asked Lucinda where they would be going.

"How about the Inn at Bay Point? I haven't eaten there in forever." When Beverly agreed, Lucinda told her that she would call her back after she spoke with Virginia. She dialed the number that Beverly gave her and waited through six rings. While she was deciding whether or not to be worried, Virginia suddenly appeared at the other end of the line.

"Hello?" The voice sounded tiny and cracked, yet still familiar. It made Lucinda realize just how much she missed pieces of her old life.

"Virginia? It's J.J. Do you remember me?"

"Oh, my gosh. Is it really you?"

Lucinda couldn't help but chuckle at the thought that some stranger would call and impersonate her. "Of course it is. Who else would want to pretend to be me?"

"Well, you never know these days. Besides, it's been so long since I've heard your voice."

"I know. I'm sorry. The reason I'm calling is that I'm in town for a couple of days and thought maybe we could get together. Beverly and I are going to dinner tonight and would like you to make it a trio."

"That would be wonderful! One thing, though. I am using a walker to get around these days. It's really a rollator, but I call it a walker. Is that going to be a problem?"

Lucinda found that so sweet, that Virginia was worried about the possible inconvenience of her walker. "I'm sure there will be no problem. I'm going to make a reservation for five-thirty at the Inn at Bay Point. I will pick you both up at the South Wing at five-fifteen."

They said their goodbyes and Lucinda called back Beverly to fill her in on the details. She then called to make the reservations, requesting a table next to the windows in the side room. The final touch, one her new situation allowed for, was to call the front desk and see if they could arrange for a limousine to be available for her at quarter to five. Once all the arrangements were made, Lucinda set about picking out something to wear. She was excited about the choice of car, as she knew that getting a ride in a limo would give the two ladies something to talk about for weeks. The look on their faces would be more than worth the price.

Lucinda put on a pair of brown slacks and a beige silk blouse. It was a lovely, warm evening, even though it was the end of September. When she arrived at the lobby, she could see the car sitting at the curb, with a tall man standing beside it. She could feel herself making the same face that she imagined on Beverly and Virginia when they saw it. *I could definitely get used to this.* When she walked out the front door, the gentleman moved to the passenger side and waited for her to get there. With what seemed to be one smooth motion, he opened the door, tipped his cap, and gave her a very polite, "Ma'am." She slid across the seat and scanned the interior. It was immaculate and she could have sworn she picked up the new car smell. The driver got into the front seat and they made eye contact in his rear view mirror.

"Good evening. My name is Roy and I will be your driver for the evening. I understand that we have another stop before our final destination?"

Lucinda was impressed by his professionalism and gave him the address to Beverly and Virginia's. She waited for him to ask directions, but he put the car in drive and headed right out onto the highway. She heard the soft sounds of jazz coming through speakers from somewhere behind her. However, when he spoke, she could still clearly hear him.

"I am familiar with this location, as my mother lives there. She loves all the activities. She takes the writing classes with a Mrs. Monahan, yoga lessons with Dee, and exercise classes with Helena."

"I am not familiar with the staff there, but I will have to ask my friends if they do any of that. It sounds wonderful."

The two exchanged small talk and the ride seemed to fly by. They turned into the complex at Southern Artery and Lucinda could see Beverly sitting on the bench and Virginia with her rollator outside the front door to the South Wing. Immediately, Lucinda realized that she had forgotten to mention this, but before she could say anything, Roy assured her, "Don't worry. I've handled those before. They actually fold down quite easily and fit in the trunk." He eased the car to the curb and she could see Beverly's eyes light up at the sight of their transportation for the evening.

This sent a thrill through Lucinda as she got out of the car to greet the two friends. As soon as Virginia released the rollator to embrace her, Roy quickly pulled a pin, folded it down, and stowed it into the trunk. As the three gave each other hugs and greetings, Roy opened the rear door and waited patiently for each to slide into the back seat.

After everyone was settled in, Roy headed out into traffic and they were on their way. It was only about a mile to the inn, and both Virginia and Beverly sat like a couple of awe-struck children. Even though they had lived in the city most of their life, Lucinda figured it looked a little different through the windows of a limousine. Conversation could wait until they were seated for dinner, so Lucinda sat back and listened to the quiet strains of jazz piano. When they arrived at the inn, Roy once again sprang into action. No sooner had he pulled to the curb in front of the main entrance, but he had the rollator out of the trunk, set up, and had the door open with a hand out to assist the ladies. Lucinda was impressed with both his professionalism and kind-hearted nature. Impulsively, she asked him if he could join them at dinner, especially since he had a fair amount of knowledge about the ladies' residence and could participate in the conversation.

"That is very kind, but I need to stay with the vehicle. However, I will be right here waiting when you are finished. Enjoy your meals." He escorted them to the door, where they were greeted by a staff member. They were quickly shown to a table with a beautiful view of the marina. When the waitress came over with menus, Lucinda asked if it would be possible to take one out to their driver in the parking lot. With a smile, the waitress assured her that would not be a problem. Lucinda felt badly about him sitting out there alone and decided that, at the very least, he shouldn't be hungry as well.

The dinner went by in a blur. Lucinda summed up, as quickly as she could, her life since leaving the East coast. The three commiserated over the loss of Annie, a good friend and grandmother. Both Beverly and Virginia reminisced about how she would come over each week to play Dominoes and Bingo with them.

Virginia said, "I miss having coffee with her every Friday morning."

Beverly added, "She was always thinking about everyone else. If you needed a ride, she would be there waiting outside your door. If you were having a hard time with someone in the family, she always seemed to know and would just show up with ice cream."

Virginia nodded. "She always worried about you, dear. When things got tough with you, when your friendship with that girl next door went bad, with your legal troubles, she swore that she was going to do everything she could to make your life easier."

Beverly jumped in. "Yeah, she said something several times over the years that you spent in jail, something I never really understood. She mentioned that she was going to help you iron out your troubles before she died." She looked quizzically at Lucinda.

Lucinda raised her eyebrows, trying to make some connection between that statement and the time spent with her grandmother after she moved back in. Nothing really jumped out at her, although she assumed that it had something to do with the jewels. She just shrugged and said, "Guess she really was a bit of a jokester, hmm? She probably wanted me to get a job at a Laundromat and clean up my act." The three of them laughed at that thought and continued with their reminiscence.

It was both sad and happy at the same time, as each of them had several wonderful memories to share and funny stories to tell. Lucinda loved hearing these stories, as it gave her a different perspective of her grandmother. Though she was a disciplinarian and a stern figure to Lucinda, she was quite the comedian to her friends. It was hard for her to picture her grandmother as a prankster, but Beverly and Virginia assured her that she had a very fun-loving side that could light up a room.

As the dinner dishes were cleared and the conversation lagged, Lucinda knew that it was time to call it a night. When they stepped out the front door into a beautiful clear night, Roy was waiting at the door to assist them. Soon, they were saying their goodbyes and promising to keep in touch. As Lucinda slid into the back seat, she was glad that she made this impulsive call. It was good to see people from her old life, to reconnect for one night to who she once was. For a brief moment, the mention of her grandmother's pledge to help her flashed through her mind. However, she was interrupted by Roy's voice, telling her that they had arrived at her hotel. She reached for the door handle, but once again Roy was there, extending a hand to help her out of the car. As she stepped to the curb, Roy thanked her enthusiastically for the evening. "You really were a wonderful client tonight. The dinner was delicious and made the wait fly by. It was a pleasure to be your driver."

Lucinda fished into her purse and pulled out several bills. She reached out to shake Roy's hand and gave him the money. When he looked down, he saw that she had just given him three hundreds. "I can't accept this. It is way too much."

She smiled. "I know what it's like to work for a living. You were outstanding tonight. Thank you for everything."

Roy reached into his pocket and pulled out a business card. As he handed it to her, he said, "If ever you need a lift, don't hesitate to call. Thank you again." He turned on his heel and was soon pulling out of the parking lot. Lucinda headed into the hotel and decided to have one last drink in the lounge before heading upstairs. She ordered a scotch on the rocks and headed for an empty seat along the wall. Sipping her drink slowly, she contemplated what tomorrow would have in store for her.

Chapter 25

Lucinda woke up well before her seven o'clock alarm, as her mind had never let her truly fall into a deep sleep. Even though she couldn't imagine what bad could come from this meeting, she was having a difficult time considering it merely some formality. She placed a quick call to the front desk, ordering a coffee and an English muffin from room service, as well as requesting a taxi for nine-thirty.

Taking a long, hot shower settled the nerves a little bit, and she spent extra time picking out her clothes for the meeting. She had originally planned on dressing casual, given what she thought would be the tone, but decided to be a bit more professional. She was thankful that she had packed a simple gray suit, a last minute addition to her travel bag. Even after all the delaying, Lucinda still found herself with a half hour to kill. She decided that people watching in the lobby would be a better way to do this than sitting in her room, watching daytime television.

When she stepped out of the elevator, Lucinda could see a taxi waiting at the curb. Looking at her watch, she couldn't imagine that it was there for her. The young woman at the front desk saw her standing there and called her over. She was a lovely girl, though Lucinda wondered if she was actually old enough to be working there. She verified that the cab was indeed there for her and asked if she needed anything else. Lucinda told her that she was all set, thanked her for arranging the taxi, and headed out the front door.

It was a beautiful fall New England day. The air was crisp, but the sun felt very warm on her face. As she approached the cab, she thought of Roy and how he would be there holding the door open for her. Instead, she climbed in unassisted, gave the driver her destination address, and settled back for the ride. Congress Street wasn't all that far away, and Lucinda was thankful for that, as her driver seriously lacked in both interpersonal skills and basic hygiene. She quickly paid the fare and jumped out of the cab.

The office of Azulai & Kendell was bustling even at this early hour. She approached the receptionist's desk and gave her name. The woman made a brief call, spoke in hushed tones, then hung up the receiver and asked Lucinda to follow her. She escorted her through a medium sized room filled with half-height cubicles, not unlike her own former office, before reaching a solitary door on the far wall. She gave a quick knock and a muffled voice replied. The woman opened the door and stepped aside for Lucinda to enter. As she did so, the receptionist closed the door behind her. Joshua Kendell rose from his desk and introduced himself. He gestured to the chair in front of the desk and she sat down. He went over to a file cabinet behind the desk, giving Lucinda a chance to take in both the man and the surroundings. The room itself was unremarkable, with a mix of furniture styles. There were old, hand-carved bookcases holding many leather bound books standing side-by-side with a modern metal rack providing a home for the coffee pot and its' accessories. There were no personal touches to be found here, which led Lucinda to contemplate the room's tenant. Joshua Kendell appeared to be an athletic man, meticulously groomed, but with an unpretentious air about him. When he turned back toward her, he gave her a genuine smile which put her immediately at ease. He had an envelope in his hand, which he placed on the desk.

"Ms. Preston, thank you for coming out to see us personally. Can I offer you a cup of coffee or tea?"

"Coffee would be wonderful. Black, please. And call me Lucinda."

Joshua moved over to the coffee pot and poured out a cup. As he was doing so, he got right to the point. "Lucinda, as you may know, my late partner handled all of your grandmother's affairs for a number of years. They eventually developed a friendship beyond her legal needs. Sometime before your graduation from high school, she came to him with a favor. She was very concerned for you, given the difficulties you had encountered up to that point. She gave him this envelope and asked that, should she not live to do it herself, he would make sure that it found its way to you when you turned twenty-five." He placed a cup of coffee in front of her and took a quick sip from his own mug as he sat down. "My partner agreed to do so and created a file in both her name and yours. It sat there for a handful of years before he was informed that your grandmother had passed. Ricardo was very fond of Ann and was most saddened to hear of her death. When your twenty-fifth birthday arrived, he tried to give you this envelope, but you had already moved away. After several attempts to track you down, he contacted a local policeman who was also a client. Detective Nelson said that he was trying to locate you for his late partner. Ricardo gave him a business card and a request to call him if you were found."

Lucinda realized that she was sitting on the very edge of her chair. Settling back into the cushion, she tried to wrap her mind around the path that this envelope had taken to get to her and how many people had been involved. Joshua pushed it over to her and said, "Better late than never, I guess." She stared at the manila rectangle, with her old name written on the front in her grandmother's script. The irony of a second mysterious envelope showing up with her former life in it was not lost on Lucinda.

She slowly reached out and slid it off the desk and on to her lap. The thought of her grandmother putting this aside for her so many years ago caused her to tear up. It had been both clasped shut and taped, so Joshua handed her a letter opener. She slit the end open and slid the contents out. On the top was a standard mailing envelope, again with Jeanette Jenkins written on it. Underneath, however, Lucinda saw a bearer bond with a value of ten thousand dollars. Not just one, however. Licking her index finger, she counted the corners in the stack of bonds until she hit ten. One hundred thousand dollars. She looked up at Joshua Kendell incredulously.

"Are you sure these are for me?"

Joshua smiled. "I would have to assume so. It had your name on it and my late partner was meticulous in his keeping of information and records. Not to mention, I have your grandmother's instructions, if you care to check."

Lucinda's mouth was still hanging open. "Why weren't these bonds listed with all her assets at the time of the reading of her will?" Lucinda wasn't angry at the delay in delivery, but was instead saddened by the thought that her grandmother had chosen to go without so that she could benefit.

Pointing to her lap, Joshua said, "I am guessing that you may find some answers in that other envelope you are holding."

Lucinda looked down at the other part of the surprise. She wondered what other bomb was waiting there to be dropped. "Do I need to open this here in front of you?"

He shook his head. "That is up to you, but it is not necessary. All I need from you is a signature confirming that this envelope was delivered and accepted." He pulled out a single sheet of paper from the now empty file with both her and her grandmother's names on it. Placing it on the desk, he produced a pen from his shirt pocket.

"How should I sign, with Jeanette Jenkins or Lucinda Preston? I legally changed my name a number of years ago."

Joshua laughed. "Yes, I know. That is why we are here today, after such a circuitous route. Sign it with both names and I will have it notarized and a copy sent to you."

Lucinda took the pen and signed the document. She decided that the letter, along with any revelations it contained, could wait until she got back to the hotel. She stood up and thanked Joshua for everything. He walked her all the way back to the lobby and thanked her for coming out to tie up a final loose end. He wished her well and turned to head back to his office. When she stepped outside, the warm sun started immediately loosening the muscle tightness that she had not noticed before. She was amazed that she could be so tense, given that she had just inherited another hundred thousand dollars. Lucinda knew, however, that the tension was in the other envelope, the one that she was suddenly both very afraid of and eager to open. She quickly hailed a cab and was soon back in her hotel room.

Lucinda sat in the center of the bed, with the unopened envelope in front of her and a freshly poured scotch from the mini-bar in her hand. She was waiting for the drink to steel her nerves. She couldn't imagine her grandmother having anything in that letter that might hurt her, but a lifetime of being on her guard wouldn't let her shake the possibility from her mind. She gulped down the rest of her drink, feeling the burn down her throat, and opened the envelope.

Chapter 26

My darling J.J.,

I am writing this to you to let you know how very much I love you. I know a lot of things haven't gone right for you. Losing your parents at such a young age, then having to live with someone who couldn't always relate to what you were going through must have been very difficult. I really did my best to fill in for your mother and father, who loved you more than life itself. Part of that role was protecting you from things in the world that were unsafe, even something as simple as information and events that might impact how you perceived yourself and the people around you. However, there are things that you should know, now that you are a grown woman.

Your father was a wonderful man and a good dad, but he got involved with the wrong types of people. Your mother and I used to warn him about the danger of associating with such people. However, he was adamant about providing for his family, even if it wasn't always the right way. He stole many precious stones from them over the years. Your mother knew about this and lived in fear. She worried that this might come back to haunt them and, subsequently, you as well. Since she couldn't get him to stop, she would take a stone or two without your father's knowledge and hide them, so that you might someday have them. I saw her doing it, and suggested that she hide them in a place where they could get to you. I was afraid that the mob would find out and come here to take back what was stolen from them. However, they didn't come. Instead, there was the accident. It was no accident, though, that your parents died in the crash. The police discovered that the brake lines had been cut. Your parents were murdered. When the car hit the stone wall, your mother was killed instantly, but your father managed to get back here. As weak and injured as he was, he made it to my door. He told me where he had stashed some gems in the house. He died in my arms.

I found the gems that your dad had hidden, but I never found the ones your mother put aside for you. He had 43 emeralds hidden away, which I sewed into the hem of my green dress. That is the reason I wanted to be buried in it and have it ironed by you. If you are reading this letter without me, it means that I have already died and Mr. Azulai has delivered it to you. You should have found the stones and used them to help you get on your feet. I am sure you are wondering why I waited to give you all this. I was worried that you might not be mature enough to handle the contents, though you have always been resourceful and thinking several steps ahead.

The bonds were purchased for me by your grandfather. He did very well in the stock market over the years and bought them to provide for me, should the need ever arise. I never had to cash in even one. I now expect that they will provide for you. I am sure that you will use them wisely.

My darling J.J., I love you so much. While I would never have wished for the events that brought you to me, I am thankful that it gave me the chance to know you and be part of your life. You have made me so happy all these years. Enjoy your life. All my love forever,

Nana

By the time she finished the letter, tears were rolling down Lucinda's cheeks. Her chest felt as though it was going to explode. She rolled off the bed and went to the mini-bar, pouring herself another scotch. Sitting on the edge of the bed, she stared at the folded letter in one hand

and her drink in the other. Several thoughts were battling for space in her mind: meeting a grandmother she never really knew all that well, one who loved her enough to risk her life by hiding jewels stolen from the mob; the fact that, in her own selfish need to get out of town fast, she hadn't bothered to follow her grandmother's instructions, put in place specifically so she could get those jewels; the fact that her parents' death was not an accident. She downed the scotch in one gulp, trying to steady the swim her head was starting to take. Reaching across the bed, she picked up the envelope and started to put the letter back in. She noticed that there was another piece of paper stuck to the inside of it. She ran a fingernail between the paper and the envelope until the two separated and she pulled it out. Unfolding the paper, she quickly scanned what was typed on it. The burn in her stomach was immediate and agonizing, and with a surge of adrenaline driving her, Lucinda propelled herself into the bathroom and vomited violently into the sink.

Chapter 27

Sitting on the floor of the bathroom, Lucinda fought to steady herself. Her cheeks were wet with tears, while her shirt was soaked with sweat. Her sides were suddenly sore and she was panting rapidly, as though something was sitting on her chest and making her work for every breath. She leaned against the wall, straightened her legs out in front of her, and laid her palms flat on the cold tile floor. She counted twenty breaths, giving each inhale and exhale a count of three, trying to get herself under control. She often counted when flying, during takeoffs and landings, to keep from having a panic attack. Today, she found she needed a count of forty before she felt like she could move without throwing up again.

Lucinda pulled herself from the floor using the towel rack, feeling it bend under her weight. She slowly walked back to the bedroom, picking up the paper whose contents had prompted the sudden visit to the bathroom. She sat back on the bed, feeling strangely exhausted, the euphoria of her most recent inheritance suddenly so far away. Pulling her legs under her, she flattened the paper out and re-read the third line.

Mother: Sylvia Jenkins. Father: Anton Lewis.

Lucinda knew her father's name was Paul Jenkins. Anton Lewis was Marlene's father. This one line answered one question and created several more. She now, at least, had an idea where the first collection of jewels had come from. The letter had said that her grandmother suggested hiding the jewels where the mob couldn't find them. Her mother must have given them to Marlene's father, so that they wouldn't be found in the house. Lucinda figured that Marlene must have given them to her detective boyfriend to give to her.

The new questions were numerous: Did her father know she wasn't his biological daughter? How did her mother and Marlene's father get together? Did Marlene know what was in the pouch? How and when did she get it? Lucinda's head began to swim again. She folded the birth certificate and put it back in the envelope with her grandmother's letter. There would be time to puzzle over all this later. She put the letter, certificate, and bonds on the bedside table, turned out the light, and buried her face in the pillow. She was asleep two seconds later.

Chapter 28

A blinding sun pierced through Lucinda's eyelids, causing little sunspots like the ones you get when you squeeze your eyes closed tight. She could hear horns honking outside and figured that it must be morning. She rolled onto her side, putting her back to the window, and opened one eye just enough to see the clock. Four o'clock! Snapping upright, Lucinda realized that she must have slept through the night and most of the day Friday. For a moment, she panicked, forgetting where she was. However, the previous day's events came trickling back to her and the disorientation turned into confusion.

As she ran through all of the information she had received yesterday, Lucinda began to wonder what in her life had actually been real. Her family had been part of the mob, this much she already knew. Her father had been stealing from these very dangerous people. However, it turned out that not only was her father a thief, but he wasn't even her real father. Her mother had had an affair with her best friend's father and given birth to his child, passing the child off as belonging to her husband. Her grandmother helped keep it a secret, as well as the fact that Lucinda's mother had been stealing from her thief husband. The mob killed her parents and made it look like an accident. Last but not least, her grandmother had hidden jewels for her and left directions that would allow Lucinda to find them. In impetuous fashion, she had not followed the instructions and allowed the jewels to be buried with her grandmother.

There had been very few times in Lucinda's life where she could honestly say that things had been easy. Most of them happened in the first twelve years of her life. Since then, it was always one slippery slope after another. Now, even as her life seemed to be turning in a positive direction, with wealth and freedom to do as she wished, potholes were appearing in the road. Lucinda took a deep breath and reminded herself that, for most of her life, she had met any obstacle head-on and that now would be no different. She just needed to decide what the next step was. Once she made this mental leap of preparation, choosing that step was easy. She grabbed her bag off the chair by the bed and fished through it until she found her planner. She found the number that she was looking for and quickly punched it on her cell phone. The voice full of sunshine picked up on two rings.

"Hello?"

"Krystina, it's Lucinda." Her friend's voice went up a decibel or ten.

"Omigod! How are you doing? I was so glad you came to the party last time. All of my friends thought you were really great and…."

Lucinda was laughing as she interrupted her. "Krystina. Krystina! Stop. I'm glad I came too, but I didn't call about that right now. At the party, I met a woman named Casandra. We swapped numbers, but I think I sent the paper through the wash. Any chance you have it close by?" Lucinda wasn't going to give any more information than she had to.

"I've got it right here. Hold on." Lucinda could hear what sounded like a purse being emptied out on the table. "I really need to get all these numbers into my phone. I have so much stuff in my bag, I think my right shoulder is lower than my left. Got a pen?"

Krystina read the number to her and made her promise to come to the next get-together before she would hang up the phone. When Lucinda finally convinced her that she would be there, they said quick good-byes and hung up. She looked at the number scrawled on the same envelope that pointed her in this new direction for a full minute before steeling herself and dialing. It rang so long that she wasn't sure if it was Casandra or the machine picking up.

"Hello, Casandra? It's Lucinda, from the party at Krystina's."

"Hey, how's it going?" She sounded genuinely happy to hear from her. Lucinda had worried that she might have forgotten meeting her.

"Pretty good. Sorry to bug you, but I needed some information. When we met, you were telling a story about a private investigator that you used to find your ex. By any chance, do you remember the guy's name or who he worked for?"

"Of course. It was called the W&F Detective Agency in Boston. The guy I used was actually the owner. His name was Bill. Nice guy, but figured himself to be a bit of a ladies' man. Good looking, but a bit older than I would like. You want the number?"

Lucinda wrote down all the info on the envelope. Casandra asked if she had a cheating boyfriend or something like that. "No. It turns out that I have a half-sister. I haven't seen her since we were kids and I'm hoping that he can find her for me."

"Family reunion. That's nice. Well, good luck. And if you think it'll get you a discount, feel free to use my name. I'm sure he took a nice vacation on the amount of money I gave him."

"Will do. Thanks for the information. Hopefully I'll see you at the next get-together at Krystina's."

Lucinda looked at the time and at the address of the agency. If she was remembering correctly, Constitution Avenue wasn't all that far away.

Maybe if she could get someone on the phone, she might be able to get in and at least start the ball rolling. She dialed the number and sat down while it rang. A very pleasant woman answered the phone.

"W&F Detective Agency, this is Iris. How may I direct your call?"

"Iris, my name is Lucinda Preston. I was referred to you by a recent client and am in town for a couple of days. I don't have an appointment, but was wondering if I might be able to squeeze in before the day's over and talk to someone." Lucinda felt immediately guilty at trying to get in so late on a Friday. However, Iris didn't even seem bothered.

"I think we could fit you in for a consult, if you are available now."

Lucinda practically jumped out of her chair. "I'm getting a cab now. I should be there within fifteen minutes. Thank you very much."

"We'll see you shortly, Ms. Preston."

True to her word, Lucinda was getting out of the cab in front of the agency in exactly twelve minutes. Since the building was so tall, the elevator ride to the 27th floor almost took as long as the cab ride. When she stepped out, she was immediately taken aback by the impressive wall to wall windows providing a panoramic view of Boston. She had forgotten how beautiful the city could be after so many years on the West Coast. She found the office and was greeted by a spacious waiting room, simply but comfortably decorated. Sitting at a desk along the side wall was an impeccably dressed woman, who she assumed was Iris. As she approached her, the woman looked up and said, "You must be Ms. Preston. Please take a seat." Lucinda sat down and began running what she would say through her head. Not more than two minutes later, the phone on the desk buzzed. Iris answered in a hushed voice, then turned to her and indicated that she could go in. Lucinda stood and headed for the door on the other side of Iris' desk. As she swung the door open, she stiffened right up when she saw the face of Bill Fadigo sitting there. He looked up and was equally shocked.

"J.J., what are you doing here?"

"I called and Iris told me that she could fit in a consult."

Bill looked down at his desk. "I don't see your name on my appointment list. I should be meeting with a Lucinda Preston right now." He looked up at her in bewilderment.

"That would be me." She couldn't help but find the look on his face amusing, but it soon turned to a smile and he got up from his chair and came around to give her a big hug. As he released her, she said, "My God, Bill. I had no idea that you were the Bill that my friend recommended."

Bill gave her a sheepish grin. "Guilty. I must be doing something right, since you found me by recommendation. But look at you! Beautiful as ever. The blonde looks great. How come you changed your name?"

She didn't answer his question, but asked, "What happened with the Boston Police? I thought you liked that job."

Shaking his head, he replied, "Ah, I was careless and messed up a pretty big case. That got me fired. However, it all turned out for the best. This agency has allowed me to do similar work, but I get to be the boss and the pay is a whole lot better." He took a pause, picked up the phone and hit a button. When Iris answered, he asked her to reschedule his last appointment of the day. As he hung up, Bill asked, "So what brings you here today?"

Lucinda looked at him seriously for a moment before answering, "Do you remember my friend Marlene?" Bill nodded and waited for her to continue. "I recently found out that she is my half-sister." He gathered up his jaw from the floor and said, "You have got to be kidding!"

"No, I'm not kidding. I just saw my birth certificate for the first time in my life a couple of days ago. It was in with some paperwork that was attached to my grandmother's estate. Marlene's father's name was on it."

"Wow! Bet you never saw that coming!"

Lucinda was slightly annoyed at this comment. "You think? I'm not really sure how to feel, but I do know that I need to find her. So are you interested in the job?"

"I'm always interested. However, I must tell you that it likely won't be cheap, even for an old friend."

Lucinda just looked at him and waited. He shrugged and opened up a desk drawer. He took out two pieces of paper and slid them over to Lucinda. The top one was a basic description of what he did, the services covered under the contract, and what the expected overall cost would be. The second one was the actual contract, with all the terms spelled out in legal-speak. Lucinda was very familiar with this kind of paperwork and just quickly skimmed it before signing on the bottom. She folded the first sheet and put it in her bag, then slid the second one back to Bill. He took out a notebook and put the contract off to the side. He wrote something on the cover of the notebook and then turned to the first page.

"So, let's start off with some basics. When was the last time you spoke with Marlene? Did she ever mention places that she would like to visit? Who were some of her close friends? Besides you, of course." When he said this last part, he looked up and smirked.

"I haven't seen her since my grandmother died ten years ago. I only knew the kids that she did theater with back in high school. She never mentioned anyplace in specific, only that she wanted to help people when she grew up. And if I knew any of this, I probably wouldn't be here talking to you." As Bill scribbled notes in his book, he laughed at the last remark. "Touché." He finished what he was writing and closed the book. "How about dinner tonight? Maybe we can catch up a little?"

Lucinda thought back to Casandra's comment. Still, she could take care of herself and she hadn't eaten in quite a while. "Fine. What time?"

"Around seven? Give me your address and I'll pick you up."

She gave him the address of the hotel and said that she would meet him in the lobby at seven. She then got up and extended her hand. As he took her hand, she said, "It's a pleasure doing business with you." Bill smiled and walked her out to the elevator. He pushed the button and said, "See you at seven." When the door opened, she gave him a quick smile and stepped into the elevator.

Chapter 29

Lucinda spent a little extra time picking out her outfit for the evening, eventually settling on a simple black dress with a black and white printed jacket, designer shoes and a matching bag. The looks on the faces of the men in the lobby told her that she had chosen well. She walked directly to the front door, where she found Bill waiting by a sleek black sports car. He whistled when he saw her. She grimaced at his response.

"You haven't changed a bit. Love your car, by the way."

As Bill opened the door for her, he replied, "I'm glad it meets with your approval." After she slid into the front seat, he added, "You look marvelous." Without looking at him, she said, "I know."

Bill was still chuckling at that when he got in beside her. The car started up with a throaty roar and they were soon headed for South Station. Lucinda had not thought to ask where they were going, but she figured that Bill wouldn't take her to just any little dive. She was not surprised, then, when they pulled up to the Harbor Restaurant. Bill must have a fair amount of influence in this town to get a reservation on such short notice. A valet came and opened Lucinda's door, offering a hand to help her out. He walked her to the curb where Bill was waiting with an arm extended. She took it and they went into the restaurant. They were immediately seated at a beautiful table overlooking the water. The waitress took their drink order and left two menus.

Lucinda smiled as she watched a ship heading out to sea. "In all the years I lived in this area, I never got the chance to have dinner here. I used to take the ferry from the shipyard in Quincy Point and get off right down there," as she pointed to the boat ramp. "I would walk over to the Quincy Market Place and spend the day poking around before coming back here to watch the ships coming and going. I would usually catch the last ferry of the night and head home. I used to wonder how it would feel to be one of the people sitting up here looking down as I am now, watching the boats leave the dock. Thank you for choosing this place."

Lucinda could feel his gaze and turned to look at Bill. "What?"

He just smiled. "You know, that was probably the most I have ever heard you open up to someone. You were always a closely guarded secret, with everything locked away. Always the tough exterior, ready for a fight. You are so different from the girl I knew then. You've changed just like the caterpillar changes into a beautiful butterfly. You really have become a classy dame." As soon as he said this, Bill looked down somewhat sheepishly. When he looked back up, he changed topic completely. "So tell me, what have you been up to all these years?"

Lucinda gave him the short version of how she arrived at this point, leaving out all the really interesting stuff that would land her in jail. When she got to the point of quitting her job, Bill's eyes got large.

"Really? You just up and quit? How the heck did you manage that? I've, uh, known some paralegals in my day and none of them ever earned enough dough to retire so young! What did you do, win the lottery?"

Lucinda ignored the pause in the paralegal reference and skipped to the question. "You know, I just recently told someone I did just that!"

They both laughed out loud, but when Bill gave her the inquisitive look hoping that she would continue, she instead changed the subject to something she knew he couldn't resist – himself.

"So, being a private investigator must have given you lots of great stories to tell!" She leaned forward on her hands for emphasis, and Bill took the bait. He launched into a series of stories involving jealous wives, cheating husbands, the occasional prostitute, and even a couple of gunfights. Lucinda was actually quite interested in his tales, but tempered her responses. She didn't need Bill thinking she was interested in more than dinner.

When the waitress returned, the two of them had decided to get a medley of items so they could pick at a variety of tastes. Among their selections were French onion soup, raspberry duck, a lobster cocktail, a Brooklyn porterhouse with Vidalia onions, and several vegetable sides. After the waitress departed, Lucinda couldn't help but be surprised at how comfortable she was with Bill. Given their history, she figured that, at the very least, she would be on her guard. She actually thought that she would be angry, but time had suppressed that wound, if not healed it entirely.

For the rest of the night, they chatted about everything under the sun except for the job. They talked about work, travels, past relationships, behaving very much like old friends. The conversation continued steadily until they arrived at the entrance to her hotel. When Bill put the car in park, Lucinda immediately got out of the car. He was two steps behind her when she got to the door. He took her hand and said, "Will I get to see you again before you head home?"

She looked down at the ground for a moment before answering. "I can't really say. I have some business to take care of and I will only be here for a couple more days. I have your number if I have some extra time." She started to turn away, but he held her hand firm. He reached into his jacket pocket and pulled out a business card. Handing it to her, he said, "My cell number is on there. Don't be afraid to use it." As he handed her the card, he leaned in to kiss her goodnight. She took the card and quickly turned away.

"Bill, I had a really great time tonight. Thank you. I'll be in touch regarding the investigation." Lucinda wanted to remind him that this was a business relationship. She heard the roar of his car as she stepped into the elevator. As she was riding up, she couldn't help but think of the feeling she got when she saw him in his office earlier that day. It was the same one she got when she saw him in her grandmother's living room the day she came home from jail. The only problem was that she couldn't forget that other feeling, the one she got when she overheard him telling Marlene that he could never fall for "someone like her".

By the time Lucinda had her pajamas on and had crawled between the sheets, she had made her decision. She would keep Bill at arm's length, use him for his investigative skills, and then move on. It was time for the next step in her plan.

Chapter 30

Saturday morning was a jolt to Lucinda's system. Each time she had come out to Boston recently, she had been lucky to get weather similar to winter in California. Today, however, reminded her why she chose to move there in the first place. Bitter winds were howling between the skyscrapers of Boston, searching every nook and cranny for any victim not prepared for the oncoming month of October. Lucinda called for a cab and waited in the lobby until it pulled up outside the front door.

The next task was already beginning to tie small knots in Lucinda's stomach. The drive to her destination was longer, as she was heading much closer to the home of her childhood, and this gave her too much time to think. She had almost talked herself out of it when the cab came to a sudden stop. She steeled herself, paid the fare, and stepped out into the cold.

Looking up at the sign on the building, she felt a sharp pang in her midsection. She could not tell if it was guilt, regret, or loss that was causing it. Another possibility was the thought of what she was about to do. Taking a deep breath, she knocked on the front door of the funeral home from which her grandmother had been buried. Lucinda couldn't hear any noise inside and considered the possibility that even death took a day off. She turned and scanned the parking lot in front of the building, looking to see if there was anyone working. Suddenly she heard what sounded like running behind the heavy oak doors. The sound got progressively louder, along with a voice asking for patience. The thud of a deadbolt opening caused an echo in the frigid parking lot and then the door swung open.

"J.J.? Is that you?"

Lucinda took in the astonished face of Mr. Schiffer, the funeral director who took care of all her grandmother's arrangements after she died. He must have been in one of the prep rooms downstairs, as he was still trying to catch his breath and was sporting a pair of bright red cheeks. "Hello, Mr. Schiffer. It's so nice to see you again. I'm very sorry to just show up at your door, but I have a somewhat urgent matter and happened to be in town. Do you have a little time?"

The director nodded energetically and stepped aside. "Of course. Please come in. It's rather brutal outside today." She walked past him and into the elegant front room, decorated with intricate woodwork, ambient lighting, and mostly earth tones. He beckoned her to follow him, and they passed through several waiting rooms before reaching an office in the very back of the building. He showed her in and said, "Please, have a seat. Help yourself to the coffee by the window. I just need a couple of minutes to finish what I was doing." He waited until she thanked him and then turned on his heel and headed back the way they had come. Lucinda walked over to the coffee pot and picked up a scent of toasted almond. She smiled and took a mug off the shelf with a picture of an island on it. She had no sooner poured out a cup and sat down in front of the director's desk than she heard the intermittent clicking of his heels on the tiled sections of the floor leading to his office.

When he entered the office, he was far more composed than he was at the front door. The flush in his cheeks had gone, and he had located the jacket for his suit. "So, what brings you back to us after, what has it been, ten years?" He made an exaggerated exhale over the length of time. He then took on a serious look. "You aren't in need of our services, I hope." Lucinda chuckled when she got where he was going with that. "No, not those services. I may need a different one, but for now I could just use some information." Mr. Schiffer poured himself a cup of coffee and settled in at his desk. "So what can I do for you then?"

Lucinda took a deep breath. "I would like to know the procedure for exhuming a body and moving it to another burial place."

Mr. Schiffer arched his brows and gave Lucinda a look that made her uncomfortable. "Certainly, but may I ask why?"

Lucinda was prepared for the question. "I would like to have my grandmother moved from Cedar Grove to Santa Barbara, California. I have been living there for quite some time now and would prefer to have her closer to me, so that I may visit."

Mr. Schiffer smiled at the thought. "Of course. I must say, though, that the process isn't simple. First you need to get a court order stating why you want the body moved. I don't see any problem there. We will need to obtain the appropriate exhumation license. Actually, we will need to get two: one from the State and the other from a religious official. The reason for the second one is because your grandmother's grave is on consecrated grounds, so you will need their permission. An environmental health officer needs to be present when the grave is opened to ensure that the exhumation is properly respectful and that the public is protected from contamination. He will verify that it is the proper grave and that the name on the casket matches the State's public records. He ensures that the workers wear the appropriate gear and oversees the transfer of the remains to a new casket. The final steps are arrangements for transport to the new burial site, as well as a purchased plot. I hope you understand, J.J., that this process isn't inexpensive. It may very well cost double the expense of her first funeral."

Lucinda didn't bat an eye. "I understand. However, it will be worth the cost to have her with me again. Will you help me with this?"

He smiled and said, "Absolutely. I think it is wonderful that you want to have her close to you. There are far too many forgotten graves that go untended and unvisited. I am sure that, if she were here, she would be more than pleased." He went over to a file cabinet beside his desk and starting pulling different forms out of each drawer. As he was doing so, Lucinda informed him of her name change and asked him if it would cause any problems with fulfilling her request. Without looking back, he replied, "I don't see any problem with that. Many people change their names for any number of reasons."

Once he gathered all the necessary documents, Mr. Schiffer sat down at his desk and began to explain what Lucinda would need to fill out. They were interrupted by a knock at the door, and a young man stepped in and apologized for the intrusion. He asked if Mr. Schiffer could spare him a moment in private. The director excused himself and asked Lucinda to skim through the documents, in case she had any questions. As she took the stack off the desk, she thought about all of the steps in exhumation and reburial and thought about when she would be able to complete the other goal of this task.

When he returned, the director explained the interruption. "My apologies. That was my assistant. His name is Jeffrey Russell. His mother, Phyllis, used to work for me. She was responsible for the dressing, makeup, and hair of the deceased. Jeffrey often came to work with her and would perform odd jobs for me. He enjoyed the experience and decided to become an undertaker himself. He attends a school in Kenmore Square that teaches all aspects of funeral business, from the retrieval of the newly deceased to the gravesite and beyond. He is learning both the interpersonal as well as the business side and has become a valuable resource. He will likely take over here when I retire. Unfortunately, his mother had to move to New Mexico ten years ago because of her health. I had a hard time replacing her." He took a deep breath and refocused. "So, where were we?"

Lucinda held up the stack of papers. "Ah, yes. Let's get started." With that, the two of them got down to business. He had her provide some basic personal information and sign some of the documents. After about a half hour, he said, "Well, I think that about does it for your responsibilities for the moment. I will get down to City Hall Monday morning and get the legal ball rolling. How long will you be here?" She informed him that she would stay as long as necessary to get everything taken care of. "Fine. I will call you in a few days. There will be other forms that will require a signature. However, I really do not foresee any problems regarding your request. I imagine that your grandmother can be laid to rest in California within a week or so."

Lucinda stood up and extended her hand. "I cannot thank you enough. I look forward to your call." He started to get up to escort her out, but she assured him that she remembered the way. She called for a cab and was soon on her way back to the hotel. During the drive, she started getting some ideas about how to finish this. There would just need to be an opportunity for her to be alone with her grandmother. That shouldn't be too hard for a granddaughter to manage as she brings her loved one home to rest closer to her.

To keep herself busy while waiting for Mr. Schiffer's call, Lucinda used the next few days to catch up on sleep and do a little sightseeing. While the Boston area hadn't really changed much in the last decade, she found that it all looked different to her now that she wasn't a resident. She was somewhat saddened to think how jaded the residents become to all of the beauty and history of their hometown. Her tourist phase ended on Wednesday morning, when the director called and told her that everything had gone as expected. He asked that she come to the funeral home the following morning at ten to sign a few more documents and he would go over the itinerary with her. The exhumation was to take place at six on Friday morning.

Lucinda was right on time the next morning and they flew through everything in short order. They started downstairs and he showed her a collection of caskets. She chose a medium priced one. Heading up to his office, he had all of the documents for signing on the desk waiting for her. She then wrote a check for the casket and the paperwork fees. He told her that he would send a bill for the balance once everything was done. Finally, he went over what she would need to do on the other end, arranging for a plot and a funeral home where they would receive the deceased. Where she had no religious affiliation in her town, he suggested that she have the funeral director there arrange for a minister to perform the gravesite service. She took a few notes and thanked him for all of the information. The rest of the day was spent making phone calls back home, and she eventually had everything finalized. By the time she had the last 'i' dotted and 't' crossed, it was dinnertime. Lucinda found herself mentally exhausted and she ended up ordering a sandwich from room service. After eating, she set the alarm for four the next morning and lay down on the bed. She had intended to flip through the TV channels, but dropped off into an uneasy sleep almost immediately.

The ring of the alarm couldn't have come soon enough for Lucinda. She was still soaked with sweat from the dreams that came to her: images of caskets, misty figures, and overgrown graveyards. Peeling off her clothes, she jumped into a hot shower, trying to wash her mind clean. By the time she got out, she felt somewhat refreshed and ready for the next step in her plan. She still hadn't worked out all of the details yet, but she felt confident that it would fall into place as she went forward. When the cab arrived to pick her up, she was standing on the curb in a simple black suit and white blouse. At that early hour, the sunglasses she wore were somewhat out of place, but she felt them appropriate for the event.

When she arrived at the funeral home, Mr. Schiffer was standing on the porch. A dark sedan and a hearse were waiting just beyond the building's entrance. Lucinda didn't recognize the two men standing by the first car, but she remembered the face of Jeffrey Russell from the other day as he stood there looking appropriately sympathetic. As she reached the steps, Mr. Schiffer came down to meet her, taking her hand in both of his. He led her to the first car and introduced her to the two men. They would be the ones driving her grandmother across country in the hearse. For now, they slid into the back seat of the sedan, while Lucinda was led to the front passenger door. Jeffrey would be driving the hearse to the cemetery. Mr. Schiffer opened the door and held her hand as she got in, closing it gently once she was settled.

Lucinda was saddened by the fact that the drive to the cemetery was so unfamiliar to her. She hadn't been back to visit her grandmother since she was laid to rest. Fall was in full swing in New England, so the ride was a blaze of color, with reds and oranges dominating the exiting green of summer. She felt like a little kid again, watching with her mouth slightly open at the beauty of it all, right up to the entrance of Cedar Grove. As the car slowed in the entrance, Lucinda tried to remember where her grandmother had been buried. She remembered standing at the grave site, not wanting to look at the casket, instead following the old stone wall that bordered the cemetery on all sides. She had thought then that she would follow that stone wall right out of town as soon as she could tie up all the loose ends of her life. It then came back to her: the old oak in the back right of the cemetery. She remembered listening to the wind in its leaves, the peaceful rustle, the cool shade. Lucinda turned her gaze to the right and, as they reached the crest of a small hill, she could see the white tent set up. As they got closer, she could make out six people: four men in protective suits, presumably from the health department; a minister reading his bible; a serious looking man in a dark suit with some sort of ID tag hanging from his pocket.

The car came to a stop about twenty feet from the tent. Lucinda could see that the grave was open. Mr. Schiffer helped her out of the car and they approached the group. The man with the ID tag came over to them and identified himself as a State official overseeing the exhumation. He requested identification, looked over their licenses, then quietly stepped off to the side to allow them to proceed. The minister came over to offer his condolences in this difficult time, as it likely brought back some unpleasant memories. However, he said that he was sure Lucinda would be comforted at the thought of having her loved one closer to her. Then the men in the white suits started to come over and she knew that it was time to raise the casket. They stood at the machine and looked at her. When Mr. Schiffer took her elbow, she understood that she would not be allowed to watch this proceeding. As soon as they were back out in the sunshine, the whirr of the machine began. She was led back to the car and, as she got in, Lucinda asked the funeral director, "Is that all we have to do?" He smiled gently and replied, "That's it. The casket will be brought back to the funeral home where the transfer will be made. We only needed to be there to make it legal and official." Lucinda was both relieved at this step being done and frustrated by the fact that she could not do the one thing that she set out to do. That would have to be done at another time.

Mr. Schiffer insisted that Lucinda let him drive her back to the hotel. The ride was quiet and uneventful. She imagined that the funeral director thought she was keeping silent in accordance with the somber nature of today's business, when the truth was that her thoughts were abuzz with the many irons she currently had in the fire. When they reached the hotel, she thanked him again for all of his efforts.

"My dear, I enjoyed and valued the friendship I had with your grandparents. It was my pleasure to be able to help you with this. And I must say, your grandmother would be very proud of the fine young woman you have grown up to be."

Lucinda felt a twinge of guilt at his last comment. She couldn't imagine that her grandmother would be at all proud of her recent actions. However, Lucinda felt sure that she would understand them, given that she too was a survivor. Life hadn't been altogether kind to her family, but they all did what they had to do to get by. She shook Mr. Schiffer's hand and got out of the car. As she was walking through the lobby, she saw the desk clerk motioning for her to come over. She weaved through the unusually crowded entryway and reached out to take what he had been waving at her. It was a sealed white envelope with her name written on the front in fine, looping script. She thanked him and headed for the elevator.

Once she was back in her room, Lucinda tore open the envelope. Bill had left a message. All it said was to call him as soon as possible. Could he have located Marlene so fast? She dialed his number and Iris answered. She informed Lucinda that Bill was in a meeting with a client and would be tied up for a while. Lucinda told her that she was just returning his call and he could call back at his convenience. Within five minutes, she was sorry she had given Bill such leeway with the callback. There was nothing in the hotel room for her to do and she didn't want to be out in public when he called. The sudden rumble from her stomach gave her the first time killer. She called room service and ordered a grilled cheese and tomato on whole wheat bread, as well as a glass of skim milk. It was childhood comfort food and it was the first thing that came to her mind.

While she waited, Lucinda ran possibilities in her mind. There were few opportunities left to complete the current task. It wasn't going to take long, but she needed privacy. The knock at the door broke her train of thought, but her lunch and the solution to her problem seemed to arrive simultaneously. As she walked to the door, she knew exactly what to do to get the legacy that her father had intended for her to have.

She sat down at the table and, for a few seconds, breathed in the wonderful scent of grilled bread and melted cheese. Simple, yet elegant. No sooner had she sunk her teeth in than the phone rang. It was Bill.

"Hlo?"

"Do I have the right room?"

"If me, Lufinda." The cheese was burning her tongue.

"What the heck did I just interrupt?" Bill sounded rather confused.

Lucinda took a big sip of milk and held it in her mouth for a moment to soothe her singed tongue and roof. Swallowing, she replied, "Lunch. Your timing is impeccable. And by that, I mean horrible. What's up?"

"I have information on Marlene's whereabouts, but I have to get back to a meeting. Iris told me you called and I didn't want to leave you hanging. Talk about it over dinner tonight?"

Lucinda wasn't thrilled with waiting, or giving Bill another opportunity to get romantic. Still, she was eager to know what he found out. "Fine. Pick me up at six." He agreed and hung up the phone. The brief interruption allowed her lunch to cool just enough and she dug in. As she ate, she thought about Marlene and this eventual reunion. Lucinda wasn't yet sure what she would do when it happened. Finding out that they were half-sisters had tempered some of the bitterness that had been festering inside her all of these years, but she still wasn't sure that she was ready to cut right to a happy-ever-after ending. There were just so many questions to ask: Did Marlene know that they shared a father? Was she aware of what Lucinda's family did and why they died? What did she know about the jewels, if anything?

Lucinda tried to clear her head and just enjoy her lunch, but these seeds of doubt were beginning to grow in her mind. She found it strange that she could so easily kill a lover or dig up the body of a deceased loved one, but she was struggling over what course to take with a friend whom she hadn't seen in years. Lucinda had always thought that, if she were to see Marlene again, she would have no problem telling her what she thought of her, with her high-and-mighty attitude. She had never confronted her over the situation with Bill, and that lack of resolution had bothered her for a number of years. When she saw him again that first day in his office, she felt that she had passed a test and put him and the whole mess behind her. Yet now, as she was about to get her first update on Marlene's whereabouts, Lucinda actually found herself feeling nervous.

She looked down at her plate absentmindedly and realized that she had eaten everything, but had no recollection beyond that first mouth-searing bite. Running her tongue across the roof of her mouth, she got up and headed for the bathroom. Stripping down as she walked, she was able to step right into the tub and turned on the hot water full blast. She stood there until she could feel her skin tingling, then quickly washed up and got out. She wrapped a towel around her head and pulled on a hotel robe before lying down on the bed. She was asleep within minutes.

Lucinda woke with a jolt and rolled over to look at the clock. It was almost five. She rummaged through her travel bag and realized that she was going to have to wear the same black dress from a few nights ago. She hadn't expected to be in Boston this long and had packed rather lightly.

At six, Lucinda was sitting in the lobby of the hotel. She heard Bill's car before she saw it and got up to meet him. Bill was just coming to the door when she stepped out.

"Wow, you look terrific!" He let out a low whistle.

Lucinda rolled her eyes. *Men! Honestly, I can't believe he can't see that this is the same dress I wore the other night.*

"Hi, Bill. Hey, isn't that the same tie you wore at our last dinner?"

"Ahh…is it?"

While he was looking down at his tie, Lucinda opened her own door and slid in. Bill caught up just in time to shut it for her. When he came around and slid behind the wheel, he looked at her and twitched his eyebrows. "Ready for GOOD Italian?"

"You know I am. North End?"

"Where else? Buckle up!"

No sooner had Lucinda clicked the two belts together, then Bill stomped on the gas pedal and they shot out of the parking lot. There was barely any time for small talk before they were passing by the restaurant. Bill was cursing under his breath, as there wasn't a parking spot to be found. Lucinda couldn't help but laugh to herself as he got more and more aggravated each time he went around the block in an ever increasing circle. Finally he bit the bullet and pulled into a parking garage. They ended up needing to take a cab. She noticed the size of the tip he gave to the cabbie and said, "Am I going to be billed for this?"

He threw his head back and laughed. "J.J., I mean Lucinda, you know I wouldn't be that unethical." She was briefly tempted to ask him for an itemized bill after the job was done, but decided against it.

They walked through a door that gave no indication as to what lay beyond it and headed down a dimly lit stairwell. At the bottom there was a sharp right and another door. When they stepped through the second door, Lucinda felt as though she had been brought to an Italian garden. There was a trellis-like structure that crossed the entire restaurant, with grape vines clinging to each beam and dangling from overhead. There were stone statues of beautiful woman scattered throughout the room and the walls were painted with one continuous image of a small villa.

The host came over and spoke immediately to Bill. "Ah, Mr. Fadigo, welcome back. It has been a while." He then gave Lucinda a quick once over and smiled. He looked again at Bill and said, "Lei ha una bell amica. It will be a few moments. Please, have a seat at the bar and I will come for you." As he turned to leave, Lucinda smiled and responded.

"Ringrazia rla per il complimento." The host gave her a quick bow and departed.

"Since when did you learn to speak Italian?" Bill looked sincerely impressed.

"I'm full of secrets." She thought of just how true that comment was.

The bartender came over as they sat down. Lucinda asked for scotch and Bill ordered a dry martini with four olives. When the drinks arrived, he raised his glass. "Here's to business." After a pause, he added, "And to pleasure." As they clinked glasses, Lucinda responded, "To business."

Bill took a healthy sip of his drink and looked at her seriously for several moments. "You know, we never really did have closure. You were so busy with your grandmother's service and settling the estate, then suddenly you were gone." She returned his gaze, but said nothing. Bill continued. "You know, I really am sorry for how things went between us. I wish….."

Lucinda interrupted. "Forget it. We were young. Things happen. I put it behind me and I think you should too. Besides, here we are, working peacefully together." She put extra emphasis on the word working. Before he could reply, the host came over and informed them that their table was ready. The waiter took their drinks and disappeared into the crowd, while the host led them through a maze of tables until they arrived at a candle-lit table for two along the back wall. When they got to the table, they noticed their drinks were waiting for them, along with a basket of garlic bread sticks. Menus had been left at both seats. The smell of the bread was tantalizing, and Lucinda took one before looking at the menu. They were still warm from the oven and soft as could be. Bill looked at her expression and removed one from the basket. They chewed in silence for a bit before opening the menus. Lucinda was amazed at the number of choices and felt somewhat overwhelmed. She ended up using the tried-and-true method of 'eeny, meeny, miney, moe' to make her choice, ending up with stuffed calamari and eggplant caponata. Bill clearly knew what he wanted, because he had already closed his menu and was watching her with great amusement. The candle on the table shed a warm reflecting glow on her face.

Feeling suddenly off balance, Lucinda shifted gears. "So, you have information for me." Bill's expression changed abruptly, as though he had just been interrupted from a very deep thought.

"Oh. Uh, yeah. Yes. Interesting things. Things that I think are going to shock you." Bill was back in business mode, but before he could begin, the waiter appeared at the table. He stood quietly with his hands clasped behind his back. Lucinda gave her order and he nodded, then turned toward Bill. She thought she was ordering a lot, but his selections were twice as many as hers. When the waiter nodded and began to leave, she accidentally blurted out what she was thinking. "Aren't you going to write any of that down?" He stopped, turned slightly toward her and asked, "Are you going to forget what you ordered?" A burst of laughter escaped her, followed by Bill doing the same. The waiter smiled, bowed, and headed toward the kitchen. Lucinda murmured, "That was amazing." Bill nodded, adding "As long as it's all correct when it comes out."

Lucinda took a sip of her scotch and then folded her arms on the table in front of her. "So. Shocking things."

Bill put his forearms on the table and leaned in close, like he was sharing a secret. "It turns out that you're not the only one in that friendship with skeletons in the closet." Lucinda sat up straighter, not sure where Bill was going with this. "Don't look so surprised. I knew about some of the stuff that went on with you. Your grandmother missed you something awful and never lost a chance to talk about what a great kid you were and how bad things happen to good people. We sat on the porch with a drink a number of times and talked. But that conversation can happen later, if you want. This is about Marlene." He looked at her sharply, as though he was trying to read her mind. She did indeed want to have that conversation, but she wasn't sure she wanted to open up again to Bill and the business with Marlene was the priority. She waved her hand, gesturing for him to continue.

"Well, after the two of you graduated, while you were endeavoring on a life of crime, Marlene went off to college. She got her business degree and got a job at a local bank. She moved up the ranks quickly, becoming an assistant manager in rather short order. While the business side of her was a source of pride for the family, the personal side – not so much. In a nutshell, she was dating a guy named Vinnie Fontana. He wasn't the go-getter type, but he had a real skill with cars, often fixing them for friends and family. He wasn't making a lot of money and his brother said that he could get him a better job. Since he idolized his brother, he said yes without any questions. Turned out that his brother was in with the Southern Artery mob. Vinnie started out fixing their cars, while doing some odd 'jobs' on the side. With the extra money he was making, he proposed to Marlene, promising her a good life. She had been in love with him almost from the beginning. They got married quietly by a justice of the peace, without telling anyone, not even her family. They never liked him and often told her that he was just trouble waiting to take both of them down." Bill paused to take a drink.

Lucinda realized that she had leaned to within a foot of Bill's face. She also realized that her mouth was hanging open. She sat back and took a drink. "How did you find all this out?" He chuckled and said, "Have you forgotten already that this is what I do for a living? Or that I was once a cop and still know a person or two?" She immediately felt stupid for the question. He continued. "And that's not everything."

"Vinnie wasn't the sharpest tool in the shed. He got a little greedy and skimmed some money off a job here and there. The mob found out and came collecting, threatening to hurt his new bride if he didn't return everything. He promised to pay it all back and they gave him a month. He knew he wasn't going to be able to do it. The cops were aware of the situation and were going to offer him a deal to roll on the mob. However, they weren't shocked to get a call from the brother saying that Vinnie had gone overboard while fishing for bluefish. They didn't find anything, but a body washed up a week later, or should I say what was left of a body. Marlene was devastated at the loss. A month later, she left a letter of resignation at the bank and disappeared."

Lucinda's head was spinning. All these years she had spent thinking about Marlene's perfect life, how everything came so easily to her. She suddenly felt very tired, but Bill continued talking. "To connect this to the here-and-now, I did some research on the last name and found that Marlene has moved frequently over the last eight or so years. She seems to have a penchant for humanitarian work. She spent some time down south building houses for Habitat For Humanity, worked with the unemployed to find government programs that provided assistance in Minnesota, then across the pond a couple of years ago. I was following a cold paper trail until just the other day, when a contact called me and said that he had found someone matching Marlene's description, only her name wasn't Fontana and she wasn't alone. She was traveling under the name St. Gaudins and, get this, with a guy. But not just any guy. A guy that bore a striking resemblance to her dead husband."

At this point, Lucinda was having a hard time catching her breath. Bill was staring at her intently, although she couldn't tell why. Was he waiting for her to faint so he could catch her in his arms, or was he merely gauging her response to this information? She began taking deep breaths for a five count, in through the nose and out through the mouth. She couldn't have asked for a better break, as the waiter showed up with their dinner. However, she found that, although everything smelled wonderful, she suddenly didn't have much of an appetite. While Bill ate heartily, Lucinda picked at everything on her plate. All that she heard tonight complicated things greatly. She had always just assumed that Marlene had gone off to have a great life while she struggled through personal loss and lack of opportunities. The fact that her half-sister spent most of her life on the run, living a life of apparent frugality and self-sacrifice, was causing some real conflict inside of her. She needed time to think everything through, but it wasn't going to happen tonight.

The rest of dinner passed in relative silence, as Bill left her to her thoughts and worked on the meal in front of him. After the plates had been cleared and another round of drinks was brought, he took a chance on continuing.

"I know you have a lot to think about, but I wanted to finish with the information relative to our business deal. Marlene and her husband were living in the Riviera when my contact came across her. He asked a few questions in the area and they suddenly disappeared. He found where they had been staying but, when he got there, the cottage they had been renting was cleaned out. Not even a scrap of paper had been left behind. My guy is really good at being a ghost, so I'm not sure that he was made. It makes me wonder if they are running from something, or someone, else."

Lucinda only half heard this last bit, as she was struggling to focus. As she finished her drink, Bill stood and pulled her chair out for her. She couldn't remember much, but she appreciated his willingness to navigate the rest of the night in peace and quiet. They walked to the car to enjoy the night air and, as they passed a small club, the sound of smooth jazz was wafting through the open door. He took her elbow and directed her in and she did not argue. She was surprised that he remembered her affinity for jazz. They sat at a high round table in the back and listened over a drink for about an hour. Then, without a word, Bill led her out and they finished the walk to the car. She became suddenly aware that they were on the sidewalk in front of her hotel. Bill took both of her hands, leaned in and gave her a gentle kiss goodnight.

"Sleep well. We'll talk soon." He walked to his car and she slowly turned and walked inside.

Chapter 31

The next morning, Lucinda woke with a headache. She couldn't decide if it was the alcohol, the smoky club, or the dinner conversation. She quickly packed her bags and gave the room a quick once-over. She was at the airport well ahead of her flight, only to find out that it was delayed two hours due to the weather. Thunderstorms were in the forecast, which made her stomach rumble in protest. She found her way to the bar, but the clock behind the bartender told her that it was a little too early for a scotch. She ordered a ginger ale, hoping that it might settle her stomach a little.

As she sat there, absentmindedly stirring her drink, she noticed a handsome man sitting two tables in front of her and off to her left. She caught him looking at her and he suddenly needed to tie his shoe. When she looked in his direction a second time, she again caught him looking at her. This time, he picked up his drink and made his way over to her table.

"Are you waiting for someone, or may I join you?" He smiled broadly.

"No, just my flight, and be my guest." She wasn't feeling particularly social, but maybe some company would help pass the time.

"Where are you headed? Someplace sunny and warm, I hope?"

She shrugged. "California. Not vacation, though. I live there."

He smiled again. "What a coincidence. I'm going there as well. I have an interview for a big job opportunity."

She returned the smile and said, "Good luck. I hope you get it."

They exchanged small talk, although most of it was centered around what it was like living on the West Coast. It helped to kill the delay, however, and soon a garbled voice came over the intercom to announce that the passengers on flight 934 to Los Angeles could begin boarding. Her conversational partner stood and picked up both of their bags and waited for her to stand up. She smiled, mouthed a silent 'thank you' and they headed for their gate. When they arrived to have their tickets scanned, Lucinda turned to him and put her hand out. He passed the bag to her and smiled. The line moved quickly and she soon found herself sitting in a window seat. Passenger after passenger came down the aisle and she mentally moved them past her. When the man with the job opportunity came along, she found herself waiting to see if he was sitting with her, but he moved past and sat two rows behind her. As the last of her fellow travelers settled in, she was thrilled to find herself alone in the row. However, when the flight attendant leaned in to ask her if the handsome gentleman behind her could move up, she quickly said yes.

He slid in to the aisle seat, leaving an empty one in between them. Extending a hand, he said, "Hi. My name is Irving O'Reilly. I know, I know. Don't laugh. My mother is Jewish and my father is Irish. The spirit of compromise, I guess. My friends call me Buzz."

Lucinda grinned and took his hand. "Nice to meet you Buzz. My name is Lucinda Preston, one hundred percent American."

The overhead sign pinged, instructing passengers to put on their seat belts. As the flight attendant went through the usual pre-flight instructions, Lucinda was reminded of the storms that had delayed the flight. She took hold of both arm rests as the plane taxied down the runway. As the plane shot forward, Lucinda closed her eyes and began to count to ten. By the time she reached six, they were airborne.

Buzz leaned over and asked, "What was that?" She looked at him with a confused look. "You were muttering something under your breath during takeoff. Praying to the almighty, by any chance?"

She smiled and shook her head. "I really don't like flying, especially the takeoff. When I was little, my grandmother's neighbor, Mrs. Casey, was going to New York City for the weekend and asked if I would like to join her. My nana insisted I go, saying that it was a great experience for anyone to have. Before takeoff, I started panicking and Mrs. Casey suggested that I close my eyes, wait for the forward motion to start, and then start counting to ten, to see how long it took for the plane to get off the ground. It was kind of like a little game. I've done it ever since."

The pilot came over the loudspeaker and informed them that they were going to be moving above the storm, but that it would be a bumpy ride for a while and that all should remain seated with their seat belts on. Lucinda found herself squirming, suddenly uncomfortable no matter how she sat. "So Buzz, let's get the focus off of this storm. You mentioned that you are going to Los Angeles for a job opportunity. What kind of business are you in?"

"I work with the FBI. I specialize in forensics with the Crime Scene Investigators."

Lucinda tried not to roll her eyes. *God, not another one. A cop, a lawyer, now a fed. I really can pick them!* "That sounds like quite a job. How come California? Not enough crime on the East Coast?"

Buzz chuckled and said, "Plenty of crime everywhere. I just need a change of scenery, both geographically and in job focus. I have spent most of my time working in a lab, but there is an opening that will give me the chance to be out in the field more often than not."

"Will your family move out here if you do?" Lucinda hoped that didn't sound as prying as it felt.

"I'm divorced. No kids. My ex couldn't handle the time that my job took. Can't say as I blame her. She remarried a couple of years ago. Guy owns a bakery. Hope she's happy and getting fat on pastry."

Lucinda smiled and shook her head. "Tsk, tsk. That's not a nice thing to say about someone who was once the love of your life."

"I know, but it makes me feel better. How about you? Heading home to a husband?"

She shrugged and said, "Always a bridesmaid, never a bride."

The loudspeaker crackled to life with the news that the worst of the turbulence was behind them and that it should be smooth sailing the rest of the way. Lucinda looked over at Buzz and said, "I'm glad you asked to change your seat. I barely even noticed the weather." The rest of the flight was spent engaging in small talk, although Lucinda thought she might have dozed off once or twice.

The landing in Los Angeles was placid, and the two soon found themselves at the baggage carousel. Buzz quickly grabbed a green gym duffel and slung it over his shoulder. "Let me know when you see yours." No sooner had he said this, then a designer bag which looked like a kaleidoscope of colors came into view. She smiled and tilted her head in its direction. Buzz laughed and said, "Why am I not surprised?" He reached out as it passed and looped his fingers through the two handles. As he handed it to her, he asked, "Share a cab somewhere?" Lucinda frowned and replied, "Unfortunately, I still have another flight in front of me to get home. Thanks again for the company. Good luck with the job." He gave her a big smile, a wave, and then turned to head for the exit. She headed up the ramp and was soon on a shuttle plane for the last leg of her trip.

By the time she opened the door to her apartment, Lucinda was exhausted. Though the exhumation of her grandmother was only days ago, she felt as though she had been gone for a month. She took a quick shower and slid into an old pair of jeans and a comfortable tee shirt. She remained barefoot, as she loved the feel of the carpet beneath her feet. She went to the kitchen and pulled the pizza wrapped in foil out of the freezer. As she opened her refrigerator, she rooted around until she found what she was looking for. In the back corner was one last can of beer. *Nothing like pizza and beer after a long day.*

Chapter 32

On Monday, she was to meet with the funeral director, Mr. Lombard. She had phoned him from Boston and they had set a meeting to go over the plans to rebury her grandmother.

It was a short drive from her apartment to the funeral parlor. As she approached the address, she was pleasantly surprised to see a gorgeous white house with pillars holding up a canopied porch. The grounds were immaculately landscaped. She was immediately thankful for Mr. Schiffer and all his help. She couldn't have found a more beautiful place. As she drove up to the parking area, she saw a tall aristocratic man waiting for her. He opened her door and extended his hand to help her out.

"Lucinda Preston, I presume."

"You must be Mr. Lombard. It is very nice to meet you."

He led her up to the building and through an intricately carved oak front door. As they walked into the foyer, she caught the scent of carnations. There was soft classical music playing. He escorted her into his office and offered her a cup of coffee. She could see why she was referred here. The two funeral directors were clearly cut from the same cloth. She was completely at ease, which was amazing given the circumstances. She took her cup and sat in the seat facing his desk. He settled in behind it and picked up a paper. "I have heard from the drivers. They expect to be here within four days. We can have a small service here on Friday before we go to the cemetery or we can have the minister do everything at the gravesite. It is your decision."

Lucinda thought for a moment before answering. "I think a graveside service would be more appropriate. I would like to make this as traditional as possible."

Mr. Lombard nodded and replied, "I understand. We have already arranged for a minister. Reverend Norman Franz will officiate."

Lucinda asked if he knew of a local florist that could provide some arrangements suitable for the occasion. He assured her that he would take care of that for her. He also informed her that a limousine would be available to pick her up at home, if she so chose. Lucinda shook her head. "I may be picking up a friend, as I am the only family here. It would probably be easier if I just drove here." Mr. Lombard simply nodded, then continued with finalizing details. He informed her that he had some paperwork for her to sign from the office of the Holy Family Cemetery. He added that he would give her contact information for a monument company, as well as their website so she could peruse the various options before calling.

Once the business end was taken care of, Mr. Lombard stood to walk Lucinda to the door. As she stood, she asked him a question that she had been preparing for the entire time. "I know that there won't be any calling hours or services here, but is there a chance that I might be able to spend some time alone with my grandmother, to say goodbye in private?"

Mr. Lombard stopped short of opening the door for a moment. The pause seemed to take forever to Lucinda, as she was waiting for him to ask why, but all he said was "Of course. We would never interfere with a grieving family saying goodbye." He then silently swung the door open before taking her hand in his and giving it a tender squeeze. "My condolences for your loss and I hope that having her close will provide some peace of mind. I will call you when she arrives." She thanked him and walked out of the office.

As she stepped out into the sunshine, Lucinda was thrilled at how well everything was coming along. In less than a week, she would have her grandmother back in the ground and the jewels in her hand. As she slipped into the front seat of her car, she caught a faint whiff of the carnations from the funeral home. It stayed with her all the way to the supermarket, where she bought a dozen of them after replenishing her food supply. She then made a quick stop at Brad's, a liquor store with the largest wine selection in the area. Lucinda picked out a Pinot Blanc and a Pinot Noir, a top shelf scotch, as well as a six pack of light beer. As she drove up to her building, she was thinking of how many trips it would take her to get everything up to her place. She was thrilled to see Mike, a college kid who lived in an apartment not far from hers. He was always happy to help, and she called out to him as she parked her car. He made three trips for her and she gave him a generous tip, more so than normal. He looked at the cash and thanked her profusely before heading home.

After getting her groceries put away and a glass of wine poured, Lucinda made a fresh cut in the carnations and put them in her faceted vase on the kitchen table. The aroma filled the room and Lucinda sat in one chair while stretching her legs out to put her feet on another. She reminded herself that there was still business to take care of, so she rummaged through her bag until she found her phone. Searching the numbers in her phone book, she found the one she wanted. Three rings later, a ray of sunshine answered.

"Hey Lucinda! I was just thinking about you. I'm hoping to have another get-together soon and was going to call and see if you could make it. I was sorry you couldn't make the last one, but....."

Lucinda interrupted, as Krystina was hard to stop when she got on a roll. "That's nice, Krystina, but I'm not calling to chat. I have a favor to ask, a somewhat unusual one."

There was a split second of silence, before her friend answered. "Okay. What's the favor?"

"I'd rather ask in person, if that's okay. Do you have a flight scheduled in the upcoming week?"

"Actually, I'm free until Sunday, which is heaven because I rarely get more than three days off between jobs."

Lucinda nodded, then realized that Krystina couldn't see her. "Good. How about dinner at La Paloma tonight? Then I can fill you in. I'll pick you up a little before six." Krystina said she would be ready and waiting. After hanging up the phone, Lucinda spent the next couple of hours puttering around the apartment and thinking about this next phase of her plan. She was equally nervous and excited, though she wondered if it would be as easy to do as she was picturing in her head. When the clock hit four-thirty, Lucinda jumped into the shower. Tonight would be a jeans and sneakers night, as La Paloma was a very casual restaurant, bordering on dive.

When she drove up to Krystina's, she was waiting on the curb and came skipping over to the car. Jumping in, she was already talking as she opened the door. "I'm so happy you called me. I love getting together with friends and we don't get to see each other that much and it's so much fun going out and having dinner. Not to mention the whole business of the favor, which sounds so mysterious and makes it even more exciting." She looked at Lucinda with an expectant look, which made her laugh out loud.

"Sorry, it's not an undercover assignment or high treason. Just a favor. But it is a favor that would mean a lot to me. Let's wait until we have some drinks and food in front of us." She eased back out on to the road and headed south. Traffic was light and they were at their destination in less than fifteen minutes. She was surprised at how many cars were in the parking lot, but when they got inside there were plenty of tables available. The hostess seated them in a corner, which suited Lucinda just fine.

The waitress brought a round of margaritas, as well as a large bowl of taco chips, two bowls of spicy salsa, and some avocado dip. Once she was gone, Krystina gave Lucinda a wide-eyed look and said, "So…..? The favor….?"

Even with the look on her friend's face, Lucinda was serious. She wasn't sure how to ask for this favor, so she cut right to the chase. "On Friday, I am burying my grandmother."

Krystina coughed in the middle of a sip and blew margarita bubbles right out her nose. Lucinda couldn't help but chuckle. She probably should have waited until her friend wasn't drinking something.

"Say that again?"

"My grandmother died ten years ago in Boston. She raised me from the age of twelve and took me in again after I got out of….college. I moved out here after settling her estate. However, I decided that I wanted to have her close to me, so I went to Boston last week and had her exhumed. She is being driven here and I am having her buried at the Holy Family Cemetery on Friday. I could really use some support, especially at the funeral home. The cemetery will be the easier part, but having a friend there will really help me get through the day."

Krystina stared at Lucinda for a moment as though she had been asked to kidnap the Pope. Lucinda was just beginning to regret asking when Krystina broke into a wide smile. "Of course I'll do it. I am so honored that you would want me to be there for you. You could have asked anybody, but you asked me." Lucinda sipped her margarita and let her friend gush a little while longer.

Suddenly, Kristina stopped. She cocked her head to one side and looked at Lucinda for a moment. Then she spoke. "Don't you have any family to be with? Where's your grandfather or your parents?" Lucinda thought for a second, considering just how much of her past she was willing to share. She decided that, out of all the people she knew here, she trusted Krystina most. She told her about her parents' death in a car accident, being raised by her grandmother, and needing to get out of town after her untimely death. She told how she never knew her grandfather, as he passed before she was born, having been cremated and his ashes were scattered in Boston Harbor. She left gaps where the demons of her life lived, hoping Krystina wouldn't feel the need to ask too many questions, but she needn't have worried. When she finally stopped talking, her friend was crying and said only, "Wow."

Lucinda immediately felt bad about bringing her to tears. She scooped up her glass and raised it. "To friends." Krystina wiped her face with the back of her hand, grabbed her glass, and forced a weak smile. "Friends." Lucinda beckoned to the waitress and, when she came over, ordered two more margaritas along with double orders of chicken enchiladas and chicken chimichangas. "The business part of the business dinner is done. Let's eat!"

They spent the next hour eating, drinking, and chatting about everything. By the time the waitress had cleared the table, Krystina was giggling, hiccupping, and slightly slurring most of her words. Lucinda loved her enthusiasm, her carefree attitude, and her happiness over just being, wherever she was. It wasn't something that came naturally to Lucinda, but she thought that maybe when this was all over, she might be able to give it a try. The final steps of her plan were falling into place and soon she could put it all behind her. She paid the bill while Krystina was in the bathroom and was standing with her friend's sweater when she came back to the table. It took a bit of work getting to the car, as Krystina was stopping at almost every table to give a thumbs up to the margaritas, suggesting that everyone have one...or ten.

It was pushing nine o'clock when Lucinda finally made it home. She had gotten her friend into bed and left a note on her bottle of aspirin, which she would certainly need in the morning, telling her that she would pick her up at eight-thirty on Friday morning. She opened the door to her apartment and was immediately greeted by the scent of carnations. It had been a long day, and she was looking forward to a good night's sleep. The smell was a good reminder that she was almost done with this journey, soon to embark on the next phase of her life. It was a good final thought before sleep.

Chapter 33

Friday morning came quickly, with the alarm announcing that it was seven o'clock. Lucinda showered and had a light breakfast of coffee and an English muffin with quince jelly. She made a quick call to Krystina to make sure she was up. A pass in front of the mirror told her she was ready – black dress with matching jacket and black flats. She went to the kitchen and found a small pair of scissors in the junk drawer, wrapped them in a dish towel, and slipped them into her purse.

As always, Krystina was waiting on the sidewalk. She was dressed in almost the same outfit, although she was wearing two inch heels. Lucinda knew that she liked adding a little height to her sub-five foot frame, and she appreciated the fact that she gave up some height to accommodate the situation. Krystina slid in beside her, gave her a small smile, and slid her seat belt across her chest and into the buckle. She stared straight ahead with a serious look on her face, which made Lucinda laugh out loud. "For God's sake, I didn't hire a professional mourner. Just pretend you're helping a friend move."

Krystina blew a bit of a raspberry at that, to which Lucinda reciprocated. The thought of moving her grandmother to a better neighborhood with a little more of a view struck the two of them as rather hysterical. With the mood lightened, Lucinda pulled away from the curb and into traffic. As they pulled up to the funeral home, Mr. Lombard was waiting at the door. He gently shook both of their hands and escorted them into a room where the casket rested. As he closed the door behind him, he said "Take your time." When the door clicked shut, Krystina said, "Beautiful flowers. Did you choose them?" Lucinda shook her head. "The director arranged almost everything. He has been fantastic." The two sat in silence for almost a minute. Lucinda wondered what her friend was thinking at that moment, while she thought about the next step in her plan. Almost as if she read Lucinda's mind, Krystina said "So what do we do now? I haven't been to a funeral in ages." Lucinda made the decision right then and there. "Well, once we tell the director we're ready, my grandmother will be moved to the hearse and we'll be taking the black limo parked out front. The cemetery isn't far from here. There will be a minister there to perform a short ceremony and that's it. They do the actual burying after we've gone, although some people prefer to watch it happen." Lucinda had done just that ten years ago, although she wasn't sure why. Though she couldn't wait to get out of town, she still wanted to be there just in case it was a joke and her grandmother was going to jump out of the box. Hearing the dirt hit the top of the casket told her that it was indeed real. She certainly wouldn't be watching today.

Lucinda turned to Krystina and said "Would you mind stepping out for a little bit? I would like to be alone with my grandmother. Maybe you could stand by the door so we aren't interrupted? I promise I won't be long." Krystina nodded, gave her a quick one-armed hug, then headed out the door. Lucinda waited for a few seconds before standing up and walking over to the casket. Now that she was here, she began having second thoughts. She didn't know what she was going to see or how she would react. She closed her eyes, took a couple deep breaths to steady herself, then took the scissors out of her bag. Holding them with her right hand, she gently lifted the top of the casket with her left. When she looked inside, her chest tightened immediately and she inhaled sharply.

Lucinda had half expected to see a skeleton, but her grandmother almost looked as though she died yesterday. Still lying perfectly flat, with her hands clasped together and her rosary beads woven through her fingers, Lucinda thought she could possibly sit up and chastise her for not following directions. However, what upset her the most was not the appearance of her grandmother's body, but the fact that she was wearing a navy blue dress. The hem of the dress was less than half an inch and still pressed razor sharp. Lucinda closed the casket and slumped back into her chair, still holding the scissors. Thoughts were running wild through her mind, but she couldn't organize even one into coherent form. Becoming suddenly aware of time, she slid the scissors back into her bag and walked to the door.

She found Krystina staring rapturously at one of the photographs on the wall opposite the door she had just come through. When she heard the door open, she turned and said "Did you know that this home used to be a golf....what happened??" She was staring at Lucinda with a look of confusion mixed with concern. "You look like you've seen a ghost!" Shaking her head, Lucinda headed for the table with a coffee pot and began pouring a cup. "I opened the casket." She heard Krystina gasp.

"You what? Oh my gosh Lucinda. Why on earth would you do that?"

"I don't know. I suddenly wanted to see my grandmother just one more time." Though this wasn't the real reason, it was partly true.

"What...what did she look like? Was she all bones, with long hair and fingernails?"

Lucinda couldn't help but smile. Krystina was, in many ways, just like a little kid in an adult's body. "No. I was surprised to see that she looked just like she did ten years ago. Even the eye shadow was still fresh."

"I wonder if they'll know you did that. Is it against the law?"

This thought hadn't occurred to Lucinda, but she doubted that they would even know. The casket hadn't been sealed in any way and she hadn't touched the body. Besides, she had been planning to do more than that anyway. She pushed the thought out of her mind, sipped her coffee and tried to sort out what the next step would be.

Mr. Lombard appeared at the end of the hallway and informed them that the limousine was ready. As they walked toward him, Lucinda let Krystina go first and she stopped beside the director.

"Mr. Lombard, may I ask you a question before we go? Did you open my grandmother's casket when it came here?"

He looked at her quizzically and nodded. "Yes. It is customary to ensure that I have the right person. Why do you ask?"

"Was she buried in a navy blue dress? She had requested that, as it was her favorite color. I wasn't able to look at her in the casket when she died and all of the arrangements had been handled by the funeral director in Boston. Most of that time is a blur to me."

He smiled gently and said "She was indeed. And, if I may say so, it was a lovely choice."

Mr. Lombard gestured toward the door and Lucinda nodded. As she walked, she thought to herself. *That solves one part of the puzzle, so how to figure out the rest?*

The driver of the limousine was waiting for her and opened the door when she approached. Lucinda slid into the backseat, where Krystina was waiting with the same look of concern. "Did he know? Did you get in trouble?" Lucinda looked at her with the most serious look she could muster and said, "Yes. When the service is over, I have to come back to the funeral home." Krystina looked at her expectantly. Lucinda held the pause as long as she could before continuing. "I have to clean the boards and clap the erasers for a half hour." With that, she burst out laughing as Krystina punched her in the arm and said, "Not funny. I was being serious."

Lucinda could see Krystina trying hard to look put out, but the smile kept creeping up. She was thankful for that, as she didn't want the day to be so somber. Besides, she was trying to keep her mind off of this newest problem and focus on giving her grandmother's re-interment the attention and dignity it deserved. She hadn't expected it to bother her, but she was surprised at the feeling of tears that seemed to be waiting at the corners of her eyes for the right moment to start flowing.

That moment came when the minister, standing next to the casket, began to read the 23rd Psalm. It was her grandmother's favorite and she wondered if this had been coincidence or not. Given the professionalism of the two directors, she could imagine Mr. Schiffer doing a little research and giving his counterpart a call to let him know a detail or two to make the proceedings more personal. She let the tears roll down her face, not bothering to wipe them away. The image of the blue dress where the green dress should have been was washed away by memories of her grandmother: rocking her to sleep the night she found out her parents were dead; consoling her when her best childhood friend took the hint and stopped calling; trying not to cringe when she wore all black to the prom; secretly digging trenches in the armrest of her 1957 Cadillac during that first driving lesson. She barely felt Krystina's hand rubbing her back as the memories threatened to flood her, knock her off her feet and wash her away. She let all of the emotions go, surprised at their power, relieved at the release. By the time the minister was done singing Amazing Grace,

Lucinda had gathered herself. She wiped her face with the sleeve of her jacket, took a few deep breaths, and pushed her chin down against her chest to loosen the knot of muscles in her neck.

As they walked back to the car, Lucinda was listening to the songs of several different birds when the next step came to her. She smiled and quietly whistled a couple of notes. Krystina looked over at her and asked, "Feeling better?" She swung open the door and replied, "By the minute."

They enjoyed an easy silence during the ride back to the funeral home. Lucinda knew that today hadn't been easy for her friend, as she found comfort in having everything be well and happy. Krystina was humming a tune she couldn't place, rocking gently from side to side and bobbing her head. Lucinda was happy to have this step behind her and the next one decided. When the car came to a stop in front of the funeral home, she gave the keys to her friend and said that she was going to go inside and tie up the last loose ends.

Mr. Lombard was on his way up the front steps when he saw her coming. He stopped and waited until she was next to him.

"Ms. Preston? I hope you were satisfied with how everything went today?"

She nodded. "Very much so. You did a wonderful job. I know my grandmother would have been thrilled." He smiled, then raised his eyebrows quizzically.

"I just wanted to take care of the last bit of business." She opened her purse.

He put his hand on hers. "We never expect a family to pay anything on the day of service. This is a day for celebrating the life of another."

Lucinda smiled and said, "I understand. However, you did provide a service, one that I appreciate greatly. I would like to take care of my side of that, if it's okay with you."

Mr. Lombard nodded and turned toward the door. She followed him to his office, where he presented her with the bill. She wrote him a check for the full amount. He stamped the bill paid and handed it to her, along with a business card. "The monument company will be calling you to set up an appointment so you can choose a stone and provide the information to be engraved. I am sure you will be very satisfied with their work." She thanked him again for everything and headed for her car.

Krystina was sitting in the front seat with the radio on when she slid behind the wheel. She turned it off, saying "Sorry." Lucinda smiled at her and replied, "Don't be. I owe you after today. I don't know if I could have gotten through this without you. How about a little lunch? Krystina nodded and Lucinda started the car. They stopped at a small restaurant named Mangos, where they each ordered a vegetable quiche.

After dropping her friend off, Lucinda rolled the windows down and hit the highway. Through the noise of the wind, she wondered out loud, "What the heck happened to that dress?" She was going to find out as soon as she got home. When she opened the door to her apartment, she went right to the phone. The phone rang twice before a familiar voice answered, "Hello?"

"Mr. Schiffer, this is J.J. I wanted to let you know that I buried my grandmother today. I also wanted to thank you for all of your help. The day went smoothly and all of your suggestions were perfect."

"I am happy to hear that it all went well. I am sure that today couldn't have been easy for you."

Lucinda twisted the cord around her fingers. "It would have been much harder without your assistance. Can I ask you a question?"

"Of course."

"After the wake, where does the casket go?"

Mr. Schiffer hesitated before answering. When he finally spoke, she could hear the curiosity in his voice. "After calling hours are over, the casket is moved into our prep room downstairs until the funeral. Is there something wrong?"

Lucinda knew that there was no reason to ask such a question unless something was wrong and tried to think fast. "I don't think so. I thought that I had put a picture of me and my grandmother at my graduation in the casket, but there wasn't one when they transferred the body. I must have forgotten it, since I was pretty out of it after she died. Sorry to ask such an odd question. Thanks again for all of your help."

"I was happy to be of service." She could hear the uncertainty in his voice. "I hope having your grandmother with you in California brings you some comfort and peace of mind."

"It does. Thanks again for everything." She hung up the phone and went into the living room. She burrowed down into the couch and tried to think. *I could have sworn that she was in the green dress at the wake, although I tried all day not to look at her. After the wake, she went to the prep room. Mr. Schiffer had mentioned that his prep person was a woman named Phyllis Russell.* Then it started to come together. *Phyllis Russell had left shortly after my grandmother's funeral. He said that she had been in ill health and was leaving for a warmer climate, New Mexico, I think.* Another memory came to her. *Her son was there the day her grandmother was exhumed. What was his name? Jacob, Jeremy, Jeffrey. That's it!*

Lucinda grabbed her phone and dialed 411. The computer voice told her that Jeffrey Russell had an unlisted number. She slammed the phone down, flipped open her laptop and did a quick search for a Jeffrey Russell in Boston. The only result was a court case pending at the Dedham courthouse regarding a suit filed by Jeffrey against a replacement window company. She stared at the screen and thought for a moment. Getting another idea, she did a search for mortician's schools in Massachusetts. There was only one such school in Eastern Massachusetts, in Kenmore Square not far from Fenway Park. When she saw the listing, she remembered Mr. Schiffer mentioning that information. She called the number and requested the Registrar's office. She was connected to a very pleasant woman named Dorothy Burnhart, who was most obliging. Lucinda told her that she was a friend of the family and that she needed to speak to Jeffrey regarding his mother. She was in the hospital and in need of medical care, and that decisions needed to be made by next of kin.

"Oh, dear, that sounds awful. According to his class schedule, he won't be on campus until tomorrow. Let me give you his apartment phone number."

Lucinda wrote the number down and said, "Thank you so much for your help. I just hope I can reach him." She smiled to herself as she disconnected the call and dialed the number that Dorothy had just given her. The computer voice this time informed her that the number was disconnected. She slammed the phone down.

It's probably better that I not involve him. I should be able to find her myself, and I don't need anyone knowing that I visited Phyllis Russell, just in case she is less than helpful in resolving what happened to that green dress and I have to persuade her a little. He would just end up being another loose end to take care of.

Chapter 34

At nine that evening, Lucinda's phone rang. Looking at the caller ID, she found it hard to believe that she had forgotten about this other iron in the fire.

"Hi, J.J., it's Bill. I have a lead on where Marlene ran off to. If you can believe this, it's a fishing village in Portugal."

Lucinda wondered what would have drawn her half-sister there. "So what do we do now?"

"Well, I am heading down there, so I can either report back or maybe you would like to go with me." She could hear a touch of hopefulness in his voice.

"Are you sure she's there?"

"I can't say absolutely, but my source feels confident that she has been there for a while."

Lucinda contemplated this for a moment, attracted by the thought of an exotic trip. However, she had a more pressing concern at the moment. She would let Bill do the hard part. "Why don't you head there and keep me informed? I have a lot on my plate right now and don't have time for the chase. Just call me in time for the capture."

"Is everything okay?" Bill sounded genuinely concerned, which surprised her. Lucinda thought for a moment before responding.

"I reburied my grandmother today."

Bill let out an audible gasp. "You did WHAT?"

"Here in Santa Barbara."

"You mean you dug her up in Boston and brought her cross country?"

Lucinda groaned. "When you put it like that, it sounds horrible. I flew out to Boston, had her exhumed, and she was driven here. We had another service, so now I can visit her more often."

Bill was quiet for a moment. "You really have done a one eighty."

The comment stung Lucinda. "What do you mean by that?"

"Don't be offended. I mean that in a good way. You just aren't the same lady I knew way back when."

"Well, I'm happy with my new self."

Bill chuckled. "So am I. So am I."

Before she hung up, Lucinda thought of a question. "If I wanted to find somebody, what would be a good first step?"

Without missing a beat, Bill replied, "Calling the W&F Detective Agency. What are you trying to do, take my job?"

Lucinda felt like strangling him. "You know what I mean. Not a fugitive from justice. If I wanted to find an old friend that had moved away, what is a good resource?"

"Anywho.com. Put in a name, first and last, city and state if you have it. It's pretty reliable, for not being a private detective. I'll call you before I leave, just in case you're interested in tagging along." Lucinda heard the click and was surprised that he didn't say goodbye. She felt badly that she might have offended him, but she didn't want anyone to be able to make a connection between her and Phyllis Russell.

She went to the kitchen, put five ice cubes in a glass, and poured the scotch over them. She shuffled into the living room, put on a CD of jazz music and settled into her favorite chair. She tried to just tune into the music, but all she could think about was New Mexico and Phyllis Russell. Finally, she got up and retrieved her laptop. She went to the website Bill recommended and put in her name and the state. While there were several variations on the name, there was only one Phyllis Russell, living in Albuquerque. She wrote down the address and phone number and, feeling rather pleased with herself, shut down the computer and went to bed.

The next morning, she called to find out about flights to New Mexico. It turned out that there was a direct flight to Albuquerque from LAX at six the next morning. She gave them her credit card number and made a reservation for a round trip ticket. Lucinda decided to drive to Los Angeles and leave her car in the airport parking garage. She called a rental agency and reserved a car for tomorrow. She requested one that had a GPS included. She then called Bill.

When she heard Iris' pleasant voice on the other end, she said "Good morning, Iris. Is Mr. Fadigo in?"

She could hear the smile in Iris' response. "He's expecting your call, Ms. Preston. Let me put you through." Lucinda wondered how he could be expecting a call that she hadn't planned on making before five minutes ago.

"So you've decided to come. I knew it. Just think: you, me, sun, beaches. Isn't there a song like that?"

"Sorry to disappoint you. I was just calling to let you know that I have some business to take care of and might be out of reach for a couple of days. Head down, do your thing, and call me if you find her."

Lucinda could almost hear the air coming out of the balloon. "Fine. Your loss. Go take care of your business. Any chance that this business is related to your Internet search?"

"As a matter of fact, it does. I'm off to Madison, Wisconsin in the morning. Thanks for the information. That site was a great help. Maybe I should have just put in Marlene's name and saved myself tons of money and aggravation."

Bill exhaled loudly. "Geez, you really know how to hurt a guy. Have a safe trip. I'll call you when I have something." Once again, she heard the click and knew that he was gone. She would apologize later, but for now it was time to prepare for a trip.

Chapter 35

Her alarm went off at three the next morning. She had packed a small travel bag the night before, not expecting to be in New Mexico more than a day. After a quick cup of coffee and a toasted bagel, she got into her car and headed for Los Angeles. As she hit the road, she noticed that the gas tank was just under half and stopped to fill up. She was shocked at what a half tank cost her. *I'll bet we hit five dollars a gallon soon!*

She arrived at the airport just before five. She checked in at one of the automated kiosks and headed off to the security line. After being 'scanned' and having her bag searched, she was allowed to proceed to her gate. She was lucky to find a seat, as the seating area was overrun by college kids, perhaps on a little R&R trip from school. She laughed when she thought about how she was the 'old lady' in her classes when she was at Arizona State. She wondered what they would think of her now.

The wait to board was short and she was soon seated in a window seat, looking out over the tarmac. The plane began rolling forward and her nerves started to kick in, so she put on a pair of earphones and tried to tune in to one of the local stations on the back of the seat in front of her. The screen worked fine, but the earphone jack was loose and the sound was breaking up badly. As she wiggled it, she found herself watching a newscast that had a familiar face in it. A rather stunning woman was in the middle of an interview with a man wearing a blue jacket with the letters F-B-I across the chest. She couldn't hear anything, but she would have known that smile anywhere. Irving 'Buzz' O'Reilly, half Jewish, half Irish, had obviously gotten that job promotion. She was genuinely happy for him, as he had seemed so excited about it. By the time the interview ended, she realized that they were in the air. She gave Buzz a silent thank you for distracting her and stretched her feet out under the seat in front of her.

The flight was smooth and passed by quickly, for which she was grateful. She was through the terminal in a flash and found the rental booth. The young man working there handed her a form to sign and then slid a key across the desk. "It's that red one over there," pointing off to her right. She located it, thanked him, and headed out the door.

When she got outside, Lucinda was shocked at how hot it was. She was glad that it wasn't humid, but she was dreading getting into a dark colored car. She pressed the alarm button and opened the door. Sure enough, it was oppressively hot and she started the car immediately, switching on the air conditioning. She opened the window until the cool air started to blow, punching in her destination on the GPS while she waited. By the time it brought up the map, the AC was kicking in and she put the car in gear.

She was heading northwest on I-85. She was quite impressed with how lovely the area was. Everything was so clean and neat. As she was thinking about what it might be like to live here, the voice on the GPS directed her to turn right in 100 yards onto route 314. As she made the turn, she saw a sign indicating that a C-Mart was up ahead. She pulled into the parking lot, locked the car, and headed inside. The moment she entered the store, she got a whiff of pizza. It smelled delicious and she decided that a light snack would do her good. She bought a slice and a soda and sat at one of the tables. She people watched for ten minutes until she finished, then headed to the ladies' room. When she was done, she walked the store until she had everything she needed: duct tape, a package of three large mailing envelopes, and a belt. She went through the express line and paid cash. Once she was back in the car, she went through her purchases. She unwrapped the duct tape and took the plastic tie off the belt, putting the tape in her handbag and the wrappings in the shopping bag they came in. Opening the envelopes, she took one out and laid it on the seat. She folded the other two and put them in the shopping bag as well. Getting out of the car, she threaded the belt through the loops on her pants. She took the bag up to the store and walked around the side to the dumpster, throwing the bag into the far corner. Satisfied, she got back in the car and continued down 314.

Thanks to modern technology, she was soon driving down Sierra Nevada Circle. The further down the road she went, the farther apart the houses were. A surge of excitement went through her. More distance between neighbors meant less chance of witnesses. Counting numbers on houses, she soon sat in front of 98652, painted in white on a black mailbox. The flag was up, indicating that there was mail to be picked up. Sitting on the back of the unkempt lot was a dilapidated trailer, with an equally beat-up truck parked beside it. As she put the car in park, the GPS announced "Destination reached". Suddenly, a big brown German shepherd ran up to the car, barking like mad. So much for the element of surprise, Lucinda thought. A frail looking woman stepped out of the trailer and shouted something at the dog. He stopped barking and ran back to the woman, then took off into a field nearby.

As Lucinda got out of the car, the woman spoke. "You lost?"

"No, I came to see you Mrs. Russell. You are Phyllis Russell?"

"Yeh. You from City Hall?"

"No, I'm not from City Hall, but I would like to talk to you about an important matter. Any chance we could step inside and talk privately?"

Phyllis turned toward the door. "I suppose. C'mon in."

Given the outside appearance, the inside of the trailer was surprisingly neat, though sparsely decorated. Phyllis nodded toward a couch, indicating that Lucinda should take a seat. As she walked toward the kitchen, she asked "Want a cup of coffee?"

"Coffee would be great. Black."

Phyllis opened a cabinet and took out two mugs. "Good. I just put a pot of water on. I hope instant is alright."

"That's fine." Lucinda had no intention of drinking it, but wanted to appear social.

"So, what's this important matter you want to talk to me about?"

Lucinda sat up a little straighter. "I know you worked for Everett Schiffer in Quincy, Massachusetts years ago. I understand that you did the cosmetics and hairdos, as well as dressing the deceased."

Phyllis had just spooned out coffee into the two mugs. She put the spoon down, turned around and leaned against the counter. "Is there a question in there?"

"According to Mr. Schiffer, you left rather abruptly about ten years ago. Why did you suddenly leave and move all the way out here to New Mexico?"

Her answer was interrupted by the whistling teapot. Phyllis kept her eyes on Lucinda, now very suspicious.

Lucinda nodded toward the teapot. "Water's ready."

Phyllis paused for several seconds before moving over to the stove and removing the pot and turning off the heat. She filled the two mugs, keeping one eye on her guest, before returning the pot to a cool burner. She brought the coffees over to the table, putting one cup at the seat closest to Lucinda and sitting at the one that faced her.

"Yeh, I worked there for many years. Had to retire because of my health. Needed to be in a warmer climate. What's that got to do with me now? Who are you?"

Lucinda got up and moved over to the table. She sat down at the seat with the second cup, keeping her eyes on Phyllis. "My name is Lucinda Preston. You were working there at the time my grandmother died and had her services done."

Phyllis squinted her eyes, not saying anything, but clearly trying to make some connection between her unexpected guest and a dead grandmother from ten years ago. Lucinda took a sip of her coffee, flinching at the heat. "May I add a little cold water to this?" Phyllis nodded. Lucinda got up and walked to the sink. She turned on the tap and put her coffee on the counter, letting the water run. Phyllis was sitting with her back to Lucinda. Turning the water off, she slipped off her new belt and looped it around her two hands and quickly wrapped it around Phyllis' neck. She pulled it tight and Phyllis started choking. She tried to get her fingers inside the belt, but Lucinda pulled tighter. She leaned down close to Phyllis' ear and whispered, "What did you do with my grandmother's dress?"

Phyllis squeaked, "I don't know what you're talking about."

"Oh, I think you do. Maybe you need a little incentive." She looped the belt over the top rung of the chair, buckling it quickly, tightly enough that Phyllis could not pull forward. She then twisted around to grab a large serrated knife from the holder on the counter. In a loud voice, she commanded, "Put both of your hands on the table!" Phyllis continued to squirm, gasping for air and pulling at the belt. Lucinda put the knife to the side of her throat and said, "Hands. Table. Now." Phyllis stopped squirming and slowly put her hands on the table. Lucinda reached for her handbag and pulled out the duct tape. She kept cutting off strips with the knife, wrapping them over Phyllis' forearms and wrists until she was firmly stuck to the table.

Phyllis was panting for breath as Lucinda once again grabbed the belt and began to pull. "Please, I'm a sick woman. I need my oxygen. I can't breathe!"

"You may be sick, but that will be the least of your worries if you don't tell me about my grandmother's dress."

"You're crazy! I need my oxygen!" Phyllis let out a hiccup.

Lucinda hissed, "You'll need more than that if you don't start talking. I am going to start cutting off fingers, one by one, until you tell me what you did with that dress!"

Phyllis began thrashing, moving only side to side because of the tape, pulling the belt tighter around her own neck. All she could say was, "Oxygen!"

Lucinda saw the tank in the corner near the bed. She walked over to it and cut the air supply hose. She turned to Phyllis and said, "Does Jeffrey know his mother's a thief?" Phyllis stopped moving, but her eyes were bulging out.

"Leave Jeffrey out of this. He doesn't know anything."

Lucinda leaned in close. "Ah-ha. So there is something to know. I'm going to count to five." She put the tip of the knife into the second knuckle of Phyllis' right index finger. "One, two, three…." She drove the knife down hard, cutting the finger off clean. "Oops, sorry. Didn't make it to five."

Phyllis let out a blood curdling scream, thrusting forward hard enough to lift the back legs of the chair off the floor. Blood was oozing out of the wound and pooling on the table around the severed digit. Phyllis was panting rapidly. The dog was now at the door, barking and scratching.

"Shall we try again?" Lucinda put the tip of the knife at the base of her right thumb and began to count. "One, two, three, four, five." She drove down the knife and separated the thumb from Phyllis' hand. Another scream came from the woman, then two words: "Under…bed" before she passed out. The dog was still barking and scratching at the door. Lucinda turned and shouted, "Quiet!" Surprisingly, the dog obeyed and sat down.

She headed into the bedroom, kneeling next to the bed and looking underneath. All that was there was a small suitcase. She slid it out and dropped it on the bed. When she opened it, she was elated to find the dress, folded neatly and stored in a plastic bag. She removed it from the bag and laid it flat on the bed. Running her fingers along the hem, she could feel each of the stones, every one seemingly having its' own little pocket. Only one pocket had been cut open, though the gem was nowhere to be found. She refolded the dress and put it back in the bag. Looking through the rest of the suitcase, she found many other bags, containing watches, rings, broaches, and earrings. There were several silk scarves folded neatly, similar to the condition of the dress. *Son of a gun, she was stealing from everyone.* She took the dress, but left the rest. She shut the suitcase and slid it back under the bed. *I wonder why, after all these years, the old lady didn't hock all these things.* Scanning her surroundings, it made even less sense why she hadn't sold it all.

Returning to the kitchen, Lucinda heard gurgling from the limp body at the table. She grabbed a handful of hair and lifted up the head. Phyllis' eyes were barely open. Lucinda had to know. "Why are you living in such a dump when you had all that stuff?" Her eyes were focused on some point beyond Lucinda, but she answered in a very weak voice.

"Tried to sell jewels, but guy wouldn't buy. Said they were mob property. Didn't want anything to do with them." She took a deep breath, then hacked out a mouthful of blood. "Told me I'd be dead if I didn't disappear. Moved here. Sold the other stuff little by little to pay the bills." Another deep breath, then she wheezed out a whispered, "Sorry," before going limp. Lucinda let go of her hair and felt for a pulse. Phyllis was gone. She shook her head. Another person on the run from the mob, living a simple life under the radar.

Lucinda made quick work of the trailer, much like she did with Andrew's condo, washing her coffee cup and wiping down all surfaces with a wet towel. She removed the tape and the belt, allowing Phyllis' body to slump to the floor. Once she removed any trace of her presence, she trashed the trailer to make it look like a robbery. She took Phyllis' purse off the bureau and dumped the contents onto the floor. She took the money from the wallet, along with a credit card, a local grocery card, license, and medical insurance cards. She stuffed them into her bag. Remembering the suitcase, she went back to the bedroom. She pondered for a moment, but didn't want to have to carry all of the valuables in it, so she wiped it down and slid it back under the bed. Once she was sure that everything was cleaned, she put all of the evidence into a large plastic trash bag. She put her grandmother's dress in her handbag and stood at the door, surveying the scene. Looking at the prone body of Phyllis Russell, Lucinda thought to herself that, regardless of how tough her life might have been, she had this coming. The whimpering from the other side of the door reminded Lucinda to do one more thing. She went to the refrigerator and, using a paper towel, opened the door and took out all the meat. She laid it out on the floor, picked up her handbag and the trash bag and opened the front door. The dog ran straight for all the meat. He must have been hungry, as he never once looked up at Lucinda. She stepped out and quietly closed the door behind her.

Once outside, she scanned the neighborhood, wondering if anyone could have heard what just went on. The fact that she couldn't even see the nearest house told her that she should be okay. She threw the trash bag on the floor in the front seat and got into the car. She backed into the driveway and, as she passed the mailbox, she put the red flag down. She wanted to give the mailman one less reason to stop at the house. Then she headed back the way she came, back toward civilization, toward the airport. She just needed to make two quick stops.

The first was at the C-Mart. She parked in the same spot, walked back out to the dumpster, and tossed the trash bag with all its' contents into the far corner. On her way back to the car, she asked a woman with a stroller if there was a post office nearby. Luckily, it was close so she didn't need to write down the directions. When she got there, she took the bag with the dress in it out of her handbag and slid it inside the manila envelope she had purchased earlier. Unfortunately, the dress was a little too bulky for the envelope and she was unable to seal it tightly. She headed inside and perused the mailing options on the wall opposite the counter. Finding a box that was almost perfect, she made all the appropriate folds to form it and put the envelope inside. She held it together until she got to the desk. The young man working there used his tape gun to seal the top and bottom. Lucinda used the chained pen to address it to herself. As she handed the box over to him, she mentally congratulated herself on being so clever. There was nothing in the package that would cause the postal service to need to open it, but an x-ray machine at the airport might raise an eyebrow or two. When the man asked if she wanted to insure it, she thought about it for a moment before refusing. If it were to disappear, how exactly would she explain that she was mailing tens or possibly hundreds of thousands of dollars' worth of emeralds to herself? She would just have to take her chances. He tossed her package onto the shelf behind him and wished her a good day.

Back in the car, she sat for a moment to mentally run through her time in New Mexico. Satisfied that she had covered all her tracks, she started the engine and headed for the rental company. It was just under two hours when she rolled into a parking space near the office. The same pleasant man from that morning was at the counter.

"Well, I hope your short stay isn't indicative of how you feel about our fair city."

Lucinda smiled and replied, "Actually, no. It is quite beautiful here. I would stay longer if I could, but I came for a meeting and need to get back home." She slid the key across the counter, along with a generous tip.

He smoothly retrieved the key and tip with one hand as he slid the acknowledgement of receipt of the car with the other. "No problem, ma'am. We appreciate your business and hope you'll be able to come see us again."

Once in the airport, Lucinda headed for the ladies' room before checking in. She was pleased to find it completely empty. Moving quickly, she splashed cold water on her face and dried it with several paper towels. She then removed all of the contents of Phyllis' wallet and wrapped them tightly in the damp towels. Stepping into one of the stalls, she threw the bundle into the sanitary dispenser. Taking a quick look in the mirror, she gave herself a satisfied smile and headed off to check in.

Chapter 36

When the plane landed at LAX, Lucinda felt exhilarated. It was a beautiful day in every respect. The weather was beautiful, she was looking forward to opening the windows on the ride back to Santa Barbara, and she had taken another step toward her new life. There was only one item left on her to-do list, and she expected that there would be a message on her machine when she got home. She found her car in the garage, paid the fee, and sped off into fairly light traffic, given the fact that this was Los Angeles. She scanned the radio stations for good driving music. *All is well, Gramma Annie. Thank you for guiding me. I promise to put red carnations on your grave every week for as long as I live.*

Though she didn't hear it over the radio, the rumble of Lucinda's stomach reminded her that she hadn't eaten anything other than a bagel and coffee that morning. She thought briefly about stopping, then decided to wait until she got home. It had been a long day and she wasn't interested in eating alone. She sang along with every song, making up lyrics if she didn't know them, to drown out the growling of her belly. The miles flew by and she was soon pulling into her garage.

Opening the door of her apartment, she dropped her bag on the floor and just stood there for a minute. Part of her wanted to scream in excitement, both because another part of her journey was done and the mail would be delivered in a couple of days. She kicked off her shoes and headed for the bathroom to wash up, scrunching her toes on the carpet with every step. She decided on a quick shower, then slipped into an oversized white blouse and black slacks. Her hair was still damp, but it felt good on the back of her neck. As she moved back into the living room, the phone rang. The ID said O'Reilly, Irving. She quickly picked up the receiver before the machine could get it.

"Hey, Buzz. Good to hear from you."

She could hear the smile in his response. "Just wanted to let you know that I landed that opportunity, so you're stuck with me now."

She remembered the flight. "Kinda figured that, since you were on t.v. and all."

He laughed heartily. "Saw that, did you? Was I twenty pounds heavier? Don't answer that. Yeah, I kinda got thrown to the wolves, but it's all good. No down time leaves no room for panic. Any chance you might be interested in dinner once I get settled in?"

She thought about the logic in hanging out with a fed. What harm ever came from dinner? "That would be nice. Give me a call when things quiet down. Congrats again on the job."

"Thanks. Will do."

As she was about to say goodbye, something dawned on Lucinda. "Hey, Buzz?"

"What's up?"

"I don't recall giving you my number." There was just the slightest pause before he answered. "Well, I know a guy who works for the FBI. He's pretty good at finding things out." Lucinda could hear the smile in his voice. "Talk to you soon."

Instead of hanging up the receiver, Lucinda pressed the button to disconnect the call, then released it and dialed Krystina's number. After four rings, she picked up.

"H'lo. It's Krystina." Lucinda couldn't help laughing. Her friend sounded like she was three sheets to the wind.

"Hi Krystina, it's Lucinda. Any chance you're free right now?"

"Only for dinner. It's six-thirty and I'm starving.."

"Dinner it is, on me." Lucinda was just happy to have company, not to mention that she could afford it.

Krystina practically exploded into the phone. "Well, what are you waiting for? Pick me up! I'm ready to go!" Without waiting for a response, she hung up. Lucinda contemplated the logistics of having dinner in a public place with a perpetual ray of sunshine who happened to be somewhat hammered. This was going to be an entertaining night.

When she turned onto Krystina's street, Lucinda saw her standing on the sidewalk talking to a rather tall, familiar looking man. As soon as she saw the car, she ended the conversation with a wave and stepped off the curb. As she slid into the passenger seat, Lucinda asked, "Who's the kid?"

Krystina had a huge grin on her face. "He just looks young because he's Swedish. He's actually our age. He's unmarried, new to the area, and I met him jogging."

Lucinda cracked, "Sounds like you should marry him before he gets away. Does Prince Charming have a name?"

"Duh, of course. His name is Carlton Pedersen."

At the mention of the name, Lucinda was shocked that she did not recognize him. However, she was happy for Krystina. Carlton seemed to be a nice guy, though she really only knew him from that one lunch. "Sounds great. I'm happy for you. So where to for dinner? Someplace we can just walk into."

"How about the Golden Chopsticks? I've been thinking about Chinese food all day."

Lucinda laughed at this, considering Krystina was the unofficial leader of all the gym devotees that attended her get-togethers. "Chinese it is."

The parking lot was packed, and it took Lucinda several laps around it before she found a car leaving. She was about to suggest going somewhere else, but Krystina was practically chanting the menu. When they got inside, they were stunned to be seated almost immediately. The hostess actually offered to take their drink orders, probably to help out the wait staff. As soon as she mentioned the word cocktail, Krystina ordered a Mai Tai. Lucinda rolled her eyes, as the image of carrying her to the car passed through her mind. "Scotch on the rocks, please."

As soon as the hostess left, Krystina started up the engines. "You know, I should introduce you to the Swede. He's really cute and funny, and I'd love to go out with him, but you need a guy, and I'm travelling all the time and don't really have the time, and you'd really like him and..."

Lucinda held up her hands, as though she were a third base coach holding up a runner. When Krystina stopped, with a somewhat shocked expression on her face, Lucinda interjected. "Actually, I met a man."

Krystina went off on another roll. "Omigod, that's awesome! Tell me all about it. How did you meet? Is he really cute? I'll bet he had a really great first line and you...."

Up went Lucinda's hands again. Krystina bit her lower lip before saying, "Sorry."

"It's okay. I met him in the airport lounge coming back from Boston. He is really cute, tall, and quite charming. He did not have any kind of a line, just asked me if I was waiting for someone. He's divorced, amicably, no kids, and was moving here for a job opportunity."

Krystina's eyes lit up. "He sounds awesome. What's the job opportunity? If you tell me Chippendale's dancer, I will fall right out of this chair."

Lucinda couldn't help but laugh at that. "No, Miss One-Track-Mind. He actually works for the FBI."

Krystina's eyes bugged out. "Wow, a Fed? That's pretty hot." At that moment, the hostess showed up with their drinks. Krystina took a very long sip, then added, "Does he have handcuffs?"

Lucinda was thankful that the waitress was coming, as she was looking to end this particular conversation. She ordered a sampler plate for two, as Krystina was too occupied with inhaling her first Mai Tai, ordering a second one, and singing some song that sounded vaguely familiar to Lucinda. She also asked if they could get two coffees, as she was going to need to be stone cold sober to handle her friend and she was hoping to get one into her as well before the night was over.

The rest of the conversation was made up of a wide array of topics, from the funeral to Krystina's upcoming flight to Portugal, to what jobs had the hottest guys. Lucinda found herself getting exhausted trying to keep up with her friend's frequent shifts in direction. They shared the sampler platter, the only thing remarkable being when Krystina cracked herself up and part of an egg roll shot out her nose. By that point, she was on her fourth Mai Tai and was slurring her words badly. When she went to the bathroom, Lucinda took the opportunity to have the table cleared, including the drinks, and paid the bill. When Krystina came back, it took little to convince her that she had finished her drink and decided to call it a night. Lucinda took her by the arm and led her out of the restaurant.

The night was comfortable, with a slight cool breeze that felt good on her flushed face. She hadn't realized how warm the restaurant was until she got outside. They loaded themselves into the car and were soon on the road. When Lucinda turned the corner, she saw Carlton Pedersen jogging down the sidewalk in front of Krystina's. She picked up a little speed and zipped by, quickly making the turn to round the block. Her friend was too entranced by her seat belt to notice what was going on. By the time she made the loop, he was nowhere to be found. She parked the car and proceeded to help her mumbling, giggling friend out and up to her front door.

"Thanksh for a great evening, Lucy," Krystina mumbled as she put her key in the lock. She stumbled through the doorway and headed straight for the couch, where she fell face first. The snoring started almost immediately. Lucinda laughed to herself and closed the door, checking to make sure it was locked. When she reached the street, she scanned in both directions and, seeing the coast was clear, she walked quickly to her car. As she got in, she thought to herself, *Lucy – I could live with that.* Out loud, she said, "Night, Krystie. And thank you. For everything."

Chapter 37

As Lucinda opened her front door, she heard the beep of the answering machine. Pressing the button, she heard Bill's voice, seeming very loud in the quiet apartment. "I'm still at the airport. Believe it or not, there has been a four hour delay. Would have been great to have company. When I land in Lisbon, I will call you." She hit the delete button and headed for the bedroom.

She kicked off her shoes and undressed, throwing everything in a pile on the floor. Stepping into the shower, she turned the temperature all the way up and stood under the forceful spray for what seemed like forever. When she felt the tips of her fingers wrinkling, she gave herself a vigorous scrub and washed her hair. It seemed lately as though she was spending an increasing number of showers trying to wash off the events of the day. Each time felt less successful, as though there was some form of dirt on her that just wouldn't come off. By the time she slipped into an oversized t-shirt and fell onto the bed, she had run through the entire trip in her mind. She remembered back to the night she killed Andrew, how exhilarated, how vindicated, she had felt. Tonight, she just felt tired. Sleep overcame her quickly.

The next morning, Lucinda felt fidgety. Having nothing necessary on the calendar, she found herself thinking about the mail. She knew it was unlikely that the package she had sent herself would make the journey in less than twenty four hours, but she made several trips down to the mail room, just in case. When she wasn't checking mail, she was ticking items off her to-do list for around the apartment. By noontime, she had cleaned the bathroom from top to bottom, organized the kitchen cabinets, done some research on Portugal online, and the mail had arrived, but nothing postmarked from New Mexico. Her frustration bubbled a bit, so she headed down to the Common to do a little food shopping. Her last trip down there had been so enjoyable that she felt that creating something unusual for dinner would be the perfect diversion. She ended up spending a couple of hours, floating from one shop to the next, eventually picking up a vintage bottle of white wine, a roasted duck (she decided that the eating would be more interesting than the cooking), and a platter of various fruits dipped in chocolate.

She returned home just about dinner time, carrying several bags filled with food. The smell wafting from them was causing her stomach to grumble in response, and she found herself tearing into different containers and making something of a sampler plate. It was hardly a proper dinner, but Lucinda couldn't have cared less. She settled on the couch, balancing a plate on the cushion next to her. She ate almost everything with the fingers on one hand, licking the remnants after each morsel. With the clean hand, she leafed through the information she had printed out earlier on Marlene's location. Since Bill didn't mention the name of the village where his contact believed she was, she had done a search on the history of Portugal. Much like the U.S., it was a country that could satisfy both the wealthiest and simplest of tastes. It had been the scene of many battles and colonizations, meaning that a tourist was apt to see a wide range of architectural styles, religions, and ways of living depending on where they chose to visit. As she read, Lucinda was trying to figure out what drew her half-sister to such a place. There were plenty of places in the world where one could disappear, places that were much closer. Still, Marlene had never been one for status or possessions, so a little fishing village actually made sense. Lucinda couldn't help but think that it wouldn't be where she would have gone, given all of the locations in the world to choose from. Though, the thought of listening to creole and jazz music in some small roadside bar sounded rather intoxicating. She reached over and grabbed the remote for the stereo, hitting the play button. The sound of a baritone sax immediately filled the room. Lucinda put her research on the table, along with her now empty plate, and stretched out across the couch.

Closing her eyes, the living room melted away as she imagined herself sitting at the bar of a dark club, lit solely by the spotlight on the stage, where a dark silhouette was playing slow, soulful notes in front of a three piece band. She could feel the tension of recent events melt away, immersed in the groove of the music. The relaxation, however, was short lived. As she sat there, Lucinda became acutely aware of the sensation of being watched. She scanned the room, trying to discern faces in the gloom, but the darkness was almost absolute outside of the cone of the spotlight. She noticed a tall figure, standing in the corner to her left, no more than fifteen feet away. He appeared to be facing in her direction, but she couldn't be sure. Though he was more shadow than solid figure, she was pretty sure that he was wearing a suit, with what appeared to be a blue windbreaker over it. Given the fact that they were indoors, Lucinda found that very odd. His presence unnerved her, so she got up and moved to a seat further down the bar.

When she settled in, she turned to face the band, but was trying to get a look in his direction out of the corner of her eye. To her surprise, he had moved into the seat she just vacated. Feeling a distinct sense of panic, she got up and headed into the crowd, moving toward the exit she could see on the far wall. Using her hand as a wedge, Lucinda wove through the mass of faceless people surprisingly quickly. When she was within five feet of the exit, she took a quick look back at the bar. Her old seat was empty, but she could not find the man in the suit anywhere. She turned forward again, only to have a shadow step into her path, blocking the door. It wasn't the man, as the person in front of her was closer to her height.

The only feature she could make out was a long ponytail. Suddenly, the spotlight swung around, illuminating the two of them for a split second, before she felt a sharp pain in her left temple. As she blacked out, the last thing she saw was a woman's face: Marlene.

Chapter 38

The sun was hot on Lucinda's face, making her head hurt even more. Even though her eyes were shut, the light made her squint hard to try and block it out. The skin on her face was taut, as the tears she remembered crying had dried. The back of her shirt was wet and cold, as though she had lay down in a puddle. She wasn't sure where she was or what happened. There were shreds of memories flitting through her mind, one by one, reassembling into a tapestry that slowly became clear. She opened her eyes and found that she was lying on her living room floor. She reached for the table to pull herself up and felt something sticky on the corner. Pulling her hand back, she found semi-congealed blood on her palm. The throb at her temple reminded her. As the memory of her dream came back, Lucinda felt her pulse rate quicken and her stomach lurch. She rolled over onto her hands and knees and thrust up into a standing position. Finding her way to the bathroom, she knelt in front of the toilet for a few minutes, waiting. When nothing came, she moved to the sink and ran the cold water. Cupping her hands, she dipped her face several times to cool the flush of her skin.

Once she calmed herself, cleaned the rest of the blood off her face, and brewed a pot of coffee, Lucinda sat back on the couch. Holding her mug, she replayed the dream back in her mind. She understood how Marlene could have ended up there, as she was now Lucinda's main focus. The tall man, however, was less clear. There was nothing about him that she knew for sure, but something told her that she knew him, that they had met somewhere before. She contemplated the possibility for several minutes, before the ache in her head became too hard to ignore. She took a large gulp of coffee and then headed for the bathroom, stripping off her sweat soaked clothes as she went.

Twenty minutes later, she re-emerged into the living room, showered, dressed in stretch pants and a t-shirt with her damp hair pulled back into a ponytail. Looking at the clock, it dawned on her that John, the postman, had probably come and gone by now. She slipped on a pair of sneakers and headed downstairs. She tried not to get too excited, as it was possible that she wouldn't find what she was looking for. However, when she turned the corner into the mail room, there on the shelf was the box she had addressed to herself just two days before. She opened her mailbox, took out several pieces, then grabbed the box and headed upstairs. Tossing the rest of the mail on the kitchen table, she grabbed a paring knife and took the box into the living room. She carefully cut the tape on the box and removed the manila envelope. Running the knife under the fold at the top, she gently shook the dress out onto her lap. She gingerly unfolded it, laying it flat on the table in front of her. She headed back into the kitchen, cleaned the knife and put it away, then rummaged through her junk drawer until she found a pair of scissors. She delicately cut along the hem, removing only the bottom eighth of an inch. One by one, she squeezed each pocket like the end of a tube of toothpaste, until she finally had forty two emeralds, sparkling in the morning sun.

Lucinda marveled at their beauty for almost a minute before heading to the kitchen, where she got two plastic bags, putting one inside the other before putting the stones in. She then rolled the dress up tightly, put it inside several pages of yesterday's newspaper, and rolled that up tightly as well. She buried this at the very bottom of her bag of trash from the kitchen, took it down to the trash compactor, and down the chute it went. With a sigh of relief, she started back up the stairs to her apartment. Feeling suddenly tired, she willed herself to grab some change from the little bowl on the windowsill above the kitchen sink and head for the pay phone around the corner. When the familiar female voice answered, she identified herself as Agent 1820 and hung up the phone. Within minutes, she had received her callback and arranged for another trip to San Francisco.

Chapter 39

Lucinda could hear the phone ringing inside as she fumbled for the key to her front door. It had rung five times before she got to it, and she hoped she hadn't missed the call.

"Hi, Lucinda. It's Gina. Are you free tonight? I'm having a few friends over for cocktails. The usual suspects, although Krystina won't be able to make it. She's on a flight to Portugal and won't be back for a week."

"Sounds great. What time?" It hadn't occurred to her before that moment that Krystina was now flying to the place where her half-sister was last seen. She wondered if there would be time to pick her brain after she came back.

"Around seven. Any chance you could bring some of those hot pickled string beans?"

"No problem. See you then." Lucinda hung up the phone. She was sorry to hear that Krystina wouldn't be there, as she was starting to feel a lot closer to her since the funeral. Still, the night would be fun. Gina's group was different from the group at Krystina's, but they were a colorful bunch. Gina ran a boutique downtown and was well known for her lavish taste in clothes, not to mention the parties. She lived near Stearns Wharf, not all that far from Ted's house. Lucinda wondered if they knew each other. Gina reminded her of one of the famous Gabor sisters, but she could never remember the name of the one she most resembled.

Lucinda decided to head out for a run. If she was going to be drinking and socializing tonight, it would be a good idea to burn some calories now. She laced up her running shoes, grabbed her keys, and hit the road. An hour later, she was back in the apartment, having worked up a good sweat. After a quick shower, she settled on the couch and flipped on the television. The noontime news was on and the newscaster was giving details about a plane crash near Islas De La Madera Y Azores. While the crash was in Spain, Lucinda knew it was not far from Portugal. She immediately thought of Krystina. A chill shot up her spine and she quickly dialed Gina's number. When the machine picked up, she left a message asking Gina to call her back. The knot in her stomach began to grow, and she went into the kitchen and poured out a glass of scotch. She leaned against the counter, sipping her drink, and said a silent prayer. The ring of the phone jolted her. It was Gina.

"Hey, Lucinda, sorry I missed your call. I had to run out and pick some things up for tonight. What's up? You sounded kind of jumpy on the message."

"Have you seen the news today? There was a plane crash in Spain."

"Can't say that I have. So?"

"Do you know the flight number of Krystina's plane?" The silence on the other end told Lucinda that Gina had made the connection.

"I'm going to call the airlines and see what I can find out. I'll call you back." Lucinda didn't wait for a response, but hung up and dug out the phone book. Once she found the number, she dialed with increasingly shaky hands, hitting the wrong numbers several times and having to start over. Finally, she got it right and soon had a humorless woman on the other end. She asked if Krystina LaForte had made her flight assignment. She could hear tapping on a keyboard, then the woman verified that

Krystina had been on flight 9002, which had departed for Portugal the day before.

"Do you know if that was the plane that crashed in Spain this morning?"

The woman answered, "I cannot give out any other information at this time," and hung up on Lucinda.

She dialed Gina's number, and she answered on one ring, as though she had been sitting with one hand on the phone. "What did you find out?"

"She would only confirm that Krystina had flown out on flight 9002 to Portugal yesterday. I guess we're just going to have to wait for information to come out."

For the next couple of hours, Lucinda sat and watched the TV, flipping channels hoping to catch more breaking news, but apparently it wasn't important enough to the local audience. Whenever she left the room, she turned the volume up so she wouldn't miss anything. Around four, while she was in the bedroom changing her clothes, she heard the familiar tones that were played before they broke into a broadcast. Running into the living room dressed from the waist down, she got to the TV just in time to hear the newscaster say, "Again, CCB Airlines flight 9002 has crashed into the side of a mountain. It appears that inclement weather and visibility issues contributed to the crash. At this time, no survivors have been reported."

Lucinda sank down onto the couch, staring at the television in disbelief. She could feel the tears beginning to well up in the corners of her eyes. Her friend was gone. The one person since....well, the one person in a long time who accepted her for who she was. The person who called her Lucy, who was happy for her and happy to see her, no matter how long it had been since they last spoke. The phone rang. When she picked it up, all she heard was the sound of someone blowing their nose.

"I take it you heard?" She knew it was Gina.

"I can't believe it. Just like that." Several seconds of silence passed. "I think I'm going to cancel the social tonight."

"Don't. I think it would be better if we are together tonight. I know it will be sad, but it's better than all of us sitting home alone." When Lucinda hung up the phone, another thought occurred to her: Could Bill have been on that flight? She dialed the number of his office, only to be greeted by the machine. "No one is in the office at this time. If you leave a name and number, we shall get back to you during business hours tomorrow." Lucinda had forgotten about the time difference. She left her name and relevant numbers before heading off to Gina's.

She stopped at The Deli and picked up a couple jars of the pickled green string beans. *Comfort food*, she thought. When she arrived at Gina's, Helen answered the door. Her eyes were red from crying. She gave Lucinda a long embrace, and then they headed into the living room. The same scene was playing out there as well. Everyone had the same red-eyed, teary look, with hugs and words of comfort being randomly given. Clearly, everyone had recently arrived, as no one was settled in. Gina was in the kitchen making drinks for everyone. Lucinda went in and put the jars on the counter before wrapping her arms around Gina from the back, resting her cheek on her friend's shoulder. Gina leaned her head back on Lucinda's for several seconds before reaching for the bottle of scotch. "The usual?" Lucinda nodded her head without removing it from Gina's back. For some reason, she couldn't tear herself away from the embrace she was giving, and Gina made no movement to end it. Someone in the room asked, "Does anyone know if Krystina has family in the area?" There were several murmurs, but no one could say that they knew for sure. It struck Lucinda at that moment just how little they all knew about each other. Even though the group had regular get-togethers and rarely lacked for conversation, no one really shared much of a personal nature. She had always kept her own life private, but never thought about how much the others did as well. Oddly enough, she still felt more connected to them than ever before. A strange little family unit they had.

Lucinda felt a cold, wet sensation on her hand which brought her back to the moment. Gina was resting her scotch on the hands clutched at her belly. She released her right hand and took the glass, raising it to her lips. The warmth of the scotch inside matched the warmth of Gina on the outside. The comfort of drink and friends was almost enough to compensate for the ache in her heart. She helped Gina pass out the drinks and everyone took a seat. They all stared at their glasses for several seconds before Lucinda raised hers and said, "May you rest in peace, Krystina." They all raised their glasses, then downed the drinks in one shot. Gina immediately got up to pour refills. While she did this, Vangie thought out loud, "I wonder if Krystina had anything prepared for a situation like this, since she did have a dangerous job."

This statement got everyone in the room talking at the same time. Helen wondered who would take care of her cats. Gina couldn't imagine who would take over her boutique. To herself, Lucinda thought about her life and what she now had to worry about. Recent events had made this an important consideration for her. She never had to worry about beneficiaries, as she was pretty sure no one would care about her old car and an apartment. She thought quietly to herself for a while before saying to no one in particular, "We should all get a lawyer and put our affairs in order. I have never given much thought to who would take care of any arrangements, or who would get my stuff." This set off another round of thoughts about what things people wouldn't want found, what relatives wouldn't get a damned thing, and what kind of services each would want. The conversation became so animated that no one heard the phone ring at first. After the third ring, Gina walked over and picked up the receiver. The sound of the phone hitting the floor quieted the room. Everyone turned to see what happened. Gina was leaning against the wall with her hands over her mouth. Lucinda noticed the tears on her cheeks and ran over to her. When she got close, she could hear a voice on the other end of the line. She picked up the phone and put it to her ear.

"Hello? Gina, are you there? C'mon, you guys!" Lucinda recognized the voice immediately and could not believe her ears.

"Krystina??"

"Lucinda? Hi. Yeah, it's me. What happened?"

Lucinda started hopping up and down. "Oh, my God! We thought you were killed in the crash! Where are you? Are you o.k.? What happened?" It occurred to her at that moment that she sounded just like Krystina.

"I'm okay. I'm in London. I got a stomach virus and was so dehydrated that I had to get a replacement."

"Thank God. We were all just drinking a toast to you and getting ready to prepare our wills!"

"Probably not a bad idea. I never bothered to before, but things have definitely changed. Anyway, sorry I didn't call earlier, but I really didn't have the energy for anything until just a little while ago. The doctors have cleared me to fly, so I'm going to catch the first available flight home. Tell everyone I love them and I will see you all soon."

"I will. We are all just thrilled that you missed the flight." As soon as she said it, Lucinda felt badly about the person who took her spot. Krystina was obviously thinking the same thing. "Me too, but I feel terrible about the crash. All those passengers, going on vacation, or maybe flying to a loved one. Not to mention, I had a number of good friends on that flight."

Lucinda was quiet for a moment. Finally, she said "Sorry, I didn't mean…"

Krystina interrupted. "I know. I appreciate your concern. I am thankful as well for missing the flight. Tell everyone I'll see them soon. I'm going to try and get some sleep. I love you guys."

"Love you back. Get home safe." Lucinda hung up the phone. When she turned around, every pair of eyes were on her.

"Well???"

Lucinda recounted the story for the group. The sense of relief in the room was tangible. Gina added, "Well, my friends, from tears to cheers. To quote from something I read recently, 'Enjoy life. It has an expiration date.' Whoever wrote it had the right idea."

The rest of the night was spent much like a typical cocktail party, with lots of eating and drinking, but the conversation consisted less of gossip and idle chit-chat, and more about the good things in their lives.

By the time Lucinda reached her apartment, it was twelve-thirty in the morning. She didn't realize just how exhausted she was until she had peeled off her clothes and slid into her pajamas. She was asleep almost as soon as her head hit the pillow.

Chapter 40

Lucinda found herself standing in the middle of an airport. She couldn't understand how she had gotten there, or where she was going. She didn't have any luggage and, when she looked down, she realized that she was wearing pajamas. She suddenly felt very self-conscious, but the people around her didn't seem to notice. Everyone was rushing to get to one place or another. A voice crackled over the loudspeaker, but it didn't sound like English to her. She could see one of those computer screens mounted to the wall across from her that displayed the different flights and their arrival or departure times. She moved through the crowd until she was standing right in front of it. Scanning the flights, she saw an arrival from London landing in ten minutes. There were departures for Albuquerque, San Francisco, Boston, and Lisbon. Ironically enough, each of those gates was within visual distance of the others.

Lucinda spun around, as the hair on the back of her neck began to stand up. The room was bright, although she couldn't tell if it was natural or artificial light. The wall opposite her was lined with windows, but outside she could see nothing but white, as though the airport was mired in a fog, or maybe clouds. The crowd around her was insistent, moving quickly and methodically through the airport, coming close to her but never actually touching her. She tried to focus on their faces, hoping to feel more connected to the scene around her, but all she could see were blurred edges. The feeling of being watched began to creep over her. Lucinda scanned the room, moving slowly in a full circle, taking everything in. Nothing but a sea of white: clothing, walls, carpet, lights. Then she saw him. The man from the bar. The only thing in the room other than her that had color. The same dark suit. The same blue jacket. The same writing on it. She still couldn't read it, but she could make out that it was three letters. Capital letters, she thought. He wasn't looking at her, though. He was reading something. She suddenly felt very exposed. Lucinda turned away from him, not sure where to go, but knowing that she needed to get away from there. She started walking past the different departure gates. She could see an exit no more than fifty yards away. She made a beeline for the door. As she pushed through the crowd, a face to her left swam into her view. Slowing, but not stopping, she turned her head toward it. The gate above the face said 'Lisbon'. The brown hair and ponytail were unmistakable, but the face itself had changed. Marlene was staring at her, watching her but not beckoning. Lucinda found herself coming to a stop. The two contemplated each other for what seemed like forever. She was struck by the changes. Marlene's face seemed thinner, paler, with a strange coloring, an almost yellowish hue. More disturbingly, the wide bright smile that she remembered seemed to be nonexistent. The look on her face seemed almost to be one of contemplation, with her lips tight together in a thin line. She appeared to be thinking hard about something. Lucinda was afraid to step toward her, for fear that she might turn and run. She opened her mouth to say something, but nothing came out. She could hear the words in her head, but all that sounded in her ears was the general bustle of the airport. She kept talking, first asking why Marlene was here, where she was going, why she wasn't saying anything. The words came streaming out into her head in a jumble, only partially comprehensible. Lucinda was truly getting lost in her own thoughts, when she suddenly realized that she was no longer asking Marlene anything. She was alternately yelling at her for letting Lucinda pull away and apologizing for doing so. She was rambling on about how they should have gone on double dates, ditched classes to go out to lunch, talked about the boys they thought were cute. She became aware that she was crying, but let the tears roll freely down her cheeks. She spewed these thoughts into her conscious, aware that Marlene wasn't hearing any of it, but stopping was beyond her control. She went on for what must have been several minutes before she found herself out of breath and with a serious case of the hiccups. She took a deep breath and stared at Marlene. The look on her friend's face had changed, from contemplative to what appeared to be surprise. It was changing again, to a look Lucinda didn't recognize right away. Marlene tilted her head slightly to the right, pursing her lips. Then she spoke, and though Lucinda couldn't hear anything, she knew exactly what had been said. 'Sorry'. Marlene gave her a thin smile, a small wave, and then turned away. Lucinda would almost have sworn that, instead of disappearing into the crowd, Marlene had actually faded away. As she searched the throngs of people weaving back and forth in front of her, a loud buzz cut right through her head, practically splitting her in two, and everything faded to black.

Chapter 41

Lucinda woke to darkness. Her bedroom was pitch black, and the darkness outside was so complete that she couldn't even find the outline of her window. She lay there for seconds, for minutes, feeling her heart rate return to normal. She couldn't close her eyes, as the dream reappeared inside her head in vivid clarity. She couldn't forget the fear that surfaced when the man in the blue coat appeared. It was subtle, seemingly out of nowhere, but everything inside told her to run. However, seeing Marlene brought on a strange sense of sadness, an emptiness. This confused her, as she had put the end of their friendship to rest so many years ago. Marlene had been out of her life for so long, she sometimes wondered if it had ever been real at all. She rolled onto her side, searching for the clock on her bedside table. Three A.M. She was wide awake now. She swung her feet over the edge of the bed and was soon pulling on shorts and a sweatshirt. A surge of energy sent her out the door into a raw, damp morning for a harder than normal run.

An hour later, Lucinda was back in her apartment. To her surprise, the light on her answering machine was blinking. *Who could have possibly called at this hour?* For a split second, she thought that some other tragedy had occurred, as calls that early or late rarely brought good news. Then she remembered: she had left a message, probably with at least a little panic in her voice, for Bill to call her as soon as possible. She pressed a button and was thrilled to hear his voice echoing through the silent living room. He had arrived at his hotel and found a message from Iris, relaying the message for him to call as soon as possible. He was going to call again at ten, West Coast time.

Knowing she now had time to kill, relieved that Bill was okay, Lucinda peeled off her soaked running clothes and jumped into the shower.

The heat loosened up knots that she didn't even realize she had. She let the water pulsate over her for quite some time before she finally washed and got out. While the message and the shower washed away much of the stress of recent events, Lucinda found herself struggling to push the dream out of her mind. The way Marlene faded, the sickly look on her face, the apology all were eating at her. She couldn't get the feeling of foreboding out of her mind. By the time she slipped into her robe, she knew what she needed to do now. She went to her desk, pulled open the top drawer and rummaged around until she found what she was looking for. Her passport looked almost brand new, having only been used once, soon after her grandmother passed away. Flipping through it, chuckling at the color of her hair in the picture, she saw the expiration date. Three weeks ago! She was both shocked at how fast the ten years had gone by and frustrated by the fact that it expired just before she needed it.

Lucinda pulled on a pair of stretch pants, a solid colored tee and, remembering the chill during her run, a hooded sweatshirt. She headed down to the coffee shop around the corner, where she ordered a large coffee and a blueberry muffin. She had about an hour to waste before the post office would open. She sat at a table where a newspaper had been left by a previous patron. Pulling pieces off the muffin, she flipped casually through the news, not really reading but scanning. More trouble in Korea, budget arguments in Washington D.C., and the Angels had won a doubleheader the day before. When she reached the Local section, a picture on the front page caught her eye. There, in a two by two inch square, was the office of Lowe and Maher. A group of men seemed to be poring over a stack of documents. Each of them was wearing a jacket with the letters F-B-I. A small turn of Lucinda's stomach reminded her of Roger's words, that agents had been surprised at her quick departure and were going to be in touch. Counting in her head the weeks since that conversation, Lucinda was shocked that she had not been contacted. She wondered if Rosaleen had given them the right information. She toyed briefly with the thought that the secretary with the icy stares was actually part of the sisterhood, had understood the situation, and sent the feds down a dead-end. Maybe she too had been infatuated with Andrew, had fallen for his charming ways, and been left behind as the flavor of last month. The thought made her smile briefly, but the picture unnerved her more. She looked at the clock over the register. The post office would be open in ten minutes. She flipped past the picture and read the comics while she finished the last of her muffin.

Ten minutes later, Lucinda was walking up to the front door of the post office just as a woman was unlocking the door. She was first in line and told the clerk what she needed. The woman, a pleasant brunette named Alyse, told her to go to the drugstore across the street. They would take the picture that she would need for the new passport. This took only a few minutes and, as she crossed back, smiled at the photo. *Not too bad for your age*, she thought. It also struck her that it was one of the few photos she had with a normal hair color. When she got back to the post office, she was able to get right back up to the same clerk. She filled out the required form and slid the two items across the desk. Alyse looked everything over, then informed Lucinda that it would take five or six weeks to process everything, and that her new passport would be mailed to her. She nodded silently, keeping her disappointment to herself. Lucinda was surprised to hear that it would take that long. She was beginning to feel somewhat claustrophobic, like the walls were closing in. Bill would be disappointed too, but that was of little concern to her.

Before heading home, Lucinda did a little food shopping on the common. Fresh fruit and a piece of salmon later and she was headed for her apartment. By the time she got home, it was almost eleven. She put away the groceries and tidied up a bit. When the phone rang, she paid no attention to it until the machine picked up. At the tone, she heard Bill's voice.

"Lucinda, are you there? Hello?"

She grabbed the receiver. "Bill? Hi. Sorry about that. Couldn't get to the phone in time."

"No worries." She could feel the pause. "Well, I found out where Marlene and her husband lived."

"You said 'lived'. Not 'living'." She sighed. "I thought you were good at this." She felt bad about saying it, but she somehow imagined that the search would have gone more quickly. Of course, her sudden need to skip town might have contributed to that.

"I don't get it. It feels like she's still running from something. I mean, since when is a move to Europe not enough? Don't worry, though. I always catch up to them in the end. I am waiting to hear from a contact. Any idea when you'll be coming?"

The hopeful tone in his voice annoyed Lucinda even more. She was almost happy to tell him about the delay with her passport. She had no intention, however, of telling him about her impending trip to see Oliver.

"Well, that's disappointing. For you, I mean. I can imagine you want this resolved soon. Anyway, here's my new cell number. No laughing, but I can't find my old phone. Somebody's probably calling Timbuktu with it right now." Lucinda stifled a laugh while she wrote down the number. "This way you won't have to call the office to get in touch with me or get an update. Keep me in the loop regarding the passport and I'll touch base with you when I have new information."

When she hung up the phone, Lucinda couldn't help but wonder what the next five weeks would bring. She was going to be stuck waiting for her passport, while Bill was going to find Marlene and then have to just follow her until Lucinda could fly out to meet him. Meanwhile, the FBI was still on the case of Andrew's murder and she was beginning to worry about just when her luck might run out. While she was stewing over the possibilities, the phone broke the silence once again. She wasn't in the mood to talk, but she glanced at the caller i.d. All it said was I.A. She was confused, but also curious.

"Hello?"

"Hi, Lucinda. It's Buzz. What's new?"

She was thrilled to hear his voice. "Buzz, it's so good to hear from you. However, it would take a month of Sundays to get you up to speed, and I'd rather not bore you with the details right now."

Buzz laughed heartily. "Wow. I'd love to hear it all. I'm going to be in Los Angeles next Thursday. Any chance we could meet somewhere in the middle for dinner?"

Lucinda was elated by the thought of dinner with Buzz, but next week would not be a good time, considering she would be heading to San Francisco. "I'm going to have to take a rain check, Buzz. Too many things going on right now in my life. I hope you understand."

"I totally understand. I have been crazy busy myself lately. I'll call you when things settle down a bit. Take care of yourself."

When it rains, it pours. First the delay in getting her passport, then a man she would really like to see asks her to dinner but she has a trip to take. If it weren't for a big payday, not to mention the tying up of loose ends, she'd have accepted the invite and delayed all of her impending flights. Considering the fact that she was going to be leaving the country soon enough, Lucinda figured that it would probably be best not to see Buzz anyway.

The sound of church bells told her that it was noontime, and she turned on the TV. The news was just starting and there was a breaking story. The attorney general was standing at a podium outside of the police station. "We have made an arrest in the murder of a partner at the law firm of Lowe and Maher. The weapon has been found and a team is searching the site for additional evidence. A press conference later today will provide more details." *Oh, my God! Who did they arrest?* Lucinda was on the edge of her seat. Her hands broke out in a sweat. Thoughts were running wildly through her mind, but that one question kept coming to the forefront: *Who did they arrest?*

As she sat there pondering the question, the phone rang and practically scared her right off the couch. Without even thinking, she answered.

"Lucinda, it's Roger. By any chance, did you see the news?"

"I just did. When did all this happen?"

"The arrest was made yesterday, but they said they were going to wait before announcing it to the media. I was hoping to call you before they did, so you didn't have to find out this way, but work has been out of control lately."

"Have they told you who was arrested?"

"No, they wouldn't tell us. All they said was that they think the person was a client. They indicated that there was a fair amount of evidence, once they knew where to look, and that this case should be closed rather quickly."

"Well, I hope they nail this guy to the wall. I feel so sorry for Andrew's family. Keep me in the loop, if you can."

Roger assured her that he would keep her up on the developments, then hung up. Lucinda thought about this news for a moment. On one hand, she was thrilled. An arrest ends the investigation and gives her the time to finish off her business and get out of the country. On the other hand, an innocent man could go to jail for her crime and spend the rest of his days behind bars. She decided that, even though he didn't commit the murder, there must have been something bad about this unknown man and his relationship with Andrew to draw the attention of the police. Being right on the edge of a new life, putting the baggage of her old one behind her, Lucinda decided that this was how it had to be.

With that, she decided to go out for lunch. It appeared to be clearing up outside, as filtered rays of sun were creeping across her kitchen floor. She grabbed her wallet and keys and headed for the door. When she hit the sidewalk, the sun was warm, with a comfortable breeze. She tied her sweatshirt around her waist and walked toward her new favorite sidewalk café, Eviddas. She covered the mile walk quickly and was soon sitting in the shade of one of the oversized umbrellas. She ordered a grilled cheese and tomato on sourdough bread, as well as an iced coffee.

While she was waiting for her lunch, a gentleman appeared at her table and stood there until she looked up. "Pardon me, miss, but you rather looked as though you might enjoy a little company. May I join you?"

Behind her sunglasses, Lucinda rolled her eyes. While the man was quite handsome and well dressed, she recognized a player when she saw one. He obviously had money, considering his well-tailored suit, but now so did she. However, Lucinda decided a little casual conversation might be nice. She smiled and nodded to the vacant seat beside her.

Before sitting, he said, "Thank you. My name is Jonas. And you are?" She tilted her head back to get a better look at her conversational partner. He had taken his hat off and Lucinda got a good look at him. After the initial shock of recognition, she decided to have a little fun. "My name is Jeanette." He put his hat on the back of the chair and gracefully sat down. With a straight face, she leaned forward and said, "You look familiar. Are you famous?" He smiled, shook his head, and replied, "Please, just think of me as Jonas. Let's not worry about who we really are." He reached out and put his hand on hers.

She couldn't help the smile that was beginning to spread. She slid her hand out from under his, pointed at him and said, "I know. You work for Lowe and Maher." The look on Jonas' face made her burst out laughing. He stared at her for a moment, then started to get up. She grabbed his hand and said, "No, Carlton, wait. I'm teasing. It's me, Lucinda." He stopped and looked at her, then a bright shade of red spread across his face and down into the collar of his shirt. He sat down and buried his face in his hands.

Lucinda had stopped laughing, but couldn't remove the smile. "What's with the 'player' routine? You're a handsome guy with a good job. I can't imagine you have any trouble meeting women."

Carlton Pederson kept his face buried for several seconds before replying. "Actually, I have a horrible time. I never know what to say and end up making a complete fool of myself. If I pretend to be someone else, I seem to be able to at least hold an interesting conversation." He looked at her with such a sincere look, she couldn't help but feel badly.

"Just be yourself. Women are suspicious of guys with lines. You have an interesting job, and I'll bet you have interesting hobbies."

Carlton laughed silently. "See, that is where they find out I'm a total dork." Lucinda shot him a confused look, so he continued. "You want to know what I do for fun?" When she said nothing, he admitted the truth. "I carve birds."

He laughed nervously. However, Lucinda was curious. When she still lived on the East Coast, her grandmother was friends with a couple who were into the very same thing. The gentleman's name was Don and his wife's name was Gloria. He would do the carving and Gloria would do the painting. Her grandmother bought quite a bit of their handiwork. She gestured for Carlton to continue.

"A number of years ago, I was living in a suburb of Boston. I was in a small bar, partaking of my original method for dealing with stress." At this, he held up his glass. "I was sitting next to a man drinking the same thing and we struck up a conversation. He told me that he taught classes in bird carving. I thought that was the silliest thing I had ever heard, but the more he talked, the more I thought I'd like to try it. His name was Charlie Murphy and he had a workshop in West Concord. While it was a small shop, his work was quite well known. He even had an extensive write-up in a regional publication called Yankee Magazine."

Carlton paused for a moment. Lucinda said, "See, just when you think you know someone." He laughed and put his hand over his eyes. "Do you ever get out to see him?" Carlton shook his head and became serious. "Unfortunately, he passed at a rather young age. His gift to me, however, keeps on giving. It is a hobby that keeps me on an even keel." Carlton glanced at his watch. "I have a meeting in fifteen minutes." He stood up and put on his hat. In his cool voice, he said, "At least let me have this moment of smooth. It was good seeing you again."

She smiled and replied, "There will always be a seat at my table for you." He bowed, pulled a bill out of his pocket, dropped it on the table and said, "Allow me" before turning on his heel and disappearing up the sidewalk. Lucinda looked down and saw the fifty dollar bill. She finished her lunch and, when the waitress came to clear the table, Lucinda handed her the money and told her to keep the change. Before the woman could answer, she too disappeared into the crowd.

Chapter 42

The rest of the week was a blur to Lucinda. She had spent a lot of time going through everything in her apartment, trying to decide what to do with it all. She had come to the conclusion that, if she even returned from Portugal, she would be unlikely to stay here in Santa Barbara. Though it appeared that she would be in the clear regarding Andrew's murder, it would be too difficult to put it all behind her knowing that she was likely to run into reminders on a regular basis. She thought about giving some of her favorite stuff to Krystina and the girls, but she knew that this would only cause questions that she didn't want to answer. Over the course of three days, she donated a majority of her clothes to Goodwill, and organized three boxes of personal effects, such as some knick knacks and scattered CD's and DVD's. The furniture could be used by the next tenant. When she was mostly done, Lucinda found herself feeling rather down. She never thought she would miss her little apartment, or the meager life she had been living here. All she had been able to think about when Detective Nelson brought her those jewels so many weeks ago was the life that they would be able to buy her somewhere warm and exciting.

Scanning the apartment, Lucinda thought about how empty it looked. Not in a 'no one lives here' kind of way, but more in the way that you couldn't tell who actually lived here. It hadn't taken her long to remove the personal touches one would find in a residence. Her grandmother's house had been full of photographs, artwork, projects scattered across tables, all items of life being lived. Her apartment never felt more like a museum than it did right now. She sat down in the living room and her mind drifted to before all of the changes, before her parents died, before she and Marlene became strangers. She had been truly happy then, would have considered herself blessed if a twelve year old thought that way. Her life had taken many strange twists through the years, culminating in this moment. She could feel the tears coming, which surprised her. Not much made her cry anymore. Before they could come, though, the moment was interrupted by the shrill ring of the telephone. She wasn't much in the mood to talk, but she glanced at the caller i.d. and was glad she did. It was Buzz.

"Hello, this is Irving O'Reilly, your friendly neighborhood porter. Any bags I might carry for you this evening?"

Lucinda laughed. Not only at his reference to the first time they met, but to the double meaning of bags. At this moment, there was nothing she would have liked better than to have someone to help carry her baggage.

"Hello there, Irving O'Reilly. No. No bags tonight." She sighed deeply. "Still, it's good to hear from you."

Buzz' tone changed immediately. "What's wrong?"

"Just getting run down. Lots of changes happening lately, difficult memories, an emotional roller coaster." She contemplated her next statement before continuing. "Though I don't really know you, I wish you were here. I could really use a hug right about now."

"Well, as it turns out, I am. I'm having a working dinner with the other agents on my case. We're down at the Santa Barbara Shellfish Company. While I can't invite you because we're discussing a case in a private room, we should be done in about an hour. I can bring you something to eat, if you would like."

Lucinda didn't hesitate. "Just you. See you when you get here. I'd give you an address, but you have that guy who can find things out."

She hung up the phone and immediately dug through the boxes she had just filled. She put her CD's and movies back on the shelves, re-hung a couple small photos she bought from a local artist selling her works on the common, and threw some clothes on the back of a chair. *Just homey enough*, she thought. She tucked the rest of the stuff into a spare closet, one that was unlikely to get opened inadvertently. She was thankful that she hadn't gotten rid of any food, or the wine that was still in the fridge. Looking through her bedroom closet, she pulled out some black slacks and a white silk blouse. She added some black dangling earrings and slid her feet into a pair of flats. A quick look in the mirror told her that the outfit was perfect.

No sooner had she sat down to wait, the buzzer at the door went off. She quickly went over and pressed the button to release the locked door downstairs. She was still standing there when there was a knock at the door. *He must have run*, she smiled to herself. She opened the door and Buzz greeted her with a giant smile. He was still wearing his suit, with a blue FBI rain jacket over it. She stepped back to let him in, but he only stepped inside the door frame before stopping.

"I hear that a hug was needed somewhere around here?" He held his arms out.

"You remembered." She stepped into his embrace and wrapped her arms around his midsection, as he was a fair bit taller than her.

"A man doesn't forget a beautiful woman making such a request. Besides, the FBI isn't just about catching the bad guy. Giving comfort when necessary comes with the territory."

They stood there in each other's arms for what seemed like forever, before Lucinda coughed quietly and said, "Where are my manners? Can I get you a drink?"

Buzz released her and said, "Just a coffee would be great. Had my drinks with dinner." He moved over to the kitchen table and had a seat. She started a pot of coffee, then took the seat across from him. Once they were sitting there, the room became quiet. Lucinda suddenly didn't know what to say. The bar had been set rather high with the greeting at the door. She asked the first thing that entered her mind.

"So, what was the big meeting about?"

Buzz shook his head. With a very serious expression, he said, "You know I can't discuss an ongoing case, ma'am. If I told you, I'd have to kill you." Her eyes widened, and he held his expression for as long as he could before he cracked up laughing. "Seriously, I can't get into too much detail, but this is the case that I came out here for. A well-known lawyer had been killed and the investigation was going nowhere. Turns out the lead investigator was close to retirement and wanted to bury this one last case. He got one suspect in mind and wouldn't consider anyone or anything else. They arrested him, over my objections, but that fell through. They released the guy today. The thinking now is that it might be a woman, which I had suggested in the beginning."

Lucinda felt as though she had been punched in the stomach. It all made sense now. Buzz was here to investigate her! This was his promotion. The man in the suit with the blue jacket. She tried to keep her composure. "Why a woman?"

Buzz got up to pour the coffee. She had forgotten all about it. As he took the milk out of the refrigerator, he continued. "There was a glass with lipstick on it. The original lead investigator was so caught up in believing it was some case of corrupt businessmen and their lawyer, while chalking up the lipstick to the guy getting lucky before he died. Early inquiries showed that this guy was a player and, in my experience, there is nothing more dangerous than a woman scorned." He placed a cup of coffee in front of her, along with the milk and a sugar bowl.

Lucinda used the time stirring milk and sugar into her coffee to process what she had just heard. Maybe he wasn't closing in on her. She remembered the glass with the lipstick. That was the woman he had in his condo when Lucinda called from the charity show. While she figured that the woman would have a solid alibi, not to mention probably no reason to kill Andrew, Lucinda hoped that this wild goose chase would take long enough for her to get out of Dodge. Five weeks was a long time to hope for, but it was all she had.

Buzz sat and watched her stir for a couple minutes. Realizing that the moment was gone, he cleared his throat and pushed his chair back. "It's late. I should really be going. Any chance you might let me buy you dinner one of these nights?"

Startled, Lucinda looked up. "Of course. I'd like that. Give me a call when you catch the bad guy, er…girl, and have some time to spare." She got up and walked him to the door. He opened and turned to look at her. "It was really good to see you again. Looking forward to that dinner." He took her hand and kissed the back of it. She smiled and replied, "Thanks for the hug. You'll never know how much I needed that." He returned the smile, spun quickly, and was gone. She closed the door and rested her face against its' cool surface until it matched her temperature, then headed for bed.

Chapter 43

The airport was bustling again. People running for gates, embracing loved ones who had driven them there, or come to pick them up. Security people with dogs, checking in travelers and porters pushing old ladies in wheelchairs. Lucinda was standing in a security line, holding her shoes and rolling one small carry-on bag. She had given everything away except what she needed to make the trip. As she waited, she scanned the airport mindlessly. The arrival/departure screen was off to her right. She watched it scroll until she saw her flight come up – on time. She was thankful for that. Looking through the wall of windows, out to the tarmac, the sun was shining. However, in the distance, a threatening wall of dark clouds was rolling toward the airport more quickly than she would like. She could have sworn that the clouds were moving quicker than the line she was in. Her palms began to sweat and she began bouncing on her toes, looking over the people in front of her to see how many were between her and the guards. That's when she saw him.

The security people in her line weren't checking people. They were talking to someone. He was showing them a picture. He was wearing a blue coat with capital letters on it. Buzz had found her. She slipped her shoes back on and stepped out of line. She began heading back to the terminal, first at a stroll, then a purposeful walk. When she heard a man call out to her, she broke into a run. She let go of her bag and sprinted forward, weaving through a throng of stunned travelers. For some reason, she couldn't find a red exit sign anywhere. Bathrooms, baggage doors, airport staff only, everything but what she needed. Finally, up ahead on the right, she saw it. Making a beeline for the door, she could hear the footsteps coming closer behind her. They were gaining on her, but she was almost there. She didn't hesitate at the door, but hit the crash bar with both hands. A loud buzz went off as she went through the opening, hit nothing but air, and plunged downward into utter darkness.

Chapter 44

The next morning, Lucinda was a woman on a mission. Everything had become clear to her. It was time to go. Her appointment with Oliver was in a little over a week, but she hoped that he might be willing to accommodate her new situation. She headed down to the payphone and went through the now familiar process. When the return call came, it was Oliver himself. She explained her haste and he agreed to meet with her the next day. She headed back to her apartment and packed an overnight bag. A quick call to the airport got her a coach seat to San Francisco in the morning. She packed up her car with the three boxes full of stuff, as well as a bag containing all her clothes except three days' worth of light clothing, and drove to the Salvation Army.

Once these errands were done, Lucinda stopped at a coffee shop for a break. Over an iced mocha coffee, she contemplated the road taken to get to this point. It shook her a bit to think about how she had evolved over the years, and not often for the better. While she had overcome many struggles, getting an education and forging a career, she knew her grandmother would not have been proud of some of her methods. Lucinda wondered if God's forgiveness would even cover some of her transgressions.

Sipping the last of her coffee, Lucinda pulled out her phone and dialed Bill.

"William Fadigo." He sounded so professional, but Lucinda knew better.

"Bill, it's Lucinda."

She could hear the smile in his voice. "So you couldn't live without hearing my voice. Get your passport already?"

"No. I just wanted to touch base and let you know that I am tying off loose ends here so that I'll be ready when it does arrive. How are things on your end?"

Bill sighed softly. "I haven't caught up to my contact yet. Seems he is off chasing a lead. In the meantime, I have been piecing together a timeline of how they spent their days here in Lisbon. I should have something to tell you in the next day or two."

Lucinda took a breath. "Bill, can I ask you a question?"

"Shoot."

"Did Marlene legally change her name or is that alias just for secretive purposes?"

The line was silent for a second. "I'm pretty sure it's just an alias. If she were to come back here, she would be back to Marlene Fontana. Why do you ask?"

"I was just doing a little homework of my own on the Internet. There was really nothing to find with either the Lewis or Fontana names, and the stuff I found related to the St Gaudins name was kind of frightening. I was just hoping to know a little more about Marlene's life before I saw her again."

"Ah. Well, maybe I can fill in some holes when you finally get here. Look, gotta go. Someone's at the door. Talk to you in a day or two."

Lucinda hung up the phone and checked the time. The day was only half over, but she was ready to get on her flight to San Francisco. With the visit from Buzz and the dream still fresh in her mind, she went home long enough to pick up her overnight bag, as well as the bearer bonds, and take the jewels out of the freezer. Once she did this, she went to a local motel and got herself a room for the night. With a little flirting and a twenty dollar bill, the young man at the desk said he would give her a wake-up call at six in the morning. She spent the rest of the afternoon watching old movies in her room before falling asleep well before nine o'clock.

The ringing of the phone the next morning brought an end to another airport dream, one where a hand had just grabbed her shoulder as she took the plunge. After much fumbling on the unfamiliar bedside table, she found the receiver and put it to her ear. "Lady, time to get up." She then heard a click, telling her that there would be no snooze alarm or second call in ten minutes. She dragged herself out of bed and went right to the shower. The hot water energized her and she was soon packed up, had a coffee and a Danish from the mom and pop shop next to the motel, and was hailing a taxi.

She was at the airport well before her scheduled flight. She checked in at one of the automated kiosks just inside the entrance of the terminal and headed for security. As she followed the signs, she remembered her recent dreams and her stomach began to flutter. She thought briefly about renting a car and driving, but had no interest in taking that much time to get there. Besides, she had an appointment that, if she were late, might not get rescheduled so favorably. She bit down on her lower lip to distract from the queasiness and turned the final corner before the checkpoint. She was thrilled to see that there was no line whatsoever, and the two guards there seemed barely awake. She handed her license to the less interested guard, who gave it a sleepy glance before marking her boarding pass and sending her on her way. Just beyond them was the x-ray machine. She took off her shoes and emptied her pockets. Remembering her efforts at keeping the stones out of x-rays while traveling back from New Mexico caused her to pause, but there was no turning back now. Putting everything into a bucket, she stepped through the scanner and picked up her stuff on the other side. By the time she put everything back in its place, the feeling in her stomach had almost disappeared. Still, she wasn't going to take her chances, so instead of sitting conspicuously by her gate, she spent the next two hours browsing through all the little stores facing the tarmac. It wasn't until she heard the announcement that they would be starting the boarding process in a few minutes that she found her way over to the gate.

She was in her seat in less than ten minutes. An added bonus was that no one was sitting in the middle seat. She had the window to her right and a bookish looking old man sitting on the aisle. The weather looked good and, for the first time in her life, she thought she might actually be getting the hang of this flying thing. She had originally hoped to sleep through the flight, but going to bed so early the night before had left her wide awake. She was beginning to feel some excitement over the future, thinking about her reunion with Marlene. She found herself struggling to remember what had driven them apart in the first place. She couldn't imagine pushing away a best friend, especially after the biggest tragedy of her life. She knew she had done it, but that was all in the past. Lucinda wondered if Marlene knew that they were related, or how she would react when she found out. She spent so much time thinking about the two of them that the flight passed in the blink of an eye.

She hustled through the airport and caught a cab almost immediately. She had the driver drop her off in the parking lot she used the first time she came. Better to respect the privacy of Oliver's business, she thought. When she took the elevator up, the doors opened and the man with no neck, who frightened her so much on her first visit, was standing there waiting. He was no less intimidating in appearance, but she found herself actually glad to see him this time. He bowed to her and said, "Nice to see you again, Ms. Preston. Please follow me." He led her into Oliver's office, poured her a coffee, and informed her that Oliver would be with her momentarily. She barely had time to re-familiarize herself with the tasteful décor of the office before he entered the room. Seating himself behind the desk, he smiled.

"Welcome. I trust you are well?"

She returned the smile. "Very much so. Thank you for seeing me on short notice."

He nodded and said, "I understand the occasional need for expedience. Shall we then get right to business?" He pointed toward the table where they had sat before. As she got up, he asked, "Are you all set with the coffee? As I recall, you were a loyal scotch drinker."

"A scotch would actually be wonderful." She sat at the table while he poured two glasses. When he put hers down, she noticed five ice cubes. She couldn't remember telling him that, but he was in fact a true professional. He sat beside her, unrolled his black velvet jeweler's mat and pulled out his loop. She retrieved the jewels from the bottom of her bag and placed them on the table in front of him. She watched as he carefully spread them out on the mat, looking at each one in turn through the loop. She heard him exhale softly at a few of the stones, as though they met some higher standard than others. When he finished with the inspection, he went to his desk and pulled out the same pad of paper. After writing something on it, he sat back down and placed the paper face down in front of her. He went back to looking at a few specific jewels, while she picked up the paper. She stifled a gasp, as the number was almost equal to the amount he paid the first time. He paused to look at her, and she smiled and nodded. He returned the smile and, while looking at one particular stone for the third time, said almost to himself, "Exquisite."

Oliver finally put down the stone and moved over to the desk. Opening a drawer, he counted out four hundred thousand dollars. "Excuse me for one moment while I wrap up your purchase." He disappeared through the door, returning quickly with a meticulously wrapped box similar to the one she had in the safety deposit box back home. When she stood, he handed her the box.

"A pleasure, as always."

She extended her hand, which he willingly accepted. "Thank you again for everything." He walked her to the door, where his large assistant stood waiting. He walked her down to the street and asked if she was parked nearby. When she informed him that she had taken a cab, he pulled out a cell phone and made a quick call. Almost immediately, a black sedan pulled up to the curb. The man opened the door and said, "Just tell the driver where you need to go." She smiled and slid into the back seat. She thought briefly about doing some shopping, but did not want to take advantage of Oliver's hospitality and asked to go to the airport.

When the sedan pulled up to the curb in front of the airport, Lucinda thanked the driver and got out. Once she was there, she found that she couldn't go inside. She was still feeling apprehensive about the dream and knew that she absolutely had to fly at least one more time, in order to get to Portugal. She now was adding the pressure of carrying almost a half of a million dollars buried deep inside her bag. She wasn't sure if that would cause any problems in security, but decided that she didn't want to risk it. As she stood there contemplating, she noticed a sign for a car rental company just inside the door of the airport. She made a spur of the moment decision and headed for the counter. A pleasant looking young man stood waiting. His name tag said, 'Hi, my name is Ian'.

Lucinda dropped her bag on the counter. "Hello Ian. I have one question."

He smiled and replied, "Yes, ma'am. Hopefully I will have an answer."

"I need to get back to Santa Barbara, but I can't fly because my sister is traveling with me and she is afraid of flying. What do I do with a rental if I'm not coming back?"

Ian raised his hands up with his palms facing Lucinda. "Not a problem, ma'am. We can rent you a car here and you can either leave it at the airport there or one of our satellite offices. Our inventory gets moved around like that all the time. What kind of a car do you need?"

Lucinda breathed a sigh of relief. Though she wasn't thrilled with taking the rest of the day to get home, at least she could stay under the radar. She rented a mid-sized car with satellite radio and was soon on her way. Ian had given her a list of the places where she could drop her car and she was surprised to discover that there was an office only two streets away from her apartment. She turned up the radio and found herself singing along to the country station. Everything was falling in place. All she needed to do now was take care of one last errand at home and lay low until her passport arrived. That last detail was the one that worried her the most. She didn't know if she would be able to stand waiting for four or five weeks, seeing as how she had given away all her stuff, had no job, and still had the FBI sniffing around on the case. For now, however, she was going to just enjoy the ride home.

It was after dark by the time Lucinda arrived at the car rental office. They were obviously closed, but Ian had given her directions about where to park the car and where to leave the key. Once she did this, she took the walk home, walking quickly and constantly looking around her. While her neighborhood was safe, she couldn't help but think that she looked like a more appealing target with so much money stowed in the bag over her shoulder. She made the trip in minutes and was soon sitting back in her kitchen. Suddenly realizing that she hadn't eaten all day, Lucinda heated up a frozen pizza and took out the last of the wine. Not the ideal combination, but she would have to make do. Shopping at this point was an exercise in foolishness. While she waited for the pizza, she rummaged through her bag, looking for the box of 'candy'. Just as she laid her hand on it, there was a knock at the door. She looked at the clock on the wall. Eight-thirty. She quickly threw the bag in one of the empty cabinets next to the refrigerator. Walking over to the door, she pressed her face to it much like she did the other night when Buzz left. She could hear breathing on the other side. Before she could say anything, there was another knock, uncomfortably loud with her ear against the door. Then she heard a voice, scratchy as though it hadn't been used in some time.

"Hello? Are you there?"

Lucinda thought she recognized the voice as the woman from down the hall. She had passed her once or twice, but Lucinda was pretty sure that the woman was retired and rarely left her apartment. She opened the door. Standing there was a woman, no more than five feet tall, with gray hair pulled back in a ponytail except for a few stray wisps that had come loose around her face. She had a pair of glasses perched at the end of her nose and she was peering over them at Lucinda.

"Sorry to bother you. My name is Wanda. I live down the hall. I know it's late, but I thought I heard you come in and I have some mail for you. It was left in my box by mistake and I hate just leaving it by your box or in the hall. You just never know these days."

She lifted up her right hand and held out a small manila envelope. The sender information was facing down, so Lucinda wasn't immediately sure what it was. She took it from Wanda and flipped it over. The return address told her that her passport had arrived. She had all she could do not to let out a whoop in the quiet hallway. She looked up to thank Wanda, but the woman had already shuffled almost the length of the hall to her apartment. Lucinda whispered a quiet thank you and closed the door behind her. She quickly pulled out her laptop and went online. Looking through flights to Lisbon, she saw that there was one seat available on a flight leaving tomorrow night. Unfortunately, it was right in the very back of the plane, likely next to the bathroom. As she clicked to purchase the seat, she thought to herself that she could deal with almost any circumstance for one last flight. Once she finished, she closed the laptop and put it and the passport in the cabinet with her bag. The smell of the cooked pizza filled the kitchen. Once she had it out of the oven, it took her less than ten minutes to finish it off, along with two glasses of wine. She went to bed feeling completely satisfied. One more busy morning to go, then she would be off to find Marlene.

Chapter 45

Lucinda was up early the next morning. She could feel the excitement coursing through her, powering her forward. She went through the apartment one last time, giving a cursory clean throughout and making sure that nothing was getting left behind. Other than a few receipts and a to-do list of her recent activity, all of which she threw in the trash under the sink, the place was spotless. She piled her remaining stuff on the counter: one small travel bag with shoulder straps, her laptop, passport, and the box of candy. She knew that she had to find a better place to hide that money, as a food container might get questioned at the airport. She took a quick run down to a store that sold office supplies. It didn't take her long to find what she needed: a day planner, about the size of a half sheet of paper, with a zipper around three sides to close it. When she got back to the apartment, she took everything out of it, leaving one big open space. She transferred all the money into it from the candy box and was thrilled to find room to spare. That led her to the next errand. She drove to the bank and was escorted into the private room with her safety deposit box. She opened it up and took out the other box of candy, the bonds, and her birth certificate. She gently unfolded it one last time, hoping that the next time she did this would be to show it to Marlene. She placed everything in her bag and headed home.

The rest of the money just fit in the day planner, along with the one document. She silently congratulated herself, as no one would think to question someone's calendar. She wondered what it would look like on an x-ray machine, but it was in fact nothing more than paper. Just really valuable paper. She slid the bonds into the pocket behind the straps of her bag, as the zipper had a fold of material over it, making it almost invisible. Looking over the pile on the counter, she was finally ready to go. She dialed Bill's number and told him that the passport had arrived. She gave him her flight information and he said that he would pick her up at the airport. She hung up the phone and looked at the clock. Not even noon, which meant that she had more than six hours to kill. An idea dawned on her and she dialed another number.

"Chic Boutique, can I help you?"

"Gina. Hi, it's Lucinda."

"Hey, Lucinda. It's nice to hear from you. You don't usually call me during work hours. What's up?"

"I was wondering if you would have time for lunch today." Her stomach rumbled in anticipation.

"I think I could do that. Let me check with the boss." Lucinda could almost see Gina holding the phone away from her ear while she got permission from herself. "Yep. Boss says it's okay."

"Great. I'll come down to the boutique at noon."

Lucinda left everything on the counter, taking only her keys and wallet. She left early, as she had one last stop to make. She headed down to the post office and put a hold on her mail. When they asked for a duration, she informed them that she wasn't sure how long, but would call them if it was going to extend beyond the thirty days.

When she turned on to State Street, Lucinda forgot just how much she loved the neighborhood where Gina had her shop. The street was lined with trees on both sides, with most of the sidewalks made of cobblestone. The shops were all small and very exclusive. There wasn't a neon sign to be found, as most were wooden and either painted or hand carved. The lights on the street were fashioned after the old gaslights. It reminded Lucinda a little of home, back on the East Coast. She found a spot almost directly in front of the Chic Boutique. When she opened the door, three little bells rang to announce her entrance. From a back room, she heard Gina call out, "Be with you in one moment."

When she appeared in the doorway, Gina was vigorously drying her hands. She looked up and saw Lucinda. Her face lit up with a smile and she said, "I'm starving. Let's eat." Leaving her two employees to run things, they got into Lucinda's car and headed for a restaurant at Leadbetter Beach. Once they were seated and had a couple of iced teas in front of them, Lucinda brought up the reason for the lunch.

"Can I tell you something?" Lucinda leaned in close, like she was telling a secret.

Gina smiled and replied, "Of course. Why so quiet?"

"I'm just very excited. I'm taking a trip!"

Gina's eyes got big with jealousy. "You're kidding! Where are you going?"

"I'm going to Mississippi for a week!"

Gina's look changed from excitement to confusion. "Really? Willingly? Why?"

"Well, my therapist suggested it. He said that, after all the changes in my life and the stress, I should go somewhere that I could unplug: no phones, no television, no computers. I'm taking a paddleboat down the river."

Gina thought about that for a second. She bobbed her head back and forth, thinking about the pros and cons. "I guess I can see that. I wouldn't mind disappearing for a week myself. Think about the peace and quiet." Then her eyes lit up. "Oooh, maybe you'll meet some rich Southern gentleman who will sweep you off your feet!"

Lucinda rolled her eyes. "Is that all you think about?" Gina flashed a mischievous smile but said nothing. "Anyway, do me a favor and tell all the girls that I'll miss them and I'll see everyone at the next cocktail party." Lucinda felt bad about lying, but she needed to cut ties quickly and completely. This was going to be hard for her as well as them. It was at that moment that she realized just how hard. She tried not to think about it during lunch, instead keeping up a steady stream of small talk. When she dropped Gina off, she did her best to keep a smile on her face and said she'd see her next week.

She pulled into the garage and activated the car alarm. She headed upstairs and keyed into her apartment for the last time. Lucinda made one more pass through each room, lingering for a few seconds in each doorway. When she came back to the kitchen, she slung the bag and laptop over her shoulder, pocketed her passport, and stood at the door. Memories flashed through her head, with the last one being the hug from Buzz right where she stood. Lucinda smiled, decided that would be the perfect memory to leave on, and shut the door behind her.

Chapter 46

The taxi was waiting at the curb. She threw her bags into the back seat and slid in on the passenger side. She was glad she was leaving early, as the commuter traffic was worse than usual. The ride took over an hour, and by the time she got there, Lucinda was eager to get out and stretch her legs. She flew through her check-in, waited through a long security line, and eventually found her gate without one sighting of a blue FBI jacket. She was thankful that she had decided to pack light, as everything qualified as a carry-on. The boarding process was quick and she soon was seated at the back right window, looking out across the tarmac and thinking about the final leg of this odyssey. She was so caught up in the visual of her stepping off the plane in Lisbon that she didn't hear the commotion coming down the aisle until it reached her.

A heavy set woman was carting two large bags, banging into almost every head along the way, throwing out a random 'sorry' or 'excuse me' every time she felt the bag meet resistance. Lucinda only turned to see what was going on when she heard a rather grating voice say "I need to get to that seat". When she shifted to her right to follow the sound, she was greeted by a rather garish dress topped off by a garishly made-up face. The woman dropped one bag on the seat next to Lucinda, then proceeded to lean over her to jam the second one in the overhead compartment. Once she had pounded it in, she picked up the second bag and flopped down into the middle seat. As she expanded over the armrest, Lucinda found herself sliding toward the window to gain a little breathing room. She looked back out the window, hoping to avoid notice and keep from getting roped into an unwanted conversation. However, luck was not on her side at the moment.

She could feel the woman's hot breath on her neck. "You're such a pretty thing. I'll bet you're going to Portugal on vacation, probably going to enjoy the beaches in a new bikini." Lucinda turned her head just enough to see the blue eye shadow over otherwise pretty green eyes. She shook her head and said, "No. Visiting family." She was sorry almost as soon as she said it. The woman's eyes lit up and she grabbed her second bag from between her feet and pulled out an album.

"So am I! I'm going to see my new grandson. He's just the cutest little thing. My daughter's been sending me pictures on the Internet and I finally got the money together to go over and see them." She dropped the album on Lucinda's lap and began flipping through pages, pointing out her grandson riding a pony, sledding down his front yard, and eating some nasty concoction with his fingers. This last picture made Lucinda glad that she had never had children. Suddenly the woman exclaimed, "Oh, my God! Where are my manners? My name is Angelena." She extended a sweaty hand to Lucinda. She paused a moment before taking it and introducing herself. The woman then picked up where she had left off, going through an endless collection of photos of the first everything: poop, party, trip to the park, and so on. Lucinda's head began to throb, and she finally spoke up.

"Angelena, it's nice to meet you and your grandson is adorable. However, I am rather nervous about the flight and would like to try and sleep through as much of it as possible. The woman looked at Lucinda as though she had slapped her. "So sorry to bother you. It won't happen again." She took the album and straightened herself in the seat. Lucinda closed her eyes and leaned against the window. She heard Angelena introducing herself to someone else and opened one eye. A young man, no more than college-aged, had just sat in the aisle seat. She had her album in his lap now, and he was nodding his head as she talked. However, he had earbuds in and Lucinda saw him dialing up the volume on his iPod. *Smart kid.*

When the plane taxied down the runway, Lucinda wedged her feet under the seat in front of her and grabbed both armrests. As they gathered speed, she began to count. By the time she hit six, they were airborne. She couldn't fall asleep with the endless chattering next to her, but she was thankful that it wasn't her on the receiving end. When the flight attendant came around with the drink cart, Lucinda asked for a double scotch on the rocks. The young man ordered a soft drink, but Angelena held her hand up, saying "It's against my religion to drink alcoholic beverages." She looked at Lucinda with a somewhat smug look, but Lucinda just smiled, held her drink up and said, "Cheers!" Angelena frowned and went back to talking to the captive audience on her left. Finally, the kid cranked up the music until even Lucinda could hear it, leaned back, and closed his eyes. Angelena packed away her album and pouted. "I should have flown first class." Lucinda thought to herself, *Amen to that.*

Aside from the length of the flight and a few pockets of turbulence, not to mention the annoying seat mate, the trip went relatively smoothly. As soon as they were given the okay to disembark, Lucinda grabbed her bag and laptop and slipped by Angelena. She thought she had moved quickly, but the young man had seemingly disappeared as soon as the plane stopped moving. Lucinda weaved through the throngs of tourists, following the signs for the exit. She had left Bill a message with her flight number and arrival time, and she was hoping that he had gotten it and would be waiting. When she got off the escalator, she saw her other seat mate at the baggage carousel. As she passed, she gave him a nudge and said, "Thank God for earphones." He smiled, grabbed his bag, and vanished into the crowd.

As soon as Lucinda passed through the doors and onto the pickup lane, she heard Bill's voice over the crowd. She followed the sound and saw him heading up the sidewalk toward her. Taking her bag with one hand, he extended the other toward her. She accepted and they walked back to his rental, a comfortable looking mid-sized sedan. She fell into the front seat, suddenly aware of how exhausted she was. Bill stowed her bags in the trunk and got in beside her.

"If you're hungry and up to it, I made reservations at a place called the Café de Sao Bento."

"I could manage a bite, but let's keep it simple. My eyes won't be staying open that long." Proving her point, Lucinda put the seat back and yawned deeply. Bill laughed and put the car in drive.

Thankfully, the trip to the restaurant was short and Lucinda didn't have a chance to fall completely asleep. Bill opened her door for her and helped her out of the car. When they got inside, Lucinda asked him to order her a double scotch on the rocks and she headed for the ladies' room. She was hoping that a little cold water would get her through dinner.

When she found their table, the drinks were waiting and Bill was looking over a menu. He stood up while she sat, and his efforts at chivalry were not lost on Lucinda. However, she was here for business right now. They raised their glasses and then each took a healthy draught. She was surprised at just how much Bill blended in. He was wearing a light cotton beige suit, with a light blue shirt, open at the collar. He was a deep bronze, a color not usually found on a Bostonian. She remarked on this and he assured her that she would look the same in just a few days.

When the waiter came over, he informed them that the special of the night was steak in a buttermilk sauce, which they both selected. While they waited, Lucinda asked for a progress report.

"There are some things to share, but why don't we save the business talk for tomorrow?"

Lucinda nodded her head. "That's probably a good idea. I'm sure I wouldn't even remember the discussion tomorrow."

The dinners came out quickly, for which Lucinda was thankful. The scotch was draining the last of her energy, so she was beginning to visualize slipping between some sheets. They focused on eating, keeping the small talk to a minimum. As she was finishing the last of the steak, which was delicious, Bill called the waiter over to pay the bill. It struck her how different it felt when she went out with Roger, who was ridiculously smooth, but she couldn't help appreciate just how hard Bill was working at being a perfect gentleman. When the table had been cleared, he stood up and moved around to pull her chair out. She stood and together they walked to the car. It was a quick and peaceful ride to the hotel.

As they got on the elevator, Bill said, "I booked you a room on the seventeenth floor. You'll love the view." He escorted her to her door. "I'm on the second floor, room 212, if you need me. Sleep well. I'll call you before lunch." He opened her door and dropped her bags inside. In one motion, he slid her key into her hand, gave her a kiss on the forehead, and got back on the elevator. Lucinda stepped into the room and closed the door behind her. She could see the entire room in the dim light of a safety lamp plugged in by the bed. Simple, yet comfortable. However, when she walked over to the window, she gasped. The view was indeed spectacular.

The hotel stood like a sentry over the entire city, with the business districts clustered close around its' feet, eventually giving way to lesser populated neighborhoods. The hotel was a stone's throw away from a dark river, which appeared to have no traffic at the moment. She took it all in for several minutes before finally falling back on to the bed and succumbing to the fatigue. She was asleep as soon as she hit the pillow.

Chapter 47

Lucinda woke up just before ten the next morning. It had been a deep and peaceful sleep, leaving her feeling more refreshed than she had felt in quite some time. The sun was streaming in through the windows, revealing a less mysterious, yet equally spectacular view of the city. She practically skipped into the shower, letting the water run over her for quite some time. After toweling off, she slipped into a light green sundress. Taking a look in the full length mirror on the back of the door, she nodded approval to her reflection. Just as she shut the bathroom light off, the phone rang.

"Morning, sleepyhead. Ready for breakfast?"

"Absolutely. I'm starving. Meet you in the lobby in five minutes."

Before she left the room, she dug the day planner out of her bag. Taking the bonds out of their hiding place, she folded them and forced them into the planner with the money. Searching the room, she found that she could pull the drawer out of the nightstand and stand it up in the back, then replace the drawer. There would be no reason for any hotel staff to go there, so it should be safe. She grabbed her room key, put it in her bag, then headed for the elevator.

When the doors opened, she was greeted by a handsome man, probably a little older than she. He smiled and said, "Boa Manha" in a thick accent, which she found very appealing.

"Good morning."

He smiled again. "Ah, an American. Welcome to my beautiful country. Vacation?"

She nodded. As the door opened to the lobby, he followed her out. "I can suggest some wonderful sites to see, if you would like."

She spotted Bill by the entrance. "That sounds great. My husband and I have never been here. There he is now. Come and meet him." The man suddenly looked at his watch, mumbled something about the time and quickly changed direction. She couldn't help but laugh to herself. *That line never fails.*

Bill looked up just in time to see the man beating a hasty retreat. When she walked up to him, he said, "You look ravishing." Pointing in the direction from which she just came, he added, "Friend of yours?"

She looked back, then laughed. "Nope. Just a friendly local, welcoming me to Portugal. How about that breakfast?"

With a confused look on his face and a quick backward glance, Bill took her by the arm and led her out the door. A valet was standing by Bill's rental with the passenger door open. Lucinda slid into the front seat. She saw Bill hand him a tip which made his face light up. When he got into the front seat, Lucinda looked at him and said, "Why do I feel like that is going on your expense report?" He shot her a sharp look. "Not everything I spend falls on my client. Trust me, you'll be happy with the end result."

The restaurant was small, but it had all the signs of a good place to eat: clean, bright, and - most importantly – very busy. They were seated in a corner booth overlooking a lovely waterfall in a well-manicured backyard full of flowers. The windows were ajar and Lucinda could hear the chirping sounds of multiple birds. *What a heavenly place.* After the waitress brought two coffees and dropped menus, they got down to business.

"So what have you found out?" Lucinda leaned forward on both elbows.

Bill took a quick sip of his coffee and then pulled out his small black notebook. He flipped through a few pages before he found what he was looking for. He informed her that Marlene may have changed her name again. A reliable source told him that she and her husband were spotted in a town less than a day's drive from Lisbon. They would be heading there after breakfast to meet with his contact.

"Good. That's what I wanted to hear." Lucinda was thrilled to be hitting the ground running.

Even with a full room, the service here was quick. Their food was on the table no more than ten minutes after they ordered. They ate quickly and were soon on their way. After a relatively scenic drive, they pulled into the town of Sintra. Bill parked in front of an old office building. They went into a dusty office on the first floor, where a man was scanning through a mountain of paperwork. He looked up when he heard the door close behind them.

"Ah, Mr. Fadigo. So good to see you. And who is this lovely woman you have brought with you?" When he said this, he stood up and came around the desk to greet them.

"This is my client, Lucinda Preston. She is the one looking for her half-sister. Lucinda, this is Ferdinand Tomissino, private eye."

Lucinda extended a hand, which Ferdinand took and raised to his lips. He maintained eye contact as he kissed the back of her hand. "Ms. Preston, it is a pleasure to meet you. Mr. Fadigo has told me so many good things about you."

Lucinda thought briefly about what Bill told this man before replying, "Nice to meet you as well."

They all took a seat around the desk, and Ferdinand opened up a manila folder from the top of one of the piles. Lucinda could see that there were a few typewritten pages, along with several photographs. He sifted through these before choosing one and handing it to Lucinda. "Is this the woman you are seeking?"

Lucinda took the photograph and turned it over. A gasp escaped from her lips. The face in the picture was definitely Marlene, but what unnerved her was that it was the Marlene from her last dream. She had the auburn hair, with some sun-lightened streaks in it. The ponytail, however, was gone. Her face was drawn, with dark circles under the eyes and overly pronounced cheekbones. Lucinda looked up at Ferdinand and nodded her head. "Does she know I'm here? Can I see her?"

Ferdinand shook his head and said, "Unfortunately, these pictures were taken some time ago in a small village called Ericeira. As Bill may have told you, they were traveling as Mr. and Mrs. Carlo St. Gaudins. They were living with one of the local fishermen for a short time, but disappeared a few weeks ago. He said that they shared very little, but did mention Sintra on several occasions. Since this town has a large number of tourists, it would be a perfect place to blend in."

Lucinda's mind was whirring now, but she kept these thoughts to herself. "I would like to be there when you find her, if that's possible. This is very important to me."

"Of course. I expected nothing less. We will begin tomorrow morning. Meet me here at nine." They shook hands with Ferdinand and left.

As Bill started the car, he looked over at Lucinda. "Told you I had a good lead." When she didn't answer, he asked, "What's on your mind?"

She thought for a minute before answering. "You said that Marlene and her husband seemed to be moving quickly from place to place?"

Bill nodded and replied, "So?"

"Is it possible that it wasn't you that made them run?" Bill looked at her quizzically. She continued. "Maybe they are still running from old enemies." It took a few seconds for him to make the connection, then his eyes opened wide. "The mob! They're not ones to give up on their money so easily. Maybe they've always had an eye on Marlene and, when Vinnie showed back up, they came looking to collect."

Hearing it out loud made Lucinda wonder if she was grasping at straws, but she was certain about one thing. Whoever was following Marlene, Lucinda wanted to find her first.

Chapter 48

Meanwhile, back in Santa Barbara, life was going on as usual. Gina had scheduled a cocktail party for that night. After making all the calls and shopping for supplies, she decided to go for a run. She was running at a steady pace and turned down Lucinda's street. As she was approaching her apartment, a good looking guy got out of his car, pressed the buzzer, and stood in front of the building. Gina ran up to him and began jogging in place.

"You look lost. Anything I can help you with?"

The man turned quickly, as though he had not heard her approach. "Just looking for a friend."

She gave him a smile and said, "Well, if your friend lives around here, I can help. I know almost everyone."

Flashing a wide smile, the man replied, "My lucky day, then. I am looking for Lucinda Preston. Do you know her?"

"Know her? We're like two peas in a pod." Gina gave him a closer look. "You're the FBI guy, aren't you?"

"Guilty as charged. Is it that obvious?" He looked down at himself as though it were written somewhere on him.

"Nope. Lucinda described you to a 'T'. I probably could have picked you out of a lineup."

He laughed and said, "Hopefully you'll be a witness in a future case, with that memory and facial recognition." He extended a hand and offered, "My name is Buzz."

Still jogging, she took it and replied, "Gina Taylor. Nice to meet you. However, you won't be able to see Lucinda. She took a trip on a paddle boat down the Mississippi for a little R and R."

Buzz scratched his chin and said, "That explains the constant answering machine and no calls back. I knew I would be in town and thought I might catch her."

Impulsively, Gina shot back, "Well, Mr. FBI man, no sense wasting the evening by your lonesome. Why not come by my place tonight? All of Lucinda's friends will be there. I'm sure she would have shown you off to us eventually, so won't this be a shock when she finds out we beat her to the punch?"

Buzz thought about that for a second. "You sure you want a stranger crashing the party?"

She laughed and replied, "Well, you're not a stranger to me. After you meet everyone else, you won't be a stranger to them either. Problem solved. Got a pen and some paper?"

Buzz fished his notebook out of his pocket and flipped to an empty page. Gina stopped jogging long enough to write down her phone number and directions to her condo. Handing him the notebook, she headed back the way she came. Over her shoulder, she called, "Nice to meet you, Buzz. See you about seven."

He laughed as he got into the car. Five minutes in town and he already had plans for the evening. Now he needed to find a place to stay for the night. He found a hotel not far away and booked a room. As the clerk handed him a key, he asked if there was a place nearby to get something to eat. She gave him directions to a café that was within walking distance. After dropping his stuff in the room, he headed back out to the sidewalk.

The directions were spot on, and Buzz was soon seated in a comfortable little place with only two gentlemen, sitting at a small table to his left, as the other patrons. As he scanned the menu, he couldn't help but overhear their conversation in the quiet dining room.

"God, I miss her." It sounded to Buzz like someone just had a bad breakup.

"So do I, Ted. It just isn't the same without her." That struck Buzz as a weird relationship.

"Roger, you don't understand. It's like someone cut my right arm off, the way she left so abruptly. You weren't there long enough to see just how much of an asset to Lowe and Maher she was." Buzz' interest was piqued at the mention of the firm, but he kept his eyes on the menu.

The first man continued. "I don't know if she realized just how much she was valued there. I know she was depressed after Andrew's death. They had had a thing going for quite some time, but I didn't let on that I knew the extent of their relationship because I knew she would be uncomfortable. That's why I tried to be subtle, and failed miserably, in telling her that Andrew had another girlfriend. I can't say I was shocked when Lucinda left. She was a very private person."

Buzz almost choked at the name. His mind started whizzing with questions and possibilities. He was lost in thought long enough that he was startled by a quiet cough next to him. The waitress was standing there, waiting to see if he was ready to order. He took a quick look to his left and saw that the two men were standing and putting their coats on. It was then that he got a good look at their faces and recognized that they were two men whom he had interviewed when he took over the case. He apologized to the waitress for taking up a table, but said that he had to get back to work. Buzz waited until the two men were gone before getting up and heading out the door.

Once on the sidewalk, he took out his cell phone and called his boss in the L.A. office. He recounted the conversation, telling him that he would like to stay in town a little longer and follow up on this new information. His boss was thrilled at the news of new information, as the investigation had stalled after the girlfriend had been cleared as a suspect. He gave Buzz permission to stay as long as necessary and told him that he would update the Santa Barbara police and make sure that they would give any assistance requested. When he hung up the phone, Buzz couldn't decide if he was excited at the new break or depressed at the direction it would be taking him. Regardless, he had a job to do. Tonight's social had just become less social and more work.

Chapter 49

When Gina arrived home, she quickly showered and gave the place a quick clean. Once this was done, she called a few male friends and invited them to come over. Even though it would change the tone of the party, she didn't want Buzz to feel uncomfortable with all women. Besides, she felt as though there had been electricity between them today. Since she never got the sense that Lucinda was interested in dating, she figured that they were truly just friends and Gina might have a chance with this handsome new addition. Any flirting would be painfully obvious if he was the only guy in the room.

Guests began showing up just before seven. Vangie and Helen arrived together, with Krystina not far behind. The guys showed up in a group, all laughing and yelling about some game from last night. By seven-thirty, all of the invited had shown up except Buzz. She was starting to feel anxious when the buzzer went off. As she hit the door release button, she said to the group, "I've invited a friend of Lucinda's and he is new to the group, so please make him feel at home."

A knock came at the door and Gina quickly opened it. Buzz was standing there holding a bottle of wine. "Never go to a party empty handed." She took it from him and gave it a quick look. The man certainly had good, and expensive, taste. She introduced him to the room and soon he was ensconced in one conversation after another. Gina was disappointed that they never got to spend any time alone, but she caught him glancing at her over the crowd on several occasions. The evening went well and everyone seemed to have a good time. As it got late, people started saying their goodbyes and disappearing out the door. Eventually, only Buzz and Gina were left.

Buzz smiled and said, "I think I've overstayed my welcome. I should be going as well. Thank you for a most enjoyable evening. You have no idea how pleased I am to have met you."

Gina felt her knees weaken and put her hands on the counter for support. She looked into those blue eyes and said, "Thank you for coming. Don't be a stranger. You have my numbers." She straightened up and repeated, "You do have my numbers…"

Laughing, Buzz replied, "Yes, I have your numbers. No, I won't be a stranger." He stepped in close and gave her a gentle kiss on the cheek. "Thanks again. I'll be in touch." It was all she could do to keep standing as he quietly let himself out.

Chapter 50

By the time Buzz arrived at his hotel, he was practically running. He quickly showered, pulling on a pair of boxers and opening up his computer. First, he searched information regarding Lowe and Maher. Bringing up a list of employees, past and present, he found Lucinda's name. He scanned his notes, as he did not remember her from any interviews. He remembered the conversation in the restaurant, which made him think that she had left between the first round of interviews and his follow-up ones after he took over the case. He made a mental note to go through those first interviews again.

When he searched Lucinda's name, he noticed that her information only went back about ten years. He found records for a college degree, two jobs as a paralegal, purchase of a used car, but nothing out of the ordinary. In fact, her life here in California seemed painfully ordinary. The lack of older information intrigued him though. He thought about doing a more intensive search, but his eyes were already starting to cross from fatigue. The clock on the bedside table said that it was almost two in the morning. He shut down the computer and made a quick to-do list for tomorrow: search warrant for Lucinda's condo, a call to the Santa Barbara Court of Records and the tax office, as well as the RMV, and a lunch date with Gina. Tossing the notebook on the floor, he was out cold within a minute.

Buzz only slept about six hours, but he was feeling fresh and excited. Working a case always did this to him, and new evidence would keep him running for hours. He had a quick but hearty breakfast at the café from the day before, then returned to the hotel to get back to work. He called his boss and relayed the information he had on Lucinda, hoping it was enough to get a search warrant. The boss told him to wait for his call. Buzz didn't have to wait long, as the phone rang in less than twenty minutes. The warrant was being issued and Buzz needed to go to the Santa Barbara police station. From there, he would be escorted by an officer to the condo. Once inside, he would be on his own.

It took less than a half hour to arrange everything, and Buzz was getting out of a squad car in front of the condo. The manager was waiting, shifting her weight nervously at the sight of a policeman and an FBI agent approaching her, unaware of why she was being instructed to open the door of one of the quietest residents. She quickly turned the key, asked if she could leave, and disappeared. The officer waited outside while Buzz stepped into the kitchen.

Once the door was closed, he scanned the room. He had a memory of standing here not all that long ago, holding and comforting her. It struck him how surreal and vague that memory seemed, given how recent it was. Looking around, he was amazed at how neat her place was. Buzz pulled on a pair of latex gloves and began a cursory search. He opened random drawers, finding the usual stuff: utensils, plates, a brand new set of pans. It didn't look like she cooked all that much. The refrigerator was totally empty, although that wasn't shocking, considering she was on a trip for a week. He moved from room to room, mostly looking for something obvious before he started pulling things apart. While there was no evidence that screamed 'guilty', it was clear that she was pulling up stakes. The closets were empty of clothing; shelves were bare of any media, though there was a dust outline where some had been recently.

Buzz pulled out his notebook and scratched a few details about the state of the apartment. Leaving it on the table, he began looking closer. Every cabinet and drawer in the kitchen was neat and organized, filled with the usual stuff. However, nothing of a personal nature had been left behind. The bathroom had been thoroughly cleaned recently. The smell of bleach was evident and there wasn't one spot on the mirror. Buzz had been in his hotel room less than twenty four hours and his badly needed some glass cleaner. Moving into the bedroom, he found only hangers in the closet, a bed with freshly washed sheets, made so clean it would pass a military inspection, and a sachet that smelled of lilac.

When he returned to the living room, he noticed a small desk against the wall by the window. Sitting in the wooden chair, he pulled open the center drawer. A small notepad with only a few sheets left sat forlorn in the front left corner. He opened the file drawer, working from the bottom up. A quick run over the hanging files told him that everything had been disposed of. However, he took each one out and opened it up, just in case. This meticulous approach paid off, as in one folder he found a copy of her letter of resignation stuck to the inside. He used his cell phone to take a picture of this, then returned it to the file. In another was a small piece of paper, with what appeared to be a sticker. It had originally been stuck to something else, but had been peeled and put on the paper, apparently for safe keeping. All it had on it was the number 617. The number sounded familiar to Buzz, but he wasn't sure why. He took a picture of this also, then put it back where he found it. At this point, he didn't want it to look as though anyone had been here. He was relatively sure that she wasn't coming back, but didn't want to take the chance for the time being.

The second drawer held nothing at all, so he gently slid it closed. When he grasped the handle of the top drawer and pulled, it resisted at first. He pushed it back in, then pulled again. It felt as though something was stuck. He opened it enough to get his hand in and he began fishing around at the back of the drawer. His hand brushed against something firm, and he was able to get a good grip on it with two fingers. When it finally came loose, he held it up and saw that it was a cheap day planner. Flipping through the pages, he noticed that it went back two years. He wanted the most recent days, though, and started from the last page and worked backward. Many of the days were blank, but others were filled with several events. All the entries were short, often just a word. One day had a list: SF – 10:30; LA – car rental; Oliver; bank. One day just said NM. Buzz took pictures of every page from the past six months that had any entries on it. Once he had everything he needed from the planner, he slid it to the back of the drawer and pushed it shut.

Feeling as though he had gotten all he was going to get, Buzz moved back into the kitchen to leave. As he reached for the lights, he noticed a small trash can under the sink. He walked over and tipped it toward him. There were a couple of pieces of paper crumpled up in the bottom. He took them out and smoothed them. One was some sort of list of things to do. He took a picture of this, wondering who the Bill was that she needed to call. The other piece was a receipt from a pharmacy not far away. He couldn't tell what was purchased, as there was only a number code without a description. Taking a picture of that as well, he crumpled the pieces up again and threw them away.

At this point, Buzz felt that he needed to make some calls and get information that wouldn't be found here. He took a quick walk around to make sure he hadn't left anything out of place, then closed the door behind him. He asked the officer if he wouldn't mind waiting for a few more minutes, then proceeded to the manager's apartment. He knocked quietly and the manager opened the door. She immediately took on the same concerned look that she had when they first arrived. Buzz flashed a smile and said, "I'm sorry to bother you, but could I have a few minutes of your time?"

She looked at him for a few seconds before opening the door and stepping aside so he could enter. He took out his credentials and showed them to her.

"I don't know if I identified myself by name before, but I'm Buzz O'Reilly. I work out of the L.A. field office." He extended a hand as he tucked his i.d. into his pocket. She took it and said, "Please, call me Diva."

"Very nice to meet you. I just need to ask a few routine questions and I'll be on my way. Do you know Ms. Preston well?"

Diva shifted uncomfortably in her seat. Buzz could tell he would need to put her more at ease if he was going to get anything from her. "We are investigating a crime here in Santa Barbara and believe that Ms. Preston, with her work background, might be able to help in the investigation."

The muscles in her face relaxed and Diva opened up. "Lucinda is a good tenant. She keeps to herself, doesn't bother anyone else. In fact, she was rarely here. She seemed to work a lot of hours, and I noticed that she traveled a lot. I assume it was for work. I am an early riser, because I like to run when it's quiet and cool. Recently, I seemed to see her leaving early in the morning, often putting a travel bag in her car. She must really love her job."

Buzz smiled at Diva's enthusiasm. "I'm sure she does. Did she ever have friends over, or maybe throw a party?"

Diva shook her head. "No parties. There was an older gentleman who used to come over at night, but I haven't seen him in months. I assumed that it was a boyfriend and they broke up. Then no one until you came some days ago."

Buzz was amazed at how much this woman saw, especially his visit, since it was late and shorter than he would have liked.

"I understand that Lucinda was going on some sort of trip. Any idea where she was headed or when she'd be back?"

Diva's brow furrowed. "I'm not aware of that, but I did see her leave early the other day."

Buzz stood up. "Well, you have been a big help. I appreciate your time and ask for one favor. I would like to keep our visit today between us. This investigation needs to be kept quiet for the time being, considering its delicate nature. Could you do that for me?" He gave her another wide smile.

Diva returned the smile and said, "Absolutely. If you would like, I could call you when she comes back." The hopeful look on her face told Buzz that she would be a valuable set of eyes here.

He produced a card from his jacket and handed it to her. "That would be wonderful, Diva. Thanks again for your time."

She looked at the card and gave him a quizzical look. "Irving?"

He just laughed and said, "That's why they call me Buzz."

As he and the officer were getting back in the car, Buzz asked if they could stop at the pharmacy. He ran in quickly and stepped up to the young woman working the counter. Showing her the picture of the receipt, he asked, "Can you tell me what this code pertains to?" She squinted at the picture on the phone for a moment, then said, "It's for a photo." Buzz looked at her with a quizzical expression. "Why would someone go to the pharmacy for one picture?" Her answer was immediate. "We often get people doing it. It's for a passport. The post office across the street does them, but they don't take the picture. We happen to be in the ideal location for that." She gave him a smile, but he was already halfway out the door, the gears in his mind spinning.

Once they got back to the station, Buzz jumped back into his own car and headed for the hotel. He wanted to make some calls and start organizing his thoughts. However, no sooner had he arrived there, his stomach began rumbling and he knew that not much work would get done until he got some lunch. He made a call to the office, requesting a warrant for six months of credit card statements, bank account information, as well as contacting the TSA about Lucinda heading out of the country. He loaded the pictures from his phone onto the computer and started a file under Lucinda's name. He then called Gina to see if she would be available for lunch. This would serve two purposes: make his stomach happy and get some one-on-one time with Gina. She was thrilled to hear from him and quickly gave him directions to her boutique.

When he turned the corner of the street where her shop was located, Buzz was struck by how beautiful it was. Much of Santa Barbara felt like a big city, but this street looked almost like it came out of a Rockwell painting. He didn't have to look for Gina's shop, because she was standing on the sidewalk waving, having seen him as soon as he pulled onto the street. She was in the car almost before he stopped rolling.

"Where do you want to eat?" Buzz was only familiar with his little café, so he wasn't about to make a suggestion.

"What are you in the mood for?" she asked.

Ignoring another thought, he replied, "Seafood. I love seafood."

Gina lit up. "Me too. Head for the waterfront. There's a lovely little restaurant called George's Clam Shack. Don't let the name fool you, though. It's excellent."

She gave meticulous directions and they were soon diving into generous portions of clams, mussels, and shrimp. Gina had two green apple martinis and babbled on for quite some time about Lucinda and their extended group of friends, her job at the boutique, and a near death experience for one of the group who worked as a flight attendant. Buzz figured out early on that he wasn't going to learn much that would be helpful to his investigation, and that he would have to watch her drinking if he was going to be able to ask some questions that would yield anything important. When Gina suddenly looked at her watch and exclaimed that she needed to get back to work, he paid for lunch and they headed back.

"Buzz, I really enjoyed lunch today. Maybe we can get together again and you can do some of the talking. I'm afraid I dominated the conversation a bit."

He laughed gently and said, "Yes, you did, but that's okay. I enjoyed hearing about your friends and your work. I'll be in touch."

Gina got out of the car and strolled leisurely into her shop, frequently looking back over her shoulder and smiling. Buzz waited until she was inside before he pulled away from the curb and headed back to the hotel.

Chapter 51

Lucinda and Bill were up early the next day, driving to Sintra for another meeting with Ferdinand Tomissino. Instead of going to his office, he had given Bill the name of a coffee shop where he would be waiting. When they arrived there, Lucinda was taken aback by the beauty of the city. The streets were tree lined and shady, with benches scattered about for taking a break from wherever you were going. Storefronts were clean and inviting, and people smiled as they passed on the street. When they entered the shop, they were greeted immediately by a tiny woman wearing a long scarf on her head that matched the simple dress she was wearing. She offered to seat them, but Bill spied Ferdinand sitting in the back and informed her that they were meeting someone.

They each took a seat, one on either side of the preoccupied private eye, and waited while he finished writing something. When he was done, he handed each of them a note card. Lucinda looked at hers and, in tight script, was written: hairdressers, boutiques, public library. Bill's had on it: RMV, car rentals, boat rentals. They each looked at him.

"I have other inquiries to follow up on. There has been no evidence that they have left the city, but my contacts have not seen them anywhere. If they have holed up, this canvassing should give us an idea of where in the city they are staying. We will cover more ground if we split up. Ms. Preston, the locations on your card should be amenable to a woman's tastes. Mr. Fadigo, yours should be equally interesting to you." He slid a picture of both Marlene and Vinnie toward each of them. "Let us meet back at my office tomorrow morning." Without waiting for an answer, Ferdinand straightened his papers into a neat pile, slid them into a shoulder bag, and shuffled out the front door. Bill looked at Lucinda and said, "How about we meet back here at six tonight? We can compare notes while we drive back to the hotel." She nodded and headed out with her card.

Once on the street, Lucinda realized that she had absolutely no idea where she was going or how to go about this. She began to feel somewhat overwhelmed. She decided to just keep it simple, look at it from a woman's perspective. She was in a new town, needed to give herself some girl pampering. She started walking in the direction that seemed to have the most foot traffic and stores. She began window shopping, trying to decide where Marlene would go. The problem was that she didn't really know Marlene anymore, but she hadn't been the type to splurge on herself and shop unnecessarily. Lucinda passed a few higher-end shops, guessing that she wouldn't have gone there. She came upon a simple hairdresser and stepped through the open door. The chairs were empty and the woman running the shop turned at the sound of her footsteps.

"Ah, you come for a new hairstyle? Maybe a wash?" She had a million dollar smile and a laid-back approach.

"Unfortunately, no. I am looking for someone and thought she might come to your shop." Lucinda walked over to her and pulled out Marlene's picture. The woman took it from her and gave it a good look-over.

"I'm sorry, no. She does not look familiar to me. She is very pretty, though. Is she a friend?"

"Actually she is my sister." Just saying the word made Lucinda smile inside. She had never left off the 'half' before now.

The woman looked again at the picture, then at Lucinda. "Ah, I see a small resemblance. You have the same smile. I'm sorry I can't help, but I wish you luck in your search. Come back when you want that beautiful hair done. I have some all-natural shampoos that will really bring out the blonde."

Lucinda assured her that she would and headed back outside. She repeated the process in almost a dozen small food shops, salons, and thrift shops. Aside from one woman who thought she looked familiar, but couldn't be sure, Lucinda had come up empty. Checking the time, she noticed that it was almost lunch time. She decided to take a break and re-fuel. She came upon a small café at the end of the street that had several tables alongside a grassy common. There were many people relaxing there and Lucinda loved to people watch. *I hope Bill is having more luck than I am.* A waiter came over and gave her a menu. After giving it a quick look, she ordered a garden salad and a glass of white wine. As she sat, Lucinda studied the people as they passed her table. What struck her was how happy they looked, how carefree. Thinking back to Santa Barbara, she was amazed at the difference. Back home, everyone was in a hurry, kept their eyes either down to the ground or off in the distance. Lucinda had said hello to more strangers on the street in the last three hours than she had in her entire time back home. She could see why Marlene chose this place. What saddened her, though, was that she couldn't even enjoy it, for fear that she would be seen. Lucinda hadn't found one person who could say for sure that Marlene had been there, sat with a coffee and a paper, or walked the dog. Always looking over one's shoulder is no way to live.

After she finished her lunch, Lucinda set back out with renewed purpose. She was determined to find some trace of her sister before she met Bill that evening. However, this was easier said than done. For the next two hours, all she got was more of the same. She was beginning to lose hope for her search. When she got to the end of the block, she came to a building unlike the others. It had a large stone façade and columns on either side of the front door. She was standing in front of the library. She wasn't sure what she had expected for a library to look like in this part of the world, but she was positive that it wouldn't look like any from back home. However, she could have easily been going in one from Boston, with its' heavy oak doors and large brass handles.

As soon as she stepped in, the cool of air conditioning greeted her and caused a chill to run up her spine. She saw a checkout desk to her right and headed over. The young man behind the desk was organizing books on a cart to be put back on the shelves. She waited for a few seconds before clearing her throat quietly. He looked over his shoulder and said, "I'm so sorry. I get so caught up in what I'm doing that I lose track of what is going on around me. What can I do for you today?"

Lucinda pulled out the photo of Marlene. Laying it on the desk, she asked, "By any chance, do you recognize this woman?"

He picked it up and gave it a good look. Nodding, he replied, "Yes. She used to come in all the time. Loved biographies and the social sciences. Voracious reader. But she hasn't been in for a few weeks."

Lucinda's heart leaped into her throat. "You're sure? Her name is Rita St. Gaudins. Does she have a card here?"

The man tapped at the keyboard, staring at the screen, before nodding. "Yes, she does. However, that is all I can say. Privacy reasons, you understand."

Lucinda thanked him for his help and strode toward the door. As she got outside, she heard the tone from her cell, indicating that she had a text message. She looked at the number, but did not recognize it. However, the message told her that Bill was texting from the new phone he had to get. It said that he was in the lounge at a hotel not far from where they had met Ferdinand that morning. She picked up speed, excited to tell him about her discovery.

By the time she got to the hotel, she was breathing pretty heavy. So much for all that running… She went into the lounge and quickly found Bill sitting at a table by the windows. When she sat down, she saw that he had already ordered her a scotch on the rocks. Grabbing the glass and raising it, Lucinda exclaimed, "She's here!" Bill was in the middle of a sip of his drink, but still nodded. When he swallowed, he said, "I know. They rented a car a number of weeks ago. I was able to weasel an address out of the girl at the rental place." He took another sip, while watching Lucinda's response over the rim of his glass. When she didn't say anything, he continued. "So what now?"

Lucinda had been thinking about this moment for quite some time, but now that it was here, she was feeling somewhat nervous. Part of her wanted to find that address right now, while another part wasn't so sure. Finally, she made up her mind. "She's not going anywhere. I'm going to see if there are two rooms available here, rather than driving back to Lisbon and having to drive back in the morning. Then we can enjoy the evening, meet with Tomissino tomorrow and let him know what we found. Then we can go see her. Besides, I'd rather not see my sister for the first time in ten years smelling like I've been herding sheep."

Chapter 52

Buzz was intrigued by all of the information he had gathered in such a short time concerning Lucinda. He had stopped by the police station after his lunch with Gina, and found that the credit card company and the bank had been most helpful in providing the requested information. There were ten faxed pages waiting with his name written on the front. Nothing had come through from the TSA yet, but Buzz was confident that he would find what he needed in the pages of financial information.

He took a fresh pack of three by five inch note cards out of his bag and tore off the wrappings. Buzz skimmed through the information and jotted notes on the cards. Once he had a card for each date and what happened on it, he organized them by the date to create a rough timeline. Lucinda had indeed been busy since her boss' death. Ironically, though few people knew about all of the travelling Lucinda had done since she kept it so quiet, the paper trail was speaking loudly and clearly. Buzz laughed to himself about this, as it continually amazed him how people seemed to forget that almost everything they do in the course of a day is documented somewhere. It's just a matter of knowing where to look. He worked well into the early morning hours before realizing that his eyes were no longer focusing and he had read the same card a dozen times. He left everything scattered across the table and went to bed.

Buzz woke about ten feeling refreshed and eager to get back to business. He took a quick shower, dressed, and headed to his now favorite café. He thought he might have to try someplace different, as all the girls there now greeted him by name when he came in. However, he really enjoyed how the infatuated 20-somethings continually stopped by his table to see if his coffee cup was empty.

When he returned to his room around noon, he only realized that he had forgotten his cell phone when he saw it still on the table, with the screen showing that he had missed a call and had a message. Dialing in his code, he soon heard Gina's ever perky voice asking if he would like to get together tomorrow. He would definitely do so, as he was hoping to ask some more personal questions regarding her relationship with Lucinda.

Scanning the cards, he started mentally putting the last several months of her life together. There were two trips to San Francisco, but one had no charges for a return flight. Maybe she had driven on one of them. Her day planner said that there was an Oliver there. He scratched notes into his notebook about leads to follow and people to contact. There was a receipt for a safety deposit box, but it had recently been closed. There was a round trip flight to Boston, along with a charge for a hotel room and a restaurant in a town called Quincy. There was a flight to Albuquerque, NM and a car rental charge made at the airport. Finally, there was a funeral home and a Joshua Kendell, along with the W&F Detective Agency in Boston. Looking over all this information, Buzz decided that he was going to start from the beginning and contact the offices of Lowe & Maher. Then he would head to Boston. He placed a call to his boss to get clearance to do some travelling. His boss told him to just follow the leads, without bothering to call, as the investigation seemed to be unfolding quickly for him. Buzz could barely contain his excitement. His childhood passion for solving puzzles had never left him, instead serving him well in his chosen career.

He placed a call to the firm and spoke to a pleasant woman named Rosaleen, whose name he scribbled into his notebook. When he identified himself, she practically bent over backward to accommodate his need for a meeting as soon as possible. She informed him that he could come after three that afternoon and he would be meeting with Theodore Maher, a partner in the firm.

Buzz was standing in front of Rosaleen precisely at three o'clock. She showed him into an empty office and said that Mr. Maher would be with him shortly. Buzz had just started scanning the office, for what he wasn't sure, when he heard the door open behind him. Turning to the sound, he realized that he was about to meet with one of the men from his first day in the café. Mr. Maher shook his hand and then took a seat behind his desk.

Buzz quickly flashed his identification. "Thank you for seeing me on short notice. I will try to keep this brief." Ted waved a hand, as though he had all the time in the world.

"So Agent O'Reilly, what can I do for you today?" He seemed genuinely confused about the visit.

"Please, call me Buzz. I am just continuing with the investigation of the death of your partner, Andrew Lowe."

Ted became even more confused. "I was under the impression that you had arrested a suspect. Two, actually, after the first one had an alibi."

"We did, but both proved to be innocent. I started somewhat from scratch, hoping to see something that was missed the first time around." Ted stared at Buzz, so he continued. "You had an employee here by the name of Lucinda Preston. What can you tell me about her?"

Ted's face lit up. "Lucinda was a wonderful asset to the firm. She came on a couple of years ago as a paralegal, but demonstrated an ability to learn quickly and work with minimal supervision. Andrew and I soon had her taking on a substantially larger workload, which she handled quite easily."

Buzz scratched a few thoughts into his notebook. "Any idea why she left, or where she went?"

He could see Ted thinking, as though he was deciding how to frame his answer. Buzz had gotten good at reading expressions and body language over the years.

"I can't say for sure where she went, though I hope it wasn't to a competitor. As for why, I can only say that she wasn't the same after Andrew died. They had worked closely for quite a while on some of our higher profile cases."

Buzz framed his next question carefully. "Did they often work outside of normal office hours? Maybe staying late or meeting on the weekends?" He knew right away that he had hit a nerve.

Ted scootched up in his chair and cleared his throat. "Uh, well, a lot of our cases require more than the normal forty hour work week." Buzz looked steadily at him and waited. "Sometimes people work together so closely for so long, there is a connection. It's like they get in a zone, thinking on the same wavelength."

Buzz got right to the heart of it. "So did Andrew and Lucinda have any such connection?"

Ted sighed and said, "After one particularly long case, one that required extensive hours beyond the norm, we could all tell that something was different. They were spending more time in each other's offices, and Andrew started consulting her sometimes before discussing things with me."

Buzz didn't suspect Ted, but he had to ask. "So did this closeness bother you?"

Ted was on the defensive immediately. "Only in the sense that I thought he was confiding too much information in her. I couldn't have cared less about what their relationship might have been." Buzz cocked his head. "Lucinda was a lovely woman, but I only liked her as a person and a co-worker. I was more worried about what Andrew might do to her. He was a bit of a player."

Buzz continued to poke. "So there was no jealousy?"

With a direct stare, Ted replied, "I have been in a committed relationship for some time now."

Shifting gears, Buzz continued. "So what can you tell me about the last time you saw Andrew alive?"

Ted looked down at his desk. "I actually hadn't seen him for a couple of days before his death. He and Lucinda had gone to Chicago to see a client. I spoke to him briefly after he landed. We were supposed to go to a charity concert that night, but he told me that he was going to be busy with a 'private' investigation at his condo. When I got to the concert, Lucinda was standing in the lobby by herself. I had been drinking and, for some reason, decided that she needed to know what kind of a guy she was getting involved with. However, when I told her what Andrew was doing, she looked completely devastated. I felt horrible. Then they started flashing the lights and I went in to find my seat. I didn't see her until the following day. She said that she sat in the back, but I assumed she went home to cry her eyes out."

Buzz took copious notes. As he finished them off, he asked Ted if there was anything else that he thought might be helpful.

"All I can say is that Lucinda was a good co-worker, meticulous, very smart, and driven. It was a pleasure to work with her." Buzz stood up, thanked Ted for his time, and showed himself out.

When he arrived back at the hotel, Buzz looked up the number for the W&F Detective Agency in Boston. A pleasant sounding woman by the name of Iris answered the phone. She informed him that Mr. Fadigo, the owner of the agency, was out of town and would not be back in the office for a few weeks.

"Do you have a number where he can be reached?"

Iris replied, "Are you a client or in need of services?"

Buzz kept his answer simple. "No, my name is Buzz O'Reilly and I am with the FBI. I have a case that he may be able to help me with."

When Iris heard that her boss might be working with the FBI, she was a little bit more helpful. "If you want to leave a number with me, I can fill him in when he calls to check in. That shouldn't be more than a couple of days."

Buzz gave her his cell number, thanked her for her time, and was just about to hang up when he thought of one more thing. "By any chance, does the name Lucinda Preston ring a bell with you?"

Iris' pause before answering told Buzz that indeed it did, though she informed him that she could not discuss anything with him without first speaking to her boss. He thanked her again and hung up.

Buzz felt the rumble in his stomach and looked at the clock. It was close to six o'clock and he was about ready to take a break. He wanted to do one more thing, though. He found information for the Schiffer Funeral Home in Boston, then made reservations to fly out the next day. For Buzz, seeing a man's face was almost necessary to ensure that he would get the truth. Once the trip was confirmed, he called Gina, hoping that she had not yet eaten. She assured him that she had not, and that his call was perfectly timed, as she was just about to heat up leftovers. When he hung up, Buzz laughed to himself. He couldn't, for the life of himself, see Gina eating leftovers.

Chapter 53

The darkness surrounded Lucinda like a blanket. She could almost feel the pressure of it on her skin. No matter how hard she strained, her eyes couldn't seem to adjust. She tentatively reached out her hand, expecting to touch something, anything. Instead, she grasped only air. She could barely see her hand as it waved in the emptiness. She rubbed her foot on the floor, extending out in small circles. The floor was solid, smooth, and she could feel no obstacles. She began taking steps forward, small ones at first, larger ones as she gained confidence. She kept her hand out in front of her for protection, and after about ten steps she came in contact with a wall. She walked boldly along it, keeping her hand there for guidance. When the wall disappeared beneath her hand, she stopped, guessing that she had reached a corner. To her right, she saw only blackness. However, to her left, she could see a doorway, lit with a bright fluorescent bulb. Through the doorway was a bed. Someone was in the bed, but she couldn't see more than a shape beneath the sheets.

Lucinda could feel her palms beginning to sweat. She was getting nervous, though she wasn't sure why. She could see no danger, but then she couldn't see much of anything. She began heading for the doorway, picking up speed, until she ran into something that made a loud metallic crash. Running her hands over it, she could tell that it was some sort of gurney. She moved around it and continued, more slowly in case there were other obstacles in the darkness. However, she soon found herself in the ring of light surrounding the opening. As her eyes adjusted, she noticed that she was in a hospital gown and a pair of slippers. She refocused her attention on the person in the bed and went through the door.

The face. The face from the picture. The pronounced cheekbones. The short auburn hair. The missing ponytail. Only now the face had tubes running from the nostrils to a beeping machine that she had not noticed before. A needle was taped into the left forearm, with a tube running to a bag of clear liquid hanging from a portable T-stand. Lucinda's heart was pounding in her ears. Marlene's face, looking even worse than the picture, was staring back at her.

Chapter 54

Buzz' dinner with Gina the night before had been largely uneventful in regard to his investigation. She started with two quick drinks and no food, which caused her speech to speed up and get less clear. They spent much time talking about his job, in which she was very interested. However, when she started asking about how often he got to use his handcuffs, he had been forced to change the subject.

As his flight touched down at Logan Airport in Boston, he was thinking about the different stops he would be making. There were still some gaps that he couldn't figure out, but he was hopeful about filling them in during the trip. The first stop was going to be the Schiffer funeral home, after he rented a car. The agency in the airport provided a nearly new Ford Explorer at a very reasonable rate. Though it had almost every amenity, all he cared about at the moment was a GPS. He plugged in the address of the funeral home and was off.

Approximately twenty minutes later, Buzz was parking in front of a small but well-maintained property in Quincy. He knocked on the heavy oak doors and then stepped back to take another look at the building's façade. The sound of footsteps brought his attention to the entrance, where the door swung open to reveal a handsome young man. Buzz stepped forward and extended his hand.

"Mr. Schiffer?"

The young man took his hand, but shook his head. "No, my name is Jeffrey. Mr. Schiffer is on his way here and should arrive momentarily. Please come in."

Jeffrey showed Buzz into an office. "Help yourself to some coffee. I will call Mr. Schiffer now to let him know that he has a client waiting." Buzz didn't bother to correct his thinking, as he didn't want to give the man any extra time to plan what he was going to say. His best shot at the truth is when the person doesn't know who he is or why he is there. Buzz chose a mug off the shelf and poured himself some coffee. It smelled like toasted almond, which Buzz wasn't too excited about, but it would still be a welcome pick-me-up. He was just finishing a first scan around the office, which was oddly decorated, when he heard voices in the hallway. An older gentleman entered, impeccably groomed and wearing a well-tailored suit. His smile was pleasant and genuine as he extended his hand, which Buzz accepted. The handshake was very solid, which was a good sign, according to Buzz' father.

"What can I do for you, Mr....?"

Buzz pulled out his credentials. "My name is Irving O'Reilly, but please call me Buzz."

Mr. Schiffer took his identification, scanned it quickly, then returned it. "So what brings the FBI here this morning?"

"I am working a case that originated in Santa Barbara, California. We have been following leads and speaking to anyone who was even tenuously connected to the situation. A woman by the name of Lucinda Preston was employed by the victim. We have been trying to contact her, but she has been doing some traveling. We know that she came out here to visit with you. Any information you could share that would help us finish this part of the investigation would be appreciated."

Mr. Schiffer gave Buzz a curious look. "I can't imagine that Lucinda would have anything to do with a crime of any sort."

"We are just covering all the bases, accounting for everyone's whereabouts and gathering all the details. Could you tell me why she came to see you?"

"I'm sure she has nothing to hide. She came to see me regarding the exhumation of her grandmother's body. She wanted to move her out to California, where she now lives. I have known Lucinda and her family since she was a little girl. That woman had a rather difficult childhood and has turned out wonderfully. Her parents died in a car crash and she was raised by her grandmother. At that time, I knew her as Jeanette Jenkins. I assume that, when she became a paralegal, the name Lucinda Preston sounded a bit more professional to her. Anyway, we handled the services for both her parents, as well as her grandmother after she had a heart attack when Lucinda was about twenty two. I took care of all the arrangements, prepared the bodies, and my assistant, a woman named Phyllis Russell, dressed them. She worked for me for many years, until health issues forced her to retire. She moved to New Mexico, but her son stayed on here to learn the business. You met him when you first arrived."

The mention of New Mexico triggered a memory in Buzz' head. "Well, that sounds pretty straightforward. Do you have a business card, in case I have any further questions?"

Mr. Schiffer reached into his jacket pocket and withdrew a card. Handing it to Buzz, he said, "I hope this has been helpful. Don't hesitate to call. And please, give Lucinda my best when you see her."

I will, he thought, *when I am putting a pair of handcuffs on her.* Once he was back in the car, Buzz was thinking about this woman and New Mexico. For some reason, Buzz had a gut feeling that a trip there was going to be a big break in the case. First, he had to take care of a couple more things on the East Coast. When he got back in the city, he found a cheap motel and booked a room for the night. He needed a home base to get organized and think out his next moves. He laid out his note cards on the bed and began putting check marks on the cards that had leads he had taken care of. He picked up one card with the name 'Stella Birch' on it. When going through Lucinda's bank statements, he had noticed a large deposit in her checking account on it, as well as a check for $45,000 made out to this woman on the same date. Curious as to whom this person was, he did a quick Google search to see what he could find out. The first item in the search results told him that he wouldn't have to pay her a visit. She had passed away two weeks ago after a long battle with lung cancer. Still, he was curious as to the relationship between the two women. Buzz placed a call to his office, hoping to get one of his colleagues to chase some leads while he flew to New Mexico. He asked one of the youngest guys in his office to look into the names of Jeanette Jenkins and Stella Birch, knowing that he wouldn't ask questions of a senior agent. He was too busy to bring anyone up to speed on the case.

Once he had done this, he picked up another card, this one containing the name Joshua Kendell. Another quick search told him that this man was a lawyer here in the city. He decided to pay him a visit now, as he wanted to get a flight to New Mexico as soon as possible. He got back in his rental and reprogrammed the GPS. The office turned out to be less than a ten minute drive. Buzz knew that time was a factor for him, so he eschewed the tactful route in getting a meeting in favor of a more forceful tone. He strode up to the desk of the receptionist, flashed his credentials and insisted that he needed to speak to a Joshua Kendell. The woman, clearly flustered, picked up the phone and had a hushed conversation with the person who answered. When she hung up, she asked Buzz if he could just wait for five minutes. Buzz needed only wait two before Joshua Kendell showed up, escorting out the members of his last meeting. He came over, shook Buzz' hand, and asked him to follow.

Once they were in Kendell's office, the man asked Buzz what he could possibly do for him.

"Sir, thank you for seeing me so quickly. I apologize for the disruption, but time is of the essence. I have reason to believe that you have a client who is part of an ongoing investigation. We have been unable to find her and are chasing all leads to find out where she may have gone."

With a very serious face, Joshua replied, "Absolutely. I will do what I can. Who is the client?"

"Her name is Lucinda Preston. We know that she came to visit you not too long ago."

Joshua's eyes widened. "Ms. Preston? Is she okay? She was indeed here, in regard to an open file that we had been trying to resolve."

Buzz' excitement was beginning to grow, but he kept an even tone. "We don't know if she is okay or not. That is why we need to find her. What was this open file about?"

Joshua was quiet for a moment, as though he was considering whether or not to breach client confidentiality. Deciding that someone's potential safety was more important, he filled Buzz in on the details.

"Her grandmother was a client of my late partner. She had entrusted some documents, as well as a sizable inheritance, with the expectation that it would be handed over to Ms. Preston when she turned twenty-five, in the happenstance her grandmother wasn't alive to do it herself. However, because of a name change, we could not locate her on the date of her birthday. Eventually, another client of ours who works in law enforcement was able to track her down. She flew out here so we could close the file."

Buzz was beginning to connect the dots. "What was her demeanor when you gave her the file?"

"She was frankly quite shocked. I didn't get the sense that she had any knowledge of the file. She didn't even go through everything here. I'm not sure of all the contents, but my partner led me to believe that there were some items related to her childhood, items that may have been somewhat upsetting."

At this point, Buzz felt as though there wasn't anything else to learn here. After assuring Joshua that the FBI would do everything it could to find Lucinda safe, he thanked him for his help and showed himself out.

Back in his room, Buzz called the airline and booked the earliest flight he could get to Santa Barbara. He would be flying out at ten that night. He spent the rest of the day going through his notes and doing Internet searches. He was hoping that his young protégé was having success looking into Lucinda's days as Jeanette Jenkins, as well as the mysterious Stella Birch. Buzz found that knowing where a suspect came from was frequently helpful in understanding how they got to be a suspect in the first place. There was little in the life of Lucinda Preston that would have pointed to so much suspicious activity.

Buzz checked out around seven and headed for the airport. After dropping off his rental and going through the tedious check-in process, he found himself sitting at his gate an hour and a half early. He must have dozed off, because he found himself being gently poked by a young kid saying, "Mister? Mister, your plane's leaving." He thanked the kid, gave him a dollar, and hustled up to the woman scanning tickets. No sooner had he settled into his seat, he resumed his nap and slept all the way home.

Once back in Santa Barbara, Buzz checked in with his boss and updated him on the progress in the case. He also touched base with his new sidekick, but he hadn't found anything yet. Buzz spread his cards out one last time for the day, checking off the completed tasks. Still a few cards to go, but a majority of them had a check mark. The gaps were filling in. He scooped up the cards and put them on the nightstand. He then went online and booked a flight for Albuquerque, New Mexico. Unfortunately, there were no available seats until the day after tomorrow. He would have to find other things to do tomorrow, but that could wait. Buzz clicked off the light and stretched out on the bed, dropping off into a deep sleep in record time.

Chapter 55

Buzz slept soundly until nine the next morning. He headed down to the café for breakfast, as he had not eaten anything substantial in almost twenty four hours. He inhaled the 'big breakfast' and had a couple cups of coffee before returning to his room. Thinking about what he could take care of today, he remembered Gina. He still had not really gotten a chance to talk to her about Lucinda. He had gotten the professional side of her, as well as the family side, to an extent. He wanted to hear what the friends had to say. He dialed Gina's cell. She was at work, but was thrilled to hear from him. They made plans for dinner that evening.

At this point, Buzz was in something of a holding pattern. He was waiting to fly out to New Mexico, waiting to hear from the office about Lucinda's life with grandma and her connection to Stella Birch, and waiting to hear back from the TSA about whether or not Lucinda had flown out of the country. He spent the day reading and re-reading his notes, just in case there was something he missed. However, he felt as though he had a pretty concrete timeline: killed the boyfriend in a jealous rage; inherited a ton of money from her grandmother; quit her job; had her grandmother's body brought from one coast to the other. He couldn't understand this last item, especially if she knew she was going to be leaving. He also needed to find out what the trips to San Francisco and Albuquerque were for. To help with the waiting game, Buzz flipped channels in his room, watching bits and pieces of several movies until it was time to pick up Gina.

At some point, Buzz had fallen asleep during a movie and woken up at an earlier point in that same movie. *Gotta love the all-day movie marathons, where they show the same movie back to back to back....* Standing and stretching, he saw that he had time for a quick shower to wake up. As he stood and let the hot water roll over him, he thought about the case, as well as the people he had met while investigating it. He was especially frustrated at the fact that he had met two women whom he could see himself wanting to get to know better. Gina was very sweet, quite attractive, and apparently quite the businesswoman. However, Lucinda peaked his interest in a different way. She was coy and mysterious, both sweet and potentially dangerous, which he liked. Unfortunately, having to arrest her in the end would probably not lead to a long life together.

Buzz shut off the water and reached for his towel. He began to hustle, not sure how much time he had wasted, not to mention water. When he headed into the bedroom, he saw that he still had an hour before picking Gina up. He began to move leisurely again, looking through the limited selection of clothes he had here. He decided on jeans and a cotton dress shirt. He should be able to fit in, no matter where they decided to eat.

When Buzz arrived at the condo, Gina was outside waiting. She looked fantastic in a simple white cotton dress. Once again, she was in the car almost before he stopped. He caught a quick whiff of her perfume, something floral, a scent he knew but couldn't place. Gina directed him to a restaurant just outside of the busy downtown, known for its' burgers and barbecue. He wondered about her choice of clothing, considering what she had in mind for dinner.

When they were seated, Gina immediately ordered a glass of wine. Knowing how quickly she could get drunk, Buzz decided that he had to bring up the topic of Lucinda early. Once they were on the subject, he could feed her drinks and she would gladly expound on her friend. He requested a glass of water.

"So, heard anything from our traveling friend?"

Gina gave him a mock-stern look. "Duh, no. She's on a paddle boat, remember? No t.v., no internet, no phone?"

Buzz hoped he looked sheepish. "Oh, yeah. Forgot about that. How long was she going for?"

Gina took a sip of her wine. "I thought she said a week. I would have loved to go on a trip like that. I was surprised she went alone."

"She didn't ask anyone? That sounds like a lonely trip."

"She really keeps to herself. In fact, we hadn't seen much of her at all for quite some time. She had gotten really busy at work and was being given more and more responsibility. Rumor has it, though, that she was seeing some guy in her firm. She never mentioned it to any of us."

Buzz leaned forward. "It sounds very mysterious: solo trips to Mississippi, secret boyfriends. I thought you girls always shared everything."

Gina downed the last of her wine and signaled to the waiter for another. "The rest of us know each other's business pretty well, but Lucinda's always been something of an enigma. In fact, just recently she had her dead grandmother brought here from the East Coast and reburied. Krystina was telling me that Lucinda asked her to attend the service, but only her. I was a little offended, since I thought we were pretty good friends, but it goes to show that you never know what someone else thinks."

As Gina started on her second drink, Buzz pushed a little more. "So none of you knew the boyfriend?"

She shook her head vigorously. "No. She never talked about anyone, never brought anyone around to meet us. I think what gave it away for sure was when she showed up to one of our parties wearing a gorgeous diamond and opal bracelet. It must have cost someone a fortune, because I don't think she could have afforded that. You see that junk she drives?"

Buzz laughed at that. "Yeah, I've seen it, but I'm jealous. It's better than what I drive."

"No chance. I like what you're driving."

"You haven't seen it. That fine piece of machinery that we came in is a rental."

Gina hiccupped, then laughed out loud. "Sorry. I just figured that was yours."

Buzz grinned, then continued. "You mentioned her grandmother and the East Coast. She ever talk about her childhood?"

At that question, Gina gave him a serious look. "Well, aren't you just full of questions."

Buzz took the hint and backed off. "Sorry. You know us FBI guys. Everything's an investigation."

The rest of the night fell into casual conversation and pleasant banter. They chatted about their work, the weather, the usual stuff. Buzz was enjoying her company immensely, but after her fourth glass of wine, she got into a giggling fit that required a trip to the ladies' room. While she was gone, he paid the bill and was standing, waiting for her when she came back. He explained that he was going to have an early morning and that he needed to take her home. When he pulled up in front of her condo, Gina impulsively leaned over and gave him a long, lingering kiss. As she got out of the car, Buzz couldn't help but smile.

The next morning, he woke to a steady rain and the rumble of thunder. He wasn't thrilled with flying in this weather, but he needed to get to New Mexico. He still had the feeling that he was going to find something big there, but wasn't sure exactly what it was. The trip into the airport was slow, as visibility went down when the skies really opened up. Buzz began to wonder if this would delay his flight. However, by the time he got to LAX, the rain had tapered to a drizzle and blue skies could be seen in the distance. He breezed through check-in and security and was soon sitting in his seat, waiting for takeoff. Once they were in the air, Buzz pulled out his laptop and did a quick search. He wanted to have Phyllis Russell's information in hand when he landed. Besides, he wasn't remotely tired and didn't want to waste this time staring out the window. He found her address and wrote it down in his notebook. Looking for more information, he could only find mention of her on one website, where she had been taken to court by a neighbor over a barking dog.

When the plane landed, Buzz stopped at the car rental place. He showed a picture of Lucinda to the guys working the counter. One of them smiled and said that he remembered her.

"She said she was here for a meeting. Must have been a short one, because she was back in a couple of hours."

"By any chance, do you keep GPS information from the cars you rent?"

The man nodded. "Just mileage. Certain rental agreements have a fee for excessive mileage. We don't track locations. Privacy laws."

Buzz asked if they had that information handy. The man told him that it wasn't in the computer. They write it on the agreement and then it gets filed. He would be able to get it, but it would take a while to find. Buzz thanked him, but didn't want to wait. He rented his own car, plugged Phyllis Russell's address into the GPS and hit the highway. It was a peaceful ride, with little traffic, and no sign of the storms he encountered in Los Angeles.

When the female voice informed him that he had arrived at his destination, Buzz found himself in front of an old trailer. He pulled into the driveway and shut the car off. When he got out, he scanned the neighborhood. Thinking of that court case he read about, he found it hard to believe that any neighbor was even close enough to hear a dog barking. He walked toward the front door, passing a beat up old pickup that was backed up alongside the trailer. He reached the front door and gave two quick knocks. He couldn't hear any noise from inside and knocked again. When there was no answer, he cupped his hands around his eyes and peered through the window. The inside of the trailer was sparsely decorated, but clean. As he scanned the room on the other side of the front door, he could see what looked like a kitchen beyond. On the floor was a dog, lying at someone's feet. This time, he banged hard on the door, then looked through the window again. Neither the dog nor the feet had moved. Buzz pulled out his cell and called 911. While waiting for the police, he took a quick walk around the trailer, looking for any obvious evidence of foul play. Within four minutes, three police cars came screeching up the street. Buzz had his identification out and explained what he saw. The officers repeated Buzz' actions, first knocking on the door and identifying themselves, then kicking the door in.

The smell in the trailer knocked the wind out of all of them. Buzz was familiar with the smell of death, but it didn't make it any easier to take. He took out a handkerchief and held it over his nose and mouth. The decaying body of Phyllis Russell was lying on the floor in a pool of dried blood. A finger and a thumb were lying on the kitchen table. The dog must have died from starvation, as it had no obvious wounds. Buzz stepped outside with one of the officers.

"This woman's death is connected to an ongoing federal investigation in Santa Barbara, California. Anything you find here could be essential to my case."

The officer assured him that their forensic team was being called as they spoke. Buzz gave him a business card with his cell phone number and requested that he be kept in the loop. He also wrote down the number for Schiffer's Funeral Home, telling him that is where they would be able to notify her next of kin, her son Jeffrey.

On the way to the airport, Buzz called the office. He first spoke to his boss, filling him in on the most recent developments. Then he was transferred to the desk of the agent doing his research for him, but only got voicemail. Hanging up the phone, Buzz contemplated this recent twist. He couldn't figure out what part Phyllis Russell played in all this. He could understand Lucinda, the jilted lover; the cheating boyfriend, Andrew; the pulling up of stakes for a new life elsewhere. Why kill this woman? Where was Lucinda going? Where did all that money in the bank account suddenly come from? Buzz was suddenly beginning to have more questions than answers.

Chapter 56

When Buzz arrived at his hotel in Santa Barbara, he was happy to find everything untouched. He had left the 'Do Not Disturb' placard on the doorknob, but had found in the past that the hotel staff didn't always pay attention. He picked up all the cards and stacked them chronologically, then clipped them together. He flipped open his laptop and added a few notes to Lucinda's file. Opening up his email, he found that he had missed a number of them while in New Mexico. The first was from the Sergeant at the Santa Barbara Police Department. He had received a fax from Lucinda's credit card company, with the most recent charges on it. Apparently there were two charges of note: a plane ticket to Portugal and a hotel room booked in some place called Sintra the next day. Buzz felt his pulse quicken. He would no longer have to wait for the TSA. That question had been answered.

The second was from Agent Wallace, his young partner and research associate. He, however, just asked for a call, as there was too much to type. Buzz signed out and immediately dialed the agent's number.

"Wallace."

Buzz chuckled at the agent's effort at sounding so serious. "O'Reilly here."

The sound of the phone being dropped made Buzz laugh out loud. He could hear more fumbling. "Sorry, Boss. I wasn't really paying attention when I answered."

"That's fine. What did you find out?"

"Quite a bit, actually. Jeanette Jenkins, now Lucinda Preston, grew up in Quincy, Massachusetts; daughter of Paul and Sylvia Jenkins.

She had a pretty normal childhood until she was twelve. Her parents were killed in a car accident and she was transferred into the care of her grandmother. After that, she went from straight A student to juvenile delinquent. She barely graduated, then got a job dishing out ice cream at a local shop. Turns out she was running a side business transporting dope and ended up doing two years. While in jail, she made friends with Stella Birch, a woman who had been in and out of jail most of her life. She was well-connected with the criminal element."

Buzz contemplated all of this new information. Wallace interrupted his train of thought.

"Seems as though she was born with a criminal streak. Her grandfather was the leader of the local mafia, and her father was working for them when he died, dealing mainly in stolen jewels. Boston police suspected that Paul was doing some stealing of his own from the mob and they killed him for it. Nothing was ever proven, though."

Buzz thanked him for the information and told him to keep looking. When he hung up, he thought for quite a while about Lucinda and her childhood. He could now understand why she decided to start over with a new name and a new life. However, it made all the recent events more puzzling. Why on earth would a woman make a new start, get an education and a respectable job, then go and kill a couple of people? And why Phyllis? Not to mention, why would she re-connect with a criminal lifer like Stella? What could that woman possibly offer her? Though Buzz was finding that he would likely have more than enough evidence to put Lucinda in jail for a very long time, he was becoming more driven to understand all her decisions. It wasn't just about getting the bad guy now. Lucinda, though she clearly had committed some horrible crimes, was beginning to appear more like a badly damaged individual to him.

Buzz felt that the next logical step for him was to follow the person, as the leads and evidence were being taken care of by other investigators. He made a few calls to find out if Portugal was a country that allowed extradition. It would make no sense to go get Lucinda if he couldn't bring her home. Once he knew that he would be able to do so, he called his boss to see how long it would take to arrange a warrant for Lucinda's arrest. Told that it could be ready in two days, Buzz booked a flight to Lisbon. No sooner had he booked the flight, the phone rang.

"O'Reilly."

"Agent O'Reilly, this is Captain Jesseric from the Albuquerque Police. We are investigating an apparent murder that was discovered earlier today. Your name was written into the notes to be included in the chain of evidence, as this case may be related to one of yours. While the investigation is ongoing, there have been a couple of things that may be of interest. First thing is it appears as though we can rule out any type of robbery. There was a suitcase in the bedroom that was filled with what appeared to be items taken from multiple thefts: wallets, jewelry, personal effects. The only thing that was truly worth anything was a single emerald. We have a guy that works in the lab here who is something of a gemologist in his spare time and he said that it is extraordinarily rare and very valuable. He said that very few people have access to such high quality stones, and he thought it odd that someone living in such conditions would have one."

Buzz was scribbling notes into his notebook. "What's the second thing?"

"We got a partial print from the suitcase, one that clearly doesn't match that of the deceased. We are running it now, but I can fax it to you in Santa Barbara. I figure the FBI could probably move it along faster than we could. I'm guessing that it belongs to the killer, as there were no other prints in the place. Just can't figure out why he wouldn't take all the loot with him."

Buzz thanked him for the update and gave him the fax number for the police station. He hung up, then dialed the station to let them know that he would be getting a fax and would retrieve it in the morning. Once again, more questions than answers, but he was starting to make some connections. Buzz' mind was swirling with thoughts, but fatigue was causing them to overlap. He would need a clear head to make sense of all these new developments. Leaving everything right where it was, Buzz shuffled over to the bed and collapsed, without even bothering to get under the sheets.

Chapter 57

Buzz woke up the next morning around ten, filled with thoughts, ideas, and a plan of action. He had little recollection of any dreams from the night before, but he suspected that his mind was working everything over while the batteries were recharging. Puzzle pieces were starting to fall into place. The fact that Lucinda came from a family of jewel thieves and there was a rare stone in Phyllis Russell's trailer was too much of a coincidence. That provided a motive for the visit. The re-connection with Stella Birch might have been to find out where to sell the jewels. Wallace did say that she had a lot of connections in the criminal community. That would explain the sudden influx of money into Lucinda's account, as well as the sizable check to Stella.

The only piece that didn't seem to fit was the private eye. What could Lucinda be looking for? Is that why she went to Portugal when she told everyone that she was paddling down the Mississippi? Buzz wasn't comfortable with unanswered questions, but he could figure them out once she was in custody. His next step would be to arrest her, then he could worry about figuring out all the loose ends.

After a quick stop for a coffee and an egg sandwich, Buzz headed for Lucinda's condo. He stopped at the manager's room and knocked at the door. When Diva opened the door, she recognized him immediately and stepped aside to let him in. However, she had a rather inquisitive look on her face.

"Is there something else I can do for you?"

Buzz smiled and said, "I was just wondering if you wouldn't mind opening the door to Ms. Preston's place one more time."

Diva frowned at this. "Is Lucinda in some kind of trouble?"

Buzz shook his head. "I can't really discuss an ongoing investigation. However, there might be some information relevant to my case in her apartment, and I can't wait for her to get back from her trip. I will only need five minutes. You can wait outside, if you would like."

Diva thought about it for a few moments before taking a key ring off the pegboard next to the refrigerator. Together, they went to Lucinda's and she let Buzz in again. As he passed her, he held up five fingers and smiled. She returned the smile and he closed the door behind him. Buzz immediately took out his dusting kit and began dusting for prints on the refrigerator door handle. He was able to lift two full prints in short order. To be thorough, he went into the bathroom and did the same thing to the knobs of the medicine cabinet and the doorknob. After pulling a couple more prints, he stowed everything into his kit. As he was about to leave, he noticed that a hairbrush had been left on the back of the sink. Buzz took several strands of blonde hair and put them in an evidence bag. *Better safe than sorry*, he thought to himself.

When he stepped back out into the hallway, Diva was waiting. He gave her a wink and thanked her for taking some time out to help him. He walked her back to her place, then headed to his car. As he opened the door, he could hear the ringing of his phone, which he had inadvertently left behind.

"O'Reilly."

"Agent, my name is David Bradley. I am the lead forensic investigator for the Albuquerque Police Department. Do you have a moment?"

"Of course. What can I do for you?"

Bradley cleared his throat. "I am just updating you on the Russell case. I see by the notes that you were faxed a fingerprint last night. I take it that it was received?"

"I am on my way to the station now to get it."

"Good. I wanted to let you know that we also found a hair. It was stuck to some residue on the kitchen table. We found the same residue on the wrists of the deceased."

Buzz waited. "And?"

"The hair was long and blonde, with a dark root. The deceased was a natural redhead. We will be doing DNA testing on it, but I thought you might want to be aware that it was found."

Thinking about his off-the-cuff decision to take strands from the brush, Buzz was elated. "I am glad you called. This information is definitely helpful. Also, I am going to send a hair sample to you for comparison. Keep me in the loop regarding anything new, please."

Bradley assured him that he would and hung up. Buzz' adrenaline was beginning to pump, as all the scattered pieces were moving together to become one big picture. He started the car and headed for the police station. As soon as he walked in the door, the sergeant happened to be at the front desk. When he saw Buzz, he said, "I have something for you" and motioned for him to follow. The two men headed through a room full of desks occupied by various personnel, before they finally came to the sergeant's office. He took a sheet of paper off his desk and handed it to Buzz. He was impressed at how good the print was. Pulling out his own kit, he asked "Do you have an enhancement magnifier for prints?"

The sergeant looked at what Buzz pulled out of his pocket and tipped his head toward the door. They walked almost to the other side of the building before arriving at a lab occupied by one man, who was busy analyzing something in a large microscope.

"Paul, sorry to bother you, but is there any chance you might be able to do a quick comparison of some fingerprints?"

The man held up one finger, continuing to look at his specimen. After about twenty seconds passed, he pulled back from the scope and scribbled a few notes on the form next to him. Only then did he look at Buzz and the sergeant. He held out his hands and they handed over their evidence. It didn't take long for Paul to get all of the prints up on a screen side by side, where he was able to overlay them. Buzz didn't need any training to see that these prints were a perfect match. He explained the faxed print to the sergeant, as well as where his came from. The sergeant told him that they would arrange for an arrest warrant for the murder of Phyllis Russell by day's end. Buzz could hardly contain himself, frustrated only by the fact that he had to wait until tomorrow for his flight.

Chapter 58

Lucinda woke up early the next morning. She had not slept well, bothered by dark dreams the night before. She remembered very little, but the feeling of panic still hadn't faded. She took a shower and put on a light dress and a pair of sandals. She had expected Bill to wake her, as he always seemed to be ready first, but she had not heard from him. She called the front desk and had them connect her to his room, but there was no answer. She chalked it up to either dealing with some last minute detail or maybe an early breakfast. She decided to go down and see what kind of fare was offered in the lounge. Lucinda hoped that she would run into Bill down there and she could give him a hard time about eating without her. However, when she got there, Bill was nowhere to be found. She got herself a cup of coffee, a yogurt, and a bagel and picked a table that allowed her to see the entire room. After an hour, she had finished her breakfast and had seen neither hide nor hair of Bill.

She made a quick pit stop at his room and banged on his door, but there was no answer. Lucinda found herself seething over the fact that Bill would find something else to do when he knew that she wanted to go see Marlene. She was glad that she had kept him at a distance. *He hasn't changed a bit, still all caught up in himself.* Lucinda had let the possibility of a romantic involvement cross her mind, but years of self-preservation kept her from giving in. When she got back to her room, she found herself pacing back and forth, thinking about what she would say when he finally showed up. As a distraction, she flipped on the television and scanned through the channels. She came across a news flash and was about to pass it by when she froze. Several policemen were standing in front of a building. She recognized the entrance as her hotel. She turned up the volume and heard a newswoman say that a hit-and-run had taken place early that morning and that evidence at the scene indicated it might not have been an accident. Lucinda's heart surged into her throat. She watched the entire segment, fearing the worst, but saw nothing familiar other than the location. Clicking the television off, she couldn't shake the feeling of foreboding resting on her shoulders. She thought briefly about calling the hospital, then decided to be more proactive. She headed downstairs and out to the curb. The area was still lined with police tape, but there were few people working inside of it. She gave it a quick scan before turning away. She was able to flag down a taxi almost immediately and instructed the driver to head to the local hospital.

The taxi pulled up in front of the emergency room entrance and Lucinda threw a handful of money on the seat before jumping out. She ran inside and stopped in front of a stern looking woman sitting at the registration desk. When she looked up, Lucinda asked if they had admitted a man by the name of William Fadigo that morning. The woman considered her for a moment, then asked if she was related. Lucinda barely paused before informing the woman that she was his fiancée. The look on her face softened immediately. She came out from behind the desk and walked Lucinda over to a vacant chair in the waiting room. She told her that he was in surgery at the moment, that he had suffered significant injuries and the doctors were trying to stabilize him. Lucinda blinked hard, feeling the tears beginning to well up. The woman rubbed her shoulder and suggested that she go wait in the cafeteria and have a cup of coffee. Once there was any news, she would know where to find her. She pointed down a hallway and Lucinda numbly stood up and shuffled off in that general direction.

The cafeteria was a dingy little room at the very end of the hall. It looked like it had come out of an elementary school from the 1960's, decorated with a checkerboard style floor, filled with straight-backed wooden chairs. Facing the windows, Lucinda saw a row of beat up overstuffed chairs, one of which was empty. As she was not sure if her stomach could take anything at the moment, she headed right for the chair. She dropped down into it and immediately sank an extra six inches. Once she was sitting, Lucinda found that she didn't have much energy for anything else. She felt like she had just run a marathon, with weak legs and struggling to catch her breath. Staring out at the beautiful day beyond the windows, she was having a hard time wrapping her mind around the news. Only two hours ago, Lucinda was thinking about what she would say when she could finally talk to Marlene. Now, she was sitting in a hospital, worrying about the life of someone who was here because of her. She hadn't realized how much of an anchor Bill had been since she hired him. He had been a calming presence, full of confidence in finding Marlene, praise for the woman she had become, and hope that maybe they could try again.

Lucinda suddenly found that she couldn't sit still. She straightened her arms up, over her head and reached for the ceiling. Keeping her arms straight, she bent over and laid her hands on the floor. All of her muscles began twitching involuntarily, forcing her to get up and walk. As she did so, she noticed the man beside her for the first time. He appeared to be American, but Lucinda wasn't sure. He was staring straight ahead, though she didn't think he was looking at anything in particular. He was holding a straw hat in his hands, giving his balding head some fresh air. She thought he looked familiar, but couldn't place the face. From the red blotches on his cheeks, Lucinda guessed that he was doing the same thing she was, waiting for news on someone close.

She walked over to the coffee machine. She hadn't had a cup of coffee from a vending machine in many years, but she needed something to calm her nerves. The sticker next to the coin slot simply said '75' and she hoped that it meant seventy-five American cents so she wouldn't have to go hunt down someone who could make change. As she dug through her handbag looking for quarters, she inadvertently pulled out half of the contents of the bag, dropping it all on the floor. Muttering a few curse words under her breath, she started grabbing everything and stuffing it back in the bag. The last item she grabbed for refused to come off the linoleum, forcing her to bend the corner to pick it up. When she flipped it over to see what it was, her mouth dropped wide open. It was one of the photographs given to her by Ferdinand the day before. She stared at it for several seconds before she stood up and turned around. Looking back over at the chairs by the window, she held it up and said, "Son of a…"

Lucinda walked back over to the man with the straw hat, still holding the picture. He didn't notice her at first, but finally sensed that someone was standing next to him. When he looked up at her, his face was filled with anticipation, as though she was bringing much anticipated news. When the look turned to confusion, she handed him the picture and said, "Vinnie."

The man stood up quickly, as though he was going to run. Instead, he took the picture and looked at it. He then turned his gaze to Lucinda's face. He stared at her for several seconds, squinting. A light bulb must have come on, because his eyes opened wide. "You must be J.J." When Lucinda nodded, he shocked her by wrapping his arms around her and holding her tight. She returned the gesture and the two stood there for almost a minute. When he finally let go, he stepped back and said, "The blonde looks nice. Much better than the neon green from the picture I saw." She couldn't help but laugh at the memory of her ever-changing hair.

"That was many years ago." Vinnie nodded. Then it dawned on Lucinda. "Is something wrong with Marlene?" His face got serious. He silently took her hand and led her out of the cafeteria. She remembered Bill and the woman's command for her to stay, but she had to know what was going on. Vinnie gently led her back to the emergency room, through the waiting area, and into an elevator lobby. They found one waiting and stepped in. Vinnie pressed the number four. When the doors opened, he brought her to room 410 and stopped. He pointed to the door, but did not go in. Lucinda hesitated for a moment, then stepped through the opening.

A surge of panic ran through her. Marlene was lying in the bed, seemingly asleep. Her very short, auburn hair framed a thin face, with highly pronounced cheekbones. Her skin was parchment white. There were tubes running from her nose and an I.V. tube was taped to her left forearm. Lucinda listening to the beeping of the machines in the room, feeling as though she had been here before. Suddenly, she turned on her heel and went back out into the hall, where Vinnie was patiently waiting.

The look on her face must have alarmed him, because he quickly took her hand again and led her down the hall. They went into a small waiting room, where there was a coffee pot and several couches. They were the only ones here and Vinnie sat her down and went over to the coffee. Pouring out two cups, he sat down beside Lucinda and handed her one. She took a quick sip, then stared into the coffee for what seemed like forever.

"What's wrong with her?"

"Well, what brought her here was a car accident. She had taken our rental car out to pick up some groceries, but the brakes failed and she went off the road. She was pretty banged up, but nothing life threatening. However, while they were taking care of her, they found out that she has polycystic kidney disease. One kidney apparently failed some time ago, as the second one was quite enlarged. Her blood work showed that it, too, was going to fail. She has been here for three weeks now, undergoing dialysis while they try to find a donor. In a strangely ironic way, that car accident was a blessing. The disease would have killed her without us even knowing that it was there. Now, we at least have a fighting chance."

Lucinda sat and processed everything that Vinnie had just told her. The car accident, the brakes failing, the need for a kidney. She was connecting the dots in her mind when the sound of someone clearing her throat came from the doorway. They both turned around to find the receptionist standing there. Lucinda's heart leapt as she remembered Bill. She got up and walked to the door. She gave Lucinda a sad look and then shook her head. "I'm so sorry." Lucinda could feel the lump in her throat, threatening to choke off her words. "Can I see him?" The receptionist curled her finger and left the room, followed by Lucinda. The two of them returned to the first floor, but headed in the opposite direction from the cafeteria. After several twists and turns, they stopped outside of a door with 'O.R. #2' stenciled on the smoked glass. She looked at Lucinda and said, "Don't turn the sheet down past his face. You don't need to see anything else." Lucinda nodded and pushed through the door.

The operating room had been mostly cleaned up, with all of the machines pushed against the walls and any life-saving materials removed. Lucinda slowly approached Bill's body, completely covered in a simple blue sheet. She folded it down until she could completely see his face.

She had no desire to go further. Other than tape residue around his nose and mouth, presumably from oxygen masks or tubes, he looked like he was sleeping. Lucinda could only think of one thing to say, something she wished now that she had said while he was still alive to hear it: "Thank you for finding my family."

As she pulled the sheet back up, a voice spoke up from behind her. "Have you been together long?"

Lucinda sighed. "Only a couple of months." When she turned around, Vinnie was standing there with a confused look on his face. She gave a half smile and said, "Let's find somewhere we can talk."

Chapter 59

Lucinda stared out the window, stretched out on her bed. It was only six hours ago that she had told Vinnie the story behind the coincidence of them being together in a hospital on the other side of the world from their home. She was replaying in her mind the look on his face when she told him that Marlene was her half-sister, and that she would like to be tested as a potential kidney donor. They had drawn blood, done some stress tests, and were now waiting for the results. As she sat there, Lucinda couldn't help but think of the irony. She had played a part in the deaths of three people: Marlene's friend in the tub; Andrew in his condo; Phyllis Russell in her trailer. Now she was hopefully going to save a life.

There was a knock at the door. Vinnie came in with a huge smile on his face. "You're a match!" He sat in the chair next to her bed, his face suddenly serious, and took her hand in his. "I am sorry for the road you traveled to end up here today. However, it was fate that brought you here, reuniting you with your sister. I thank you, from the bottom of my heart, for saving the love of my life." He gently kissed the back of her hand, got up, and headed for the door. As he opened it, he looked back and said, "I'll see you when it's all over."

Lucinda stared at the door for a long time after Vinnie had left. So many things had happened in the past several months, so many things had changed. People had come into her life, while others had gone. She thought about Ted and Roger, having to keep their love a secret. She had done the same with Andrew, although she wasn't so sure that there was ever love between them. Marlene and Vinnie had to run in order to keep their love intact. Her own mother had a secret love, one that she took to her grave. Lucinda thought about her parents' end, Marlene's near miss, even Krystina's. Remembering that night when they all found out that she had missed the flight, Lucinda swung her feet over the side of the bed and stood up. She went out to the nurses' station, returning with a pad of paper, an envelope, and a pen. First, she found her handbag and began rooting around. When she found what she was looking for, a small key, she put it on the bedside table. She then stretched across the bed and began to write. By the time she finished, the nurses were coming in to get her prepped for surgery. She took the key off the table and folded it inside the letter, stuffing both inside the envelope. After sealing it, she wrote one thing on the outside: Marlene.

Chapter 60

By the time Buzz landed in Lisbon, he was feeling conflicted. Normally, as he proceeded in an investigation and began gathering evidence, he would get more excited in anticipation of the capture. However, there were many things about Lucinda Preston that made this very different for him. The fact that she was beautiful and intriguing was not the issue. He had encountered those situations before. Those people were clearly guilty and motivated by greed, jealousy, or vanity. Lucinda didn't really fit into any of those categories. As far as he could tell, her life after the age of twelve had been one of challenges, loss, and apparent loneliness. Losing her parents caused a downward spiral, one that culminated in jail time. After starting a new life, changing names and locations, she gets involved with someone and finds out that he is cheating on her. In a moment of anger, she lashes out and kills him. Her friends say they barely know her, and an apartment manager says she seemed married to her job. What he found in New Mexico, however, was disconcerting. Buzz had a theory about that, but couldn't be sure. It couldn't be coincidental that Lucinda, whose family stole jewels from the mob, killed a woman who worked at the funeral home from which her family was buried, and that the woman had a rare emerald in her possession. The bread crumbs that led him here, though, were most confusing. If she were taking the money and disappearing, she was doing a bad job of it. Lucinda was too smart to use her own credit card for hotels if she were trying to vanish. Not to mention, there was the business of that private eye, Fadigo. He still hadn't figured out what this last piece of the puzzle was about.

Once he was out of the airport, Buzz hailed a cab. Noticing that the hotel in Sintra was not booked the day she landed, he wondered if she stayed here for a night. He asked the cabbie if there was a hotel nearby. When he nodded, Buzz directed the driver to take him there. Less than ten minutes later, he was standing in the lobby. He scanned it quickly, though he didn't expect to see her just sitting there with a cup of coffee. He went up to the registration desk and pulled out both his identification and a picture of Lucinda. The woman took a quick look and nodded. She tapped at the keyboard, scrolled through a list, and informed him that she was in room 1717. Another thought hit Buzz, and he asked the woman if they had a William Fadigo registered there. More tapping, more scrolling, and she informed Buzz that he was in room 212. He thanked her, then asked if there was a room available for the night. Intentional or not, he couldn't tell, but the woman slid a key across the counter with the number 1715 on it.

As he rode the elevator up, Buzz found himself happy that they were in two different rooms. *At least it isn't a romantic involvement.* He keyed into his room and dropped his bag on the floor. He was exhausted and badly in need of a shower, but there was one thing that he wanted to take care of first. Taking only his key, he stepped out into the deserted hallway. Standing outside of 1717, he listened intently for almost a full minute. Stepping back, he could see no lights on in the room. Thankful that the hotel hadn't moved into the 21st century and installed key cards, he pulled out a small file. It only took seconds for him to pick the lock and he quietly entered the room and closed the door behind him.

By the safety light plugged into the wall socket, Buzz could see that the room was devoid of personal items. The closet had only empty hangers in it, the bed was neatly made, and the towels in the bathroom were fresh and folded. He wondered why Lucinda was still renting the room. There had to be something here that she was coming back to get.

She had that room in Sintra, so there was no need for this one. That would be his next stop, but first he needed to find what was waiting here.

After half an hour, Buzz had opened every drawer, pulled apart the bed, unfolded every towel, and looked inside every lampshade. Frustrated, he sat down on the side of the bed. As he stared out the window, he had a strange thought: did the hotels in Portugal have bibles in every room like they did back home? He laughed to himself as he pulled the drawer open. Sure enough, a small, leather-bound bible stared back at him. He took it out, flipped through it absent-mindedly, then put it back. He slid the drawer shut, noticing that it didn't shut all the way. Opening it again, he shut it forcefully. It closed a little more, but still not all the way. He pulled it out, lifting at the end until the drawer came loose from the nightstand. He got down on one knee and turned on his flashlight. There, in the back of the well, was a small black rectangle.

Reaching in, Buzz felt the smooth texture of the rectangle and pulled it out. *A day planner.* He gently unzipped it and opened it flat on the bed. His jaw dropped when he saw the contents: a stack of bonds and countless thousand-dollar bills strapped together. He quickly zipped it up and headed back to his room, without straightening up the mess he made. Given what he now possessed, Buzz wasn't worried that Lucinda would find out he was here and disappear. She wouldn't be going anywhere without this.

After a hot shower, Buzz stretched out on the bed and began running the details of the case over in his mind. He didn't expect to be able to sleep, especially not considering what he just found. However, as soon as he was horizontal, he found himself struggling to keep his eyes open. Exhaustion finally got the better of him and he turned out the lights. He was out cold ten seconds later.

Chapter 61

Lucinda stared up at the huge overhead light, which filled her vision and made the rest of the room invisible. At first, she squinted to try and diminish its intensity, then gave up and closed her eyes altogether. The nurse had given her several shots of a medication that would make her drowsy. Then she had been given an intravenous injection, which they said might cause some hallucinations before putting her completely under. As she lay there, she became aware that the sounds in the room had faded. She opened her eyes again, and the light had diffused and taken on different colors, like a sunset. A shape appeared in her peripheral vision. She rolled her eyes to the left, and Marlene's face swam into view. Lucinda tried to tell her that she shouldn't be there, that she needed to be in her own operating room, but she couldn't get her mouth to work. All she could do was stare, at how healthy Marlene looked. Her ponytail was back, the dark circles under her eyes were gone, and her face looked full and healthy.

Lucinda smiled at her and Marlene returned the smile. Then Lucinda became aware that the light was changing again, as it began to concentrate in dozens of pinpoints. She thought she heard music playing. The cold table beneath her fell away, and she felt as though she were floating. The air around her became crisp, with a salty smell she remembered from her times going to the sea with her parents. A feeling of peace washed over her and she extended her arms, as though she were flying through the air like a seagull with its wings outstretched, letting the currents of the wind lift her higher and higher. She could see her mother above her, reaching out to her, beckoning her to come. Then everything went black.

Chapter 62

The next morning, Buzz woke up early with the feeling that things had taken a strange turn. Something felt wrong, but he chalked it up to his mixed feelings about arresting Lucinda. The bottom line was that she had murdered at least one person and there would be a price to pay for that. He quickly got dressed and headed down to the lobby. He grabbed a coffee and a bagel from the continental breakfast, then hailed a cab, giving the driver the name of the hotel where Lucinda had booked two rooms only days before.

When Buzz stepped out of the taxi, he was struck by the sight of police tape stretched between parking meters and light poles, cordoning off an area about one hundred square feet in size. As he passed it, he noticed what looked like a stain on the concrete where blood had been spilled. Not what he liked to see first thing in the morning, but he was used to it. He went inside and walked up to a young man standing at the registration desk.

"Looks like you had some excitement out front recently."

The young man looked up at Buzz, then toward the door. "Yes. Hit-and-run, early yesterday morning. It was very sad. I heard it happen."

Buzz glanced toward the door. "Any idea who it was?"

Looking back down at his paperwork, the man replied, "The person who got hit was an American, like you. The police didn't know who did it, but they didn't seem to think it was an accident."

Buzz felt like he had been punched. "Did the victim survive?"

The man shrugged. "Don't know. Whoever it was got taken to the hospital, but there was a lot of blood on the sidewalk."

Buzz ran out the door and was thankful that his cabbie hadn't picked up another fare yet. He jumped back in and told him to floor it. When they arrived at the hospital, Buzz was jumping out of the cab before it had even stopped. The driver yelled at him and he realized that he hadn't paid him. He tossed a twenty through the window and went into the hospital. He went up to the first person that passed him wearing scrubs and flashed his badge. The nurse took him to admitting and pointed to a desk in the far corner. He strode right over and dropped his badge on the desk.

"A hit-and-run victim was brought in here yesterday morning, correct?" Buzz was being more abrupt and authoritative than he would have liked, but he wanted answers.

The woman looked at him with wide eyes. "Yes, sir. Brought into the emergency room."

"I need to see this person, as soon as possible."

The woman's face softened. "I'm afraid that is impossible. The person died while in surgery. There was massive internal damage."

Buzz pulled out Lucinda's picture. "You're telling me that she is dead?"

Looking at the picture, the woman shook her head. "No, I'm not."

Utterly confused now, Buzz blustered, "But you said that the victim died."

"Yes, sir. I did. However, it was not her. It was a white man, about forty."

"Have you seen this woman?" Buzz tried not to raise his voice.

"She is here. It was her fiancé that died. She was scheduled for surgery late last night."

Buzz shook his head. "I thought there was only one person in that accident."

"There was. Her surgery was unrelated to that."

"Is she out of surgery? I need to see her."

The woman told him that she would need to look into the situation and directed him to a waiting room. Buzz flopped into one of the chairs, his head swimming with all of this new information. He couldn't figure out what kind of surgery Lucinda would be having, so far from home and on the very day that her private eye had been killed. He didn't have to wait long for that answer, however, as the receptionist who had directed him there showed up in the doorway. She wore a serious expression as she beckoned him to follow her. She led him to a small office down the hall and told him that the doctor would be in shortly to talk to him.

When the doctor entered, he wore a similar expression as the receptionist. Buzz could feel his heart sink.

"I understand you are here for a Lucinda Preston?"

Buzz shook his head. He opened his mouth, but nothing would come out. The doctor sat with his hands folded and looked up at Buzz.

"I'm afraid there was a complication during her surgery. She volunteered to be tested for compatibility in order to donate a kidney to one of our patients. The test was expedited and she was a match. However, further testing should have been done. It turns out that Ms. Preston had blocked arteries to her heart and the stress of the surgery caused her to suffer from cardiac arrest. There was nothing we could do at that point to save her."

As Buzz was processing this sudden twist in the case, the doctor picked up a box that he had brought into the office with him when they first met. He reached across the desk and dropped it in front of Buzz. "These were the only possessions she had when she came in. Given the fact that we don't really have the means to search for next of kin, not to mention you were here searching for her in some legal capacity, I feel that it would be safe to hand it over to you."

Buzz focused his eyes on the box, staring at it for a few seconds before finally deciding to pick it up. As he did, he asked the doctor, "What will happen with her remains?"

Sitting back in his chair, the doctor told him that, if unclaimed for two weeks, it would be buried in the common cemetery just outside of the city. Buzz nodded his head and told him that he needed to step out for some air. He excused himself from the office and walked aimlessly until he happened upon a cafeteria with access to a small courtyard. He threw three quarters into the coffee machine and waited while it spit out eight ounces of the thinnest coffee he had ever seen. He grabbed the cup and winced. *At least it's hot.* He found the door and stepped outside into the warm morning sunshine. Scanning the area, he found that he was alone, save for one older, balding gentleman sitting on a marble bench. Buzz chose a second bench, a little farther away, as he thought he heard the man praying. He closed his eyes, feeling the warmth on his face, and took a sip of coffee. As he sat, a voice nearby spoke to him.

"That is a look of peace you wear."

Buzz opened his eyes and turned to the voice. The balding man had apparently finished his prayers and was now standing less than ten feet away, holding a straw hat with both hands. He flashed a warm smile. Buzz closed his eyes again and replied, "No peace here. Just the end of a long journey."

The man's look became one of consternation. "Friend or family?"

Without looking at him, Buzz replied, "Close acquaintance, I guess? Not quite a friend, although I would have liked that."

The man shuffled his feet. "Loss is never easy. My condolences."

Buzz opened his eyes to find that the man was extending his hand. Buzz reached out and accepted the gesture. When he did, the man said simply, "Carlo."

"Buzz. I take it your prayers were answered?"

Carlo's face lit up. "An unexpected angel came and saved the love of my life. I can say it no better than that."

Buzz smiled and said, "I am very happy for you. Enjoy the second chance."

Carlo bowed and said, "I surely will. I will leave you with the peace and quiet of this beautiful morning." With that, he went back into the cafeteria and disappeared. Buzz sat for a moment, then decided that he should report in to the boss and let him know what happened. Pulling out his phone, he realized that he had never turned it on after he landed. When he did, he found that he had several messages waiting. All of them were from Agent Wallace, his bloodhound looking for clues stateside. All of them basically said, 'call me', although some of them used more colorful language than others.

Chuckling at the young agent's increasingly hyper messages, Buzz scanned through his contacts and hit speed-dial. While he waited for the call to connect, he opened the box and looked at the contents: a bracelet, a small handbag, and an envelope marked simply with 'Marlene'. The phone rang about six times before a sleepy voice answered.

"Lo."

"What a professional way to answer, Agent Wallace."

A loud cough followed, then the response. "Sir. Sorry, sir. I just didn't expect a phone call so early in the morning." Buzz winced when he realized that he had forgotten about the time difference. "Sorry, Wallace. I forgot I was on Portugal time. I can call back later."

"No need, sir. I am up now. I just wanted to update you on the case. After finding out some of your suspect's background, I started looking into more recent stuff. I was reading your notes and saw that she had hired a P.I. When I called, I spoke to a woman named Iris. She said that she had spoken to you about her boss helping you with a case." Wallace paused before continuing. "I might have stretched the truth a bit, as I told her that their client might be in trouble and she needed to be very open with me about the details of what the job was. It turns out that Ms. Preston was searching for a half-sister by the name of Marlene Lewis. Iris' boss had tracked her down to Portugal, living with her husband. They were going by the names of Carlo and Rita St. Gaudins. I thought that might help you locate your suspect, knowing what she was looking for."

Buzz looked in the box again, then blurted out, "Outstanding job, Agent. Gotta go. You just gave me another lead to follow." He hung up and dug out the letter. Fortunately, it hadn't been sealed, but the flap had merely been folded inside. He opened it and quickly read the pages. By the time he finished, Buzz was nearly jumping out of his skin. He grabbed the box, stuffed the letter back in, and ran into the cafeteria. Scanning the room, he did not see who he was looking for. He bolted into the hall, looking at every face as he went, until he reached the receptionist. Pulling out his identification, he asked, "Do you, by any chance, have a Rita St. Gaudins as a patient here?" The woman tapped at her keyboard and said, "Yes, sir. She is currently in recovery. Sixth floor, room 617."

Buzz ran to the elevators and, when he saw that both were nowhere near the main floor, bolted into the stairwell. Taking the steps two at a time, he was soon on the sixth floor, panting rather hard for a federal agent. He walked quickly down the hall until he reached 617. As he got there, he could hear crying. He peeked around the corner and saw Carlo sitting on the edge of the bed, holding a small auburn-haired woman while she cried into his shoulder. Buzz waited for several moments, but finally had to knock.

When he did so, Carlo turned around with a surprised look on his face. The woman looked at him with confusion.

"I am sorry to interrupt, but I am afraid we need to talk." Buzz came into the room and sat in the chair on the far side of the bed.

Carlo let go of his wife and stood up so he could face Buzz. "It is good to see you again, but this is a bad time. My wife and I have just received some bad news about a family member."

Buzz nodded and replied, "I know. I am aware of what happened to the donor of the kidney. I have something for you." He pulled the letter out of the box and handed it to the woman. "After you read this, I will be able to help you with what comes next." The woman looked at the front of the envelope and gasped. She looked at Buzz with wide eyes. He nodded toward the letter and she opened the flap and unfolded the single sheet inside.

Chapter 63

Dear Marlene,

God, there are so many things to tell you! I still can't believe that it has been about twenty years since we last said anything meaningful to each other. I have to admit, I hated you for a long time, for a number of different reasons, none of which were really your fault. Seeing you, with your complete family, while I had to make do with my grandmother drove me crazy in the beginning. However, I came to realize that I had a woman who loved and cared for me as much as any parent could have. I watched you live the life that I thought we would live together, playing sports in school, having friends, being popular. I, however, embraced my role as outcast, even playing it up as much as I could. Losing Bill to you was a turning point in ways that I don't think I'll ever be able to tell. However, I know now that I needed that, as I wasn't in a place to be able to have a healthy relationship. I needed to start over, to reinvent myself, which I did after my grandmother died.

Clearly, we have both traveled long roads to get to this point. Even though I have had a pretty good life up to this point, I always imagined that yours was just better, a little more interesting. Over time, I was able to let you slip out of my mind and begin really living my own. It wasn't until recently, when I discovered something rather shocking, that you came back into my consciousness. In case your husband didn't share it with you, it turns out that you and I are half-sisters. Since it was kept from me, I can only assume that it was kept from you as well. Apparently, your father and my mother had some sort of relationship that produced me.

When I first found out, I knew right away that I needed to find you. I just didn't know why, or what I would say to you. During the search, I learned some things about myself, most I wish I didn't. I have done many things that I regret, some things that may come with heavy consequences, but it is this one thing that hurts me the most. I regret the fact that I used a horrible experience in my life to push away the best friend I ever had. You tried so hard to be there for me and all I could do was wallow in my self-pity. I think of all the life milestones that I couldn't share with you, as I had shut myself off emotionally from everyone. I wasted years thinking that you had gotten the better deal, the better life, while I fought for every little opportunity. All I can do now is thank God that I am being given a second chance to spend time with my best friend, my sister, though I know I don't deserve it. I only hope that you are willing.

If, by chance, I am not sitting while you read this, waiting to have the longest catch-up session in history, then there is something else you need to know. I am aware that you have been moving frequently, which tells me that you may have figured out that the mob has been looking for you. I know that your husband stole from them years ago. It was no coincidence that it was your brakes failing that landed you in this hospital. My parents were stealing from the mob and their brakes were tampered with, causing the accident that killed them. The investigator that I hired to find you was killed in a hit-and-run soon after we discovered where you were.

In the envelope you will find a key to my hotel room in Lisbon. I have left something behind the top left drawer of the desk that may help you resolve your issues with the mob. I only hope that you can move past that old history and start a new life somewhere.

I hope you can forgive me for being such a fool, and for throwing so many years away for such childish reasons. If I don't get the chance to say it to you, know this: even after all these years, you are still the best friend that I ever had.

Love,

J.J.

Chapter 64

Marlene looked up at Buzz, with tears flowing freely down her cheeks. Her mouth was open, but nothing was coming out. He smiled at her, then looked down at the floor.

"Your friend was very intriguing. I didn't know her for all that long, but I enjoyed the little time we spent together."

Wiping her face on her bedsheet, Marlene could only muster one sentence. "I don't understand."

Standing up, Buzz replied, "I will do my best to fill in the gaps and answer questions, but that will have to wait." He reached into the box with Lucinda's personal effects and retrieved the planner, which he had brought with him rather than leave it in his room. "I can save you a trip to the hotel. This is what she had left behind." Buzz placed it on the bed beside Marlene and sat back down.

Reaching out with trembling hands, Marlene picked up the planner and stared at it. She glanced at Buzz, but all he did was nod his head. She grabbed the zipper and slowly ran it along three sides. When the planner fell open, the noise from Marlene's mouth made Buzz laugh to himself. While he had never received such a gift, he could well imagine that he would have made a similar noise.

Marlene dumped the contents onto the bed, where Vinny picked up the bound packs of thousand dollar bills. While the two were exchanging incredulous looks, Buzz took the opportunity to explain.

"The most important thing for you to understand is that your sister went to great lengths to find you. She was going to let nothing stop her from doing that. Clearly, she regretted choices that she had made and was hoping to make amends. I think it is safe to say that she has done that. Where the money came from really isn't important. As far as I'm concerned, it is legally yours with the passing of your sister. What we need to think about now is the next step."

Marlene shot a hard look at Buzz. "What next step? Who are you?"

Buzz stood and pulled out his identification. He flipped open his wallet and said, "I am going to speak to your doctor now. You read the letter. The mob doesn't give up. There's only one way to get them to stop. It's time for both of you to die, and I am going to help you with that."

34116825R00187

Made in the USA
Lexington, KY
23 July 2014